CAN'T TAKE MY EYES OFF YOU

AIMEE BROWN

Boldwood

First published in Great Britain in 2023 by Boldwood Books Ltd.

Cover Design by Alice Moore Design

Cover Photography: Shutterstock and iStock

The moral right of Aimee Brown to be identified as the author of this work has been asserted in accordance with the Copyright, Designs and Patents Act 1988.

Every effort has been made to obtain the necessary permissions with reference to copyright material, both illustrative and quoted. We apologise for any omissions in this respect and will be pleased to make the appropriate acknowledgements in any future edition.

A CIP catalogue record for this book is available from the British Library.

Paperback ISBN 978-1-80426-836-0

Large Print ISBN 978-1-80426-835-3

Hardback ISBN 978-1-80426-834-6

Ebook ISBN 978-1-80426-837-7

Kindle ISBN 978-1-80426-838-4

Audio CD ISBN 978-1-80426-829-2

MP3 CD ISBN 978-1-80426-830-8

Digital audio download ISBN 978-1-80426-833-9

Boldwood Books Ltd
23 Bowerdean Street
London SW6 3TN
www.boldwoodbooks.com

To all of those who find their love 'young' and grow up together.
It isn't always easy, but the heart wants what it wants.
This one's for you.

1

BERKLEY KAINE

June 2020

'Where's your boy toy?' Mike, Will's older brother, asks, disrupting my peace as he walks onto the dock with me.

I squint open a single eye, groaning at the sight of him. He's standing in front of the sun, the light glowing around him like he's the golden boy. In this family, he is.

Currently, I'm lounging lakeside at my boyfriend's parents' place on Oswego Lake. The summer sun warms my front as I close my eyes again. This almost feels like a vacation if I block out Mike. If I wanted, I could text Sylvia, the Adlers' house manager (who has a freaking house manager?), and request a drink. She'd even hand-deliver it to me.

My family was lucky to have name-brand Cap'n Crunch on top of our lower-middle-class fridge. I don't belong in this neighborhood. For sure, my bank balance doesn't even qualify me to be on this side of the city. I'm only sitting here because my grandparents decided to spend their life's fortune on my fraternal twin sister, Bianca, and me to go to a ritzy private high school. That's where I met the love of my life, my boyfriend of nearly eight years, William Adler. He belongs in this neighborhood, bank balance and all.

Time to speak to Mikey. 'Your parents wanted to "talk" to him,' I say.

He smirks. We both know they're giving him an ass-chewing over something. Usually, it's one of three things. He's not acting the way they think an Adler should. They're disappointed in how he's spending his trust fund money. Or, and this is my favorite, they disapprove of his choice of woman, i.e. me. I'd take a proud bow, but I'm sitting down.

Mike laughs as he makes himself comfortable in the lounge chair next to me. The arrogance that oozes from him is cringy. He's older, shorter, darker and douchier than Will. A sleazy rich boy. Outside, he's a handsome-as-fuck douche-lord that women hope to make their sugar daddy. Inside, he's a wealthy grease-weasel with no morals and far too much confidence. I suspect he eats gold coins in milk for breakfast, Scrooge McDuck-style.

'We can't *both* be the favorite son, can we?' he says with a sneer.

'You two do have a very "heir and the spare" essence about you.' It's hard not to notice at times too.

'Like royalty.' He bellows a laugh. 'Fitting. He must've finally told you, eh?'

I prop myself up on my elbows, suddenly interested in his words. 'Told me what?'

He crosses his ankles over one another and clasps his hands behind his head like he's settling in for a long chat.

'He *didn't* tell you?' He chuckles an evil-sounding *he-he-he*. 'That pussy.'

'Again, tell me *what*?'

Mike waves a hand. 'It's nothing. I'm sure they're just in there drilling him over the same shit they've been up his ass about for years.' He rolls his head my way, lifting a single manicured eyebrow. 'You.'

Ass. Hole.

I stand up, refusing to even waste the time on telling him how I truly feel about him, and make my way into the house. I should have known this was about me. *Me*. The barely twenty-two-year-old, five-foot-three woman who generally keeps to herself and avoids talking to any of them unless absolutely necessary. I'm the thing they're drilling him about today. Perfect. And here I thought this dinner was in my honor for graduating college next weekend at the top of my class. Nope.

'Hi, sweetheart,' Sylvia greets me as I walk into the kitchen from the back deck. She's a sweet woman, heavy-set, graying shoulder-length hair, always a smile on her face, and she's the most 'motherly' woman I've ever met, yet she has no children of her own. To her, Mike and Will are 'her' boys. 'Looking for William?'

I nod. 'Mostly I'm escaping Mike, but yes, Will was on my mind.'

She grins, patting my back as she passes me by. 'He's in a heated discussion with Jacob in the den.'

My stomach drops as I glance towards the door to the den at the far side of the kitchen, instantly worried. A heated discussion? Over *me*? Shit. It's worse than I thought. What did I do this time to warrant a chat in what they affectionately call the war room? AKA the den. The room they retreat to when planning out their evil affairs. There are hidden cameras to film whatever deal they're making and then use it against people when they default upon their previously agreed-upon terms. Making a deal with the Adlers is like dealing with the mafia. If you attempt to screw them, you might disappear. They probably won't kill you, but you'll mean nothing in your previous circle of high-powered assholes, so you might as well be dead.

'Heated?' I ask Sylv, just to make sure I've heard her right while popping a cherry tomato from a container on the counter into my mouth.

Before she can answer, I jump at the sound of his dad yelling his name. '*William!* For God's sake, enough about Berkley! Whether you want to be or not, you're in this now, so don't embarrass us in front of the whole damn world! For Christ's sake, grow up already, and act like an Adler!'

I heave a sigh. That's a lot of audible exclamation points. Sylvia notices my disappointment.

'Berkley,' she says, sliding an arm around my shoulders and hugging me to her side. 'You're a lovely woman. Which means you're far too good to be an Adler.'

'There's only one I want to be with; unfortunately he shares DNA with the rest of them.'

'William's not like the others, sweetheart. He's a good man. He'll do the right thing.'

The right thing? Why am I getting the feeling I'm in the dark on something everyone else can see?

I tiptoe to the den door to eavesdrop – I'd say it's allowed considering I heard my name – but the room is suddenly silent. Maybe Will killed him? If so, bravo, boyfriend. Let's bury this bitch. I'm kidding. Mostly.

What would they do if I slid the door open and made a drama-filled entrance, standing up for myself and my man, acting shocked to discover they hate me with the passion they do?

'William.' His mom, Melinda, says his name sternly. 'Do not make us pull the plug on your trust.'

'Go ahead and pull it!' Will yells. 'You've been threatening it for years so let's get it over with already.'

They're threatening his trust again? That's it. I'm standing my ground and Will's. I can't let them continue to treat him this way. They never do this to Mike and last I knew he bought a small yacht just to party on; it literally never leaves the dock it lives at. Will doesn't deserve this. I step forward, reaching for the door, ready for battle. I can do this. Will's my best friend, and he'd never let anyone talk to me the way they're currently talking to him.

Ding-dong – the front doorbell echoes through the massive home.

'I'll get it!' I yell, even surprising myself – the voices on the other side of the den door suddenly silence again. I'm being a coward, I know, but me interrupting wouldn't have done anything but given them more ammunition against me. That's the last thing Will needs.

A bit defeated and honestly a little relieved, I walk through the foyer, pulling open the front door to faces I don't recognize. An older woman, dressed as fancy as they come, pulls her designer sunglasses to the tip of her nose, peering over the top, disapproval plastered all over her tight face.

I glance down at myself, following her line of sight. Black tank top, check. Gauzy white sleeveless blouse unbuttoned but tied at my waist, check. Cut-off jean shorts, check. Black flip-flops, check. I'm completely dressed, with everything in its place – no obvious faux pas.

'*Where* are the rest of your pants?' the woman asks slowly, like English might not be my native tongue.

'They're shorts?' I say, equally as slowly to match her asshole-ism. 'Are the Adlers expecting you?'

'Probably more so than you,' the woman says with a haughty laugh. '*Who are you?*' Even her tone irritates me. She pushes past me. Her three overdressed companions follow, making their way into the home like they've been here before.

'I'm Berkley, Will's girlfriend. *Who are you?*'

The youngest woman stops, doing the same peep over her

sunglasses. *Please, woman. Judge me through your dark lenses like a normal human – no need to make it a show.*

'*You're* William's girlfriend?' she asks, the hint of a laugh in her voice as if something about that is funny. She stops before me as I close the door behind them.

'Guilty.'

She lifts the sunglasses from her face, revealing big blue eyes and a splatter of freckles across her nose and cheeks. Jesus, she looks like a real-life Disney Princess with her long, platinum-blonde hair braided over her shoulder. Her disapproving gaze travels over me, stopping with a smirk as her eyes meet mine again.

'Enjoy that spot, honey, because William's about to move into his grown-up life. Which means childhood puppy love will be left at the pound.' Her eyes dart over me once again. 'Where you belong.'

What?

I grunt in offense, but words evade me. Who is this woman, and how does she look so sweet on the outside? I look her over for anything insult-able, but she's flawless. Short minidress, higher than high heels, legs as long as a giraffe's, zero visible cellulite, and a waist so tiny I'm sure she's got a Kardashian-recommended drawer full of waist trainers in her closet. Damn it. She's gorgeous.

She bats her long fake lashes, waiting for me to respond to her little dig. I have to find *something*. I look her over again. Maybe that waist trainer will suffocate her – wait. I lean to the side, noticing the junk in her trunk.

'*Who* are you, and *where* did you buy that ass?' Eh, not my best material considering her ass is actually perfect, but it'll do.

She smirks, completely unoffended.

'I'm Felicity Harper, the *future* Mrs William Adler. And I pay money to have a beautiful man at the gym sculpt this ass.' She fishes around her oversized bag, pulling out a business card and shoving it my way. 'Looks like you could use a session – or thirty.'

What is this woman's problem?

'Thanks, but no thanks.' I hand the card back to her. 'I don't need it because Will adores my ass exactly as it is.' I pretend like she doesn't bother me. But she does. I'm bothered.

Finally, with an uninterested sigh, and a dramatic roll of her eyes, she walks away from me.

'The future Mrs William Adler,' I groan, repeating her words under my breath. 'The balls on this bitch.'

'Dinner!' Sylvia yells through the house.

I'm starving. And if we're all busy eating, there won't be time for words. Before I can make it past the foyer, Will suddenly storms through, grabbing my hand and pulling me out the front door with him.

'What's going on?' I ask, stopping in the driveway full of expensive cars. 'And who's the girl that claims she's your future wife?'

He groans loudly, seemingly not listening as he runs a hand through his hair with frustration, resting it on the back of his neck before finally turning to me. 'This isn't a graduation party.'

'I'm gathering that. It seems they've lured us here to arrange your marriage instead.'

'What?' he asks, confusion all over his pretty face.

I throw a thumb in the direction of the house. 'Felicity Harper says she's here to marry you. I don't want to seem troubled over this, but I never got my invitation.'

Expecting a laugh at my joke, I'm surprised when he plants his hand on his forehead. 'They invited the Harpers? *Fuck*.'

'OK, you seem super stressed by this. If not a graduation party or a surprise wedding, then what?'

'An intervention.'

I rock my head back and forth, hoping this doesn't hurt his feelings. 'I mean, I have been meaning to talk to you about your binge drinking...'

He lowers his chin with a guilty grin. 'That's not it. It's, uh...' He stalls, searching my eyes for whatever words he's looking for.

'Just say it, Will.'

'You.' He says the word before I can even finish saying his name.

'Me?'

He grabs my hands, pulling one to his lips while I process, kissing it softly, his eyes on me the entire time.

'What do I need an intervention for?' I ask. 'I barely drink. I'm graduating top of my class. So I have to work for every dollar I earn – that hardly seems intervention-worthy.'

'They want us to break up. Again.' He says the words gently as he tucks my hair behind one of my ears, his eyes begging for forgiveness.

I drop my head into his shoulder with a groan.

'I know, it's ridiculous,' he says, sliding his hands to my back and hugging me close. 'How can they look at you and *not* see the most amazing woman on the planet like I do?'

The anger building inside of me fades with his sweet words. He does it every time. No matter what I'm irritated over, he can always fix it. Always. Which means I can't be mad at him because he didn't choose his asshole parents.

'With all their scheming, you'd think they'd figure out how to drive us apart for good, right?' He laughs, then notices I'm not. Sweet words can't change that I'm pissed – at his family.

Will releases me from his hold, running his hands down my arms from my shoulders. 'Berkley, look at me, please.'

Reluctantly, I look him in the eyes.

'We're not *really* breaking up. You know this. It's just for show, to get them off my back.'

I nod. 'Oh, I know, but it's exhausting considering it's not the first time we've "broken up" to keep them happy. It's time to face it, Will, they'll never stop trying this. One day you may have to choose between them and me.'

He shakes his head. 'I don't think they'd ever go that far.'

I laugh. A laugh that says, *you're an idiot* – with love. 'Will, they've brought down people way more important than us. A blind spot in your judgment is what they're looking for. Once they find it, they'll best us. It's only a matter of time.'

He says nothing, just frowns. He knows I'm right.

This family. How dare I try to steal away their youngest son and force him into a life of middle-class chaos. In their eyes, he's worthy of a woman who comes from money and power – someone at his level who orders a second bottle of Dom Pérignon at dinner on his dime without asking permission first even though she can afford it on her own. Not a peasant like me who has a boyfriend with millions in the bank and still buys six-dollar wine, ate a gas station hot dog last week and runs a measly little bookstore I've worked at since I was fifteen. Clearly, I am the gum on the bottom of their Louboutin heels.

'Let's get this over with, I guess,' I say. 'Word of warning: I'm probably going to swear or, at minimum, make fun of Mike.'

'I fully support any words that leave your lips. Especially when they're less than stellar and directed at my brother,' he says with a sly smile. 'Berx—' He stops me from walking away, pulling me back to him by my hand. He kisses me softly, his hand on the side of my neck, forcing me to melt into him the same way I always do. 'I love you. You know this, right?'

'Yeah...'

'No matter what's said or how ugly things get in there, I absolutely love you. I need to know you understand this?'

He seems serious as he says the words, sending a pang of worry through my chest. What the hell does he mean? No matter what's said or how ugly things get?

As he awaits my answer, he slides his thumb along my jawline, stopping at my chin, kissing me again, making my brain fizz, not to mention my loins burn. Bye, worry. Lust is taking over, and I need to rein it in before I do him on the driveway and really make a name for myself in this neighborhood. Instead of the poor peasant dating Will, I'd become the hussy who fucked him in front of the house. I feel like the former is a little less damaging to my reputation.

'I know *you* love me,' I confirm. 'But for your family, it was hate at first sight. I'll never fit in with your world.' I sigh, frustrated by all of it. 'I can hold my own; I'm just saying I'll be fighting this battle until the end of time.'

'No you won't, because as your Prince Charming, I will fight it for you. Besides, you fit in with *me*, Berx. That's all that matters.' He kisses my forehead sweetly. 'Come on. Let's act like we want to be here, put on a show, then go back to my place and pretend they don't exist. Alright?'

I nod, forcing a smile that feels sadder than anything else. Will we ever be able to just live our lives without the Adlers interfering and demanding he play by their stupid rules? I don't know anymore.

2

BERKLEY

Will laces his fingers through mine, squeezing my hand tightly as a silent reminder that my 'Prince Charming' is right by my side and not afraid to talk back to his family, as he leads me into the house. We stop in the formal dining room, everyone already seated and only two chairs left. The two furthest apart and on opposite sides of the table. Subtle.

'Berkley, you're sitting by Finn, and William, you're next to Felicity. Doesn't she look pretty this evening?' Melinda pats Felicity's shoulder. I can't remember a single time she's called me pretty.

Before we part ways, Will stops, pecking a soft kiss onto my lips, possibly just to piss off his parents, though I don't hate it.

'I love you,' he whispers into my ear, squeezing my hand tightly before finally walking away, allowing our hands to drop only when our fingers can no longer touch.

Truthfully, I may put on a hell of a *fuck the world* exterior, but inside, I'm not as secure as I pretend and Will knows this. I mean, who really is? We've all got insecurities, and mine seem to shine the brightest when I'm around his picture-perfect, never-suffered-a-day-in-their-life family.

I walk to my chair at the end of the table, all alone in Timbuktu, sitting between Jacob at the head to my right and Finn to my left. One of these men scares the hell out of me, and the other I've never met. Finn's an unusual-looking guy, tall, messy black hair like he just rolled out of bed to join us, with a hook of a nose and eyebrows that meet in the middle.

My gaze wanders back to Felicity. She's chattering to Will in a hushed voice, leaning into him, looking smitten as a kitten. Her gestures, the way she speaks, the way she looks at me like I'm trash. She's so clearly one of them. She continues talking to Will – quiet enough I can't overhear her words, but she makes sure her giggle at whatever he's just said is audible and I catch her glancing my way.

Will, however, looks like he's at a job interview and already knows he's not interested – he's humoring her and his parents by being nice. That's Will, *nice*. And so, *so* handsome. Six-one, strong shoulders, dark brown hair that's a tad too long on top right now so it's swept to one side, clean-shaven, and his eyes – wow. Big golden-flecked whiskey-colored eyes that could convince me of absolutely anything.

'Hellooo.' Finn drags out the word, somehow making the two syllables sound dirty as I reach for my water glass.

'Hi?'

He leans into me, our shoulders brushing against one another. 'In twenty, you should meet me in the bathroom upstairs, end of the hall.' He says the words into my ear like a sweet nothing that makes my skin crawl. The way he waggles his eyebrow sends a creepy shiver down my spine.

'Choked the can and don't know how to use the plunger?' I ask.

'They never use that bathroom so it would give us an opportunity to get to know one another, intimately.'

I grimace, leaning away from him. 'I uh, think your parents' money is giving you too much confidence.'

'Berkley.' Jacob coughs my name as he clears his throat. Apparently, that was rude?

Will glances over, worry on his face. I shrug. *Just disappointing your parents, once again.*

'Let's get this evening started, shall we?' Jacob stands, tapping his fork on the fancy-schmancy crystal I better not drop or they'll surely bill me for it. 'First, a toast,' he says. 'To the future of the Adler family, the Harper family and Portland. We've got exciting things coming our way.' He lifts his glass, the table following suit.

Considering neither of those are my last name, it's abundantly clear that Will was right. This isn't a graduation party.

'*And* Berkley,' Will says.

I bite back a proud grin as he stands from his chair, his eyes on me as he lifts his glass.

'You're graduating college next weekend with a higher GPA than probably any of us. I'm so proud of you.'

How is he this good at continuing to sweep me off my feet so many years into our relationship?

No one at the table acknowledges his words; they just stare like he's spoken without permission. He's the black sheep of the family – the one they have to chase and bribe into behaving whatever way they want. They're always disappointed in him. It's hard to watch and probably even harder to go through. He doesn't love talking about what goes on between them, and I don't push. It's probably why I've never heard of the Harpers.

Thank you. I mouth the words to him. Then he does this thing he's done the entire time we've dated. He points to his chest, then to me. A silent *I love you* that's consistently earned some weird swoony sigh from me. He's a total romantic, and I love it so much.

'What he said,' Jacob says, tilting his drink my way before tossing it back in one swallow. 'What are your plans going forward, Berkley?' he asks, sitting back down at the head of the table.

'Um...' I didn't expect him to ask about me. This almost never happens.

'We do not start our sentences with *um*,' Melinda corrects me. 'I thought you were a writing minor?'

Rude.

'Um...' This time, I repeat it just to annoy her. Because why not? 'I was a writing minor, but right now, I'm speaking. Did you know people use "um" as a filler while they find the right word or to break into a conversation without being rude and using something inappropriate like "listen up, fuckers".'

Will snorts a laugh as his water glass is headed towards his lips, missing his mouth completely, then gasping as he accidentally dumps it down his shirt. Every head at the table turns to him. Clearly he'd die if he was choking to death because no one is attempting to leave their seats and help him. Finally, he pulls himself together, forcing away one last chuckle.

'Sorry.' He dabs his napkin to his chest.

Knowing he'll live, all eyes turn back to me, horror on their faces like I've just publicly murdered a kitten we will now eat for dinner.

'As for my plans,' I continue like I didn't just offend nearly everyone in the room. 'Our apartment remodel is nearly complete and we're moving in in three weeks. Frank's retiring, and I'm now store manager. I hope to one day own it.'

'Is it a grocery store?' Felicity asks, like grocery store employee is less than respectable. I bet she's never even stepped foot in one.

'It's a bookstore,' I say. 'You know, books?' I push my hands together to represent an open book. 'Those things people read to make themselves smarter. We sell those. If you can read, you should try one sometime.'

Yes, I'm being a snotty bitch to her. In my defense, not only does she want to steal my boyfriend, but she started this with the puppy-love pound comment. Now I'm just making sure she truly hates me, so I never have to converse with her again. My behavior's completely logical.

'I suppose you read the sad single woman porn too?' she asks.

'If she doesn't yet, she's about to...' Mikey says with an evil chuckle, his eyes on Will. They shoot one another a glare. Note to self: ask Will what that was about when we get home later.

'First of all, I'm not sad or single. Second, Will does an unbelievable job of keeping me romantically and sexually satisfied, thank you very much.'

Felicity frowns but Will grins with pride. And horror now lives freely on Melinda's face as she glances between us. Is she truly only just realizing we sleep together?

'But to answer your question, sure,' I say. 'I read some. Erotica, spice, fluff, romance, guilty pleasure, or whatever you need to call it to make yourself feel important, we stock it.' I stab a fork into my side salad, going for a crouton but failing. 'For the spicy stuff, Will and I try it out to see how possible it is. If it's not, I copy and paste the scene into an email I send to Mike from an anonymous account that he literally responds to. He's been begging "Amanda Mount" to come over and show him how to have sex for years.'

Mike snorts at this revelation. 'That's *you*?'

I nod, a proud smile plastered on my face.

A deep disappointed sigh leaves Melinda's lips. 'We're setting Felicity up with William,' she says, her eyes on me. 'It's been our plan all along.'

It's been her plan? I can't believe she just said those words out loud. To the entire table. Like she's arranging a fucking marriage.

'No way on God's green earth will that ever happen,' Will argues.

Felicity gasps, pulling a hand to her chest, like she didn't expect to be rejected.

'You can't be serious about the woman who just used both the F word *and* referred to erotica at the dinner table, are you?' she argues with Will. 'She's catfishing your brother.'

'*We* are catfishing my brother,' Will informs her. 'That account was my idea.'

Melinda's jaw drops. 'Why would you do that to your brother?'

'For laughs, mostly, but also because he's a dick,' he says, shooting Mike another glare, then turning his attention to his plate.

Melinda's brow furrows. 'Michael is *not* a dick.'

'At least not a big one,' I say under my breath, flashing Jacob a smirk as he side-eyes me.

Mike shakes his head. Oops, he heard me. All eyes are now on me, probably expecting me to apologize for even existing in their world.

'Um,' I say, just for fun now. 'I take full responsibility for the F word, but Felicity used the word *porn*,' I remind Melinda. 'If we're going to chastise someone for talking about a specific topic, let's at least hold accountable the woman who brought it to the table.'

Melinda glares my way. 'Sweetheart,' she says, turning her attention to Will, patting his hand, which is the closest she's come to hugging one of her sons since she birthed them. 'Berkley just isn't the quality of woman we hoped to see you with.' She continues speaking like I'm not literally sitting two chairs away from her. 'I didn't want to say this in front of her, but Felicity is more your type for the long term.' She side-eyes me, lowering her voice, probably in a last-minute attempt to spare my feelings based on whatever my face is doing right now. 'She's from a great family and knows how to behave in a way that won't embarrass us. You'd have beautiful babies.'

Babies? She's planning their children too?

'Berkley's the kind of girl you lose your virginity to and then move on,' Mike adds.

O-ffen-sive. They don't expect me to sit here silently and take this abuse, do they? 'Cause if so, they obviously don't know me well.

'Must be true,' I say, lifting a shoulder. 'Considering Finn just asked if I'd take his virginity in the bathroom upstairs later.'

Mike bursts a laugh but Finn shoots me a glare.

Will's entire aura changes from annoyed to pissed. He tosses his napkin onto his plate. 'You *what*?' he barks in Finn's direction.

Finn shrugs, shaking his head like he's no idea what I'm talking about.

'Why would you say that to her?' Will yells.

'*Let her go*, William,' Melinda pleads with him. 'It's the right thing to do. Tell him it's the right thing to do, Michael.'

'Do it,' Mike says, staring at his phone, not paying attention to even one word. 'Get you some rich ass.' He glances my way with his usual douchey arrogant grin.

How. Fucking. Dare. Him.

I reach across Finn, grab Mike's phone from his hands, and drop it into his sparkling water. Ker-plunk, asshole.

'Damn it, Berk!' Mike yells, grabbing the phone from his glass and shaking it out, sprinkling sparkling water all over Felicity, who's sitting across the table from him. She lets out a horrified squeal that would make you think it was acid, not water.

'*This is Valentino, you idiot!*' she yells at Mike, standing up so urgently she sends her chair to the floor with a crash, startling everyone.

Will and my gazes meet, both wide-eyed and unsure how to react to any of this. This dinner is suddenly chaotically unhinged, like a Griswold family get-together. I hope we laugh about it later but presently, I'm low-key terrified of how this will end.

'Blame Berkley; *she* did it,' Mike says, like we're twelve and he played no part in all this.

Melinda turns her attention to me, her face pinched in a way that might hurt. 'Since you're insistent on ruining the dinner we're throwing you, I might as well get this over with. Here.' She pulls a card from under her plate, handing it to me via Felicity. 'Perhaps this will help you not leave here completely broken-hearted.'

'You got me a gift?' I act shocked as I peel the envelope open, pulling out a graduation card, signed *The Adlers*. God, she should be a fucking poet. It's the same heartwarming message they wrote on my high school graduation card. Inside is a check for twenty-five thousand dollars.

Wait.

What?

I look at it again, heat rising from my chest to the top of my ears, and tears burn my eyes as they attempt to surface. Her words play back in my head: *maybe this will help you not leave here completely broken-hearted.* Will was right. This is an intervention to rid the family of me.

'Is this...?' I blink back tears threatening to spill over.

'A small bribe, darling.' Melinda pinches her fingers together like it's no big deal. 'Nothing worth crying over. You just made more than you'll make all year!'

'Jesus, Mom!' Will yells, standing from his chair and making his way to me. 'I told you, I can do this without losing Berkley.'

'Do *what*?' I ask, desperately trying to pull it together. I glance at Will, completely confused.

'You still haven't told her?' Jacob asks, his face full of amusement.

'Based on the convos Berkley and I have had today, I can confirm he has *not* told her,' Mike interjects, an evil grin on his face as he frantically taps at his phone screen because his lifeline to the world has recently drowned and he needs to resuscitate it.

'I'm working on it,' Will snaps back. 'I was going to talk to her tonight—'

'Talk to me about *what*?'

Will kneels next to me, glancing at the check and card in my hand before dragging a hand down his face.

'If he won't say it, I will. We're doing a show,' Felicity says like I'm the dumbest girl in all the land. '*PDX Royals*. It's about a lifestyle you wouldn't understand, *book* girl.'

She calls me 'book girl' like it's supposed to hurt my feelings. 'Thank you, *rude* girl.'

Will says nothing at all. He just looks vocally constipated in a way that's pissing me off. I turn my attention back to the table.

'*PDX Royals*? What is this show? *The Real World: Trust Fund Edition*?'

'I can't believe she guessed it,' Mike says flatly, a smug smirk on his stupid face.

'Don't worry, muffin,' Finn says, nudging me with his elbow. 'After you dump Will, you can bunk with me.'

Gross.

'One more word from you, and I'll hurt you,' Will says, pointing a finger at Finn.

'*William!*' Melinda bolsters. 'We do *not* threaten violence in this house.'

'Bullshit, we don't,' Will counters.

'Can everyone just... *stop... talking*!' The table silences at my raised voice as I throw my hands out in front of me, attempting to focus on everything being said. I feel like my head is on a swivel as different information comes at me from different people. I look to Will, still kneeling beside me, frustration on his face as he stares at the check in his hand.

'You're *doing* this show?'

He shakes his head, his hand on my knee, fixing me with his eyes. *Don't do that. Don't sweet-talk me with your beautiful smoldering face.*

'I, uh...' He swallows hard before finishing his sentence. 'I don't know yet.'

'You don't *know*?' Mike bursts a laugh. 'You signed a contract, a lease, and we start filming in two weeks. You're definitely doing it.'

A contract and a lease? But *we* had plans to move in together three weeks from today. We designed the place together, and Will insisted he pay the contractor. They've nearly finished. Oh, my God. *This* is why he wanted to make sure I knew he loved me? So I wouldn't be mad? Well, he's in luck. I'm not mad. I'm fucking livid.

I stand up, tossing my napkin at Will. He stands with me, casually grabbing the napkin before it can hit his face. I yank the check from his other hand, wad it up and throw it at his father, watching it bounce off his forehead and onto his plate.

'Well, this was fun,' I say sarcastically.

'Berkley—' Will attempts to grab my hand, but I pull away.

'You know what? I don't *need* money to leave this family alone. The lying and reminders I'm not worthy are plenty to make me never want to step foot in this house again.'

I turn to Will, my heart utterly full of pins, like a voodoo doll. I blink back tears as I attempt to find the words I need, but they're angry and I know they'll do more damage than good. Will's the only person I've ever stopped and considered my words with because I never want to hurt him, yet now I'm about to tell him off in front of his family.

'I can't believe you're actually one of them. You lied to me, William. Just like a fucking Adler. We had plans for our future and you go off and make this kind of decision without even talking to me? Not even a heads-up. Just a family dinner to toss me aside so you can live life on some ridiculous fucking show.'

'Berkley.' Will repeats my name, his voice weak, extending a hand my way. 'Let's go talk.'

'I have nothing to say to you.'

'She's a little overly dramatic considering they're not married, isn't sh—'

'*Shut. Up.* Felicity,' Will barks at her.

This. Woman. She'll be lucky if I don't drown her in that sparkling water. I want to tell her off, but my head is all over the place and my heart is in pieces at my feet. I can't stay here for another second as I am about to have a really ugly cry and this is not the place. The whole room would undoubtedly film it and air it on their stupid show.

I dodge Will and storm out of the house, heading straight for his Jeep. The only place I can disappear since I didn't drive myself here and it's too far to walk home.

I yank the door handle repeatedly, setting off the alarm, which Will flips off with the clicker in his hand as he walks my way. Without a word he pulls open the passenger door for me. As I get in, our eyes meet, and we stare at one another for a moment. He's never lied to me before and this one changes everything, my entire life, *all* our plans – gone. Ugh. Talk about worst graduation dinner ever.

3

WILL ADLER

What a fucking nightmare. I should have expected this, yet somehow, I didn't. Berkley's right. I lied to her. A big fucking lie that changes all the plans we'd made.

She and I have been together a long time. I know all her faces, moods, everything about her. She's pissed in a way I've not experienced directed at me before. Sure, we've been in some battles with my parents in the past, and we've had some fights. But she's never called me one of them or stormed out of the house like she just did. Then again, they've also never tried to pay her to dump me or announced they're pairing me off with a woman I've got zero interest in. Then, without warning, they spilled the fucking tea about the show. I knew if I didn't tell her soon, she'd find out another way, and I was desperately trying to prevent that, but things moved so quickly. Now it looks like I was a part of the conspiracy against her. She must feel terrible.

I get into my Jeep and start it, glancing over at her, but she's scowling out her window, her arms crossed over her chest tightly as she leans into her door, staying as far from me as possible.

'You might spark that tree on fire with that glare if you're not careful,' I joke, attempting to lighten the mood.

'Guess I better stare at the house then so that'll go up in flames too.'

'Berkley, I'm sorry.' I reach over to touch her, but she leans further into the door. Ouch. 'I was going to tell you tonight. I didn't expect those loudmouths to come out with it like they did.'

Silence, but an eye roll so I know she's listening.

'Nothing we're planning for our future is ruined; we can still move in together. I'll film from our place.'

'Did you ever think that maybe I don't want to be a part of this show? You know I hate the spotlight and now you want to move into our apartment *and* have cameras following our every move. Nope. I'm out.'

I sigh heavily. 'You still want to come over and we can talk more about it?'

Head shake.

'Want me to take you home instead?'

Nod.

'You want me to shut up?'

Another nod.

My heart slows with each of her wordless responses. The silent game is a first for us and I don't love it. Yes, as Mike and Felicity so harshly informed her, I did sign multiple contracts to participate in the *Royals* show. *Without* discussing it with her first. How do you bring something like this up? *Hey, Berx. I've decided to take the shallow rich-boy path and attempt fame* The Real Rich Kids of Portland-*style. What do you say? Up for my annoying family and friends and airing our dirty laundry for the world to see?*

Berkley isn't an air-our-dirty-laundry kind of girl. Sure, she's got a mouth like dynamite and can be absolutely fearless, but she's also private. She hates having her emotions on display or being the center of attention – two things essential for reality TV now that I think about it.

Why did I think she'd be good with this? In my defense, my parents and the production team talked it up like a lifetime opportunity and convinced me she'd eventually be all in. That does not appear to be the case. I'm not sure I can even talk myself out of this, but I have to try; I love this woman.

After we've merged onto the freeway, she speaks. 'Was this you or your asshole family?'

'Both?' I answer honestly.

'Explain.'

Here we go.

'A couple months ago, a production company approached my parents and pitched a reality show idea centered around Mike, me, Felicity and Finn. The Harpers are old family friends and some of the richest assholes on the west coast, along with my parents. They got the ball rolling and didn't even include me in it until a few weeks ago. I've meant to tell you about it every day since I found out, but my parents kept telling me that these things don't often close, so I wanted to wait until I knew it was a sure thing. When I ended up signing, it was rushed and chaotic, and my head was spinning with all the info I was presented with. I kind of did it because everyone else did, and they were looking at me like I'd ruin their lives if I didn't participate. It was all four of us or no one. You know how my family is. What was I supposed to do?'

'I dunno, maybe tell them that you need to discuss this with your girlfriend of seven fucking years?'

I nod. 'You're absolutely right. I should have done that, but I didn't and I'm sorry.'

The way she shakes her head, staring out the windshield, her lips pressed together tightly, visibly pissed, hurts my heart.

Keep talking until you've talked your way out of this, Will.

'Reality TV is hot right now, Berx, and fuck knows what else I'd do with my life. I feel like a total loser living off my parents' money like some rich brat. Look what Mike's turned into. I can't become that guy. I wanted to do something to provide for myself. For *us*. And apparently, following around four trust-fund kids seems to be something people want to love to hate, and more importantly I can get paid for it. A *lot*. It seemed like an easy way to replace my trust before my parents really do take it.'

Her head swivels my way slowly. 'You *want* people to love to hate you?'

'I don't know that I *want* it, but—'

'No, no,' she says quickly, cutting me off. 'It's perfect because it's exactly what I'm doing right now.'

A disbelieving chuckle leaves my lips. 'No way do you hate me.'

She shoots me a glare. 'I don't understand. Does what I think not mean anything to you?'

'What you think means *everything* to me.'

'We met with a contractor months ago. They're nearly done with the remodel, William. You wrote him a check in full. Contractors are in the apartment now. I ordered furniture! And now you're suddenly moving somewhere *else*? I guess I'll cancel all that then.'

'Do not cancel anything, Berx. You can't live there the way it is. It's been vacant for decades. When the show is over, I can still move in. It's just temporary. I'm not doing this forever.'

'How long?'

'Two years.'

'Two *years*?!' She stares out the windshield, her face blank. 'So, I'm just supposed to go on without you and wait for you to become a reality star and then we can get on with our lives?'

It sounds *so* bad. 'I know, it's bad, I realized that this morning when they threw another "rule" on me.'

'There are *rules*? Like what?'

'Like, only bathrooms are private spaces. Drama is encouraged. And...' Fuck. This is why I was fighting with my father earlier. She might dump me for this and I wouldn't blame her. I'd be heartbroken, but I'd get it. 'The network thinks the show will be more successful if the four of us go into this... single.'

For a moment she says nothing, just silently seethes. 'Well, that's just perfect for your girlfriend, isn't it? Did you even tell them I exist?'

'Of course I did, Berx. I begged for you to move in with us, but they weren't keen on that idea.'

She slaps a hand onto her forehead and groans. 'My God, I'm an idiot. The love of my life wants to bone other women on camera. I'll be humiliated.'

'Bone other women? Are you out of your mind? I may go into this seeming single but obviously you're still the only girl I ever want to bone.'

Tears slide down her cheeks and she wipes them away quickly, probably hoping I won't notice.

'Baby...'

'Do not *baby* me, Adler; you can't fix this by being sweet. I can't believe you did this. Do you have any idea what this will do to you?'

'What do you mean? I'll still be me, Berx.'

'No, you'll be some Kardashian wannabe whose world suddenly revolves around yourself and I'll become a distant memory. The girl who took your virginity, just like your mom said. Holy crap!' she says. 'They did it! Your asshole parents bested us and found a way to control you, make money *and* get rid of me. And you fell for it.' She drops her head into her hands.

'I don't know what to say to make this better.'

'There's no words to fix this, William, so to save yourself, I'd shut up.'

Ouch. She's never told me to shut up before. Not seriously,

anyway. I drive through the city, towards the apartment she's currently sharing with her sister, silently, as she's requested, but my mind is wandering. I've loved this woman since I was fifteen years old. I fell for her the moment I walked into sophomore homeroom and saw her sitting in the back corner, doodling in her notebook. It was love at first sight for me.

I remember it like it was yesterday. She was wearing bright pink shorts and a white sleeveless blouse with colorful stitched flowers across the top. Her then long hair was colored pastel purple and pulled over one shoulder. She was adorable, and when I wrote the words 'you're pretty' in her notebook after claiming the desk in front of hers, she looked me dead in the eyes and wrote the words 'no thanks, Abercrombie'. I don't know if it was the flirty smirk on her face or the fact that she made me laugh, but I was utterly smitten with her from that moment on.

Every day after that, I'd walk into homeroom, beeline right to her and try again. I'd tell jokes, compliment her, tell stories; I even juggled office supplies one day. Writing in her notebook always got her attention when nothing else would work. Each day it was some version of 'you're pretty', then I'd wait for the words she'd write next. Once, she wrote, 'fuck off, rich kid'. Another time it was 'go away, dork'. But each time it was with a grin that said she didn't really mean it. She seemed to like our flirtatious game so I continued on.

After weeks of mutual flirting, and her pretending to play hard to get, I brought her a present. I had Sylvia teach me how to make cupcakes, and after a few failed batches, I got some that were perfect. I spent forever attempting to keep a steady hand and write 'you're pretty' in icing across the top of two. When I got to school the next day (early, that's how excited I was) I sat the cupcakes on her desk and waited for her to get to class. After a silent moment of her behind me, she jabbed me in the shoulder with her pen, smiled and wrote the following words in her notebook: 'you're pretty too, thx'. Success! We've been inseparable ever since.

My eyes linger on her as I drive. How's she still so gorgeous and getting prettier by the day? Five-three, slender but curvy in all the right spots, big brown eyes, light brown hair falling just below her shoulders that she now fades into blonde, and completely kissable lips. This girl can take care of herself, is well read, sweet as cupcakes and has a huge heart. I trust her entirely, with my life, money, everything I have, and I've just let her down so badly she won't even look at me. It's beyond painful.

I can't give up, though. Hesitantly, I reach over the center console, slide my hand down her thigh and caress her skin with my thumb. She doesn't look at me but lays her hand on mine, tucking her fingers under my palm. It's not much, but it's something.

'I'm sorry,' I tell her. 'I really am. I fucked up, but I'll fix it. I promise.'

'We'd planned our entire lives, Will. The apartment, my job, a future engagement – we've even named our kids. I guess that's all off now.' She cries, dabbing her eyes with her shirt collar.

'None of that's *off*; I'm just taking a couple years to focus on my career. This'll be good for our future, Berkley.'

'How exactly is you becoming some reality TV playboy good for our future?'

That's an excellent question. One I don't exactly have an answer for and considering my situation, it's lame. The money. I can't explain it, but I have this deep-seated need to be independent from my parents, which means making my own living.

Duh, the money! That's right, maybe this will help. I pull the check I kept from my back pocket and hand it to her.

'Take the money. This is nothing for them. Tomorrow, we'll open a new account. One for our future wedding.'

'I don't want that money.'

'Why?'

'Because there is no future wedding, *William*. That's the one part of us that we haven't nailed down because I don't want to ask a guy to propose to me and I don't want to just decide to do it. I want the big, unexpected proposal. But now that dream is dead. By the time the show is over I'm sure you'll be living your best life with your future wife, Mrs Felicity Adler.'

'I'm never marrying that weirdo – we're just working together.'

She groans in frustration. 'Have you seriously never watched reality television, William? Once you become some heart-throb assface that every girl in America wants, you won't even remember my name.'

'Ass-face?' I ask, a little offended. She's never called me an assface. 'Considering you're my number one, forever, there's not a chance I'd ever forget you or your name.'

As we pull into her apartment building, she lets out a heavy sigh. 'I thought that too, but apparently I was wrong.'

'What do we do?' I ask, as I pull into a spot near her apartment and put my Jeep in park.

'Well, I think there's only one thing to do.'

I stare at her, waiting for her to spell it out for me because right now my head is full of what feels like cotton.

'I'm setting you free so you can experience your shallow-as-fuck show as a beautiful single rich douche, so you can focus on your "career",' she says, air quoting 'career'.

'You're setting me free? What's that mean?'

'It means I'm breaking up with you so you don't break your contract, *William*.'

'Will you *stop* calling me William?' I ask a little too aggressively.

She grunts, clearly not liking my tone. 'Go, *William*.' This time she says it just to piss me off as she grabs her bag from my back seat.

'Go live life on this stupid, shallow reality show and fall in love with the most pretentious woman I've ever met.'

'Berkley...'

Is she seriously considering leaving like this?

'Good luck, Adler.' Her voice is small and soft as she says it and I know she's fighting back emotions she doesn't want me to see. Her calling me by my last name is never good either.

'Don't go like this, Berx.'

'I sincerely hope it's everything you're expecting.' Her eyes glaze over with tears and even though she's doing her best to hold them back, she can't and before I know it she's got a hand over her face, covering a sob.

I am an *asshole*. My heart. Jesus. If it stopped right now, it would feel better than this. How could I hurt someone I love this much?

When she grabs the door handle, I panic. This can't be the last time I ever see her. *Do something, Will. Don't let her leave thinking you don't love her.*

Before she can get out, I slide my hand around the back of her neck and pull her to me, kissing her with everything I've got. To my surprise, she kisses me back without hesitation, almost desperately, like this might be our last. Her hand moves to the side of my face, sending clouds of butterflies through my chest. There's no way someone else could cause every nerve in my body to jump to life when they touch me like she does. I can't lose her.

After an unexpected make-out session, she pushes me away, gripping my shirt momentarily before she wipes her lips with her thumb like she's attempting to wipe me away.

'I know you're mad. Break up with me if you need to; this is my fault, and I deserve it, but I can't just quit loving you. Ever. I don't want to know what life's like without you, Berx. I know the show seems crazy and shallow as fuck, but I did it for us. I'll make my own money, to get my parents off my back and I'll do whatever I can to prove that I still want everything we've planned for our life together. I just need to do this, for me. I can't live under their rules our whole life. But I promise, baby, I adore everything about you; hand to God, you're the only woman for me.'

She softens a bit as she stares into my eyes. 'We'll see,' she says, disheartened. After a moment, she hops out of my Jeep, slamming the door shut behind her.

With every step away from me she takes without looking back, my heart sinks slowly through my chest like an anchor thrown off a ship to the bottom of the ocean. Water may as well be filling my lungs as I feel like I can't breathe. I sit in the parking lot even after she disappears into her apartment, phone in my hands as I try and think of anything I can say to save this. But she's right. There are no words. I toss the phone onto the passenger seat and pull away from her building. I fucked up big.

4

WILL

I've been lying here for two weeks unless I have to use the bathroom, eat or get another beer. My phone is next to me, the volume as high as it goes, wishing Berkley would just call me back. She would hardly even talk to me when I showed up at her graduation last weekend. Just took a couple photos with me and then asked me to leave. Like a sword to my heart and I plunged it into my chest all on my own.

The door to my room swings open suddenly. 'Dude.' Bryce, my best friend and roommate, walks in, yanking open the curtains, allowing the sun to assault my vision that's now adapted to the dark cave I'm wallowing in. 'You still alive, man?'

'Unfortunately.'

'Mikey's here.'

'Uggghhhh,' I groan.

Mike here is just adding salt to the wound, considering his big mouth is part of why I'm in this mess. Had he not helped break the news the way he did, maybe I could have saved myself. Who knows? What I do know is that it's always about Mike when he's around.

The man can do no wrong in our parents' eyes, and I can do no right. We aren't exactly friends. Brothers yes, buddies no.

'Mike can fuck off.'

Bryce laughs. 'Already told him, but I get the feeling he ain't going away until you talk to him.'

'*Wil-ly!*' Mike bellows as he invites himself into my room, a beer in his hand. 'This is good,' he says, inspecting the can. 'What is it?'

'Uh, *not* yours?' Bryce answers with attitude.

They aren't friends. Mike doesn't have many friends so he claims mine by default of being my brother. He goes through 'friends' like no one I've ever witnessed. Using them until there's nothing left in it for him, then ghosts them – super stand-up guy.

I roll onto my stomach, pulling the comforter over my head. 'Go away, ass-face.'

'If you don't get out of this bed, the network will cancel the show.'

'Boo-fucking-hoo.'

'You were excited about this until Berkley told you not to be. The whole world will laugh at you if you don't lose the pussy-whipped thing.' He steps onto my bed, jumping up and down to annoy me. 'Come on, Willy. You were supposed to move in two days ago. Stop being a heartsick baby. She didn't die. You're not in mourning.'

'I am too.'

'*Get up*, turdpipe.' He throws a pillow at my head, slowly getting more aggressive – a reminder of our childhood. He would demand I do something, I'd tell him to fuck off, then he'd attempt to beat the hell out of me. Round and round we'd go. 'We start filming in two days.'

'*Leave.*'

'*Ugh*,' he groans like I'm the frustrating one. 'What do I gotta do, little brother?' He lies next to me, repeatedly jabbing me in the side, his elbow pinning my head to my pillow.

I swing his way but don't get a good hit. 'Why don't you crawl up my ass and die?' I shove him over, dumping the beer still in his hand all over us.

He laughs, shoving my head into the puddle of beer on my pillow like the bully he's always been. 'He's feisty when he's heart-broken, eh?'

Bryce is leaning against my door frame with his arms crossed over his chest, watching this scene play out with a blank face. 'He asked you to leave.' He repeats my request.

'Not leaving. I'll drag his ass to our new place if I have to.'

'And I'll *kick* your ass if you try it,' I respond.

'Fine,' he huffs, finally leaving my bed. 'You want to do this the awkward way. I'll play. I called her.'

This gets my attention. I roll over and sit up, turning to him. 'You did *what*?'

'I called Berkley. Told her it was an emergency – asked her to come over urgently.'

I drop back onto my wet pillow, dragging a hand over my face. This asshole. 'What is with this fucking family constantly being in my business?!' I yell. 'Why would you do that?'

'Because it's her fault you're like this. So she needs to come over here, show you her tits, forgive you, do you, whatever, and drag your ass out of the pit of despair you're in so you don't fuck this up for me.'

For *him*. Nice.

'First of all, it's *my* fault I'm like this, not hers. Second, *never* talk about her tits again. Third, you're a selfish prick.'

His slimy laugh irritates me. 'If you're trying to insult me, say something I don't hear daily.'

'People regularly call you a selfish prick?'

He smiles smugly, like he's proud of what he's about to say. 'Not everyone loves a loaded, handsome, important man.'

I roll my eyes. Please. Important? To who? 'That's very humble of you; now leave, assbag.'

Once again, he does not leave, just laughs as he paces in front of me before yanking the comforter from me and tossing it on the floor across the room.

'*Mike*,' I growl. 'You're such a bitch.'

'Now, is that any way to talk to your brother who just convinced your bimbo to race over here and save you from yourself? I suggest you drag your rank ass to the shower before she gets here. You smell like beer and BO.'

This time I jump out of bed. She's racing over? No.

'She said the words she's coming over?' I ask, glancing at my phone. ''Cause she should be closing up the shop right now.'

He nods his head, lifting a single shoulder. 'Apparently, you're worth dodging out of work for. Who fucking knew?'

That's all it takes. I'm in the shower two minutes later, and Mike's throwing my shit into the boxes accumulating in my room like I'm actually moving into this condo. I've barely got pants on when I hear a frantic knocking at the front door. I glance into the living room as I search my dresser for a T-shirt, but it's empty, and my clothes are strewn all over my room. I grab one randomly from the bed, sliding it over my head.

'Why are you knocking?' Bryce asks as he opens the door for her. 'You have a key.'

'We're not exactly a thing anymore so using the key felt wrong. Is he OK?' she asks, talking quickly, her voice panicky. 'Why didn't *you* call me? The last thing I wanted to hear – without warning – was assbag's voice,' she snaps at Bryce.

'Thanks!' Mike yells from my room like he's offended.

She sighs in relief when she sees me walking out of my room, shoving past Bryce and practically running to me, throwing her arms around my neck. Jesus. I wrap my arms around her, lifting her off the floor, kissing her cheek and holding her to me tightly, finally feeling complete again. I didn't expect this greeting, but I feel exactly the same way, sweet girl.

'You're alright,' she says into my ear. 'Mike said you were hurt?'

'He said what?' I set her down, allowing her to inspect me carefully.

'That you were so depressed, you tried to hurt yourself. Did you?'

'No. I mean, I'm depressed, yes, but not hurt-myself depressed. Though I suddenly feel like hurting *someone*...' I glance over at Mike peeking out of my room.

A relieved smile crosses her face, then she hugs me again. 'Mike's such an asshole.'

'Yes, yes he is,' I retort, my gaze moving back to my brother, who's lifting his hands like he's sorry. Liar. *I should hurt you*; I mouth the words as he smirks like the smarmy piece of shit he is.

'I'm gonna give you two a few,' Bryce says, backing out of the room towards his bedroom on the other side of our apartment. I'm glad he's good at reading the room. 'Mikey!' he yells. 'Get out!'

'Later,' Mike says, dodging past Berkley like he's afraid of her. He should be, 'cause if she wanted to murder him right now, I'd gladly help. 'I got your lady here, now pack your shit,' he orders as he exits. 'Or I'll be back with Finn to drag your pathetic heart-sick ass over, and that's not a threat; we'll do it. You're not ruining this for us.'

I flip him off. He might be an asshole, but that asshole somehow got Berkley here when I couldn't. He shuts the front door behind him, leaving the two of us standing only inches apart, one of her hands loosely in mine. Now to figure out what to say.

5

BERKLEY

For a moment he stares at me, a not-so-subtle smile on his face. 'You look good.' The words tumble from his lips as if he's at a loss, or unsure how I'll react. If he had a tail, it'd be between his legs right now.

'We both know I look like shit, but thanks,' I say meekly.

'Nah,' he says sweetly. 'You've never been anything but beautiful.'

'Will—'

'I'm miserable without you, Berkley.' He cuts me off, squeezing my hands in his.

Why's it so hard to hide my feelings from this man? Maybe because before now I never have. He *looks* miserable. He hasn't shaved since I saw him last, by the looks of it, and he needed a haircut two weeks ago; now it's just unruly. But adorable. I want to kiss the hell out of him.

No, Berkley. Do not let him in already! Stand your ground. He made a giant decision that ruined your future together and lied to you.

'I'm gonna blow off the show,' he says. 'Everyone will hate me but I can't lose you—'

'Will, don't,' I say, a painful twang shooting through my heart. I've thought long and hard about this and I've got some things to say.

'*Don't?* I thought that's what you wanted? For me not to do the show.'

'What I *wanted* was for you *not* to lie to me about something this huge. But that didn't happen, so...' I cross my arms over my chest. 'I assume you lied because you *want* to do it? You don't seem very happy about it now.'

'I lost the best thing I've ever had because of this show; nothing about that feels happy.'

As I walk to his couch, I heave a sigh, tossing my bag onto it before sitting down. He follows, sitting on the coffee table to face me. We've been in a lot of fights. Mostly small things. He's so organized it annoys me. His tone was wrong. *My* tone was wrong. I put the milk back in his fridge with only a swallow left. I'm overly stubborn (so I'm told). He uses the toilet – for both numbers – while I'm in the shower. Little things, ya know? Annoyances. This is the biggest fight we've ever had and the only time we've ever broken up for real.

I don't even know what to say so instead I start picking the bright blue polish off my nails. Why am I ruining a perfectly good manicure? *Just talk to him. You've rehearsed this five hundred times over the last couple weeks, Berx. Say it.*

'I'm miserable too,' I admit softly, glancing up at him with only my eyes. I wish I could lie and say I'm fine, but I can't. I can't lie to him so how he did it so easily I don't get. He looks relieved to hear the words. I couldn't not say them. I'm here wearing not a stitch of makeup, and my hair's pulled into a messy ponytail. I rarely leave my apartment like this. I haven't even worked since we parted ways that day and until an hour ago, I couldn't even remember the last time I showered.

'You shouldn't have lied to me.'

'If I could take it back, I would.'

'If only time machines were real,' I kid.

'Ha-ha,' he laughs softly. 'Not gonna lie,' he says, a hint of a guilty grin on his face. 'I looked 'em up. I had high hopes for that Elon Musk, but he disappointed me again.'

I stifle my smile. 'You're not allowed to make me smile right now.'

'It's my only talent, Berx. To me, your smile is brighter than the sun. I love seeing it.'

This time I can't hold back a laugh. 'Laying it on a little thick there, aren't ya? You going to hang the moon for me next?'

'I could probably build a really big ladder. I got a lotta change in the bank.'

I roll my eyes playfully. Time to steer this boat into serious-ville. 'All I've done for two weeks is overthink all this,' I say. 'I need to talk. Only the person I want to talk to is you. But, warning, it's about you.'

'About me or not, please never stop talking to me. I craved hearing your voice so much I listened to your voicemail a couple dozen times—'

'Forty-seven,' I say. I counted. With each ring another piece of my heart dropped to its death.

'Then I called your sister. You may not look identical, but your voices are. About killed me.' He dramatically grabs his chest.

'I talked to Bianca yesterday and she didn't tell me you called.'

'I asked her not to. I didn't want you to think I was pathetic.'

I sigh, staring into his eyes. He's sweet and maddening all at once. I can actually see why a network might think he'd be entertaining. *I* on the other hand am *not* TV material. Nobody wants to watch a girl eat an entire bag of SkinnyPop popcorn while reading a book about love for eight hours straight.

Wait a second, he missed me but also asked my sister to keep a secret from me? How many more secrets are there? Or will there be by the time this is all over?

'I hate that you're hiding things from me. That's not you. Usually, you're sweet and honest, and you hate upsetting me. Now you're lying, scheming with your psycho family behind my back, and disappointing me like it's your job.'

'There was no scheming,' he says, attempting to defend himself, but I'm not buying it.

'I gotta ask, Will, is this the first big lie you've ever told me?'

'Yes,' he assures me. 'I promise, there was no Adler-style scheming, Berx – at least not on my part. It just... I think...' He stumbles over his thoughts. 'The whole thing got away from me, and I didn't know how to tell you because I didn't want to let you down. I thought this would be an easy, quick way to make some money so we could get out from under my parents' thumb. I want to take care of us, Berkley. *Me.* I don't want my parents being more of a man than I am. But I swear, lesson learned. Trust me, baby, I'll never lie to you again, and yes, I realize how ironic that wording is.'

Damn my heart for forcing through a smile. I sigh. Having no control over your heart is exhausting.

'This is like, what, an inner struggle? Some kind of life quest your heart thinks you need?'

'Well, you own my heart but my soul is telling me I need to make my own way. Create my own life. This is a way to do that and it seems fun. I'll only live a few blocks away, and since you want no part of this, we can totally still see each other as much as we want.'

'Or as little,' I say, watching him frown.

'The contracts are iron-clad. I fought with my parents about it that day at their house. The network owns my ass for at minimum two years. What if you don't live there, but play the part of my on-screen girlfriend?' he suggests. 'Let's show the whole world what true love really is, Berx.'

His adorable crooked smile right now. I can't even. The man is going to break me.

Stay strong, Berx. Being a part of this would for sure ruin you. Think about all those failed reality stars attempting to resurrect themselves or worse yet, in jail. Ya don't need that.

'No. I'm not turning into the Kardashian family to boost your ego. This is *your* thing. Mine is the bookstore and the apartment remodel I'm now the lone boss of.'

His brows squish together as he thinks. 'How about... you *don't* be a part of the show, but you're still my behind-the-scenes girlfriend?'

I burst out a disbelieving laugh. '*Behind the scenes*? You really have lost your mind, haven't you? Will, that implies there will be a different on-screen girlfriend. No. Break-up still on.'

He glares playfully, or maybe painfully.

'You know that feeling you have right now?' I ask, poking his chest. 'That's the guilt of making a decision without even asking my opinion. Who knows? Maybe I'd have been on board. But instead, you sinned first and asked for forgiveness later. That doesn't work for me, Will. What will you fail to tell me while you're living this life? How much stuff will I find out along with the rest of the world? My heart can't do it. This is already life-changing and I got absolutely no opinion on it.'

'It's not just guilt,' he says, now holding my hand to his chest. 'I miss you. I honestly don't know who I am without you.'

'Well, maybe now is a good time for us to figure that out? I mean, who really ends up with their first love anyway?' I ask, my heart sinking through my chest like a rock tossed into a pond. 'Maybe we need a two-year break and after we can meet up for coffee and see if what we thought was love really is.'

We stare into one another's eyes – I hate that this hurts so much. *This!! Sucks!! Will!! How could you do this?!?* That's what I want to scream at him if you were wondering if I'm at all mad about this. I am. For the record – I'm pissed. But broken-hearted trumps pissed. Then there's the fact that love doesn't just go away; it's part of why it's one of the most painful emotions of them all. It lingers long past its arrival.

'You don't want to talk to me for two years?' he asks, his voice rising with each word.

'Talking leads to laughing and laughing leads to flirting and that leads to my pants dropping to the floor on their own. So *no*, we should probably just legitimately move on and have new experiences – figure out who we are as independent adults. That's what you wanted, remember? Independence.'

He cocks his head. 'From my asshole family, not you.'

'This decision affected me more than it will them. I was expecting a blissful summer with my best friend and boyfriend, in our brand new, beautiful apartment. But now I'm doing that on my own and you're going to be creating a new life that the whole city will fall in love with.'

'Maybe they'll hate me; you don't know.'

'Yes, I do,' I say. 'I know because it's exactly what I did.'

'Berkley,' he says with a sigh, dropping to his knees from the coffee table in front of me. 'You're my best friend. How do I live any life without you? Tell me how.'

'I don't know, Will,' I say, sudden tears burning the backs of my eyeballs.

'Wait a second,' he says, his face suddenly lifting. 'We're best friends. Maybe friends don't do some of the things *we* do but one thing they always do is talk...'

'And that means?'

'It means we can still be friends while I do the show.'

'Friends?' I ask. I think about this for a moment. 'I dunno...'

'Don't mull it over silently – speak.'

'I *don't* want to be on the show, Will. If the world only knows you, the tabloids have no way of ruining us. Your family will be attempting that already and I can't stand up to the wrath of the all-powerful Adler name.'

'Tabloids?' He laughs, moving to sit on the coffee table in front of me. 'You think this is going to fly into popularity? Have you met Mike, Finn and Felicity?'

'Yes,' I remind him. 'They're a train wreck, all three of them; that's binging material. You'll be mingling with reality-show greats before the apartment is even finished.'

'No way,' he says, shaking his head.

'You do realize you could have gotten a job at McDonald's, and I'd still love you, right? I'm not with you because you have an outrageous trust fund.'

'I think you'd love the discount you'd get on food if I worked there most,' he jokes.

So I have a palate of a five-year-old. It's comfort food.

'But yes, I know. I'm in this now, and I'm sorry I hurt you, truly. I also hurt me in the process. I've lain in bed for two weeks, mourning our relationship while trying to find some way to apologize properly and get you back.'

'I've got a hundred and sixty-eight of those apologies in my apartment right now.'

He's sent me flowers every day since I tossed him to the curb. He and the florist are probably on a first-name basis.

'Yet I know you're still the most beautiful thing in that apartment.'

'Bianca's going to be offended,' I joke. We are living together until our apartment is ready. *My* apartment. God, that's weird. Who knows if he'll ever even live there. I can't think about it or I'll be in a ball of tears on the floor of my shower when I get home. A place I've been too many times over the last couple of weeks as it is.

'Friends don't call each other beautiful,' I say.

'Yes they do.'

'Well, *you* can't because it makes me miss you.'

He smirks. 'Missing me is bad?'

'In this situation, *yes*.'

'Do you think I'm capable of not missing you every second you're not around? We text two hundred times a day. Our Snapchats are *busy*. Who are you going to call at two in the morning when you wake from a bad dream? Hell, who will I call throughout the day to say something I know you'll love just because I know it'll make you smile? *Miss* isn't even a strong enough word. For you, Berkley, I pine. Covet. Desire. Need. Crave. Yearn. Thirst.' He's listing off words as he grabs my hand, pulling it to his chest like he's acting out a Shakespeare scene. 'Shall I go on?' He pauses the dramatics.

'No, no, I get it. Maybe we make some rules?'

'Rules?' he asks, finally back to his serious self.

'Yeah,' I say, standing from the couch and pacing around the room. It's what I do when I'm mulling things over. Things I already know the answer to but am trying to justify that answer to guarantee the outcome I want. I'm human. 'You know how sometimes I have terrible ideas, and you go along with them?'

'Most of those ideas end up low-key brilliant; however, the truck-stop sushi to save on time is suddenly racing back to me.'

I gasp. 'I forgot about that one. Worst getaway weekend ever.'

'Worst *sushi* ever,' he corrects me. 'Nicest hotel bathroom, though. Thank God that you love me no matter what, right?'

Our eyes meet as we both freeze. I love him no matter what? Damn it. *That's* why this is so hard. I want to love him through this but I know I should walk away. Then again, like he said, we are friends and friends support friends.

'This might be crazy, but what if... We're breaking up, I get that, but isn't there usually some leeway in that?'

'Leeway?'

'Yeah.' He nods enthusiastically, now standing in front of me. 'You wanted to make rules – let's do it. Rule number one: friends do tell one another they're beautiful.'

I roll my eyes. 'Fine, beautiful boy. Rules number two, three and four: friends do not flirt, friends do not date and friends definitely do *not* say the L word.' I lift a finger with each new rule.

'L for lettuce, I agree, moving on.' He tries to blow past it but I hold out a hand to stop him.

'*Love*, Will. I'm talking about saying we love one another. We're spending the next two years broken up, so no lovey-dovey stuff. My heart can't take it.'

He frowns hard, rubbing the back of his neck frustratedly. 'Rule number five: the closure clause,' he says suddenly. 'May I present my idea?'

'I can only imagine what this is going to be.'

'Imagine it, Berx. This is going to be difficult. You may pine for me too. And if you do, we can use the closure clause. I've heard when people who've dated long-term break up, they often have a few relapses before the break-up takes. After that they walk away.'

'And if I do the math you did on the phone calls earlier, I'd assume a few is like twenty-five in your mind?'

He steps closer, a crooked smile on his face as he grabs one of my hands. 'Berkley, I'm serious. We've dated for seven years. I hurt you, and ruined our plans for the unforeseen future, but I'm in this and it's going to be hard for us to just stop seeing one another. If I had to guess I'd say there might be times where we can't help but call one another and why can't we be who we were in those moments. I want to be able to wean off of you if I have to do this.'

My heart slows. This is really happening. He really can't get out of this and everything is going to change.

'We get three relapses and after that, we stick with the meeting up for coffee when it's all over to see if anything is left.'

Three relapses? It sounds so sad, yet kind of romantic. Like a romance book.

'OK?' I say, unsure if it's the right answer or not, but not knowing how else to do this.

'And tonight we get a freebie,' he throws in, sliding his hands around my waist.

'There it is, the road to more than three: freebies.' I laugh. 'We can't break the rules on day number one.'

'Why not? Only we will ever know,' he says, lowering his voice.

'I have a sinking suspicion that I will regret this, but alright, I'm in. Those are the rules. Shall we shake to make it official?'

'No,' Will says, pulling me against him and planting a kiss on my lips and just like I always do, I melt into him. God, I missed him.

Here we go. *PDX Royals* vs. Berkley Kaine. How bad could it possibly be?

6

BERKLEY

Six Months Later, December 2020

PDX ROYALS FANS – MEET THE STARS

HELLO, *PDX ROYALS*! Apparently, giant trust funds are all you need to be considered American royalty, and these four singles fit the bill. This brand new show has captured the heart of reality-television lovers all over the country and has secured four guaranteed seasons of chaos you can't look away from. With only three episodes airing so far, the show has garnered the highest rankings on the E! since we started keeping up with the Kardashians.

Based in Portland, Oregon, the show follows the lives of siblings Mike and Will Adler along with Finn and Felicity Harper. All bets are off on future storylines as the cast find their way into adulthood – and possible love – while living life off trust funds their parents have rules on and partying at the most elite clubs in the city. Which of the four will grab your heart? Let's meet our stars!

48

AIMEE BROWN

Finn Harper is the oldest at twenty-seven. As a gourmet food blogger and chef, he is focused on finding the best food in the city while looking for love in all the wrong places. Club bathrooms and fancy cars are the settings for his romantic shenanigans – careful googling that. Finn's already made quite the name for himself online. Let's just say that Kardashian sex tape is nothing compared to what we've dug up on Lord Finn of PDX.

Next up is self-proclaimed 'King' Mikey Adler, twenty-six. As a club promoter-slash-property investor, the 'big dog on campus' is on every VIP list in town and sees himself as the show's star. After all, it's one of his viral videos that caught the attention of the network to begin with. Swagger and charm are Mikey's game, and women flock to this stunner – or maybe it's the way he throws around that black card? Either way, watch out because money and power are the keys to his heart, and if you get in the way, you might find yourself at the mercy of his powerful parents, Jacob and Melinda Adler, who own half the city and protect their eldest son fiercely.

Felicity Harper is the lone princess of the group. At twenty-five, she's already proved to be quite the fashion and makeup influencer. Felicity's social media following dwarfs the guys' many times over. Between clubbing almost nightly, working on her ever-expanding brands and posting to her dedicated social media followers hourly, she wears heart eyes for none other than Willy Adler. The two have a love-hate thing that we can't wait to see play out.

Speaking of Willy Adler, he's the youngest of the group at twenty-three and the most mysterious of the four. He hates the 'prince' title his brother has given him and seems reluctant to interact with the cast more than necessary. We dug into his background and discovered he graduated from PSU with a masters in business management last year but hasn't yet put his newly acquired skills to work. Willy's head appears to be some-where else, and he drowns his sorrows with many alcoholic beverages. Do I smell a drinking problem on the way? Possibly. We're here for the drama that will follow this cast twenty-four-seven while filming.

The show airs on E! every Sunday at 9:00 p.m. PST. Who will you fall in love with?

* * *

Only three episodes have aired and just like I predicted, it's an instant hit. His face is everywhere. Online. Social media. Tabloids. I've even seen promo billboards on the freeway. I will never get used to seeing him like this.

I throw the tabloid onto the front counter. Why'd they have to go and make him look like the lost-in-life loser of the bunch? How dare they make Felicity look like she has any chance with him, too. Though I am glad they nailed Mike and Finn's douchey personali-ties, that only tells me they plan to focus on the two who have the potential for the most drama. Sigh. I have a feeling I'm up for some heartbreaking Sunday nights.

The rules between Will and I still stand. We've been broken up for six months now and had one relapse night (not counting the previous 'freebie'). My phone still blows up with his texts and he tells me everything as it happens – so he says – so I'm not entirely in the dark, but we try to keep our interactions phone-based and not face to face. Too many chances to screw things up.

'Ooh,' Olivia says excitedly, approaching the counter where I'm working, her eyes on the magazine. 'This is *so* weird! We know famous people! You've had sex with a famous person!'

I laugh. 'Say it a little louder, would ya? I'm not sure Gunner's reading group heard you.'

Olivia is my assistant manager and life-long best friend. We run To Be Read, the bookstore I fell in love with as a teen. Will, Olivia and I all worked here as teenagers. We're far more professional now, mostly. She and I each run a section, and things run relatively smoothly.

Liv's one year older than me and a chronic dater of all the wrong guys. Her natural dark-as-night hair flows down her back in big beach waves I'm jealous of. She's tall, curvy, wears a lot of eyeliner on her big brown eyes and has the most beautiful dewy light-brown skin. She's absolutely gorgeous. Her parents met when her mother was on a girls' vacation in Mexico and claimed it was love at first sight. She swears in Spanish, has perfected the eye roll, and she's not afraid of anything.

Her specialty within the store is mystery, thriller and crime. She loves a whodunit and is currently attempting to write her own. I've read what she has, and I'd buy the hell out of it. She's a true-crime junkie whose knowledge of how that world works is so extensive I'm sometimes a little scared she might one day be able to carry out the perfect murder. And I'll be the girl helping dispose of the body.

Originally, To Be Read was Frank's shop (the owner). But after his last stroke, he retired, and Olivia and I took over. He allowed me to refurb my apartment upstairs and now To Be Read is my happy place. If only everywhere I looked I didn't see a certain someone who helped design said apartment. I'm dealing. Kind of.

Liv rolls her eyes playfully. 'I can't believe they made the cover! But, ugh, why must they all be so picture-perfect?'

'All their flaws are internal, remember?'

She laughs, nodding her head. 'While our flaws are visible, and we're perfect on the inside. Did you read it yet?'

'Yep.'

'And?'

'They made it seem like a love story will be their main focus. One I will not be involved in.'

'Eh.' She grimaces. 'That's no good. I told you you should have been on camera some.'

I lower my chin, shooting her half a glare as I straighten up the front counter. 'I'm not competing for him. I broke up with him so he wouldn't expect me to do exactly that and so my name would stay out of articles—'

'Exactly like this.' She finishes my sentence for me. 'So, you're just going to continue a digital forbidden love affair when really, you're madly in love, and fighting this break-up like nothing I've ever witnessed?'

'It's complicated, Liv. He's my best friend, but I can't be his girl-friend through this because I don't know if I can trust him on the show. I've seen exactly three episodes and he's already broken his record for how much he can drink; the award for stupidity isn't that far a reach now.'

'Yeah, yeah, he may as well have a double life. I know, we've had this conversation daily since it happened,' she says like it all annoys her, but really, she asks for those daily updates.

She flips the tabloid open to the article, holding a single finger in the air – her *shut the hell up* finger. Clients approach and Liv scoots down the counter, tabloid and all, never once looking up.

'Did you find everything you were looking for?'

'We did,' one of the young women says, setting half a dozen magazines onto the counter.

I ring them up one by one; each has Will's gorgeous face staring back at me. *PDX Royals* and the cast is the headline on all of them and each one pisses me off a little more. Two years of this won't be annoying at all.

'They didn't even mention you!' Liv says a little too loudly, star-tling the woman working the card reader. 'Can you believe that?!

They call themselves paparazzi, and they don't know you're in the background doing the star of the show?'

'Liv... *shh*.'

She shakes her head. 'I'm telling you, Berx, you two gotta use one of those free bones over at Will's place, so the whole world won't think he'll eventually fornicate with "Princess" Felicity. Blech, I can't believe they titled her that.'

'Wait,' one of the women in front of me says. 'You two *know* them?' She points at the tabloid in Liv's hand, her head flipping between us as she awaits our answer.

'Uh, no?' I keep my cool while lying, but Olivia doesn't play along. She nods her head obnoxiously.

'This one here's been sleeping with Prince Willy for seven years, ladies. Spread the word. For all we care, Princess Felicity can be locked into a castle tower by an evil dragon.'

Prince Willy. When it was announced that a douchey video of Mike's smug self was what attracted the network to them – episode one – he named himself King Mikey. You know, because of the show's title, *PDX Royals*. Finn was quick to call himself Lord Finn, even applied to become one like Scott Disick did once. Stupid as fuck. But that meant by ridiculous rich-boy rules made up by the king himself, Will needed a title too, and by default of Mike being king, he proclaimed his little brother Prince Willy. A name he's come to loathe but has developed a party boy personality for in front of the cameras in only three episodes.

'*Liv!*' I bark, lifting my hands palms up when our eyes meet.

'What?' She heaves a sigh, turning to the women. 'Strike that, ladies. William Adler is a jobless liar and probably a future cheater, so trust me when I say you don't want anything to do with him.'

'Not better,' I groan.

'*Maldito!*' Liv exclaims.

'Forget you heard any of that,' I tell the women. 'We *don't* know

them. We're fans daydreaming, just like you. Thanks for coming in.'
I hand them their receipt and pray to the tabloid gods that they
don't know a single reporter.

As soon as the doors close, I shoot Olivia a glare. 'No more
public chatter about Will and me,' I command. 'I don't want
cameras up my ass or my name floating around in these magazines.
God knows what they'll say.'

'The attention could be a free advertisement for the shop. Did
you ever think of that?'

'Yes, I did. *Not* worth it. We're now known as the most popular
bookstore in town because of our skills, not because my legs open
like saloon doors for the city's newest prince.'

She laughs. 'Like you don't enjoy it.'

'We're broken up,' I remind her; it's the only way to keep a leash
on my heart. Remind myself we're broken up. He's free to date
whoever he wants. As am I. And eventually, maybe we will. 'You're
encouraging me to date, so if you want that to ever happen, I'd stop
reminding me of the sex I occasionally have had with Prince Willy.
It's absolutely nothing; we're just weaning apart.'

'Seven years is a long time to go cold turkey from – I get it.'

The front door dings open. 'To Be Read welcomes you!' Liv and
I say in unison. The little greeting Frank developed two decades ago
lives on.

I glance over at the customer headed my way, dropping my head
dramatically. He's dressed in disguise, a dark oversized hoodie, the
hood pulled over his head masking part of his face, and big
sunglasses. The cherry on top is the fake mustache glued to his
upper lip. It's handlebar style so he fits right in with the hipsters
around this neighborhood.

'Speak of the devil and he pops right in!' Liv says with a
beaming smile. 'How is it? Do they feed you caviar for breakfast and
lobster for dessert?'

He laughs. 'We buy our own groceries and this morning I had leftover Chinese for breakfast. And a mimosa, because I'm classy and my world is so weird Lis serves booze for breakfast.'

Lis. He has a nickname for her. Like the article said, they have a love-hate relationship. When Will's drunk, which seems to be often, they get along just fine. He won't touch her with a ten-foot pole but they have some laughs and seem like friends. I have no love for her so I'm just sporting hate in my heart watching it play out. Hate, or jealousy – the line is fine.

'What are you doing here?' I ask.

'Snuck away from the cameras and we weren't shooting far away so I thought I'd come say hello. I haven't seen you in person in forever.'

'Is she as good as you remember?' Olivia asks.

He shakes his head, a wide smile topped with a mustache with curls at the ends. 'Every time I see her, she's prettier.'

'You're violating rule number two: no flirting.'

'But I'm following rule number one: calling you pretty.'

I shake my head. Do I love hearing him call me pretty? Yes. But my heart grasps on to things like that like a lifeline, so I try to limit it.

'You're not even a little happy to see me? It's been months, Berx.'

Of course I am. That's the problem. I adore seeing him. Right now, I'm desperately stopping myself from throwing myself at him and doing him on this counter. I want to confess my undying love for him. I want to beg him to choose me over the show. But I can't, and not only because it seems desperate. He made his choice and he's locked in. No use fighting it.

I grab the tabloid from where Olivia left it, slapping it on the counter between us.

'All the tabloids,' I say. 'Your face is on them. The women who just left had bought half a dozen magazines with articles about you. They're dreaming of doing you.'

'Really?' he asks, a smile growing until I lower my chin. 'I'm kidding.' The way he blows out a breath as he leans on the counter with his elbows, flipping to the article, says he hadn't seen this yet. He reads it silently, making awkward faces at the same spots I did. Finally, he stands. 'I mean, we kind of knew it might be coming, but I get it. It's weird for me too. At least they didn't mention you. Must mean we aren't doing a terrible job at keeping our previous relationship under wraps and you out of the spotlight.'

'Yep. Now I'm just your dirty little secret. Your side ho who says yes to ridiculous relapse amendments like "holidays are freebies" because *we* make the rules. I'm pretty sure we're the only Americans who celebrated Finland's Independence Day.'

Yes, there's one intimate moment I didn't mention. It's like we can't count. His job has become finding ways to throw in freebies and I've gotten pretty good at saying no, but the Finland freebie was too good to say no to.

'Hey.' He points at me seriously before finally cracking a smile. 'That was the best Finnish holiday we've ever had.'

A grin spreads across my face. 'See, I can't resist your arrogant charm.'

'I am *not* arrogant,' he argues with a laugh.

'*Yet*,' I say. 'I've no doubt after two years of this' – I tap the photo on the front of the tabloid – 'you'll get there.'

'Berx...' He says my name gently, lovingly, breaking all the rules with his tone alone and jabbing at my heart like a fire poker stoking a wood stove. Heat radiates through me as he steps around the counter, resting his hand on the small of my back and dropping his head onto mine. 'I might have lied to get here but losing you was never in my plans, remember? I'm still yours. Just not "out loud".'

'Why, uh...' I step away from him like I've got something to do at the other end of the counter. 'Did you only come by to tell me I'm pretty?'

'No... I know you've turned into a total hermit, and possible workaholic, and rarely take a lunch.'

My gaze shoots right to Olivia, who's pretending to be busy at her counter, looking away from me quickly. They still talk so he's still got insider info because we share a circle of friends.

'Actually, I was just planning to go to lunch.'

'Perfect timing then, I came to take you.'

My head wanders to the dirty version of 'take you' and I'm suddenly in the middle of a daydream of us at a restaurant, somehow adding a bathroom freebie to our loose list of rules. An afternoon delight will only make things worse.

'Rule number three: *no* dating.'

'Friends have lunch. Back me up, Liv,' he hollers her way.

She nods. 'Sorry, but he's right. Friends do have lunch. We had lunch yesterday.'

I glare. 'Fine. We can have lunch but somewhere quiet, *away* from the cameras, and we are only allowed to eat. No second locations. No disappearing to the bathroom together. And *no* freebies. Got it?'

He lifts a single hand. 'Hand to God, Berx. I just want to catch up face to face.'

Fifteen minutes later and we're seated in a tiny Italian restaurant halfway across the city, sitting at a table near the back, far from any windows. Will doesn't waste a second; there's food in front of him and he has an appetite. I, on the other hand, am struggling to not be reminded of old times and realizing it's easier to fake when we only talk via phone. Now I'm stuck here in awkward-ville.

'How's things?' Will asks.

'We talk every day. You already know how things are.'

'Humor me, Berx. I just want an hour with you. Please,' he begs, his eyes pleading along with his words, practically melting my heart on the spot.

'Things are good. I'm settled into our, er—*my* apartment.'

He frowns to himself. 'But you're happy?'

'With the apartment? Yeah. It's everything we dreamed.'

'When do I get the tour?'

'Never,' I say without missing a beat. That's my new talent. *No*s come easily, because if they don't, *yes*es cause problems.

He jerks his head up, a look of confusion on his face. '*Never?*'

I shrug my shoulders. 'You *have* a key, Will, and since all this started you've yet to even see if it works. You saw the plans; the place looks just like that, only I opted for a queen-size bed as opposed to a king. No need for a huge bed when I'm all alone.'

'Right,' he says softly. 'Makes sense, considering you're the queen of my heart.'

I shake my head, now biting into my sandwich. 'Rule number two, Adler. *No* flirting.'

He rolls his eyes.

'Let's talk about bigger things,' I suggest when I'm done chewing. 'You have a theme song! They picked a good one as you *are* stunning.'

He groans. 'Let's *not* talk about that. I came here to get away from the show, not chit-chat about it. I needed a moment to decompress and there's only one place I feel myself...'

'I know.' I soften, because I can tell he's struggling with the show, and I'm not a total bitch. 'It'll get easier. Life changes take time, but eventually you'll be comfortable there. I don't know how you couldn't; the place is to die for.'

'Are you comfortable at the apartment alone?' he asks sadly.

'Um... yeah. I mean, are reminders everywhere? Yes. But I'm making it work. I even took a chance and tried something new the other day.'

He looks at me curiously.

'Black pepper popcorn – it's so good. I'll pick you up a bag.'

'Alright,' he says with a smile. 'See, this is what I mean. I needed this.'

'You needed to talk about popcorn?'

'I needed normality. To be treated like I'm not Prince Willy but just some guy who used to live completely under the radar with his best friend at his side. You make me feel normal.'

'I'm gla—'

Before I can finish my sentence, I notice half the waitress staff at this restaurant are at the front counter, giggling and whispering and before I can even remember what I was saying they're approaching our table. As soon as they speak to him, he's suddenly all smiles for his fans. These are the moments that remind me he's no longer mine anymore. Two years is starting to feel like a lifetime.

7

BERKLEY

Work was long today. We had two author signings and I've only just gotten the shop cleaned up and am now lying in bed, with a seven-layer chip dip that won't survive to the new year. What I didn't do was go out and party like Will wanted me to. Instead, I'm watching *Dick Clark's NYRE* alone. I couldn't possibly miss it, yet watching it alone isn't the same, and the book on my nightstand is also calling my name. But it's romance. Am I up for reliving my own heartbreak through someone else's love story? Not yet.

Will did beg me to come to a party with him tonight but I can't handle being out with the *Royals* idiots. They're too desperate for attention. Yes, I wanted to be with the Will I used to know. I wanted to kiss him at midnight like I have every year since I met him. But I only see little bits of that guy so it looks like this is officially the year I start without him.

I click the volume of the TV up louder to drown out the ticking clock on my bedroom wall. Just get to midnight, Dick, so I can cry myself to sleep and then wake up refreshed, renewed, and in a brand new year.

The slam of the downstairs side door to the outside startles me, and I sit straight up, muting the TV I just turned up, listening. I locked up the shop, right? I jump out of my bed, grab the baseball bat I keep for security, and tiptoe into my living room as heavy steps come up my stairs. *Why* are they coming up here when there's a whole bookstore to rob, and my office they had to walk through to get to my stairwell has the money. Jesus, I locked my *front* door, right?

My door handle shakes as someone tries to open it. Am I starting the new year dead? My heart is beating so hard I can hear it in my head. What to do? Hide! I run across the dark room, standing where I know the door will open, and whoever is breaking into my apartment won't see me. I jab Will's contact, calling him as I stand against the wall, baseball bat in one hand, phone against my ear in the other.

'Hi, baby,' he answers, his voice soft.

'Someone is trying to break into my apartment,' I whisper as the door opens.

'Berkley, it's me,' he says into the phone, his voice carrying through my apartment. When he closes the door, he jumps back, noticing me standing behind it, baseball bat already in full swing.

'Don't hit me,' he blurts, dropping his phone and reaching for the bat now en route to his head.

'Fucking hell, William!' I half yell, the bat now in his hand after a successful defensive catch on his side. 'You finally decide to try out your key and scare the shit out of me! Why didn't you tell me you were on your way?' I ask, still talking into the phone as I try to recover from thinking I was moments away from being murdered.

'You seemed down on the phone earlier so I wanted to surprise you,' he says. 'There was no way I could leave you here alone to ring in the new year without me.' He glances around the apartment he's never seen completed and smiles.

It's one big L-shaped room, with a living room on one side and a kitchen on the other, a long island separating the two. At one end of the island are three doors. One to a bathroom. One to a closet. The other to my bedroom.

Everything in here is vintage, most things from the fifties besides the electronics. A flat-screen TV sits on a fifties box television as if it's a TV stand. One of those arched silver ball lamps sits over the green velvet couch. A wall of bookshelves displays books in a rainbow of color. A bright pink shag rug pulls the whole colorful, retro room together. Had he lived here, maybe it wouldn't be as girly as it is. Still, he doesn't seem disappointed as he looks around.

I drop my phone, breathing a sigh of relief, wrapping my arms around his neck.

'I brought fancy expensive champagne, the kind I know you love. It's pink,' he says as he hugs me.

I perk up. He's enticing me with pink champagne?

'Really?'

'Yeah. We have to toast the new year.'

'Right,' I say, not letting him go when he expected me to so he continues to hold me.

'I'm sorry I scared you. I just...' He kisses the top of my head as I lean into him, so glad he wasn't a total stranger. 'God, Berx, your heart is racing.' He has a hand on my back so he probably feels it. He pulls away, looking at me seriously. 'You were legit terrified.'

'I probably wouldn't have been if someone hadn't pounded at the door last week at like three in the morning. Was that you too?'

'No,' he says firmly. 'As you reminded me recently, I've got a key. I wouldn't pound on the door. Are you serious? Someone was trying to get in downstairs? In the middle of the night?'

He holds me out at arm's length, looking me right in the eyes as we talk. Why must he be so damn handsome? I just want to shut him up by covering his mouth with mine. But nowadays I make him work for it. He no longer gets 'easy' Berx. It's against the rules.

I take the champagne from his free hand and meander towards the fridge, putting the bottle in to chill before closing it and turning back to him, my kitchen island now safely between us.

'It was probably someone headed home from the bar. I dunno. There was definitely pounding on the door, but it woke me up out of a dead sleep, so I don't know how long it had been happening and I only heard it a couple times after that. The whole event was maybe a minute long.'

Exasperation is what his heavy sigh sounds like. 'You *have* to tell me stuff like this, Berx.'

'*No* I don't because *we* are no longer an item. Had you been an intruder, you'd be headless right now. I can take care of myself.'

'I know you can,' he says, following behind me as I head back to my bedroom. 'You're fearless but I'd never forgive myself if something happened to you. I'm putting in a security system next week.'

'You don't need to do that.'

'Consider it done. It's the least I can do seeing as I worry about you.'

I roll my eyes as I crawl back into my bed, turning onto my side away from him to continue watching the countdown. The TV is the only light in my room, flashing to whatever band is now performing in Times Square before the ball drops. If he was really worried about me, he wouldn't be living ten blocks away in a swanky apartment with his idiot brother.

Will sets the bat behind the nightstand by my side of the bed, then kicks off his shoes, pulling his wallet, keys and phone from his jeans and tossing them onto my dresser before stripping off his T-shirt. There's a mirror on the wall I'm facing so I can see as he gets undressed, and there's not a chance I'm looking away. He glances up at the mirror as he pulls off his pants, leaving only his boxer briefs; his eyes meet mine. He flashes me a smile that makes my insides all warm and fuzzy. I miss him.

He slips into bed with me, sliding his hand around my waist, pulling me against him, kissing the back of my shoulder where I've tattooed a capital W next to a black heart, King of Hearts style.

I got the tattoo when we were in college as a surprise for his birthday because I love how he kisses my shoulder when he spoons me like this, always in the same spot. He loves seeing a W for Will on me like it somehow makes me his no matter what. I branded myself before I knew we'd break up, like an idiot, and now he's half naked and in my bed with me.

'What are you doing?' I ask, pretending his presence bothers me, but my body snuggles into him without me even trying.

'It's a holiday, Berx. We agreed we could be the old us on holidays. It's in the rules, remember? New Year's is important. It moves us into an entirely new time dimension and you're who I want to see the second that gets here. *And...* I miss you. Seeing you at lunch recently has me thinking about you non-stop and I'm now realizing why you don't want face-to-face visits. It makes walking away too hard.'

'Yet here you are breaking every rule.'

He sighs into my hair. 'I have no control when it comes to you.'

This break-up has not done great things for me. I'm struggling. He doesn't want to be broken up, and he makes it known (if tonight wasn't a tell). But I can't invest in us because his new life is partying, and it's only a matter of time before he does something stupid. He's a twenty-three-year-old guy with way too much money. He's *going* to fuck up and I need to protect my heart.

But... I'm also weak so I wiggle in his arms, turning towards him so we're face to face. Maybe I wanted to give him the cold shoulder in public or earlier when I realized he wasn't an intruder, but now I just want him.

'Hey, beautiful,' he says, kissing my forehead, then my lips. After a minute, he breaks the kiss, lifting the blankets and looking me over. 'You're wearing my shirt,' he says, his eyes stopping on the words *Kiss Me, I'm Irish*, an arrow pointing towards my groin. 'Want me to follow orders?'

'Only if this counts officially as number two and not a freebie,' I admit. 'But not yet.' I reach up, running a hand through his hair and staring into his eyes. 'I hate this. I feel like your side ho.'

'You're my main ho, baby.' He chuckles.

I don't. 'Not funny.'

'I know, I'm sorry.' He kisses me again.

'I didn't think I'd get to see you tonight since I refused to go out.'

'We're filming,' he says. 'If they want us to go out, we go out, but I kept an eye on the time and slipped out when I had the chance. I was going to text you, but time got away from me, and after our phone call didn't go the way I'd hoped, I wasn't sure you'd *want* to see me tonight. It's why I snuck in. I wanted to surprise you.'

Our phone call wasn't that bad. Just the usual me refusing to hang out with him and his ass-face friends and residual feelings that I fight off, so I feel I'm in control of the situation.

'We can't keep doing holiday freebies, Will. Do you have any idea how many there are? Next thing I'll know we'll be honoring Grandparents' Day with an old-fashioned freebie bang. I can't.'

He laughs, but then goes serious. 'You really want me to leave?'

'No,' I say quietly.

'Tell me what you want, Berkley.'

Finally, I give in, sliding a hand over his ribcage, to pull myself closer to him, kissing his chest. He closes his eyes as I do, breathing out what feels like a sigh of relief.

'I want to be with you,' I say truthfully. 'But it's counting as our second relapse, because as you just said, it's getting too difficult to walk away.'

He frowns. 'Alright. So for tonight, we're the old us again?'

'Yep,' I say.

'Then I can finally say the words I want to. I love you,' he says, hopeful.

'I know, Will. I know.' I might not be able to say the words, but that doesn't stop me from kissing him back when his lips meet mine because I apparently have zero willpower. Pun. Intended.

8

WILL

'What can I get you two to drink?' a waitress says as she stops at the end of our table.

I glance at Berkley, her hair braided and pulled over her shoulder as she looks at the menu. Even fresh out of bed, with yesterday's makeup on, she's still gorgeous. I insisted I take her to breakfast because I hate leaving like I'm a one-night stand for her and even though last night was otherworldly, that's what this morning feels like.

'Coffee?' she asks.

I hold up two fingers to the waitress.

'I'll be right back,' the waitress says, flashing me an *I know who you are* smile.

'Another of your fans,' Berkley says, with a roll of her eyes. She hates the fan thing. I can't say I blame her. If random men were swarming our table for a moment with her, I'm sure I'd be jealous as hell.

'A part of the gig I can't control,' I say.

She's looking over her menu at me, her eyes lingering as she studies me. 'It's that pretty face of yours,' she says with a coy smile.

'By the way, I still like the glasses more than the contacts. I almost forgot how super-hot Clark Kent they make you.'

I reach across the table to touch her hand. 'I love that you think I'm super-hot 'cause I think you're super-*duper*-hot.' Now that she's given me a window of opportunity, am I going to flirt like a kid in love? Abso-fucking-lutely.

She grins.

I do usually wear contacts. When I don't, I have nerdy black-framed glasses she helped me pick out years ago. If I'm going out and don't really want people recognizing me, which has only become a problem recently, these glasses, baseball caps and my favorite hoodies help me hide. And the occasional fake 'stache. I gotta make my girl smile.

'Flush my contacts more often, and the glasses will magically appear,' I say. Lucky for me, I keep a backup pair in my Jeep.

She grimaces. 'I can't believe I did that. I'll buy you more.'

'No, you won't. I have plenty at my apartment.'

For a second we sit silently, looking around the diner, waiting on our coffee to wake us up completely.

'Do you think we'll be like this forever?' she asks, suddenly changing the subject.

'Describe *this*?' I say, sitting back when the waitress brings a pot of coffee and two cups to our table.

The front door of the diner dings open, interrupting our conversation and earning a groan from each of us at the sight of the newcomers. Mike, Felicity and Finn walk in. This is a regular haunt because the diner is open twenty-four-seven, but I didn't think they'd show up this early on New Year's Day.

'Well, throw some toes in the air. Spanky and the rest of the fuckwit gang is here,' Berkley says under her breath, making herself busy pouring us each a cup of coffee.

I laugh to myself, but keep my co-stars in my sights. Felicity's gaze is on Berkley. She walks across the room like she's walking a runway, wearing the same dress she was last night, so I bet they haven't even been home yet. Her heels tap on the floor as she struts our way.

'I swear that woman exists just to be my nemesis. Why's she hate me so much?' Berkley whispers.

'Because you own my heart and she wants it.'

'The balls on that girl. She's got some big ones, I'll give her that.'

The two women's faces drop when their eyes meet. Yep, they are not and will never be friends. That's what this looks says, clear as day. Comparing them would be like comparing cucumbers and oranges. There are no similarities. Berkley is prettier by a mile, she makes me laugh, she has a soul and I'd rather be sitting next to her than Felicity any day.

Mike and I acknowledge one another's presence silently as he leads the double Fs through the place like he owns it to a booth at the back. Behind us, thankfully. Jonah, our lead camera guy, follows them. He gives me a nod, panning the camera to Berkley and me as he walks past. Heads of other customers turn, glancing between the five of us, attempting to figure out why the camera is even here.

Felicity stops at our booth, her eyes on Berkley. 'Well, if it isn't my least favorite person in the world, buzzkill Berkley,' she says, her tone less than thrilled. 'I thought you'd finally jumped off a cliff.'

'And I wish you'd swim into a boat motor,' Berx says with a smile. '*Farcical Felicity*.'

I can't help but chuckle. I'm one thousand percent certain Felicity doesn't even know the word 'farcical'.

'You're a waste of mine and Will's time. You should really think about that cliff thing.'

'I'll rent you a boat.' Berkley doesn't back down and finally Felicity wanders off, towards the table Mike and Finn are at.

'Ugh. I hate her, Will. I feel like there's about to be a gang shooting,' Berkley whispers to me. 'I should probably just go,' she says, attempting to scoot out of our booth, but I'm bigger than her and sitting right next to her, blocking her in. If I wasn't, she'd be out the front door already.

'Stay,' I tell her, sliding my hand down her thigh. 'With you is where I want to be and I don't care who on the planet knows it.'

She rolls her eyes. 'As sweet as that is, do you have any idea how much hate mail I'm going to get when this airs? Two of my photos have gone out into the world connected to you and fans didn't hesitate to let me know they hate me. I had to lock down all my social media accounts recently.'

We, er, I, in particular, make the tabloids pretty regularly, so I get why she's nervous. Berkley's only made a couple accidental appearances on season one. Brief – mostly because the first time she showed up while filming, Cole (one of our producers) rushed her through an appearance agreement without explanation. She meant to cancel it, but figured her identity is now out there as someone in my life, and you can't really take that back. Felicity also hasn't exactly made it a secret that they both pine for the same guy. I can't believe people are harassing her.

'Why didn't you tell me?'

''Cause you don't get to know everything anymore, William. Plus, it's humiliating. They think *I'm* the loser here.'

'You are *not* a loser.' I lean into her, kissing the top of her head. 'Top-of-the-line security system. By the end of the week. I promise.'

'That'll definitely fix everything, thanks,' she says sarcastically like she's lost all hope.

'Berx, look at me.' I throw an arm over the back of the seat behind us.

Reluctantly, she glances at me. Berkley's never been a do-as-I-say kind of girl. I love that about her. I also love that she knows despite my fucked-up way of showing it, I'd never let anyone hurt her. Maybe I've made all the wrong decisions lately, but my whole heart belongs to this girl.

'Promise me you'll tell me when you're scared of something, alright? Call me. Text me, whatever. I will drop everything to help you.'

Her laugh isn't jolly.

'We both know that's not entirely true.' She looks away from me as she says the words, stirring her coffee with her spoon.

I have failed her in the past; I know this. Not only was doing the show a total mistake, but a few times, she's called, and I either wasn't near my phone, had it on silent, or was too intoxicated to help her.

'I fucked up, baby. I know this, but I can't go back. None of us expected the show to blow up like it did. I have to see it out now.'

'Have to or *want* to?' she asks, our food being delivered interrupting us.

'I'll check back in on ya, sweetie.' The waitress winks at me, touching my shoulder, completely ignoring Berkley, who lets out an irritated groan.

'I love you, Berkley,' I say into her ear. I know she's asked me not to say those words as it's a violation of rule number whatever, but I can't *not* say them to her. It's like an urge I can't stop and technically we're still living relapse number two. '*Please* let me in a little more?'

She closes her eyes momentarily before sitting up, ignoring my request and picking up her fork.

I sigh, a little discouraged, planting my hand on her thigh again and sliding it down to her knee. A hint of a smile turns her lips as she looks my way. We don't say anything. We don't have to. We feel exactly the same way, and the fact that we can't figure this out is killing us.

9

BERKLEY

Six Months Later, June 2021

PDX ROYALS FANS – CAT-FIGHT ALERT

Did you see last week's episode, *Royals* fans? We've finally discovered where Willy's head is at. On his longtime girlfriend (now ex), Berkley Kaine! She's been spotted a couple of times now as being closely related to someone on the show but looks like that relation isn't by blood. We did some research and we know these two dated since their teen years and broke up just before Will decided to do the show. Bryce and Bianca, friends of Willy's, have been in the background of the show since the start, but we had no idea Bianca had a fraternal twin sister who holds Willy's heart. The woman is beautiful too, unsurprising considering Will is a stunner himself.

What we didn't know, until recently, is that she and Felicity are not fans of one another. We don't know the exact story, but if we had to guess, who could blame them? They're pining after the same man! And I'm not sure Willy's going to let Berkley go so easily even though it seems she is attempting to keep her distance from all things *Royals*. This smells like DRAMA and we love it!

I have a feeling we'll be seeing more of her soon with the way Willy has latched on to a bottle of booze. (We previewed tonight's episode – trust us, she's there.) Can she help him? Or will Felicity swoop in and save the day? We don't know, but we can't wait to find out.

The show airs on E! every Sunday at 9:00 p.m. PST.

* * *

My phone dings with an incoming text on the counter in front of me. Will's face flashes across the screen. I tap his text, clicking on the link he's sent over. It takes me to a tabloid magazine website, where my face stares back at me. I knew that stupid fight would make the show.

CAT-FIGHT ALERT

Shit.

'Liv!' I yell her name through the shop. Longtime *girlfriend*? Where the hell did they get that? If Bianca blew my cover, she will hear about it.

After a minute, Liv pops out of an aisle in her section. 'What?'

'There's a photo on a tabloid site of Will and me.' I watch the stupid show; I knew it was coming. I just didn't think the tabloids would pick it up the way they did.

'Oh yeah?' she asks excitedly, speed-walking my way, her arms overloaded with books she's stocking. She dumps the books onto the front counter, grabbing my phone from me and looking at the photo.

'How'd you find this?' She backs out of the website and frowns, glancing up at me with a disappointed look on her face. 'You're *texting* Will? I thought you were trying to quit him?'

'I *am* trying.' We no longer speak every day. I've limited it to once a week and texting mid-week is against that new rule. Usually, we text on the day the show airs because he gets to preview it first and warn me of whatever will piss me off.

'Did you read the headline?' I ask her, ignoring her chastising of my and Will's relationship. Whatever it is. 'Longtime *girlfriend*?' I ask. 'That's the first time they've ever referred to me as Will's girlfriend.'

'They were bound to find out at some point. Honestly, I'm a little surprised it took them this long. At least it's a good photo.'

'I guess. I mean, this makes it a bit weird, doesn't it? Not to mention that I'm on tonight's episode as well. How did this spiral out of control when all I wanted was to *not* be a part of the show?'

'You can't quit the star,' she says like I'm a dumbass. 'That's the problem. If people are jealous, screw 'em. Is it your fault you can pull in some hot-as-fuck tail? *No, it's not.* People would be high-fiving you in the streets if you were a dude.'

I scrunch my face. 'But instead, I'm seen as his backup girl. The one fighting the princess for him. Ugh.'

My phone buzzes in her hand. 'It's him,' Olivia says. '*Prince Willy.*' She grimaces as she says his name. 'He says, "Call me please". Pfft, she'll call you when she wants to call you, and you'll deal with it,' she says to his message.

'*Stop,*' I say, grabbing my phone from her. 'We're grown-ups. *And* we're friends. We talk shit out.' I lift the phone to my ear and wait for him to answer. One ring.

'Hey.' His voice alone melts me.

'You do know *your* phone dials out too, right?' I ask. 'You could have just called.'

'It's completely my fault you've been identified so I thought that warranted a phone-call apology. My publicist wants a straight answer: are we or aren't we an item?' he asks hesitantly like he's unsure he wants to know the answers to any of his questions.

'We are *not* an item and you *know* that.'

He's silent for a moment, contemplating my words. 'Alright,' he finally says. 'Can I at least confirm we're friends?' He sighs heavily. I can almost see him running his hand through his hair in frustration.

'I mean, I guess you have to, don't you?'

'It'd be smart to get on top of it.'

'That's what she said,' I say with a laugh.

He chuckles. 'For what it's worth, I'm sorry this is headed the exact direction you didn't want it to but my feelings haven't changed. I didn't cringe seeing us together until Felicity walked into that diner and ruined our moment.'

'I know. Next time I'll be smarter about being in public with you. Perhaps we should just cancel our final "relapse" and call it quits now before this gets worse?'

'Are you serious? During our birthday month?'

My heart sinks. Will's birthday and mine are a few weeks apart and they're both coming up.

'We're one year in, William, and things have gone awry. How much worse will it get if we keep going?'

He thinks on this before saying, 'I'll agree on one condition.'

'What's that?'

'You come over here for one night. I'll sneak you in. No one will ever know you're here and afterwards, we'll take a break until the show is over. Fair?'

I sigh heavily, looking up from my phone to Olivia. She frowns, reaching out to touch my hand.

'Fine, but under the dark of night, William. Promise?'

'Absolutely,' he says.

'Then I guess it's set. Text me the details and I'll be there.'

'Alright, and Berkley... I still love you.'

'Yeah, that's what you keep saying...' I moan. Love sucks. Like truly. Zero stars.

10

BERKLEY

I'm at Bianca's with Olivia at her and Bryce's apartment. It's about six blocks from my bookstore and four blocks from Will's apartment building, sitting near the middle ground. We have *Royals* watch parties so I don't have to go through it alone. Plus Bryce loves to see himself on television.

It seems I've acquired some fans recently because I've appeared on a few episodes now. Barely. Like glimpses, yet the paparazzi misses nothing. Because the show sometimes hurts, we've even created a drinking game to play while we watch. Anytime Will refers to me on the show, we drink. I leave here either tipsy, or a little bit heartbroken, a lot.

Tonight, I'm making an appearance. One of the producers, Cole, has befriended both Will and me, taking a personal interest in the complications of our relationship. When Will gets overly intoxicated, Cole will call me and have me talk him down. You could say I'm his drunken fairy godmother.

After the little diner incident, I called another 'no face-to-face visits' penalty for fear that exactly what happened would happen. Not long after, I got a call from Cole that Will was not in a good place and had been in a fight in a bar. I did see him that night but only long enough to find his car, then drive him home and into bed. This is the scene on tonight's show. I then snuck out when he finally passed out.

My phone dings when I set it on the table. I glance at the notification. *Will Adler* flashes across the screen. Ugh. He's been texting me all day after we fought earlier. Sweet things that usually would make me smile but tonight, they're just killing me inside. I need to drown them out.

'Who's that?' Olivia asks as my phone buzzes *again*.

She sets three beers on the coffee table in front of us. Bianca sets the tray of six shots before us. I down one immediately.

'Uh, I thought we were playing the Berkley game?' she asks.

'Well, now we're playing the Will-is-shish-kebabbing-Berkley's-heart game, and I need to get said heart intoxicated so it won't hurt as much.' I cock my head, finally picking up my phone.

'*Oh...*' Olivia says, figuring out who's continually texting me. 'Bad?'

'No.' I shake my head. 'He's being completely charming and saying all the right things. "I'm sorry, baby. I love you."' I read his words aloud, sighing heavily. He's sorry that he looks like a drunken idiot on tonight's show and got me involved.

Olivia pulls a hand over her chest with a groan. 'Gawd.' She balks. 'Why must he be so Casanova and imbecile at once? A real Cascile.'

I laugh to myself. 'They are literally just words he says to make himself feel better about always doing the wrong thing.'

'Forward them to me; I'll talk to him.'

'No.' I laugh. Olivia doesn't have much of a filter when it comes to Will and me. She hates him when I hate him. And her hate is much more murder-y rage than mine.

When the show's theme song starts, I cringe. *Work faster, tequila!*

'Blech,' Olivia says, tossing a handful of pretzels at the screen when it flashes to a clip of Will and Felicity in the intro.

The episode moves to their apartment. Will's lounging on the couch in the background, an Xbox controller on his knee, but his eyes are on the phone in his hand. Felicity is sitting on the arm of the couch near him, talking his ear off about her newest business venture.

Olivia gasps. 'What do you wanna bet he's texting *you* right there? And why does *she* have a theme song? Do *you* have a theme song?'

'I only save his life once a season. I'm not important enough to have a theme song,' I remind her, lifting my shoulders.

The scene moves through him out on the town with Felicity, Mike and Finn. When he's not playing the part of drunken party boy, he's overly emotional and calling me over and over; parts of my voicemail play through the television speakers. Finally, we see him drinking. A lot. They even air the fight he had, him yelling at someone that Felicity isn't his girlfriend, Berkley is.

We all do a shot.

That's what started the fight that night? Honestly, I didn't know this part. When I asked him what he fought over as I drove him home, he claimed he didn't know.

The second my face appears, a song blasts through the speakers, making both Olivia and Bianca burst out a laugh. My jaw drops open that they would choose *this* song.

'You *do* have a theme song!' Olivia says as she squeals a laugh.

'Oh my God.' Bianca laughs with Olivia, her hand now on my shoulder. 'I'd have paid money to be in the room with Felicity when she heard they chose Billie Eilish's "MyBoi" as your theme song.'

I let out a groan, with a bit of a laugh because, yeah, it's funny. Humiliating in so many ways, but I'm sure it rubbed her the wrong way when they screened the episode this morning.

'Bitcher alert!' Mike says on screen.

Mike calls me a multitude of names: buzzkill Berkley, 'the bitcher' and loads more. Which as far as I can tell translates roughly to the woman who can control Will when he can't – aka the fun police. I yell at Mike, Finn and Felicity for almost letting him die at minimum once a season so far, ruining their 'fun'.

'Mike!' My voice carries through the apartment from the TV as I yell at him on screen. 'You can't maybe encourage him to quit drinking when he starts slurring?!' I yell. 'He now has a court date!'

'Pfft.' Mike waves a hand my way. 'Just drive him home, and don't ruin our night like you always do, would ya?'

'God forbid you act like his brother and help him.'

The *I don't care* laugh that comes from Mike's lips pisses me off *now*, and this scene was filmed a while ago.

'He's a grown man, Berkley. I'm not his fucking babysitter. No one is making him drink until he blacks out. He starts all on his own. Usually, after he talks to you. Here's an idea: leave him alone so he can quit worrying he's doing you wrong all the time.'

Fuck-er. I cross my arms over my chest as I watch the scene unfold. Instantly pissed again.

'Here's another idea,' I yell back at him. 'Why don't you step in front of a bus and die?'

Mike stares at me, the two of us standing in the middle of the bar they were at that night, in a stare-down that neither of us back down from until Felicity approaches, baby-talking Will like she's worried about him. My new theme song obviously takes front stage for a moment as the camera focuses in on our reactions to seeing one another. Me rolling my eyes at the sight of her. Her groaning at the sight of me.

'Boo, bitch!' Olivia yells, throwing more pretzels towards the TV.

I storm off the screen, disappearing with Will out the front door of the bar. The camera pans to Felicity and Mike now talking about what a bitch I am. Like I'm the bad guy here.

'On a high note, you *look* fantastic.' Bianca rests her hand on my shoulder. 'Sun-kissed, hot, *way* prettier than Felicity, who is totally jealous of you, by the way. Look at her,' she says. 'Your name leaves her lips more than the show portrays too.'

Bianca would know; she appears on the show a lot because she's dating Will's best friend, Bryce. I know Bryce hates when Will drinks and turns into douche Lord Willy, but he still comes around because they've always been close. Secretly, I think Bryce is hoping that between the two of us, maybe we can help Will get his drinking under control and get our friend back.

'And here I am, the idiot who's jealous of *her*,' I say, admitting it to both Bianca and Olivia.

I've never said it aloud. I pretend like it's not her that bothers me; it's him. Because it's *his* fault. But I can't stand her. I want her to have all the bad luck, and yet she lives on like one of the chosen ones.

11

BERKLEY

Olivia and I are waiting for the Uber to pick us up. Sure, the bookstore is only half a dozen blocks away, but Liv can't drive home as buzzed as she is. They can drop me off on their way. I'm a little giggly but the extra-large order of cheesy fries helped sop up the tequila in a way that I feel almost sober.

My phone dings with an incoming text. Olivia glances at the screen like the nosy nelly she is. *Cole Davidson* flashes across the screen. I tap the text; a photo of Will pops up. He's sitting on their rooftop balcony ledge, his new BFF, Jack Daniel's, in his hand, lifted to his lips, as he drinks it right from the bottle. My heart speeds in my chest. Damn it, Adler.

'Uh-oh,' Olivia says, leaning in, looking at the photo with me. 'Is the good prince having a meltdown? I can't imagine what that rich boy is tormented with now...'

I tap the screen, calling Cole and pulling the phone to my ear.

'Hey,' he says on the first ring.

'*Don't* let him sit there,' I say frantically. 'He'll fall over backward.' Worry races through me. 'How bad is he?' I ask, suddenly hearing him yelling in the background.

'He's currently hollering for me to call you. He threatened to jump earlier. Said he feels like he's ruined your life. Hang on,' he says to me. The phone shuffles then settles. 'Hey, bud, Berkley's coming over. What do you say you wait for her here?'

'She's coming?' Will asks anxiously, slurring his words.

'Here,' Cole says. 'Talk to him while I get him to a chair.'

The phone shuffles again and I hear him breathe into the phone. I know him so well I know his breathing. Ugh.

'Hey.'

'Berkley.' He says my name with a sigh of relief. 'Can you come over?'

'You *need* me to come over?'

'I *need* you, baby.' The way he says it, like he's desperate, pulls at my heart in a way I wish it didn't.

My head is fuzzy from the couple shots I did earlier so it's not making any stellar decisions this evening and out of the three organs that run me, it's the only chance I had to do anything smart when it comes to Will. My heart and loins are his biggest fucking fans.

'Sure, I'll come over.'

'Berkley's coming!' he says excitedly, the phone dropping to the ground with an audible thud.

I wait a second to see if Cole comes back. Finally, he does. 'You're headed this way?'

'Give me like ten minutes, and distract Jonah, would you? I don't need a repeat of what I watched tonight,' I say.

'Yeah, neither does he. It's why he's drunk right now. He feels like he's let you down. Again.'

I sigh, ending the call and slowly turning to face Olivia, who I'm sure has plenty to say. I scrunch my face, ready to take the heat.

'You're seriously going to go save that idiot?' she asks, perturbed.

'He's not an idiot, Liv,' I defend him. 'I mean, he *is*, but he's not doing well.' I tap my head like it will help me explain it. 'I can't just ignore that. I lo—' I stop mid-word when I realize what I'm about to say. 'I dunno anymore.' The words leave my lips somehow feeling like defeat.

'Maybe he should consider healing your heart.' She taps my sternum, looking me right in the eyes. 'Then he could feel good about himself again. You're letting him manipulate you.'

'He's not doing it on purpose. I can't just turn my back on him when he's like this. No one else cares if he lives or dies. I'm the *only* person with a soul that he knows.'

She lets out a huge groan. '*I know. Go,*' she says, 'I'll be fine. The car's almost here.' She waves me away from her. 'Go nurse him back to health and get your fix and make it the last one so you can finally move on. He's like the drug you just can't quit. It's not healthy.'

I hug her until she laughs and shoves me away. Then turn around and walk the four blocks to Will's apartment building.

My chest is filled with anxiety and excitement at the same time. I hate that he's so drunk he'll likely pass out once I get him into bed and I'm *totally* mad at him right now, but I'm excited I get to see him again. Like I said, we're a total mess.

I don't know how to stop this cycle. I mean, I'm starting to get scared for him. His binge-drinking bouts are getting more frequent. Maybe tonight I'll mention rehab again? Not that he'll agree to go.

The elevator doors open to his and Mike's apartment, and I walk into chaos. There are easily three dozen people here. Women. Hipsters. Someone playing a random guitar. Loud music blasts through the place. A remake of 'Tainted Love'. Actually, that seems to be the one thing fitting in this situation.

I glance around the room, spotting Mike across the way with his group of misfit friends. Felicity is one of them. Giggling at everything he says while sitting in his lap.

Wait a second. *Why* is she sitting on his lap? Fucking hell, this girl is hard up for attention. I spot Cole, sitting in a chair he's turned to face the balcony, his back to the room.

'Cole.' I say his name as I walk through the kitchen towards him.

'Buzzkill Berkley!' Mike yells.

'Say, masturbation Mike...' I groan, ignoring him altogether and giving him the finger, including the camera guy, Jonah, now following my every move.

'Is he OK?' I ask, stepping up in front of Cole and glancing out the window.

Will's lying in a lounge chair, his eyes closed and his head slumped to the side. The neck of the bottle of whiskey is still in his hand but sitting on the ground. His apartment is full of people and not one of them is out there with him or even paying attention to him, except Cole.

'I'm sure if you get him to bed, he'd be OK sleeping it off,' he suggests.

I nod, staring out at Will. 'By the way, I'm not thrilled with my new theme song,' I say, glancing back at Cole before I step out onto the deck.

He laughs. 'You like that? That was all me; it seemed fitting.' His arrogant nod makes me wanna smack him, but I actually like Cole, so I won't.

I shake my head. 'It's humiliating to the tenth level. Remind me to pay you back one day.' I push open the door, walking to Will slowly. Jesus. I blow out a breath. How is he *this* good-looking when he's absolutely hammered? I sit on the chair he's in, facing him, our hips touching.

'Will.' I say his name, touching his chest. He groans something, rolling his head across the back of the lounger but never opening his eyes.

'*William*.' I say his full name louder. Shaking his chest.

He opens his eyes slowly, smiling when he sees me. 'Berx.' He slurs the word, reaching up and resting his hand on mine.

'Hi,' I say, giving him a shy smile. 'What, uh... What's going on?'

He sits up, dropping the whiskey bottle, his hand now on the side of my neck as he leans his forehead against mine. He smells like a distillery. Yuck. Jack Daniel's mixed with his usual cologne. Not a good mix.

'I miss you so much.' He slurs every s. 'I'm sorry I...' He bumbles through some words that make no sense then presses his lips to mine.

For a second, I close my eyes, wishing this was the Will I used to know. It's not. Even so, my heart skips a beat to feel his lips on mine. Is it a love spell, or is it a curse? I can't tell anymore.

'Do you want to maybe sleep it off?' I ask, pulling away from him, my hands now on his shoulders.

'Stay with me?'

'Um...' I shouldn't. I *know* this. But the bit of tequila lingering within disagrees. 'Sure,' I say, standing from the chair and offering my hands to help him up. Will and I need to have a serious talk tonight, and the only way I can do that is by being in the man's presence.

He doesn't hesitate to take my hands, letting me pull him off the lounge chair, leaving the booze where it landed when he dropped it. Thankfully on its bottom.

I steady him, which isn't easy considering he's got about eighty pounds over my hundred and six.

Cole pushes the door open, holding it as I steer Will through it.

'We should really start paying her for babysitting,' Mike says to his friends with a laugh.

'Fuck you, Mike,' I yell. 'Why don't *you* go jump off the roof?'

'You sure do tell me to die a lot,' Mike says.

'May the odds be ever in your favor.'

'Yeah, fuck you, Mikey.' Will repeats my words on a ten-second delay, flipping him the bird with both hands as we slowly walk through the living room.

'I'll kill him for you, baby. You want me to kill him?' The way he slurs it makes me laugh to myself. Even hardly able to think, he's standing up for me, threatening his brother's life.

'Not yet,' I tell him, patting his chest. 'We don't need murder on your record. Plus, if I ever want to get rid of Mikey, I'd rather torment him a while, demand a ransom even your parents probably wouldn't pay, then end him with my bare hands.' I glare at Mike as we walk past him.

My eyes dart to Felicity, her ruffled skirt so short I can see her bright blue panties as she sits on the couch next to Mike, her legs resting over his lap.

'I thought you were hot for Will?' I ask her.

'He's still not over you, and I don't do seconds.'

I burst out a laugh. '*You don't do seconds*? Newsflash, bimbo: he was *always* my boyfriend first,' I remind her. 'But ya know, math is hard, I get it.'

She rolls her eyes slowly like speaking to me physically pains her. The feeling is incredibly mutual, sweetheart. Please, gods of the universe, let that bitch get hers. Break a heel on camera, fall head-first into a well, drown in a mud puddle: whatever works, I support.

When we get to Will's room, I kick the door closed behind us.

'First stop, bathroom,' I tell him. 'If you gotta puke, puke. But you're brushing your teeth either way.'

'Why?' He stumbles into his bathroom, turning towards me as I lean against the door frame, watching him.

He rests his hands against the bathroom counter, glancing at the toilet, then back at me. His hair falls over his forehead as he stares at me.

'I don't need to puke,' he slurs. '*Yet*.' He laughs like he's just told a joke. 'But I do need to kiss you, and you don't like the taste of Jack, so I'll brush my teeth for you.' He's wagging his finger my way as he opens every door on the medicine cabinet, not finding what he's looking for.

I hand him his toothbrush, then pull open one of his bathroom drawers. Will's one of those guys who buys backups for his backups. This drawer is full of contact lenses, two pairs of the same glasses, two tubes of toothpaste and three unopened toothbrushes. I open one, tossing the garbage into the trash can.

'I'll join you because tequila breath is kinda rank too.'

'You've been drinking?' he asks, staring at me through the mirror, surprise on his face.

'The show aired...' I remind him.

'I'm sorry, baby.' He drags a hand over his face, dropping it to rest on the small of my back.

Tissue paper, meet water. I can already feel myself caving.

He laughs to himself for a long time, over absolutely nothing but whatever is going through his head, staring at me with heavy eyelids.

'I *might* try to kiss you,' he finally says. 'I *want* to kiss you, Berkley. *Bad*. But I don't want to use up our last relapse lay.' He's now behind me, pressed against me, his hands on my waist and his lips on my neck.

My heart literally flutters. There he is. My Will.

Here's the thing about drunk Will. He's not a happy drunk. He likes to throw out insults and fight. I've even heard Felicity talk about what a douche he is when he drinks. Will getting wasted is a truth pill no one in his life enjoys.

Then, when I show up, his bedroom door closes and it's just the two of us, he turns into the sweetest man I know. He once again worships the ground I walk on and is so gentle and sweet that I *want* to be here because I see the guy that I knew. That's why

I keep doing this. I miss the Will he was, and right now, he's here with me.

'We're supposed to be brushing our teeth, remember?' I reach up and pat his cheek, leaning into him.

He grabs my hand, bringing it to his lips, staring at me, then at himself in the mirror, clearly not remembering what he's supposed to be doing even though I just said it again.

I get both our toothbrushes ready, handing him his. He shoves it in his mouth, brushing his teeth slowly.

'Ugh.' He grimaces, nearly gagging. 'It's like brushing your teeth and drinking orange juice.'

'Why are *you* drinking tonight?' I ask, looking at him in the mirror.

'Because the show aired and reminded me of what an ass-face I am,' he slurs, now speaking around the toothbrush in his mouth.

'You're *not* an ass-face, Will – at least not completely.'

'Yes, I am. You can say it.' He's now brushing his teeth in what seems to be slow motion as he desperately tries to stay awake. 'Say it, baby. I deserve it.'

I heave a sigh. 'Fine,' I say. 'You're an ass-face,' I tell him, throwing out my arms in frustration. 'An ass-face I *don't* want to die on camera because he feels bad about the decisions he's making in life.'

He spits the toothpaste into the sink, leaning over and drinking right from the faucet. I do the same, rinsing my toothbrush and putting it in his medicine cabinet, hoping no one else touches it.

'Come on.' I direct him out of the bathroom, his hand now in mine, towards his bed.

He strips off his shirt and stumbles through pulling off his pants before finally dropping onto his bed in just his underwear. He rolls like a drunk log to the middle, patting the side I usually sleep on, reaching for me.

'I need you.' He points at me obnoxiously. 'Here.' He stretches out an arm, pointing at it.

Fight it, Berkley. Tell him to sleep it off and go home. Or, ya know what? Don't fight it. Let this be your last.

He stares at me, big brown eyes gazing up at me. Damn it, he's handsome. I sigh. I did convince him to leave the roof by saying I'd *stay*, and he's in no condition to be alone right now.

I slip off my flip-flops and climb into his king-sized bed with him. Fully clothed. And by fully clothed, I mean still in the short shorts and tank top I've been wearing all day. It's not enough to ward off wandering hands. I'd have to be sewn into a snowsuit for that. As soon as I'm in his bed, he pulls me against him, kissing the top of my shoulder.

'I'm sorry I'm an ass-face,' he says into my ear. 'To make it up to you, I did something for your birthday.'

'Oh, God, what did you do?'

He rolls over onto his back, pointing at his chest.

'You got a tattoo?' There it is. The letter B followed by a purple heart, Queen of Hearts style on his chest, above his heart. B♥. My heart beats through my chest like it's just seen a ghost.

Last summer, he pierced his ears. He now wears two black small-gage earrings. At first, I hated them because they represent his party-boy phase, but they've since grown on me. This summer, he got a tattoo.

'It matches yours,' he says.

'When did you get this?'

'A couple days ago.'

Damn it. That's actually sweet as hell. I run my fingers around it. It's not very big, maybe an inch tall and wide at most. He even did the purple heart. My favorite color.

'Damn you, Adler.'

'You're mad?' he asks, worry in his voice.

I am the opposite of mad and that's what's pissing me off. I *love* this moron. And I can't tell him because we're both such a mess it'll only make things worse if I do.

'Why would I be mad?'

'Because I tattooed your initial while we're broken up.'

I sigh. 'I'm not mad, Will,' I say. 'It makes me...'

This is your heart, Berkley. I know I talk a big game, and then somehow melt for this dude every chance I have, but I'm serious when I say: do not tell Will that you love him right now. This guy needs some work. Of the professional kind. You alone can't save him. You just can't. When he's sober, use up your third life and be done with this so he can possibly live through the next year.

'It makes you what?' he asks.

'Sometimes I can't believe you still have a heart in here.' I touch his chest.

He flashes me a sad smile. 'Can I see your tattoo?'

'Sure.'

I roll over, now facing away from him, literally snuggling my back to his front. He slides his arms around me and pulls me against him, kissing the tattoo I got in college, W ♥. I blink back tears as he holds his lips to my shoulder, sending electricity through my soul. I love lying like this with him. I crave it so much it physically pains my heart now that it's happening.

'I miss you so much it hurts, Berx. I don't wanna be here anymore. I'm not happy.' He buries his face into my neck and hair as he starts to cry.

I sigh, hugging his arm around me to my chest, kissing his fingers now resting on my left collarbone.

Do not cry, Berkley. This room can handle exactly one sobbing fool, and he's already arrived.

Drunk Will gets goofy, pissed, depressed, fighty, emotional, handsy, then passes out. A pattern that never changes. We're moving through the drunk Will phases quickly tonight, so it's only a matter of time before he tries to make out with me and then literally passes out mid-kiss.

'Will, if you're unhappy here, move in with me. I hate watching you do this to yourself.'

He starts to snore, and I know I've lost him. My heart sinks in my chest a little. He's just blown by the flirty portion of the evening. Maybe me saving him all the time is only making things worse? Maybe *I'm* the one holding on here? Shit. I hold his arm across my chest tightly, pulling his hand to my face and crying into it while he's passed out.

12

WILL

I wake up to the sun shining through my windows. Wait, how the—
did I even get here? The last thing I remember, I was on the balcony,
wallowing in self-pity that the *one* woman I want doesn't want me
back. I embarrassed her on television, then I had to watch her,
while we screened the show, literally save me from a night I don't
even remember. She even went to court with me. I am a *dick*.

I squint, one eye opened, reaching up and massaging my
pounding head. A blurry mess of brown hair lies on the pillow next
to me. Wait a second? Brown hair, who the *hell* is this?

'Ugh,' I groan. Damn it. Did I do something stupid in a drunken
stupor?

'Hello?' I poke her back with my forefinger. 'Miss? You gotta go,'
I say to her, shadowing my face from the sun. 'I fucked up.' I poke
her again. 'I was drinking so I wouldn't call a woman and shit
clearly got away from me.' I jab my finger into her shoulder blade.

'Can ya stop poking me?' She groans, pushing her ass into my
groin. Her voice triggers something in me, a tugging at my heart
that makes me forget my own name.

'Berx,' I say with a sigh of relief, sliding a hand around her waist, pulling her against me, kissing her shoulder. I throw a leg over hers, like I won't let her get away from me. 'My God, *why* are you here? I thought I fucked up again.'

She settles into me, holding my arm across her tightly. She missed me; I can feel it. I can't believe she's in my bed. I kiss along her shoulder to her neck.

'You did,' she says, moving her head back and allowing me access to continue up her neck. 'Fuck up again, I mean. You got blackout drunk and threatened to jump from the balcony. You don't remember asking me to come over?'

'I don't,' I say. 'We didn't use up our last relapse night, while I was *that* wasted, did we?'

'Technically, we didn't.'

'Phew,' he says with relief. 'What stupid things did I say?' I ask, nuzzling my head into her hair, breathing her in deeply. She always smells like vanilla shampoo and raspberry body spray. A summer day in the form of the most beautiful woman I've ever known.

'You said you missed me,' she says. 'That you're not happy here. You said you were going to try and kiss me—'

'Am I a good kisser when I'm hammered?' I ask, interrupting her with a laugh.

Suddenly she goes stiff. I feel her let out a disheartened breath like she's near tears. I hold her tighter. What did I do this time?

'I honestly don't remember anymore,' she says, her voice flat. 'You passed out after the crying phase.'

The crying phase, *fuck*.

'Baby, are you... *mad* about that?' I ask, confused by her words.

She lifts a single shoulder. 'I don't know,' she says, her voice wavering as she speaks. 'I haven't seen you – and I... I...' She can't finish her sentence for some reason, and I can hear *why* in her voice. 'Last night, you said you were unhappy, and... and, I don't know how to fix that.'

'Berkley.' I scoot away from her, encouraging her to face me.

Finally, she rolls onto her back, glancing up at me, tears in her eyes.

'I can't do this anymore.' She cries with legit tears streaming down her face and it tears at my heart. 'Seeing you hurts too much. It makes me miss you, and I have no right to miss you because *I* called this off.' She covers her face with her hands. 'I think we should call it.'

Fuck. I brush her hair from her face, resting my hand on the side of her neck, kissing her lips gently.

'You want to call it? Our relationship?'

She cocks her head, narrowing her pretty eyes at me. 'Yes, our relationship, whatever it even is anymore. To the whole world, you're a rich single Portland Royal, and I'm the woman in the wings saving you from yourself while the woman the tabloids once called "Prince Willy's queen" is lounging around on your brother's lap when you're too drunk to notice.'

'I could give two shits about Felicity.'

God, my head is pounding. It's hard to be smooth when your brain feels like it's on fire. How much did I drink last night? I rub the back of my neck, the hangover moving over me like a wave.

'Hey.' The door to my room swings open and in walks a woman Berkley's never met. Felicity's best friend, Danika Frost, and she's wearing her underwear and a skimpy slip only. 'Which dress should I wear, the red or the black? I know it's not dress-up worthy, but I like to look my best when standing next to the most handsome prince in all the world.' Finally, she looks up from the dresses in her hands. 'Oh. You have company... I didn't know.'

There is nothing going on between me and Danika. But she's trying harder than Felicity is so guilt washes over me.

'And this is my cue,' Berkley says, climbing out of my bed, still clothed, and slipping on her flip-flops. She's mad. I can sense she's mad. But it's because she doesn't know nothing's going on between Danika and me.

'Berkley, don't go,' I say, following her out. 'That's not what it looked like—'

'I'm sorry,' Danika says to me as I race past her, following Berkley from my room towards the front door, in only my underwear – which is an opportunity that Jonah doesn't ever miss.

Me calling her name doesn't do a damn thing, and I watch as she storms out of my apartment and disappears into the elevator. Why must my life look so much worse than it really is? There's no way she'll be answering my calls now.

13

BERKLEY

One Year Later, June 2022

PDX ROYALS FANS

BOILING HOT! Every last one of these Royals is burning me right to my core in the best and worst of ways. From the bikinis to the Speedos (YES! Mike actually wears Speedos, viewers – warning: they're leopard print and at least one size too small), add exuberant amounts of alcohol, and this show is the exact drama you never want to live. Let's do a recap of what's gone on so far.

King Mikey has lost his ever-loving mind. Shame is not a trait he understands. One moment he's attempting to charm the swimsuit off Felicity in the pool during daylight hours (we all watched that make-out scene – CRINGE), the next second she's begging Mike to talk her up to Will romantically. Though the aftermath of that did not go over well. 'You want that little fuck, get in there and seduce him already, then.' Do I sense a touch of jealousy on Mike's part that the princess is smitten with his little brother?

Lord Finn is most certainly not lord of the dance, this much is clear. Elaine Benes can finally relax because after that club party a few weeks ago, Finn now holds the title of best bad dancer – EVER. Word of advice to you, Finn: be a wallflower. Where are all these women he claims he knows, anyway? For a guy with a sex tape, he spends an awful lot of the time flying solo. He is lord of the kitchen, though, as he's been cooking up a storm and the crew had their first official 'dinner party' recently. I think Gordon Ramsay would have been proud of the way Finn handled himself in the kitchen. He wasn't shirtless, washed his hands and actually seemed to be confident with good reason.

Princess Felicity is absolutely beautiful, elegant, successful and a real head turner, however... if I was given the opportunity to be her new BFF, I think I'd pass. (No offense, Felicity!) Never in a million years have I seen a woman throw herself at a man like she has Willy. My advice to you, Felicity: rewatch these episodes and take notes, sweetheart. We're quite certain Willy has eyes for someone else.

Speak of the devil, Prince Willy. What is going on with you, darling? Between the drinking, the hiding out in his room or sneaking looks at his cell phone, I'd say he's got more of a life outside the show than on it. Out of the group, he avoids the cameras the most, unless he's completely smashed (which is often), then he's a real hoot. Security tells us he's very good at sneaking away from the cameras. Where is he going? Fans suspect another woman and we've got our sources on the hunt. Perhaps we'll find out soon!

Maybe you've noticed the new gorgeous face around the Royals' condo recently. She began as a walk-on character last season but she's now an officially casted Royal! She's not exactly a personality to be missed either. Sweet, smart and beautiful, she even graced the cover of *Cosmopolitan* magazine recently with an article about her entrepreneur ways.

Danika Frost! (Yes, that Frost family.) Felicity's longtime BFF has moved into the condo this season as she and Felicity start a health brand: Harper Frost. Vitamins, supplements, work-out and yoga gear – soon your medicine cabinet and gym bag will be full of Harper Frost products and we can't wait!

The show airs on E! every Sunday at 9:00 p.m. PST.

* * *

'Finally, she's ready to move on and we're out in the world living life again!' Olivia says happily.

Have I become a hermit in the last year? Sort of. Work is my escape and everything else is just me surviving. But I did it. We did it. Will and I finally let one another go and after a year, I'm ready to move on.

'But *soccer*?' I ask Gunner and Olivia as they lead me to our seats. 'I don't even know the rules.'

We're walking sideways in front of people to get to our seats in the center of the section.

'The rules are easy,' Liv says. 'Kicky dudes kick the ball into the net without hands while running. Did I mention they're usually hot kicky dudes?' she asks, glancing over at me, waggling her eyebrows.

'Kicky dudes?' Gunner asks, clearly not impressed with her description.

Meet Gunner. He's twenty-seven, a little nerdy but in a 'he's pretty cool' kind of way (a joke he does not enjoy) and has spent his adult life in creative writing class after creative writing class. He claims peer feedback is why his hair went gray prematurely. He writes sci-fi dystopian comic-style fanfiction online, publishing in chapters or 'episodes' that readers eagerly wait for.

After Frank's exit, I needed a new employee because neither Olivia nor I were versed in fantasy, sci-fi or superhero. When Gunner walked in, résumé in hand, in full costume of some fantasy character I'd never heard of, he blew me away with his knowledge so I hired him on the spot. He's worked at To Be Read for a year now and has built his section into something movie-worthy. Even Sheldon Cooper would be proud. An entire wall built of never-been-out-of-the-box action figures separates his department from Olivia's. He does weekly meet-ups with a group of regulars that read every book he suggests, then come in for discussion hour. It's easily the busiest reading group we have within the store.

'You got a problem with kicky dudes?' Olivia asks him, attitude galore.

He laughs nervously. 'Nope. Perfectly explained. What else do you really need to know?'

With the foam finger shoved under his arm, the armload of food and beer, not to mention the team jersey on his back, you can hardly tell Gunner's a fan. Olivia knows messing with his love of soccer or superheroes is the fastest way to irritate him. She's pressing those buttons methodically. It's their thing.

'I'm just here because I like the food,' Olivia says. 'And obviously the hot kicky dudes. This was mostly Gunner's idea, so if you hate it, blame him.'

'Hello from under the bus,' Gunner says, clearly offended, glancing past me and shooting a glare at Olivia. 'I don't remember you having any better ideas.'

'I am thankful you chose a safe place.' She ignores his tone, continuing her conversation. 'We probably don't have to worry about "someone" from *Royals* showing up unexpectedly and distracting us.'

They both stop walking, each giving me a cold look.

'If you're going to continue to bring him up, I'll never truly get over him.'

He sent me a text a few days after that last night I saw him and asked:

Was that *it* it? Like we're *done* done?

And I ignored him. It was so hard, and I cried as I deleted his text but he doesn't really need me to answer because I know he knows already.

Olivia took the reins and texted him herself, telling him to accept it and move on. That didn't go over great, but she handled it. Since then, I haven't heard a single word from him. I read about him in the tabloids like everyone else.

The three of us slide into our seats, situating everything, so we're comfortable.

'Mm-mm. So, freaking good. It's like movie-theater popcorn. You can make it at home, but it's not the same.' Olivia swoons over a hot dog, the sole reason she came today.

'They are goo—' I start to say, then freeze, my drink partway to my mouth as I internally panic, a familiar voice invading my head. I glance around for him, worry filling my insides like bumblebees.

'Uh-oh...' Liv points to the jumbotron now running a *Royals* commercial.

Will's gorgeous face stares back at me, stopping my heart. Damn it. He's the face of the show. The face of Portland. I thought he was everywhere six months into the show – God, was I wrong. Now, two years later, he really is everywhere – tabloids, billboards, commercials, walk-on acting spots, radio shows, advertisements and local news. I even saw one of their posters on our way into the stadium today. Now his stupid beautiful face is looking back at me along with a woman who could give Angelina Jolie a run for her money. Danika Frost, a rich girl who is attempting to take over the world with her entrepreneurial ways. I saw an article recently that predicted if those two (she and Will) 'got together', they could be the power couple of the city. Just stick an ice pick through my eye already, would ya?

'Four more seasons, Portland,' Mikey says, the rest of the group toasting him.

I glance at Liv, who forces a ridiculous smile but forgets her *oh shit* wide eyes. 'He must've signed another contract,' she suggests.

She said the words that were at the tip of my tongue but I didn't want to say out loud. Yes, this is news to me. I shouldn't be surprised, considering I officially 'walked away' a year ago, but I feel like he's a part of my soul and there's no way to get rid of someone once they've become embedded into who you are.

'That abstruse dickbag!' Gunner says with disappointment. Only he would mix an obnoxious word with a swear. He's definitely not wrong in this case.

Honestly, I feel like I might puke. The day I found out he signed up for the show flashes through my head, and somehow this feels worse.

'I guess I need a new life path.' Not that I was holding out hope any longer.

Liv frowns, but I wave her off.

'I'll be fine,' I reassure her, reading her mind. 'We broke up a long time ago. It may have taken us some time to finally part ways for good but we did it and I'm... *happy*... for him.' The word literally did not want to leave my lips, but I forced it and that's exactly how it sounded too. Actress of the year over here, folks. Where's my Emmy?

'That didn't even sound happy,' Gunner says matter-of-factly.

'Yes. It did,' I insist. 'If he's happy, I'm happy for him.'

'It totally sounded happy.' Olivia backs me up. 'Shut up, Gunner.'

Luckily, he knows us well enough to know when he shouldn't get involved and he turns his attention to the field, ignoring us completely.

Deep breaths, Berx. You aren't dying. You just wish you were. It's no big deal because you are completely over Will. He can sign as many contracts as he wants. Be the fucking Bachelor for all you care! You're on to bigger and better things!

Finally, the ad passes, my heart rate levels and I can breathe again. That was far more emotion than I was expecting today. I prop my feet on the empty chair before me, sipping my drink and diverting my eyes from the screen. A man with Will's hair a few rows ahead of me stops my heart again but when he turns to talk to his friend I exhale. Not him.

Focus, Berkley. You broke up with Will because he lied. He ruined all the plans you made for your futures and he just lied again. Proof you did the right thing.

'Which one is your favorite?' I ask, distracting myself with anything possible.

'Alex Donovan, number nine,' Gunner answers.

Olivia's been talking about Alex for a week. We went to school together, but I haven't kept up with him. All I knew about Alex Donovan was that he and Will were on the same soccer team in high school and had some kind of rivalry from a fight they had over a girl in their earlier school days together.

Honestly, I didn't even realize he'd gone pro until Olivia told me. She's a professional internet stalker in her free time so of course she and Alex have kept up on all the socials.

I hunt for number nine, spotting him talking to someone as he kicks a ball back and forth with a teammate.

'Whoa,' I say with a laugh. 'Alex grew up, didn't he?'

He used to be tall and scrawny but those days seem to have passed. When I met him he was one of those cocky I'm-the-best-on-the-team fourteen-year-old boys. I wasn't impressed at all back then, but I'm sure he's grown up just like I have. Good for him to be so gifted at soccer he got to go pro.

'Yes. He. Did,' Liv says. 'I'm glad you said it like that because he's your rebound boyfriend. He's going to ask you out today.'

I whip my head in her direction. 'I can't go out with Alex, Liv. He's Will's arch enemy.'

'Anyone who doesn't have a superpower has no arch enemies,' Gunner says casually.

'We talked about this months ago, Berx. And you agreed to a rebound guy. Well, there he is, I found him. The fact that he and Will aren't exactly friendly is even better. We all know Will's still in love with you; if you're dating his enemy, maybe he'll finally pull his head out of his ass.'

'If he signed another contract, his head is going to be there a couple more years so that's doubtful. Plus, I'm over him.'

She and Gunner both laugh. They don't even try to hide it.

'You just nearly had a stroke at the sound of his voice on TV. You're not over him.'

'This is where Alex will help!'

'I can't do it, Liv.'

'Why? Because of Will?' She balks. 'Honey, I didn't want to say this to you because it's uncomfortable, but have you seen how he and Danika get on? I think Will might be moving on too. Why not make him jealous while he does?'

'I worry about you sometimes,' Gunner says to Olivia with worry on his face.

'You need to date more because if you request I buy another jumbo pack of batteries with the store inventory again, I'll have them delivered care of "Berkley's love stick" and make you sign for them.'

Gunner suddenly chokes on his drink, coughing as if he's dying.

In case you're a total prude, what Olivia affectionately calls my 'love stick' is a motorized vibrating contraption meant to de-stress women in the privacy of wherever the fuck they want and lives in my nightstand drawer.

'Thanks for filling Gun in on *that* little tax violation. Not at all embarrassing,' I say, feeling the heat rise to my cheeks. Yes, he and I are close but not that close.

'You're going out with Alex.' Liv brings the subject back to the date.

'I said I was ready to live life again; I don't know if I'm ready to date, Liv.'

'It's been long enough, so *get* ready. I'm not asking you to marry the guy. I'm simply suggesting you let a handsome, hot dude take you to dinner and maybe give the love stick a night off.'

Gunner grunts an uncomfortable laugh. 'Can we stop saying the words "love stick"? Please?'

'Prude,' Liv says.

'I'm not a prude,' he defends himself. 'It's just way more than I need to know about my friend and boss. Moving on, I worry a love triangle between these three may result in a Norman Osborn, Peter Parker and Gwen Stacy issue,' he says, stuffing his face with popcorn.

Olivia and I both glance over, confusion on our faces.

He lifts his eyebrows, his eyes now wide as he stares back. 'The original rivalry of Green Goblin and Spider-Man?' he asks, concern growing on his face. '"The Night Gwen Stacy Died"? A two-part issue: numbers 121 and 122, released in June and July 1973? You two seriously don't listen to anything I talk about, do you?'

'We do too,' I insist guiltily.

He rolls his eyes. 'They were two friends who became mortal enemies who literally tried to destroy the world over a woman. Does that not seem a little similar here? Berkley will have two rich, influential men fighting over her because we all know the second word of this gets out to Will, he'll show back up into our lives. The Clark Kent of Berkley's world. Only one person loses in this. In *Spider-Man*, it was Gwen. In this' – he glances at me with an uncomfortable look – 'it's you. But I know you two, and I know this is happening no matter what I say, so here's to you surviving another terrible idea.' He lifts his beer in the air.

I consider Gunner one of my best friends, and moments like this are why. He doesn't hate Will with the fiery passion that Olivia does. Liv and I follow the BFF rules when it comes to hating people. If she hates someone, I hate them equally and vice versa. Her hate towards Will is a little more ragey than mine – proof in the fact that she wants me to date someone to both 'get over' Will *and* make him jealous – but she's only being protective.

'Will has apparently re-signed a contract to extend the show, and has heart eyes for the newest city Royal,' Olivia reminds Gunner. 'Pretty sure that means he couldn't give a flying fuck about who Berkley dates so I highly doubt there will be any love triangles.'

'Men fighting over me? I can't even imagine that,' I say with a laugh.

'Perfect, then you literally can't say no,' Liv says. 'He likes you too. Look...' She shoves her phone my way, turning her attention back to her hot dog.

I glance down at Olivia's phone now in my hand, a thread of text messages between Alex and her on the screen. I read through them. He thinks I'm pretty. He wonders what's up with Will and me. Am I a part of *Royals*? Because if so, he's out.

Well, we at least have that in common, I suppose.

'After the game, we're headed down to say hello,' Liv says. 'So, prepare yourself. Give him a chance. You need this, Berx. If for nothing else than to prove that you're an amazing woman that any guy would be lucky to love.'

I sigh heavily – she's the best best friend and that's no exaggeration. I need to make her a mug.

'Look at him,' Olivia says, pointing to the field where Alex is. 'Gunner's already in love with him.' She nods to Gun, whose eyes are steadily fixed on his idol. 'Who wouldn't be? He's beautiful, talented, gainfully employed and *not* an ass-face.'

'I'm *not* in love with Alex,' Gunner says flatly, defending his man-crush.

'Oh-kay.' She laughs, dramatically rolling her eyes to the sky.

'So, he's cute,' I say, my eyes now on Alex. 'That's not the only thing that matters.'

'Yeah, Liv. Berkley prefers arrogant rich dudes with growing drinking problems who she refuses to tell how she really feels because every woman on the planet now wants him, and she's afraid he won't pick her in the end...' He looks my way slowly, raising a single eyebrow like he just doesn't understand me.

I'm a little offended he knows me this well. 'I'm *complicated*.'

'You're pertinacious and too wrapped up in Prince Willy the moron,' he says.

'Words like "pertinacious" are why we don't listen to you when you speak,' I say, winking Gunner's way.

'He lied to you,' Gunner reminds me. 'And he just signed another contract without ever even speaking to you. *Again*. That to me says he's choosing the show and moving on.'

'I thought you were on team Gwen Stefani?' I ask.

'*Stacy*,' he says. 'Gwen *Stacy*. And after another thought on it, I figure Olivia's probably right. Why the hell not do something that might piss him off? He hasn't had a lot of concern about how he's made you feel.'

'Yes, he has.' They don't know him like I know him.

'Nope!' Liv yells. 'Do not defend him. We're moving on, remember. To that!' She points at the field again.

'Fine,' I say, slouching back in my seat. 'I'll give Alex a chance.'

'*Woo!*' she hollers, high-fiving the stranger in front of her. 'The rightful princess of Portland is about to bag another successful, handsome man, and I am the genius matchmaker.'

'Don't quit your job yet, Cupid,' Gunner teases. 'This could be a total disaster.'

14

BERKLEY

The game was long and I saw that stupid *Royals* ad twice more. I've never been more thankful for an event to end. We're now standing with a bunch of children, waiting for team members to come out and sign autographs. There must be fifty kids here – and Gunner.

'Liv,' he says excitedly, a tad buzzed from the three super-sized brewskis he threw back. He throws an arm around her neck. 'I can't believe you pulled through with something cool, and we get to meet Alex Donovan! You think he'll sign my shirt?'

'He's signing my cleavage whether he wants to or not, so I don't know why he'd refuse your jersey.'

'You realize you're fangirling over a footballer that Olivia has demanded I fall in love with?'

'SLEEP,' she corrects me, loudly. 'I demanded you *sleep* with him, but if love brews, one more point for matchmaker Liv,' she says with a wide grin.

'The more beer I knocked back the more I realized that I've got zero problem with you falling for my idol. My only request is that you put in a good word for me as best man at your wedding,' he says drunkenly.

I snort with laughter. 'Wedding? We haven't even been on one date. I haven't talked to the guy since high school and barely even then.'

People around us suddenly erupt into chatter as the players head our way. Gunner's jumping up and down like a kid waiting to meet Santa. I back away from the crowd, standing behind them with the parents as the kids, Gunner and Olivia get their autographs.

Alex is kneeling in front of a little boy, chattering away as he signs the ball now in his hands. OK... so he's not unpleasant to look at. Ruggedly handsome with an unshaven scruff on his pretty face. He glances at me several times, moving in my direction when the kid he was busy with runs off.

'Berkley Kaine.' He says my name slowly as he walks over, a coy grin on his face. 'I haven't seen you in years. Wow,' he says with a chuckle. 'You're hot, girl.'

'Hot?' I repeat. Not exactly the romantic meet-cute I'd envisioned as a story to tell my grandkids one day. 'Thank you?'

Alex smirks, stopping in front of me and looking me up and down. 'Olivia says you like what you see.' He motions down, winking my way.

'Um...' She said I liked his penis? What a weird thing to say. How do I respond? *You're OK too. Five stars. Solid ten. Total smoke show. I'm sorry, but you can't compete with the guy who ran off with my heart years ago?* Ugh.

'You know what, I never told you this because you always had a boyfriend but I always had a bit of a thing for you back in high school.'

'Really?'

'Yep. You're gorgeous, girl. Always have been. Willy might have got to you first but if he hadn't, I'd have given it a shot.'

That's... oddly sweet?

'Let's get dinner,' he suggests, grabbing my hand, pushing my jacket sleeve to my elbow, and scribbling his name on my inner forearm in black Sharpie marker that I'll have to scrub for days to remove. And I was worried his vanity-laden come-on line was the douchiest part about him. Maybe he's just nervous? I mean, this is awkward. I'll give him the benefit of the doubt.

'You like Italian food?' he asks.

'Sure.' I nod, staring at his signature across my skin. He made the Os in his name into little hearts. Maybe he's a romantic deep down?

He smiles when I look up, his face lighting up when he does. Tall, blond, handsome, fit. Maybe he's a little into himself but is looking at him painful enough to say no? Olivia's right. Will and I are clearly over. Perhaps Alex and I will somehow click?

'Olivia gave me your deets,' Alex says.

'Perfect,' I say, glancing at Olivia, who's staring at her chest where Alex did indeed brand her directly under her face. She already gave him my 'deets', did she?

'I'll call you. We'll set it up,' he says, backing away from me towards another kid with a proud grin on his face. 'I'll see you later, gorgeous.'

A weird schoolgirl giggle bubbles up and out of my mouth. He smiles wider then disappears into the crowd of fans once again.

'Ugh.'

I grip my chest, glimpsing his autograph on my arm again. Why does my chest hurt? Like I'm somehow guilty.

Calm down, Berkley. It's just a date, not a marriage proposal.

Olivia, Gunner and I all watch Alex walk away when the after event is over. Each of us silently daydreaming about him probably very different ways. Beautiful, arrogant, yet somehow charming? God. I think I have a type? The three of us head towards the stadium exit together and as we walk I hold out my arm for them to see the signature that literally goes from elbow to wrist.

'You were right,' I say to Olivia. 'He does seem to like me and he doesn't make me wish I didn't have twenty-twenty vision. He does seem kind of conceited, though.'

'Isn't that your thing?' Gunner laughs.

Asked and answered. Olivia laughs along with him, lifting a hand that Gunner meets with his, high-fiving right in front of me.

'This feels weird,' I say, shoving my hands into my pockets.

'You've dated one person your entire life; of course it feels weird. Shockingly, I'm with Gunner on this one. If you want to know if Will will follow through on your future life plan, this is how you do that. By bringing an equally successful, handsome man into the mix. Will's too drunk now for that life you're dreaming of, Berx. Who knows if he'll snap out of it. This may well be the new and not-so-improved Will Adler. Experience new things. Go out, be seen, end up in the tabloids with a new handsome man. Will is. Let him hurt a little. It's only fair.'

'There are times when you terrify me,' Gunner says to Liv, who looks as if he's just complimented her.

'Let me get this straight. You two think I should date Alex and *tell* Will this?'

'Yes,' they say in unison.

'Sleep and tell, girl. We'll spread the word.' Olivia motions between her and Gunner.

'Oh, great. Gossip. That's not at all weird when you're a dude in his late twenties,' Gunner says, shaking his head.

Olivia flips her head his way, her eyebrows raised. 'You just fangirled over a soccer player who's going to sweep our girl here off her feet and treat her like a queen. That's where you should be embarrassed, not over gossip. You fangirl like a lady, by the way,' she says, jabbing his internal buttons intentionally.

Gunner laughs, but walks away without saying a word. They totally like each other. This is middle-school flirting at its worst. I've been noticing it for a while now.

'How about this?' I say when Gunner is far enough ahead of us that I know he can't hear me. 'I'll date Alex when you finally admit you're into Gunner.'

'What?' She acts appalled, yet interested.

'Please. You could cut the sexual tension between you two with a knife.'

'I am not into Gunner,' she insists but her gaze moves to him and the smile creeping up on her face right now isn't convincing me I'm wrong.

Gunner's truck beeps to life, alerting us to change the subject before his spidey-senses pick up on us talking about him.

Liv walks straight to him and holds her hand out. 'Keys, ya drunk...'

'No one drives my truck but me,' he says, before eventually caving and dropping his keys into her hand. The two stare at each other for an uncomfortably long time. Finally, I yank open the back door of the crew cab truck, hitting Liv in the process – intentionally – to break the tension.

Gunner clears his throat as he walks away from her towards the front passenger seat. Looks like someone else does drive his truck.

As we drive, my mind wanders. Only this time, I'm wondering if they might be right. What could dating Alex hurt? I'm single; he's single. Maybe Will's not the only man I could love with. If I fall for Alex, I'll quit holding on to hope that Will might come to his senses and follow through with our life plan, and I will finally be able to get him out of my head. Seems simple enough.

15
WILL

'Condoms, condoms, ma'am, can you help me?' Mike yells it through the store, obnoxiously *and* intentionally. After that one time a woman didn't know who he was, he makes sure people know in advance to save himself the embarrassment of that scene he'll never live down because it's out in the world on film forever.

'You have to be as loud as you can get? Jesus. *Shut up.*'

He punches me in the shoulder as we walk through the CVS, stopping at the older woman who's now talking to Mike.

'I'm looking for the *big* boxes. Magnum preferred, *obviously*—'

'He's King Mikey!' Finn finishes his sentence then they snicker like they're thirteen.

The woman directs us to the correct aisle but as I pass by the first aid aisle, I get a glimpse of her. I stop. Holy fuck, she's as gorgeous as ever, even more so if possible.

'Berkley.'

Her head snaps my way.

'Will.' She sets a bottle of hydrogen peroxide back onto the counter in front of her.

'Hi,' I say, a smile involuntarily spreading across my face.

'Hello. How are you?' she asks flatly.

'I'm alright. How are you?'

'Never been better!' she says, but I can read right through her.

I glance around at the aisle we're in. 'Are you alright?'

'Yeah,' she insists. 'Didn't I just answer that? I've beyond good. Why?'

I point to a box of Band-Aids and she laughs uncomfortably. She plants her hands on her hips. I've never seen her this nervous around me.

'Right, we're in the first aid aisle. No, I'm fine, everything is perfectly fi—' As she motions to over herself she suddenly stops, her eyes on her arm. I follow her gaze and see it.

'You got a *tattoo*?'

She has the one, but I had no idea she was even thinking of getting another and can't even imagine what it could be that she'd want it that big.

'*No*,' she says pulling down the sleeves of her jacket. 'I did not get a tattoo.'

'Then what is that?' I ask, reaching for her hand and lifting her sleeve. 'Al-ex Don-o-van?' I read it out loud slowly as I push up her sleeve. My brows squish together and my face is doing everything I don't want it to do. Why does she have his name on her arm?

'It's Sharpie marker, not a tattoo. Liv, Gunner and I went to a game yesterday. He was signing autographs, Gunner is fan, and I didn't have any paper so since I didn't want his name across my chest, like Liv, he signed my arm?' she asks like she's not sure of any of it. Explaining herself in a way that says she's afraid of my reaction.

'That's cool,' I say, pretending my heart's not on fire right now at the thought of her with Alex Donovan. 'Is it serious?'

'Serious? Nope. Nothing serious about an autograph I'll have to buy product to get off before I work on Monday.' She grabs the hydrogen peroxide and a bottle of rubbing alcohol, then breezes by me towards the checkouts.

'Berkley, we can't even talk for a minute?' I ask, following behind her.

She stops suddenly, turning towards me, causing me to nearly mow her over, but I save it by grabbing her shoulders and holding her up, and we're close. Way closer than we've been in the last year. Her vanilla shampoo clouds my head.

'Fine,' she blurts. 'He asked me out, but it's nothing *serious*,' she says, speaking quickly, nervously. 'I don't know why it's a big deal when you have *two* more years of Danika. Congratulations, by the way. On both the new extended contract and your new lady friend. You two seem to have clicked.'

'Well, the show is heavily edited so—'

'Let's go, little bro, we got the goods! We grabbed a box of child-sized rubbers for you—' He stops in his tracks when he spots her in front of me. 'Oh. My. God.'

Berkley steps away from me. She probably wishes she could step right in a new life right now and I don't blame her.

'Where you been, girl?' Mike asks Berkley like they're old friends. 'Sometimes I hear Will in his room trying to call you when he's slopping drunk to get a piece but you never answer. You got a back line?' He and Finn laugh at this.

'Just check out,' I say, shoving him away from us and towards the register.

'Where's Jonah?' Berkley asks. 'Shouldn't you three have a camera up your ass?'

I laugh. There she is, my spitfire Berkley, pretending she has no heart.

'He's around here somewhere. Guy's gotten pretty sneaky over the years.'

'I've noticed. Every time I turn on my TV there's an image of you and Miss Frost and I don't know about all the other fans but pass the ice pick, please, I need to shove it into my eyes.'

God, even pissed, she's adorable. I wish I could fix this.

'You *wanted* to move on and I've no doubt Alex will attempt to be your knight in shining armor soon enough.'

'And Danika will be your princess,' she snaps back.

'Let's go, Willy or we'll leave your ass here,' Mike yells on his way out of the store. We can't go anywhere and not alert the whole damn place that we're there. How would people adore him? The 'king' of Portland. Ugh.

'Sounds like your ride's leaving,' Berkley says, walking away from me towards the front counter.

'Call me sometime,' I say into her ear as I head to the door, touching her back as I do and feeling her stiffen up at me being so close to her.

'No thanks,' she says, never looking at me as I leave.

'Hey,' I say, stopping in the doors.

Finally, our eyes meet and I do the one thing she can't unsee. The one thing I know to do that can say what my heart wants to scream but shouldn't because it breaks all her rules. I touch my chest, then point her way. Immediately her shoulders drop and she sucks in a breath.

HOOONNNKKK. HONK. HONK. HONK.

That's my cue. If I don't leave now, Mikey'll have a press conference in the parking lot about his purchases and then publicly beg to be the face of their companies.

I get into the back of Mikey's SUV next to Jonah, who's apparently filmed our entire encounter. Great. They shouldn't use it but the show's become a little 'sin now, apologize later'. I've got zero privacy and of course that'd be when I ran into her for the first time in a long time.

What did I even just accomplish doing what I did back there?

It's not like she's going to ever take me back. I signed a *second* contract.

'Stop by the liquor store on the way back,' I say to Mike.

'Yeah! Last-minute party, good idea, Willy,' Finn says as we speed away from the CVS. If I gotta have the memories, maybe my friend Jack can comfort me.

16

WILL

Four Months Later, October 2022

PDX ROYALS – CALLING DANILL FANS!

Willy and Danika are officially dating! That's right, not only did their publicists confirm, but that was quite the make-out sesh last episode. My loins were on fire, folks!!

Sure, as usual Willy was overly intoxicated when it happened but when isn't he lately? Deep down something is very wrong and until he goes on some drunken rant letting us in on whatever that demon may be, we may never know what is going on in his troubled head (or possibly heart?)

We spoke with Danika earlier this week and she excitedly let it slip that there 'may' be a change in sleeping arrangements in the coming days. I feel a steamy, sexy scene coming our way and we are here for it! Like any of us look away when these two strip down to nearly naked to take a swim. Take my breath away, E!

The show airs on E! every Sunday at 9:00 p.m. PST.

* * *

PORTLAND TIMBERS WATCH

PDX soccer star Alex Donovan dates Berkley Kaine?! She tried to avoid the camera but we snuck a shot anyhow and caught her gorgeous face. Hand in hand, they exited the swanky event put on by the team that raised over four million dollars for youth sports sponsorships. While his pockets are deep and we're not surprised to see him donating, we've learned over his pro career that blondes are Alex's 'type'. Many, many, many, many (you get my gist) blondes. Short ones, tall ones, loud ones, shy ones. So we've got to ask, why the beautiful dark-haired maiden this time, Alex? And what did go on between her and Prince Willy last year? To our knowledge they've not spoken or been seen together. Did their relationship go sour? With the way Willy drinks, we wouldn't be surprised. But this article is about Alex and Berkley, and boy do they make a fine-looking couple!

Support the Timbers here – Portland Timbers (https://www.-timbers.com)

* * *

Well, that's just grand. If I'd have known what I was about to stumble into by simply stopping into a convenience store to grab a drink, I would have died of dehydration instead. The headline caught my eye immediately: *Alex Donovan dates Berkley Kaine*. My arch nemesis. And I don't just say that because I'm dressed as Superman's alter ego, Clark Kent, heading to a costume party. I say that because we all went to high school together. Alex and I were on the same soccer team from age five to eighteen and we just never saw eye to eye. We were always neck and neck, same skill set because we always had the same coaches. We are both from wealthy families so nothing was out of reach and I was as good as he was. When we got to college, I decided not to play soccer anymore so, finally, he won that particular war. Now he's decided to twist the knife by dating the love of my life? Asshole.

'You look *so* handsome in glasses! Did you buy those at the costume store?' Danika's voice distracts me from my trip down memory lane.

'My glasses?' I ask, readjusting them like there's something wrong.

'Yeah,' she says, putting the finishing touches on her Lois Lane look in the mirror next to me.

The woman doubted I could pull off Clark Kent until five minutes ago when she entered my room without an invitation. You could say we're 'casually' dating, unless you watch the show, then we're nearly married. (UGH.)

'I bought my glasses at the optician's.'

She spins to face me. 'You wear glasses?' Her face is blank. 'How did I not notice that until now?'

'Because contacts are invisible?'

'Contacts?'

Jesus criminy. I'm dating a woman who doesn't know me at all. I am an idiot. Every day I believe it more. I gave up perfection for a shot at what I thought would be happiness, a career, a fun story I could tell later in life. Now I'm drunk all day, and 'with' a woman who wasn't even aware I can't see.

'Oooh! Lois Lane has never looked better!' Felicity squeals as she walks in.

She's finally calmed down about not being the next Mrs William Adler. After living with me for nearly two years during the most unhappy time in my life, she's decided I'm a drunk asshole and Danika deserves better. It's like I planned it myself.

'Meeting in Will's room!' I yell, joking but knowing full well that where there is noise, there is everyone. I've got zero privacy in this apartment and it's starting to drive me insane. At least with everyone in here, Danika can't get handsy. The last thing I need tonight is the guilt that I'm seeing someone else when I know the woman who owns my heart will also likely be there, also with someone else.

Just as I predicted, Mike and Finn join us, bringing in an ice-cold beer for me.

'Thank you, boys. Now I'm going to need just about ten more of these to be drunk enough to face "you-know-who".' I say that last part under my breath so the ladies don't overhear.

'You need to face a therapist,' Mike suggests. 'You're too obsessed with her.'

'I'm not *obsessed*, just nervous. I haven't seen her in a while and the last couple times I have it didn't go well.' I crack open the beer and down it in practically one long swig.

'Whoa,' Mike says, preoccupied enough that I grab his still nearly full bottle and do the same.

'I think "nervous" was an understatement,' Finn says.

'Whoa, whoa, *whoa* – I think we know who's not driving.' Danika sidles up to me, sliding her hand across my back. 'How about we don't focus on you-know-who and then she won't be a worry. Just relax, babe. I'll be there too, so no need to be nervous. You're happy now, remember?'

My heart does its usual cringe at the word 'babe'. I've asked her repeatedly not to call me that but she never listens. I thought since Berkley insisted we break up that dating someone else would force me to move on. I hoped maybe it would help heal my heart. It hasn't. And despite what she says, I'm definitely not happy.

'Pretty sure those weren't his first two of the evening,' Finn says, now pointing around my room at littered empties.

'Captain Obvious is here, folks!' I bellow. 'Newsflash, I'm drunk again. Is anyone really surprised?'

The whole room shakes their heads.

'How many have you had, little brother?'

I shrug. 'Well, I couldn't sleep last night so I invited Jack over. When he ran out at lunch, I switched to these.' I take Finn's partially drunk beer and down it too.

I was a mess knowing I might see her tonight *before* I saw the article earlier. Now I'm straight up losing my mind.

'You're gonna have a long-ass night, bro.' Mike shakes his head but looks pleased that I'm about to be miserable. Figures.

'Dani is going to kill you if you focus on Berkley tonight.' Felicity hangs back as the others leave my room, warning me of something I'm already aware of.

'Bring on the bullet.'

I'm kidding – kind of.

'That's a little morbid, don't you think? Maybe dial down the wasted Will show; you're starting to embarrass us,' she says nonchalantly as she exits my room.

'*I'm* starting to embarrass *you*?' I ask with a laugh. 'That's rich!' I slam my door shut, locking it so they can't re-enter.

Should I call her? I mean she's got me blocked but I could at least ask if she's going to prepare myself more. I dial her number and as usual, it rings through to voicemail. Again.

'Hi! You've reached Berkley Kaine. I'm currently unavailable but leave a message, and I'll get back to you.'

Just the sound of her voice has me rubbing my chest like it hurts.

Beep.

'Hey, Berx. I'm, uh… I'm getting ready to walk out my door heading to Bryce and Bianca's party and I assume you will also be there. Considering what I read in the tabloids today, I'd also guess

Alex will be with you. I don't really know the situation there. Nor am I asking to. God, this message makes no sense, which is a good lead in for me to say what I called to say: tonight's going to be awkward and I'm pretty well already lit so I'd like to apologize for whatever I say or do now. I'm sorry. For all of it. Words. Actions. Everything. Bye.'

Ugh. That was a disaster. Hopefully she'll delete it without even listening. According to Bryce, that's her usual move.

* * *

We're at a popular bar downtown, Kelly's Olympian. It's small and narrow, has neon lights everywhere and an entire motorcycle hanging from the ceiling. You can't be afraid to get close in this place because people are streaming in and out and it's packed. Pretty much the whole room is in costume too. I feel like Ted in that episode of *How I Met Your Mother* where he's hunting for his date at a costume party only the whole room recognizes me in an instant, flocking to our crew in a second, and I've yet to catch even a glimpse of the girl I'm looking for. Which is probably best for now considering Danika is hanging off my arm, insisting we stay together.

'Look,' Dani says, motioning around the crowd. 'We're easily the most believable Clark and Lois here.'

'You forgot best-looking. You two could play the parts in a TV show.' Felicity encourages the idea.

'Ohh! There's Evan!' Felicity squeals, grabbing on to Danika's arm. 'Come on,' she requests. 'He's so unbelievably hot, and loaded, that you have to help me seal this deal.'

'I thought you were boning Mike?' I ask, just out of curiosity 'cause he claims they're 'unofficially' a thing. But only after dark, which he doesn't see the problem with.

'Please,' Felicity groans. 'He's an easy lay and a woman has needs.'

'Needs that he *actually* provides for?' I laugh. 'Ain't buying it.'

'Go get us drinks and I'll meet you at the bar,' Dani says, she and Felicity walking away, arm in arm towards this Evan that Felicity is pining over.

As I head towards the bar, I see her, alone, sitting on a stool stirring her drink with a tiny straw. God, she's gorgeous, as usual. Dressed in a vintage-style black pencil skirt that falls just below her knees, black stilettos (my favorite ones that I bought her), a low-cut white dress shirt, and a badge around her neck.

You can do this, Will. Talk to her. See how she is.

She's got her back to me, and suddenly her sister, dressed as Wednesday Addams, appears at her side. Bianca notices me first and of course her face can't hide the fact that I'm headed their way and Berkley spins on her stool, following her line of sight.

'Oh,' she says with a gasp. 'You came?' She shoots a glare at her sister.

'We couldn't *not* invite him; he's Bryce's best friend,' she defends herself.

'I suppose all your BFFs aren't far behind?' Berkley asks in a snippy voice. That's when she allows herself to look me over; her eyes fall down my chest, noticing the partially unbuttoned shirt revealing the Superman logo.

'*You came as Clark Kent?*'

'*You* came as *Lois Lane?*'

We stare straight-faced at one another, each waiting for the other's response before giving our own.

'I didn't want to waste money on a costume and I had everything I needed for this one. Plus, I never get to wear these shoes.' She holds out a foot, displaying the sexiest black stilettos I've seen in my life. I fell in love with them the day I bought them and she used to wear them to dressy events we'd go to just because she knew how sexy I think she is in them. If I had to guess, I'd say this was intentional. She expected me to be here just like I did her.

'You threw that costume together yet I know for a fact that Lois Lane has never been this beautiful.'

She groans. 'Says the man who likely walked in with an entirely different Lois.' The smile she's attempting to keep at bay finally starts to emerge and, lucky for us, the folks lingering around us, Bianca included, disperse, leaving us to talk. 'By the way, you're not supposed to call your ex-girlfriend beautiful.'

I sit on the stool next to her. 'You want me to take it back?'

'Yes,' she insists.

'Can't.'

'Why not?'

"Cause it's not a lie. You're the prettiest girl in the room, Berx. As usual.'

She drops her head, a smile finally shining through. 'Fine,' she huffs, her gaze once again meeting mine. 'Then my only option is to match your "beautiful" and one-up you.'

'Alright,' I say with a stupid grin on my face. I can't wait for this. We haven't talked in how long and now she wants to match my compliment. Maybe I should be scared here?

'You make the hottest Clark Kent I ever did see. Handsome, debonair and dashing. If I wasn't here with an equally handsome man, I think I might want a villain to walk in so you could save my life.'

I chuckle. 'How about I just save you from the villain you came with? Where is he, by the way? Shouldn't *he* be here complimenting you instead of me?'

'Do I sense a touch of jealousy?' she asks.

'I'll answer that if you do.'

'Never happening. You are dating the most influential, beautiful woman on the west coast. Why would you be jealous of Alex?'

'Pfft, you practically have the ability to read my mind, woman. You know exactly why I'm jealous and I know exactly why you are.'

She shakes her head. 'You know no such thing.' She lifts her drink, motioning for the bartender to bring her another. 'It's ten in the evening; shouldn't you be slurring your words right now?'

I smirk. 'Seriously, Berx, Alex Donovan? You know I hate him.'

'Yes, I do,' she says with a laugh. 'And I have a feeling you're gonna be real mad when you find out you and he accidentally wore the same outfit. I know how faux pas that is in your world.'

I glance around the room, looking for another Clark Kent, but my gaze lands on a blond man dressed in a full Superman costume. Suit, cape, all of it. I laugh like it's the funniest thing I've seen in all my life.

'*What* is funny?' she asks.

'He's a *dumbass*, that's what. Lois Lane doesn't even know Clark Kent *is* Superman.'

She pinches her lips together, obviously irritated with me. 'Well, he originally rented a Spider-Man costume so I'm just happy Gunner was able to convince him to return it. He's not one to allow superheroes to mix and mingle.' She looks like she regrets telling me this the moment the words leave her lips. 'Now be quiet, he's coming and I don't want this to be weird.'

'You think *I'll* be the one to make it weird?'

'Yes, Prince Willy. I can smell the booze on your breath. Bite your tongue.' She shoots me a *shut up* look.

'Willy!' Alex says suddenly, like he's only just noticed me. He looks me up and down. 'My alter ego. You play the dorky reporter well, but now it's time for my superhero self to whisk my woman away.' He rests his hand on Berkley's lower back.

'I'm waiting on a fresh drink,' Berkley tells him.

'What's the matter, Alex? Worried your lady will fall for the brains and not the brawn? That's a tad cowardly for Superman, don't you think?'

Alex turns towards me, annoyance all over his face. 'What's your deal, Adler? Don't you have a girlfriend? Give up.'

Berkley grabs Alex's shoulder. 'Can you give me and Will a minute?'

He glances between the two of us. 'Don't try anything,' he warns me, wagging a finger in my face like I'm going to be afraid of him. Please.

As he turns to leave, I turn my attention back to Berkley. 'Annoying.' I laugh.

'Yes, you are.'

'*Me*? Why?'

She rolls her eyes, accepting her fresh drink from the bartender and standing from her stool. 'Let's go outside and talk, can we?'

'I'd like that,' I say, following her through the bar and down the street to a parking garage where things are quieter.

'I'm not your biggest fan right now.'

'Tell me something I don't know.'

'*What* is with your attitude?' she bellows, obviously allowing that anger she had for me to release. '*You* chose this life.'

'Temporarily,' I remind her. 'For us.'

'No, William. You did not make this decision for us. This was for your soul Kelly's Olympian – or probably ego, truthfully – *remember*? Extending the show is only proof of that.'

'I extended the show because you wouldn't take me back and *insisted* we part ways. *Remember*?' I snap back.

'Do *not* have a tone with me, William!'

'Don't have a tone with me, *Kaine*!'

'UGH! You are impossible!' She stomps a heel on the ground in frustration. 'I only see one dumbass here tonight, and that's the guy who won't stand up to his parents and be the person he *wants* to be, as opposed to the rich dicklord they've turned him into.'

'*Finn's* the lord,' I say, immediately wishing I hadn't.

She points, her jaw dropped, anger on her face. 'You can't even be serious for one second! I don't know this Will. You're drunk all the time. Crying into my voicemail with ridiculous memories from our past. Yet you strut the streets with perfection at your side and the whole world thinks you're blissfully happy.'

'It's an *act*, Berx. I'm on a TV show.'

'A *reality* TV show, *William*! Do you not see how this whole thing has changed your "reality"? The world does not see the sweet man I once knew. They see Prince Willy. The rich, drunk "*prince*" along with his beautiful, talented princess, Danika, and his kingdom of pretentious dicks. Why are you even worried about me anymore? I don't fit anywhere into your new life.'

Now I'm mad. Or maybe frustrated. 'We're really going to do this, right here on the sidewalk?'

'If not now, *when*? I'm tired of worrying about you. I'm sick of being afraid I'll run into you. I'm completely over Cole calling and begging me to come talk you down out of a drunken stupor, and I want no part in any of what this show has become. *Zero*.'

'Cole *calls* you? *Still*?' I thought that stopped a long time ago.

'Yes.'

'Why?'

'Oh, I dunno, maybe because he's afraid you're going to drown in your pool with a bottle of Jack in your hand. The whole world is concerned; do you never read the tabloids?'

'I read one recently,' I snap back. '*You* were the headline.'

'Ugh, please. I make *one* tabloid and suddenly there's a problem? I run a bookstore and have to walk past a magazine rack with your stupid face on every one, all day long. The paparazzi talks about you like you're a drunk idiot and you've literally become exactly that.'

'Now you think my face is stupid?'

'I think *you* are stupid for ruining my life.'

'You seem to be blissfully happy with Alex, so how did I ruin your life?'

She shakes her head, frustration on her face. 'Are *you* happy, Will? I want to know. Nearly two years into this, are you still happy with your choice to do this and now commit to two more years? You better answer honestly because in case you forgot, I know you as well as I know myself and I'll *know* if you're lying.'

I rub my forehead, dragging my hand down my face. 'I'm an absolute fucking mess, Berx. I'm living with people I hate. I drink too much because I don't know how else to deal with my constant bad decisions. I've got people around me all fucking day, and yet I've got no one to turn to that won't manipulate me when I need to talk. I don't even know who I am anymore.'

'There's only one person you can blame for that.'

A heavy sigh emerges. 'You're right,' I say. 'My misery is my own fault. And the only way I can deal with it is to forget. So, on that note. I'm sorry I hurt you. I'm pissed I hurt myself and I can't handle one more second so I wish you luck with Alex. I hope he makes all your dreams come true and I'm now going to disappear and forget all this ever happened.' I back away from her, knowing nothing I can say will fix what I've done. It's over between Berkley and me and she's right, I did that myself.

'Yeah, go drink some more, that'll help!' she calls after me angrily, and even though I'm refusing to turn around, I can tell she's in tears. 'Why don't you figure out what the hell you really want in life and what makes *you* happy. I'm pretty sure that's what you're constantly asking your good friend Jack Daniel's. Maybe ask your *sober* self instead?'

I storm past Jonah, who's just exited the bar, likely looking for me.

'Hello?' he calls. 'Where ya going?'

'Out,' I bark. '*Don't* follow me!'

17

WILL

'William Adler!' An officer yells my name as he approaches the cell I'm in, unlocking it and pulling open the door. 'You're free to go.'

I sit up from the hard metal bench I was sleeping on and realize my back and my head are killing me. Jesus. How much did I drink last night, because this is the worst hangover yet. I barely remember why I'm sitting in a jail cell this morning. A vague recollection is slowly coming back to me of fighting with Berkley, then getting into a fight with a guy who called me Prince Willy the Pathetic, then I decided to go home, get my Jeep and drive to a bar across town where no one knew me. I made it just fine; it was the drive home when all hell broke loose.

The officer was not even a little bit impressed with 'who I was' (but my drunk self actually asked him the question). After I failed the DUI test miserably, I was hauled into jail, my Jeep was towed, and I don't even remember who I called with my one phone call. I can't imagine who I'm about to walk out to, and if it's Berkley – FUCK.

Dragging a hand through my probably disastrous hair, I stand from the bench and follow the officer directing me, his hand on my bicep like I'm a hardened criminal too risky to let walk on his own. Jesus, I used to just be a danger to myself and now I'm walking out of a jail cell as I endangered everyone on the road too.

He shoves open the door to the area where arrests are processed, walking me through to the main lobby. He hands me a plastic bag of my belongings and without a word shoves me out then walks away. I stop in my tracks, completely ashamed of who's staring back at me. She being Berkley's mom, Laura. Shit.

'Well, well, well,' she says in a motherly tone I'm not familiar with. 'You have no idea how shocked I was to get a call requesting I come bail you out of jail after being arrested for drunk driving.' She looks me over. 'You're hurt too?' She touches my eye, which stings as she does. I reach up, feeling a lump.

I shrug. 'I probably deserved it. Is it bad?'

'It's a bruised eye; it'll heal. I'm more worried about how bad it is in here.' She presses a finger to my chest, just over my head.

'Real bad,' I admit. 'Scary bad.'

'Oh, honey. Let's go.'

'I'll pay you back whatever this costs,' I say sheepishly as I follow her out to the front of the station.

The flash of a camera startles me, mostly because I feel like my head is filled with Jack Daniel's.

'I know you will; now get in before you make headlines all over the world.'

If there was ever a time I felt like a kid in trouble, this is it. I've known Laura since I was fifteen. She treats me like her own kid. Which means she's not afraid to tell me off when I act like an idiot and I am absolutely certain now is one of those moments.

'You hungover?' she asks, her tone insinuating she's hoping my answer is yes. Which I totally deserve so I get it.

I crawl into her SUV slowly, proving that I do indeed not feel great. 'You've got no idea, so if I ask you to pull over, please don't question it,' I say, giving her a knowing look.

'If you puke in my car...' she warns sternly.

'I won't. I hope.' I dig my shit out of the plastic bag in my hands – my wallet, phone, watch, hat, jacket, keys. I pile it all in my lap, ready to use the bag to barf into if I gotta. Until that moment comes, I rest my head on the headrest, my eyes closed as Laura pulls away from the cameras still outside my door.

'Did I call you?'

'No,' she says. 'You called Bryce, but he worked all night, so Bianca called me. We agreed your parents and newfound friends would be useless in this situation, so here I am. I considered coming when I got the call, then I chatted with Brian and we thought maybe a night in jail to sober up and think about things is what you needed.' She's proud of the decision she and her husband have made and it shows.

I'm mortified. I'm twenty-five years old, millions in the bank, living a life I shouldn't have a single complaint about, and right now, I feel about as grown as an infant. Berkley's dad is involved. Good fucking God. I'm sure the only reason he's not here too is that he's at work. But I don't doubt he'll have thoughts that I will hear later. Even so, I'd rather deal with Brian and Laura over my parents any day.

'I suppose that's fair,' I say, my eyes still closed to block out the light of day that feels as if it's burning my brain. After a few silent minutes, I squint open one eye and glance Laura's way. 'Does she know?'

Laura shakes her head. 'You've got her all sorts of mad, I can say that. She won't be happy with me for keeping this from her either.'

I snap open both eyes. 'You're not going to tell her?'

'This is your problem. I'm just making sure you get home safely and alive. I do need to ask, though, what's going on with you, Will? You wanted this: the show, the freedom, the money, the fame, all of it. Now you're destroying yourself on camera because you're not happy. Why not save yourself and walk away?'

'I'm bound by contracts written partly by my parents,' I explain.

'Is there nothing you can do to get out?'

'I could lose everything.'

'You're pretty close to that right now, honey.'

'Trust me, I feel it. But you know my parents, a deal is a deal. If I break it, they ruin me.'

She groans in frustration as she drives. 'I know,' she says, shaking her head like it pisses her off. She's not a fan of the way my family treats me, but I've warned her to never get involved, and so far she's respected that. If my parents have the audacity to ruin me – and they would – they'd destroy the Kaines and enjoy every second of it.

'Can I be honest?' I ask, nervous to put this all out there.

Laura nods.

'I don't know how to live without Berkley. She's been my best friend for over a decade. She's the only person I trust, and when she's not there, I've got nobody. I fucked this up so bad. I keep signing contracts and I know she doesn't want me to. I'm acting like a true Adler whose only concern is what's best for me. Like she means nothing at all, which couldn't be further from the truth. I don't know how to fix this.' I look at her sadly, desperate for someone to help me.

She pulls up to the curb in front of my building, parks her car, and turns off the engine. After a moment, she gives me a slight grin. 'You've got to make a choice. There are two paths in front of you right now. The show and all that comes with it: money, fame, drama, partying, and the mistakes. Or the life you'd planned with

Berkley, the woman you've loved since you were a teenager and who, to use your own words, is your best friend and the only person you trust. She wants to be your forever, Will, but she's lost hope. Watching you self-destruct while turning into someone she no longer knows is killing her.'

'I don't know why I keep doing what I'm doing. She should be forefront of my mind and I'm so intoxicated all the time she's not.'

'Tie a string around your finger. Tattoo her name on your forehead. If your life with Berkley is important at all, you'll make sure she's your number one.'

For some reason the day I ran into Berkley at CVS flashes through my head. Alex's name was written on her arm that day. I glance down at my forearm. Maybe I won't tattoo her name on my forehead, but if I did it on my inner left arm, I couldn't sign a damn thing without thinking of her.

'You do have one huge battle to fight before you can choose any path, Will.'

'What?' I ask nervously.

'*Stop* drinking. You could've killed someone last night, and the exact same situation nearly killed you not long ago. This is no longer you binge drinking on the weekends. I know this is hard to hear but you're a full-blown alcoholic, sweetheart. It's barely ten in the morning and the tabloids are already chattering about what a mess you are.'

The cameras outside the police station are proof of that. Somehow they know shit before I do, and are like vultures to get their story. I can only imagine what's being printed right this second.

'If you truly love Berkley, you'll choose yourself first. Get sober. Not a sober week, or month. Stop begging her back. None of that's enough at this point. See a counselor. Figure out the issues you have with your family, face your demons and climb out of this.

Then grovel, Will. Grovel hard, and try and win her back. I don't think you're too late but if you keep going the way you are, you're going to miss your chance altogether.'

I nod. 'You are a wise woman, Laura. Tell Brian I'm sorry and thanks. I'm going to fix this. Somehow, I will. I promise.'

18

BERKLEY

Five Months Later, March 2023

PDX ROYALS FANS

Ay-ay-ay! Two years in and the show is getting HAWT, viewers. So much happened last season that one paragraph might not sum up each of our stars but we'll give it a go.

King Mikey finally convinced Felicity to skinny-dip with him in the hot-tub ('for shits and giggles' was his exact bribe) and things went exactly where we thought they would – XXX. Mike celebrated the next morning by going out for a big breakfast with Finn at the crew's favorite diner to talk details (that we all had to hear – remember, Finn is Felicity's brother… EW) but where was Felicity? Was Mike the gentleman who let his lady sleep in after a night of rambunctious shenanigans? Nope. They didn't air this next part but a little mouse on set has told me that when Mikey woke that morning, Felicity had already left the apartment. Not his bed – THE ENTIRE APARTMENT. Did she sneak out before sunrise, because if so, ouch.

Lord Finn has sweet-talked his way into being a *Playgirl* centerfold. We're not sure whose idea this was but if you're looking for a full Finn 'spread', it's on its way. We're not going to lie, viewers, we're scared and I think you should be too. If his eyebrows look like that, I can't imagine what his – oh, never mind, this is a PG-rated article. On a brighter note, Finn has created a menu to die for at a soon-to-open upscale restaurant. We'll have more details on that soon.

Princess Felicity's publicist has officially denied any connection between her and Mikey. 'It' never happened, according to the tabloid headlines. Nothing like paying a magazine to reject a guy. She and Danika are still in business mode, pitching products to local businesses and their online store is practically ready for business.

Prince Willy is on a spiraling decline. For the last few months we haven't seen him sober even once. Rumors of secret meetings between him and the network are swirling around and we're beginning to worry about his wellbeing. We are far past party-boy status and wonder if medical intervention might be necessary for the young reality star. The fighting between him and his housemates is next-level concerning as well. What is bringing Willy down? Talk to us, Will!

The show airs on E! every Sunday at 9:00 p.m. PST.

* * *

PORTLAND TIMBERS WATCH

Alex Donovan and Berkley Kaine (Prince Willy's childhood love) have officially broken up. We've never been too sure how serious their relationship has been but word is it's over.

Perhaps it has something to do with the altercation Alex was in with one of our photographers who asked about Berkley and Will's current relationship. She didn't have an answer and when Alex stepped up to speak for her, things took a turn for the worse. (Don't worry, our photographer, Aiden, is fine and has decided not to press charges as Alex has openly volunteered to pay for the camera he destroyed.)

We have to compliment Berkley for her ability to nail down two very desirable men in the city, but why aren't things working out for her? She seems like a sweet girl. We'll keep our eyes and ears open and let you know as soon as we know more.

Both Alex and Berkley declined to comment when we contacted them but Alex's publicist says all is well in Donovan's world and he's excited about this season. As are we! Go Timbers!

Support the Timbers here – Portland Timbers (https://www.-timbers.com)

* * *

The continual knocking at my apartment door after business hours tells me this unexpected visitor is one of four people with access to the building. Bianca, Olivia, Gunner or Will. Not that the last one has direct access anymore. I yank the door open just as Bianca starts to put her key into the lock.

'Christ on a cracker, woman. *Why* are you not answering your phone? I thought you were dead!' she half yells as she and Bryce invite themselves in. I'd turn them away, but Bryce has a pizza in his hands, and a girl's gotta eat.

'Good Lord,' Bryce says, looking around the place. 'You just gave up with life, eh? Because of a break-up with *Alex*?'

Yep, I dumped him. I don't like when men try to speak for me and the way he talked about Will and my previous relationship made me look just as bad as him so I told him I needed a break. He wasn't thrilled but considering he's on the road right now, he peacefully left the city and the whole thing has brought every relationship misery I've ever had to the forefront of my mind. I don't even know how these reporters put it all together unless someone gave them the 411 and I've no clue who that could have been, besides Alex. He's competitive; it makes sense if it was him trying to get under Will's skin.

'What makes you think I gave up?' I ask, offended.

Bryce laughs. 'Well, the thirty empty Chinese take-out boxes. The overflowing garbage. The pile of Kleenex on your coffee table. The army of dead flowers all over the room. Shall I go on?'

I shake my head. Part of the problem is that the flowers aren't from Alex. The card is always signed with a heart only, no name. I started getting them a few months ago and at first, Alex claimed they were from him. But when they kept coming and he was surprised each time, I figured out he isn't a flower kind of guy. But I know a man who is, and I haven't talked to him since our blow-up at the Halloween party.

'The flowers aren't from Alex. I've got a secret admirer,' I lie, glancing around the full vases of droopy, dead flowers, drying out a little more each day. They match my heart and are a visual reminder of what love really feels like. A slow, painful, ugly death of your once-pretty soul.

'It's no secret...' Bryce laughs.

'If you're not sad about Alex, why are you crying buckets?' Bianca asks, gathering up all the used tissues and carrying them to the kitchen, where she gets a fresh trash bag out and dumps them all in, now wandering my apartment, throwing things away.

'Can't a girl just have a good cry? I've been watching a sad show,' I lie.

'Might it have anything to do with Portland Royalty?' Bryce asks, grabbing my remote, hitting play at an unfortunate moment where Will's getting out of the pool. 'I *knew* that was one of his old sweatshirts hanging off your shoulders.'

I grimace. 'This doesn't look innocent, I see that now, but in my defense, when I miss him, his voice is comforting. Currently, I'm in distress after my break-up and I needed comfort. So sue me.'

'And his near nakedness?' he asks with a smirk.

'Also, somehow comforting?'

'*Why* are you watching this? You're tormenting yourself! Come on,' Bianca says, leading me away from the TV towards my bathroom. 'You need to take a shower; I'll clean.'

'He posted a TikTok earlier,' I say to her, glancing over at Bryce. 'He says he's doing something important and going away...'

I flash my phone with the video Bryce's way. I've only watched it five hundred times. He's a reality star for a reason. I can't look away. He's got this bewitchery that just sucks you in. It's what I imagine the apple in the Garden of Eden was like. Tempting, beautiful, shiny and enticing you in all the right ways even though you'd been warned it would for sure fuck up your life. I mean, I just pushed replay without even trying. Apple-in-the-Garden-of-Eden dangerous is what Will is.

'So?' Bryce asks, clearing a spot on my coffee table for his pizza box, pulling out a slice. 'He's doing what he needs to do.'

I pause the video. 'What he needs to do? I can only imagine. Answer me this, what is on his left forearm?' I stare at the video, unable to make it out.

'Tattoo,' Bryce says.

'He got another tattoo? If those are the words "Prince Willy", I will fucking die.'

'It doesn't say "Prince Willy",' Bryce says, his tone hinting he's tired of me after being here only five minutes.

At the end of the video, Will points to his heart, then to the camera. A silent message I know well. 'I'll see ya soon, baby,' he says, exiting the screen and leaving a cryptic message I'm afraid to decode.

My eyes move to the watch and like counts. Over a million already, and he just posted it an hour ago. The comments are all women telling him they love him. I sigh.

'Where is he going?' I ask Bianca, hoping she'll pity me, unlike her stubborn boyfriend.

'He wants to surprise you,' she says.

I roll my eyes. 'With what? A heart attack? He's intentionally enticing me with his stupid pretty face as he speaks in code and now you're going to honor the best friend and boyfriend secrecy rules?'

'Yep,' Bryce says with a nod, relaxing into my couch, *Royals* still playing on the screen in front of him. 'Hey, I'm in this episode. Damn, I look good,' he says smugly.

'Whatever he's doing, I'm sure it's too little too late. I don't doubt he's signed a brand new contract for something. Did he and Danika break up and he's on his way to being the next Bachelor? Ugh. You guys. He needs celebrity rehab, you realize this, right?'

I drop onto the vintage chair in the corner of the room, pulling the hood of Will's hoodie over my head as I do. This thing still somehow smells like him. I tuck my face into the neck and breathe him in.

'I bet every woman watching that video who's ever met him now thinks it's for them,' I say, my voice muffled by the fabric covering my nose and mouth. I pull my knees to my chest, pulling his sweatshirt over them too. Will's hoodie now completely wraps me in a hug. A Will-less, loveless hug.

'They do not,' Bianca says, squirting grapefruit-scented cleaner onto my island bar top.

'How do we know that message was for me at all? It's probably for his fans.'

'He only calls one person "baby", and you know that. You're acting unhinged, woman,' Bryce says between bites.

'What does he want me to do? Wait years more for him to pull his head out of his ass? Am I waiting for him to retire? If he needs to tell me something, why doesn't he just call me like a normal human being?'

Bryce laughs. 'Maybe because you've got him blocked?'

'Do you *want* me to waterboard you?' I ask, tossing a pillow towards him that he slaps away, knocking it to the floor before it can hit him. 'Of course I blocked him. Look what a video of him does to me!' I motion to my swollen eyes. 'Bianca, help me out.'

'I'm helping you out by cleaning this trash hole.'

'What's going on, though? Did he sign on for something else? Please tell me now if he did. My heart can't take another surprise.'

'Yes and no,' she says.

I sigh heavily, my patience wearing thin. 'This is one of those moments where I'm going to say something mean,' I say to my sister.

'How rare,' she says with a laugh, scrubbing my counters with a force I've rarely witnessed from her.

'Ha-ha. All his secrecy is doing is reminding me that Will has turned into a big fat drunk liar and I'm tired of it. And you two certainly aren't making me feel better.'

Bianca bursts out a laugh. 'We're here because I hadn't heard from you in a few days. Liv warned me you're holed up in your apartment alone because you spiraled after this break-up. You're not answering emails, calls or texts. It was either I come over, or *Mom*. So, be glad it's me.'

'My heart is missing, Bianca,' I say.

She and Bryce exchange worried glances as she walks into the living room, bright yellow dishwashing gloves on her hands. 'How can we help? We're worried about you.'

'I'll be OK,' I say, leaning forward and grabbing a slice of pizza. 'I mean, my heart fell through my chest like glass shards multiple times over the last few years that now jab at me anytime I move, but I'm sure, eventually, I'll get used to the pain and move on. *Somehow*.'

Bianca's face is sincerely sad as I say the words; even Bryce frowns.

I feel like a part of me is missing. A part I'll never get back. Like a puzzle with a missing piece. That's me.

Once Bianca has forced me in and out of the shower, they leave and I lie in bed for hours, watching every TikTok video he's ever made until I finally fall asleep to his voice. Love. Sucks.

19

WILL

Three Months Later, June 2023

ROYALS NO MORE?

Say it ain't so! Not only did Willy Adler storm off set mid-season, go radio silent concerning Danika (who's sworn off 'rich assholes' forever in a recent interview) and go MIA for months, he's now had his lawyer cancel all current *Royals* contracts. A meeting between production, him and the network went nowhere, and it's official: *PDX Royals* might be coming to an end. They have one more partial season ready to air, and it may be their last from the looks of it. Unless the rest of the cast can save themselves, it's all over. I'm sorry, *Royals* lovers. We've reached out to Willy and his publicist, but both have declined to comment. Come cry on my shoulder, *PDX*ers, we're sad too. We're on the hunt for answers and will update as soon as we know more.

The show airs on E! every Sunday at 9:00 p.m. PST.

* * *

'Hi.'

She rolls her eyes. 'What do you want?'

'I want to spend my life with you, Berx.'

'Please.' She turns to walk away and I do what I came to do, dropping down on one knee and when she spots the ring in my hand, she shakes her head. 'I'm over you, Will. Get the hint already, would you?'

Over me? 'Berkley, baby—'

'Don't "baby" me, Adler. I'm no longer yours. I can't marry you because I already said yes to Alex.'

My heart explodes right there in my chest. I should be dropping dead right now, but I can't take my eyes off the massive rock on her finger. She's marrying my nemesis and her face as she told me was stone cold. She truly doesn't love me anymore. Holy shit. I'm too late.

'Folks, we're headed into Portland for landing in...' The words leave Berkley's lips but they don't make sense.

'I don't understand?'

Suddenly, I jerk awake in a cold sweat, with a gasp, realizing I'm still on a plane, not in the middle of proposing to a woman who seemingly hates me and is marrying Alex. I lean forward with a heavy sigh, attempting to recover from heartbreak that's never felt so real.

'You alright?' asks my seat-mate – a middle-aged balding guy. 'Did she say no?'

'What?' How in the hell could he know that?

'You've been talking in your sleep for twenty minutes. Berkley this and Berkley that, and truthfully, I'm completely invested now, so, did she say no?'

I was talking in my sleep? That's new. Must be a stress thing. 'It was a firm no; she's marrying someone else.'

'That hurts, bud. Does this woman actually exist or is she just the woman of your dreams?'

'Both?' I say, unsure of how else to answer.

'Is she really marrying this Alex?'

'God, I hope not.'

He lifts a copy of a book I've never heard of. 'I finished my book,' the man says. 'I've got all the time, and I'm an old romantic. Tell me about her.'

What could it hurt? It's not like I have anyone else to talk to and maybe this guy is some kind of love guru.

'We dated for seven years and I decided to make some stupid decisions that affected the life we were planning, so she dumped me.'

'Sounds painful. What'd you do?'

'I signed some contracts without her permission that required me to live somewhere other than where we agreed upon. For the last three years.'

'Whoa. You didn't just make a bad decision; you lit a stick of dynamite in your own world.'

'Yep. I'm a real moron.'

He laughs. 'Everyone is, whether they admit it or not. She never forgave you after three years?'

I shake my head. 'Not even a little bit. Mostly because I continued being an idiot until I hit rock bottom and here I am. Three years later and on a plane back from rehab ready to prove she's all I want and I'm finally in the right state of mind for our future.'

Besides Bryce, Cole and my family, no one knows where I've been the last three months. After I was arrested, I tried to straighten up but it wasn't as easy as I had hoped. Once my housemates heard I was considering leaving the show they started treating me better because they aren't ready for the Royals to end. But that didn't last long. So I went down the path of total annihilation of my own life – all on camera – before finally deciding to stand up for myself. If I didn't, I knew I might end up dead.

In a drunken stupor, Laura's words came back to me and I took a chance, went to rehab, endless counseling and put myself first so I could maybe do the same for her forever.

'You think she's decided this Alex is her new future?'

'It's literally all I think about so it's become my worst fear.'

'That's rough, bud. Women are complicated creatures. Take it from an old guy like me. I've been married four times. Interested in knowing what I've learned?'

Married four times and he's offering relationship advice? Not sure I do want to know, but I've got a feeling he's going to tell me anyway.

'Women don't want a man to parent, son. They want a man they can depend on. A partner in life, not an anchor. Put her first, listen when she speaks and do more supporting and less "fixing". Make sure she knows she's your one and only. Be her friend and her lover. Never let chivalry die. Don't stop dating her. Romance her for no reason at all. Respect her. Be both gentle and dominant depending on the situation. Figure out what she likes and do it without her asking... I could go on and on, but these are the ones that come to mind the quickest.'

'That's a lot of lessons.'

'Yes it is, kid,' the man agrees. 'Top secret tip: if the fight is real bad, call a time-out, strip naked and continue. In my experience you'll either be making love in minutes or you'll be wishing you don't die stark naked as she chases you through the house telling you what an idiot you are.'

I laugh out loud. 'You speak from experience?'

'Yes, I do,' he says with a wide grin. 'Trust me on this, bud. I'm not married because I'm terrible at it. I've got issues I don't want to fix. I don't want kids. I hate being tied down. I want to do what I want to do without permission, and women don't love that. Relationships fall apart because people don't really want to try, but floating through life will get you nowhere. You need to decide what kind of life you want and then put your all into it.'

'For a guy with four failed marriages under his belt, you are surprisingly insightful when it comes to romance, thanks...' I hesitate when I realize I don't know this man's name yet.

'Calvin Klein, the lawyer, not the fashion designer. My friends call me Cal.'

I take his outstretched hand. 'William Adler. I play an idiot on both television and real life. My real friends call me Will.' I'm cutting the 'y' right now. No more Willy. That's the guy I no longer want to be.

'You're on the TV?' His eyes are wide with wonder but I can tell he's no idea who I am. Thank God.

'Reality show, but I walked away to take care of my issues and now I'm headed home to Portland to win her back.'

He raises an eyebrow. 'Attempting a second go after epic failure. You're a brave man, Will Adler.'

I nod, agreeing completely considering it feels like I'm on my way to slay a fucking dragon for the woman I love.

'Tell me you've got a plan.'

'What I've got is a rough draft, though I can't pretend I haven't rehearsed it every night I lay in a rehab bed for six months.'

'Run it by me; maybe I can help,' says the man four marriages deep.

'Well, first I plan to grovel. GROVEL, in all caps, Cal. Then I hope to remind her who I really am, worship the ground she walks on, earn back her trust, and hopefully give her this...' I pull the ring box from the front pocket of my carry-on bag and flip the lid open.

'Whoa,' Cal says with a nod. 'That might do it.'

'Man, I hope you're right,' I say, my voice shaky.

Cal pats my leg. 'Just don't forget to take responsibility for your part in this. Women love a man who's not afraid to admit he was wrong.'

The seatbelt lights flash on.

'You're a smart man, Cal,' I say, strapping on my seatbelt.

Before he puts on his seatbelt, he pulls a business card from his wallet, handing it my way. 'I don't often put relationships back together, so perhaps you could let me know how it goes?'

I take the card. *Calvin 'Cal' Klein – Divorce Lawyer – Los Angeles.*

'You're a divorce lawyer?'

He nods with a huge smile. 'Like I said before, deep down I'm an old romantic. I blame my first wife. If she was still here, I'd be a very different man.'

'Is she how you found out you enjoyed divorces enough to make it a career?'

He shakes his head, his face more serious than I've seen so far. 'Brain aneurism. She was my college sweetheart. The absolute love of my life. Died just three years into our marriage when we were twenty-nine. I could go through thirty divorces and doubt I'll ever feel heartbreak that could compare.'

God, she died? How awful. 'I'm so sorry.'

He nods. 'If this Berkley is the one you can't quit thinking about – the woman who consumes your soul – do whatever it takes. Those women don't come around often and I'd give anything to spend another moment with my sweet Clara.'

I blow out a breath, glancing out the window next to me at the Portland airport below. I thought I was nervous before, but now I'm realizing I can't fuck this up. Cal here lost the love of his life and he's never been the same. I'd really rather not end up in those shoes.

20

BERKLEY

PDX ROYALS

Prince Willy sighting!

We got word that Willy might be on a flight back to PDX yesterday afternoon. Guess what? He was! And we've got the photos to prove it. From what we could see through the hood pulled over his baseball cap, head down as he walked through the airport, he looks good! We contacted his publicist and she had no comment but take a look at our photos: he's alive and back in the city!

Though Willy's publicist wouldn't comment, we did get in touch with one person in Willy's life and that's his ex, Danika Frost. You read that right, *Royals* fans. Danika and Prince Willy have officially split and she wasn't overly pleased to hear he was back. In fact, her exact words were, 'Willy needs to grow up before I'll consider taking him back.' Is he on his way to her place to grovel his way back in? We'll let you know!

The show airs on E! every Sunday at 9:00 p.m. PST.

* * *

'Did you see this?' Olivia speed walks across the store, slapping a tabloid on the counter. Will's face is on the front. It's recent – a photo of him walking through the airport, pulling his suitcase behind him. In three of the four shots, you can hardly see his face. But in the last one, they caught him looking up, making eye contact with the camera. My heart stops.

'He hasn't graced the cover of a tabloid since *last* winter, Berx. He walked away from the show. He's finally tossed Danika Frost to the curb where she belongs too. That's why we haven't seen him. Not even his publicist will comment so it must be true. You should call her and ask.'

'I'm not calling his publicist. I've only ever met her once. She exists in the part of his world he keeps me far away from, remember?' I ask. 'It's all bullshit, Liv. Likely, it's some kind of publicity stunt for the upcoming season. All of it. From his disappearance to this. He better keep walking this city with his head down because if his eyes meet mine, I might punch him.'

That's probably a lie considering how my heart just practically seized up in my chest seeing his face on the cover of a magazine. Dropping dead would feel better.

'I can see this irritates you,' Olivia says. 'So, quick question, if I bump into the man, should *I* punch him too? Am I giving him a chance to explain? Letting you two have some moment? Do we hate him, tolerate him, forgive him? Make the rules, Berx.'

I laugh. 'This is why I love you, Liv. For now, we hate him. He disappeared instead of figuring out his shit and fighting for the *us* he supposedly couldn't live without. Looks to me like he's doing just fine, and is probably on his knees at Danika's door as I speak.'

'Done. Prince Willy sucks. I'll have shirts made.'

The front door of the shop dings open; Olivia and I both snap our heads that way to see Alex walk in. I blow out a heavy breath. Why am I suddenly *not* in the mood to see the guy I'm somewhat dating, once again? Boyfriend and girlfriend doesn't seem to work for Alex and I. He's gone too much and I've got heartache issues. But we see one another twice a week, mainly for the sex, which sadly isn't great but better than nothing. (I'd hoped it would get better, in my defense.) We're not very serious. He's busy; I'm busy. Really, he's a nice enough distraction, but there's no *magic*. I want the magic! The fireworks! The shivers, ooh, the shivers! But nope, even fireflies are steering clear of this friends-with-benefits situation.

Don't get me wrong: I could look at him all day long and not find anything to complain about. Then he opens his mouth. I truly thought the smug essence he had when we first met would fall away as we got to know one another, but apparently, that's just Alex. He's not afraid to get into a referee's face during a match and he's not afraid to let his true self show. I'm just not into that kind of guy as much as he wants me to be. We've got no real chemistry. Nothing in me *yearns* for him. I want to *yearn*! We've never even exchanged the L-word.

'*Alex!*' Gunner yells through the store, like he's here for him.

Gunner is Alex's private fan club of one. He goes to *every* home game. He DVRs matches so he and Alex can watch them together and figure out where he can improve, knowing he already has coaches who do this for him but apparently Gunner's got shit to add. I'm convinced Alex and Gunner's bromance is more substantial than Alex and my 'romance'. Alex loves being doted on by fans, and Gunner is his super-fan.

'I'm coming for the birthday girl in a minute,' Alex says, pointing my way with a wink as he heads to greet Gunner before me.

'Will's back in town,' Liv says. 'How do you think Alex will react to that?'

I shrug. 'It's not something I'm going to worry about because in *three* years not once has Will made *me* a priority. Why would that change now?'

'Maybe he's back for your birthday?'

'Trust me, he's not. Last year he didn't even call on my birthday.'

'Kinda hard to call a girl when you've blocked his number.'

'Technicality,' I say, sick of talking about this, honestly.

'Ladies,' Alex says, handing me a single daisy as he walks around the front of the counter. 'How are you, sweets? Happy birthday!' He pecks his lips on mine.

'Thank you.' I lift the flower to my nose. 'I'm good,' I say forcing a smile. 'How are you? I thought you'd be at practice still?'

Here we are, dating off and on for a year now and we're still playing the *hi, how are you, I'm good* game. Our entire relationship feels very small talk-ish. Partly because I don't give a rat's ass about soccer, and he doesn't want to hear about Will. Will's in almost every story I have, and soccer is in pretty much all of his.

'I'm about as good as I'm gonna get, sugar,' he says. 'He-he.' He slaps my ass before giving it a squeeze. 'What's this?' He grabs the tabloid still sitting on the counter between Olivia and me. We exchange guilty glances.

'Willy's a *joke*.' Alex rolls his eyes, tossing the tabloid into the trash can next to me. 'He's got everything a guy could ever want, and he'll still drink himself to death. You should be glad you moved on to a *real* man, Berx. I'll never let you down like he did.' He pulls me against him in a way that's not sexy or romantic, with his hands gripping my ass as he slams us together like a couple of Legos. I feel like I need to take a second to evaluate whether or not I'm injured.

'Who are you playing tomorrow?' Olivia asks, changing the subject when she notices how uncomfortable I am.

It takes two seconds for Alex to be wholly immersed in talking about soccer and himself. His two favorite subjects.

As they talk, my gaze wanders to the trash can. Will's big brown eyes stare back at me and my heart pangs in my chest painfully. I shouldn't still miss him. I *guarantee* he's not still thinking about me.

'Damien's OK. McConnell sucks ass.' Alex is boring the hell out of Olivia with details of other players. If she could prop her eyes open with toothpicks right now, she probably would; that's how interested she seems. I've been there.

'I'm not at all worried,' he continues. 'You guys are coming, right? I know Gunner's on board.' Alex glances at me, his eyes pleading. 'You're coming tomorrow, right, sweets?'

Don't show up for a couple games and the guy acts like he needs to beg me for my support. I was legitimately busy those two nights. I was considering adopting a cat, and it was cat open night at the shelter. Right when I thought I was bonding with a rough-looking dude named Simon, he bit me and reminded me that I don't need a cat. The second time I was on my period. Enough said.

'Of *course*,' I say, looking to Olivia for support.

She nods, picking up on my wordless plea. 'I can hardly resist those stadium wieners,' she says.

'Yeah,' Alex says with a laugh. 'That's why this one comes too...' He slaps my ass again. 'Pun intended.'

Ugh. 'Well, ladies, I gotta run. I'll see *you* tonight – *before* your party.' He waggles his eyebrows, winking at me obnoxiously like no one else will read what this means.

Liv turns her head my way slowly after the front door closes behind him. 'Why *before* the party?'

'He wants to *give* me something. A *gift*. In *private*,' I tell her in the same way he told me earlier on the phone.

'His stadium wiener in a box? It's been done, Alex. We're all so over dick-in-a-box.' Her eyes roll so hard it hurts me. 'Good fucking

God. I really thought he'd be more romantic than that,' she says, fake swooning. 'He just needs a little coaching. I'm on it.'

'Good luck with that,' I say, my phone ringing on the counter and Frank's name popping up on the screen. 'It's Frank,' I say to Olivia. 'I talked to one of his daughters recently and his health is steadily declining.' I take a cleansing breath and prepare to take the call. I knew this day could come. 'This might be him announcing he wants to sell. *Or* he's dead. Either way, our dream of owning this place might be about to come true! So, *be quiet.*'

Olivia zips her lips closed, her hands firmly covering them, just in case, while standing at attention as she listens in, the phone on speaker.

'Hi, Frank,' I say.

'Berkley.' He says my name flatly, my heart slowing in my chest. Olivia and I exchange a grimace. He's still alive but he doesn't sound great.

'Is everything OK?'

'Don't grow old, sweetheart. It's not as much fun as the movies make it seem.'

'I'm sorry to hear that...'

'I'm not doing great healthwise—'

'Is there anything I can do?'

'Not at the moment, no. I just called to let you know I've decided to leave selling the store up to my daughters since this is their inheritance. I've suggested they give you girls first opportunity but you know how kids are these days – greedy as hell. They're talking to realtors and I know you have some interest so I thought I'd give you a heads-up. Maybe don't hold your breath, honey. The place may blow up; it's in a desired location.'

These are the exact words I did and didn't want to hear. His daughters aren't as keen on ensuring the bookstore survives the transition of new owners. I caught on to that the first time I met them and they called the store a dusty old bookshop – a dying trend. I disagree to the nth degree. But even I could see they seem to be in it for the money. But I'm ready. I've got financing secured and Olivia and I are going in together, though if they're going to open the bidding to the whole world, there's no way we'll win that war.

'I'd love to keep the store any way I ca—'

'We'll be in contact, dear,' Frank says, ending the call abruptly.

I drop the phone from my ear slowly, laying it back on the counter.

'*Viejo estúpido*,' Olivia shouts, then does a quick Hail Mary. 'Forgive me, Lord, for I have bespoketh the living wishing they were dead. I don't really.'

'Now what?' I ask, a mix of worry and dread sinking through my body like thick mud sliding down a hill.

'This royally fucks us, because besides my apartment, the place is rundown and not worth a bidding war. *How* do we compete with a bidding war, Liv?'

'*Puta madre!*' she yells, stomping her foot. 'There's got to be a way.' She taps a single finger to her lips, thinking. Suddenly she smiles wide. 'I know what to do!'

'What?'

'Say I said I know a guy, and money is no object for him.' She lowers her chin.

'I'm *never* asking Alex,' I tell her. 'I can't owe the guy money.'

'I was talking less Alex and more Adler.' She walks around the counter, grabbing the tabloid from the garbage, holding it in front of her face. '*I'd give you all my money for another chance, Berx. Call me, baby*,' she says, mimicking Will's voice, pointing to her chest then to me.

'You're making me *feel* things, Liv. Please, stop. And no way. Absolutely not.'

'He *owes* you, and you know he can't tell you no.'

'He doesn't owe me *money*. Just one slightly destroyed heart. Plus, ever since we met I've insisted he not spoil me rotten with money. I don't know why he feels like he needs to be his own person and make his own money but asking would violate whatever bothers him about that. I can't ask him for money. It's too... Adler-ish. I want to do this on our own and he *knows* that. I'm *not* asking him because then I would owe him.'

Olivia nods her head slowly, a frown now emerging. 'You're right. I've spent three years telling you to dump him, and now that you finally have, I suggest you call him when the store is in peril.' She blows out a heavy breath. 'That's not fair. I'm sorry.'

She hugs me tightly, my arms at my side until she pretends to choke me out, then I hug her back.

'Don't be sorry. Either we win the bidding war, or we don't.'

'And we all find new jobs... Gunner's smart, I bet he could come up with something to save us, because I can't spend my days without you. It'd be boring as hell!' Liv says frustratedly.

'If it is meant to be, it will be. That's a saying, right?'

'Yes, it is. And I claim it now, sister: it is meant to be.'

'Amen!' I say with a grin – but deep in my gut is a whirling mass that feels a little thunderstorm-ish.

Honestly, I don't know how fine I'll be if I lose the store. Where will I work? Where would I *live*? I've put ten years of my life into the place. *Gawd*, I pretty much gave up the *love of my life* for this store and the life we had planned here.

21

WILL

I stand on my parents' porch, flipping through the photos that Bryce just sent me via text. I'm back in the city? How the fuck did they find that out? Vultures, these tabloid reporters. I swipe out of the article and shove my phone into my pocket.

There's zero way the rehab center leaked this. The place isn't one of those rehab centers looking for a dollar selling patient names and risking privacy violations. I pretty much kept to myself while I was there so I doubt any other patients would've talked. How did I think I could leave this city unnoticed and come back the same way? It's like I'm wearing an ankle bracelet that reports my every move – probably right to my parents. The alarms are probably going off right this second.

I walk in the front door, wandering through my parents' foyer and into the kitchen.

'William!' Sylvia says excitedly, dropping the dishtowel in her hand onto the counter and hurrying my way.

'Hey, Sylv! Long time no see, eh?'

'Too long, sweetheart.' She hugs me tightly, patting my back in the way a mother should.

My mom won't hug me, which is why Sylvia has been my mother-figure my whole life, literally since I was brought home from the hospital. This is a hug I need. I've been on my own for three months. Not a single call from my family. Only Sylv, Bryce and Cole have checked in on me.

'Do you know how thankful I am for you, Sylv?' I ask quietly, in case my mother is standing close, eavesdropping as she has in the past. Trained from a small child, I believed, *Sylvia is not to be mistaken for my mother; she is my caregiver only*. Yeah, those were my mother's actual words – such a sweetheart.

'Careful,' Sylv says. 'You'll make me cry with talk like that!' She pulls away, swatting my way playfully. 'You ridiculously sweet boy.' She gets serious, looking me in the eyes now. 'How are you doing? Rehab went alright?' She stands with her hands on my arms, looking up at me with a curious grin, eager to hear whatever I have to say.

'I'm doing good. Rehab though, *phew*, yeah...' I shake my head and think back on it. 'That was a lot more working on myself than I expected.' I laugh under my breath, like it was no big deal, but damn, how did I not know that getting sober wasn't just about putting down the bottle whose spell you were under?

'But you did it, and you're sober?'

'Three months,' I say with a nod.

'I am *so* proud of you, sweetie,' she says with a beaming smile.

'I'm proud of myself, truthfully.'

Weird. This is the first time I've said that out loud and it feels good. I *am* proud of myself. Getting sober is the second hardest thing I've ever done.

'You're going to be so much happier. Does Berkley know you're back?'

A painful stabbing feeling just shot through my chest – probably just another arrow to my heart. I didn't expect hearing her name to hurt. I should have prepared more because I knew it would take less than a day of me being back for someone to mention her.

'No,' I tell her with a sad sigh. 'We've barely talked since that fight we had at the Halloween party ages ago.'

Sylvia frowns. 'Maybe it's not too late?' she says, her voice hopeful.

'Looky who it is.' Mike interrupts us, his smarmy voice pissing me off immediately. 'The asshole who ruined my life. I can see why your old bimbo hates you now.'

'Language, Mikey!' Sylv scolds him like he's twelve.

'Ruined *your* life but saved my own?' I pause a moment, rocking my head back and forth like it takes actual thought to answer this question. 'Worth it,' I say, grabbing a water bottle from the fridge.

Mike's still living a douchey rich boy life, only now he does it without a theme song at our parents' place because the show is on hiatus until they can attempt to sweet-talk me into coming back. Never happening.

'You're such a selfish fuck, always have been,' Mike says.

'Oh yeah,' I groan. 'How super selfish of me to choose to live instead of drink myself to death. What will my fake friends think of me now?' I ask sarcastically.

'You've changed,' Mike says with disappointment.

'I grew up, Mike. You should try it.'

He flips me off, shoving me into the fridge as he walks past.

'Just as I thought, you're still an immature bully.'

'Cry me a river, baby brother.' Another finger thrown over his shoulder.

'Where are Mommy and Daddy dearest?' I ask, glancing around the place. 'I'm here for one reason only so let's get this bitch-fest over with.'

'War room,' Mike says, nodding towards the closed door to the den as he approaches it.

I should have known. God forbid they treat me like their kid and not some business deal.

Mike leads the way, sliding open the pocket door and walking in, me right behind him. We step down the single stair into the room decorated like a lake house. A big fish hangs on one wall (a fish none of us caught). An antique canoe hangs upside down from the vaulted ceiling. Leather furniture. Heavy rare-wood coffee table imported from some tropical country, and a wall of books. Books nobody wants to sit and read as they're all antique, or encyclopedic in nature.

'William.' Dad acknowledges he still knows my name. 'Welcome home, I suppose.'

'Heartwarming,' I say with an irritated smirk. Obviously, I should have expected less from these people than the very low bar they've already set.

'How are things, William?' Mom asks.

'I'd say it's good to be back, but I'm sure we all know that'd be a lie.' I drop onto their leather couch, propping my feet onto the coffee table. 'I'm sober, by the way, three months, thanks for asking.'

Neither of my parents acknowledges what I've done for myself. They just stare at me blankly like they aren't sure what I want from them. How did I end up a part of this family? I think we all wonder that.

'Sorry, was that too deep? Forgot where I was for a moment. Continue; how may I disappoint you today?'

Mike laughs, but it's not joyful. 'It's like he's *proud* of ruining the Adler name.'

'It's not *like* I'm proud,' I correct him. 'I *am*. I hate this fucking name. It's a curse.'

'The Adlers are *not* cursed,' my mother says defensively, her eyes narrowed as she glares my way. 'We are by far some of the most blessed folks in the country. You've never wanted for anything. *Ever.*'

'Well... I think never *ever* is a bit strong. Since I was fifteen, I've wanted one thing, but I lost her because I listened to you throbbing knobs for so long.'

Mike grunts like I've offended him but he's the biggest knob of them all and he knows it.

'Boo-hoo, asshole.' I pretend to cry, fists to my eyes, just to irritate him. And here I *just* said I'd grown up. It comes and goes, I guess.

'William Alexander!' Dad scolds me.

Man, I didn't expect to be this pissed to be here, but I am. I knew I'd be standing up for myself today, for the first time ever, so I expected to be angry. But hearing the name Alexander as Dad middle-names me for harassing my dickhead brother isn't helping.

Do what you came to do and get the hell out, Will. Keep. Your. Cool. You can only control your reaction. Not theirs.

'That rehab didn't have a manners class?' Mike asks.

'It was more morals, less manners. Morals means you have a fucking soul, by the way.'

Mom rolls her eyes.

'It did teach me thou shalt not kill,' I continue. 'And if I were you, I'd shut the fuck up before you force me to choose whether that sin is worth it or not...'

Cool. It. Will.

'*Fuuuuuuuck...*' Mike groans. 'Now he thinks he's better than us.'

Dad lets out an exhausted sigh, a hand to his forehead. 'My God, it's like you two never left middle school! Can we have *one* conversation where you act like adults and where Berkley doesn't come up?' he asks, glancing between us but settling on me. 'She's a piece of your past you need to leave behind.'

I shake my head. 'I will never leave that girl behind. *Ever.* And how do you three feel no remorse? You helped ruin our relationship.'

'Doesn't affect us now, does it?' Dad says as if I should see the light and ignore her too because she's but a bumpkin in the Adler kingdom.

'It affected *me*.' I touch my chest where my heart used to be as I stand from the couch. 'You've been preaching this same ridiculous "you're too good for her" bullshit since I was a teenager, and I'm not taking it for another second,' I say, my voice raised. I've never yelled at my father before – but it feels good.

'I'm nearly twenty-six years old, and the last three years I've discovered what never meeting her might have been like and I never want to know what that's like again. Losing Berkley ruined me! I can only hope I've still got a chance because she makes me a better person. And with that being said, I've concluded that I'd rather give up being an Adler than lose her forever.'

'*Pfft.*' Mike sticks his nose where it doesn't belong, as usual. '*Pretty* sure you've already lost her, dude,' he says with an arrogant laugh. 'She dumped you and moved on to a professional soccer player. Alex Donovan, at that. He-he, that guy hates you so I doubt you have a fighting chance now.'

'I'm *this* close to murdering you,' I say, pinching my fingers together closely.

'William!' Dad says, frustration in his voice, approaching me with his hands out as if he's going to comfort me. We all know that won't happen.

'You don't mean that,' he says, his voice low, now stopping in front of me. 'Giving up being an Adler would also mean giving up your inheritance and trust.'

Not *one* mention of giving up the three of them. Maybe they think they're excluded from this deal. Or more likely they just don't care.

'Take it. I'm here to ask to be cut off.'

I've done the work to build my accounts over the last three years. I was taking outside job after outside job. If someone wanted my presence for their brand, as long as it wasn't offensive, I did it. I've built up the same amount of money I had in my trust to begin with. I've also done my research. Yes, I spent a lot of time drunk over the years, but I'm not a *complete* moron unless it comes to love. When I started all this, I hired a financial guy who's the best in the city. Lloyd Marino. A guy known for dealing with large amounts of money and not ending up in the slammer.

He's read through the trust fund details extensively; they can't take back the money already given to me. They broke it into two payouts rather than giving it to us all at once, so if we blew through it like coked-up rock stars, they could hold back on the next payment until they had us under control. That next payout is my twenty-sixth birthday in three weeks. But I don't want it. Since the day I was born, I've been under their control, and today, I want out. Out of my trust. Out of the will. *Out of my family.*

'Ah.' Dad laughs. 'He *wants* to be cut off,' he tells my mom obnoxiously.

'Do you have any idea how that will make us *look*?' Mom asks, concerned only with their reputation.

'He has *no* idea how lucky he is to even *be* here right now. That's *your* doing!' Dad barks at Mom.

She furrows her brow, her lips pinched together uncomfortably as she shakes her head.

'What the hell does that mean?' I ask.

The two of them are now in the middle of some weird stare-down. If we were in the old west and it was sundown, I'd probably look away.

'On second thought, I don't care what that meant. Just know, I'll start leaking info to the press if you want to fight my request. What should I start with?' I ask Mom, glancing at my father, kind of enjoying the panic on their faces. I rub the scruff growing on my face like I'm deep in thought as I await their answer.

My mother's eyes go wide. The look of horror that they've raised a son who might go against them.

'That's right,' I say. 'I'm no longer a pushover and I know everything about this family – the good, the bad and the stuff that would ruin you. By unfortunate way of DNA, I'm an Adler, remember? And like a true Adler would, I'm not afraid to pull the plug on all your bullshit. If you want to go there, say the word. Leave me alone, take whatever money you need and forget about me. I don't want to live *this* life anymore. It's nearly killed me twice, already.'

Dad walks through the room to the wall of windows overlooking the lake. He stares out the window for a few long, silent minutes where I literally listen to the seconds tick by as no one in the room seems to be breathing.

I've just made a big threat that could ruin all of us, and with my history of letting them down, I think they're all three finally realizing I'll follow through if I have to.

'Have you ever seen the financial books for To Be Read?' Dad finally speaks.

That's a weird turn.

'No,' I tell him. 'That's Berkley's store.'

'That's too bad.' He walks to the bookshelf, pulls a cigar from a box, rolling it in his fingers as he heads to his smoking chair. 'Cigar?' he asks me, offering it my way.

I shake my head. 'Fine, I'll take the bait. Why's that too bad?'

Dad smirks as if he knew I'd cave at the mention of Berkley. 'Because Nicholas, our realtor, got wind that the owner's daughters are considering putting it on the market. Frank's health isn't doing well. Besides the apartment you wasted tens of thousands of dollars on to renovate, the building's old and in rough shape, but it's in a *great* location. We could fix it up and put anything there.'

'*What?*' I step towards him. Why didn't Berkley call me about this? '*No!*' I bark. 'Do *not* fuck over Berkley to get to me. That store is her dream.'

'I wish you'd do this the easy way but you never want to. This seems to be the only way you *listen*,' Dad says like it's common knowledge. My silver bullet, and he's got the metaphorical gun cocked and pressed to my forehead.

'Why the fuck would I need to listen when I'm twenty-five? Screw you people. I'm out. Pretend I died,' I say, now marching towards the door.

'We've already put in an offer!' Mom calls after me, stopping me in my tracks. I turn back. 'To Be Read is about to be a distant memory.' The way she waves her hand like it's dust in the wind is ice-fucking-cold.

So much of Berkley's and my history is in that store. Our future was supposed to be there too. I can't possibly let her lose it to my parents, who are insistent they ruin her just to control me. I've never been this pissed. How fucking dare they treat me like a child. This ends now.

'I will burn this world of yours to the fucking ground if it saves Berkley,' I growl at them. 'That is *not* a joke.' I storm out of the room. My *God*, that felt like a Superman-defending-Lois thing to say. Berkley would have loved that. I wish she was here but I can't focus on that. Instead, I pull my phone from my pocket on my way to my SUV, calling Lloyd.

'Willy, how are ya?!'

'Listen.' I shut myself into my car, locking my doors just in case. 'I need you to do something for me urgently – as in *right now*.'

'Well, this isn't making me nervous at all...'

I blow past his worry. 'To Be Read, Berkley's bookstore downtown, it's owned by Frank Kensington. His daughters are considering selling and I know Berkley's dream was to someday own it, but there's no way she can compete with my parents so make sure I win.' I speak fast, knowing my father is probably making a similar call right this second because I doubt they've made an offer yet. What they have right now is a threat to keep me in line. To shut me up.

'*OK...*' Lloyd drags out the word. 'How high are you willing to go?'

'Spend everything I have if you need to. I don't care, just outbid my parents and keep my name out of it. I'll get Berkley in there to put everything in her name when it's over.'

'Will do; I'll give you a call when it's done.'

I end the call. But my phone rings again, Cole's name flashing on the screen. We've kept in touch because he's more than just a producer of the show. We've become friends. I tap the speaker button.

'Hey.'

'You make it back?'

'I did.'

'Sounds like shit's blowing at the Adler household. I just got calls from your brother and your mother,' he says, irritation in his voice.

'I'd say I'm surprised but...'

Cole is the head producer of *Royals* now. If he wants something to happen or not happen, he gets to make that call. He's the great and powerful Oz that stands between my parents and the network, who've requested they no longer have a direct line of communication with them. A detail I've laughed over more than once. Apparently, they're 'aggressive'. Understatement of the year. Cole's not enjoying his position since I walked off mid-scene, telling the whole room to fuck off and disappearing unexpectedly.

'They've requested I lose all tapes of illegal shenanigans or anything that could further strain the family name,' he says, clearly annoyed.

'So, lose *everything*?' I ask with a laugh. 'Guess I should apologize to you now, as I've lit a fuse that could soon implode their world.'

'You make my life complicated, Adler. Day one of your new life, and you toss in a live grenade. Sobriety has made you fearless. You call her yet?'

'How am I supposed to call her? She's had me blocked for ages.'

'That's right, you ass-face. I guess you'll have to quit being a coward and go see her.'

'I'm not a coward; I've been back less than twenty-four hours.'

'Your timing is perfect because Bryce invited me to Sing! for Bianca and Berkley's birthday tonight. Come by. I'll text you the details.'

'Will Alex be there?'

Cole laughs into the phone. 'To my knowledge they're casually dating again, so yes, I assume he'll be there. Do you want to wait in the wings or would you rather fight for her?'

'Just show up uninvited and crash her party?'

'*I'm* invited – *with* a plus one. Wanna be my date?' He laughs. 'Come on, man, this is *your* circle of friends that I've been added onto *only* because of you. All I'm doing is inviting the guy that connects us all.'

I've spent the last few months figuring out how to fix what I've broken in me and thought *that* was scary – this is downright terrifying.

I could've stayed at rehab for any amount of time, but I chose three months because I didn't want to rush through it and end up in a worse place down the road. Finally, I felt good enough to maintain my sobriety without being contained within a fancy rehab center. I know what makes me happy. I see what's missing and I have a plan – sort of. No way will my being intimidated by her 'casual' boyfriend stop me.

'Show up and move slowly,' Cole suggests. 'I won't even tell anyone you're coming. You know her better than anyone on the planet, Will; try not to forget that.'

I used to know her best. God, I hope I still do.

22

BERKLEY

'Finally,' Bianca says when Alex and I walk into Sing! 'I thought you were never coming.'

'That makes *two* of us,' I say, irritation dripping from my tone as Alex makes his way across the bar to where Gunner is sitting.

'What took you so long?'

'Alex wanted to give me a birthday "gift" since I seem stressed lately.' I drop my purse onto the table they've claimed. Balloon bouquets are placed along the center of the table, the number 25 in silver mylar balloons and lavender and periwinkle plain ones as fillers. My and Bianca's favorite colors.

Bianca scrunches her face. 'Seriously?'

'Yep, but I give up. He just cannot figure it out, and it takes forever until finally I fake it and disappear to the bathroom for a quick "shower".'

Bianca blows out a breath, glancing across the bar to where Alex is now laughing at something with Gunner, Bryce and Cole. 'Does he know he's bad at it or—'

'Or.' I cut her off. 'Definitely *or*. I mean, how do you have that conversation?'

'You don't, you just dump him for good,' she says like it's no big deal. 'Your mid-twenties are no time to settle for mediocre. This might be the best you ever look.'

'Um, *what*?'

She smirks. 'You should be having the best sex of your life at this age. You should *want* him. Your clothes should be throwing themselves off. Find the guy who does *that* for you.'

I let out the heaviest sigh in all of history. 'What if you only get one of those guys in a lifetime, and mine was an idiot?'

She glances over with a frown. 'Crap. I'm sorry. I shouldn't have said that.'

I wave a hand like it's not a big deal. 'Forget I asked. That was one of those questions no one else was actually meant to hear. I don't want to talk about it. Or him. Let's just get hammered,' I joke. Mostly.

The group of us do a round of shots. Bianca and I do two because it's our birthday, and those are the rules.

Thirty minutes later, the tequila has successfully annihilated my inhibitions, and Bianca and I are on stage, belting out a rather terrible version of 'I Will Survive'.

Midway through the song, it happens. The front door of the bar opens and my 'idiot' walks in. I stop singing mid-word, but Bianca keeps going. Music dances around the room until my mic drops to the floor with a thud that blasts through the speakers, startling the whole room.

Suddenly I'm in Medusa's gaze, and Bianca follows my line of sight. He's got everyone's attention like a spotlight from heaven is shining down onto him, but his eyes are on me.

'Holy Moses and burning bush,' Olivia states.

He walks in slowly, his hands shoved into his jean pockets, glancing around nervously. Nervously? He's Prince Willy of *PDX Royals*. I've never seen him nervous a day in his life.

Bianca steps off the stage, but I'm frozen as I try to figure out what the hell to do. Do I run? Hide? Cry? Homicide? Hug him? Ugh, my emotions are all over the place.

Cole, Bianca and Bryce greet him enthusiastically, leaving Olivia, Gunner and Alex stunned at the sidelines.

Olivia steps up to him, squaring up like they're about to brawl.

'*Man*,' she says, her hands now on her hips. 'You've got some big ole fucking bo-jangles to show your face here. *Estúpido chico rico, polla en un palo.*' Her hand gestures drive it home as he steps back from her.

I don't know what she's just said, but it was undoubtedly a string of profanity-laced insults based on Gunner's shocked face. He glances between her and me, grimacing. He points to himself then Will, silently asking if he should do something here.

They are the best friends ever. Both of them nurture that part of me they know still loves him, but when it comes down to it, the way he hurt me pisses them off enough to attempt to protect me in a moment like this where my brain has suddenly seized up.

I shake my head at Gunner, who breathes a sigh of relief. We all know he's a lover, not a fighter.

'Liv,' Will says calmly.

'*Why* are you here?! 'Cause it's certainly not in response to an invitation,' she snaps.

Cole lifts his beer. 'Yeah, it is,' he says guiltily. 'Will's my plus one.' He glances my way, raising his shoulders like he's silently apologizing.

'*You* invited him?' Alex asks. '*Why?*'

'Isn't a birthday party open to the birthday girls' friends? Will and Berkley have been friends for over a decade.'

'He relinquished that title,' Olivia reminds him. 'I study murder for a living, buddy. Don't you dare think I won't make you disappear if need be.' She jabs a finger into his chest that he just takes, like he knows he deserves it.

Will's gaze once again meanders to mine. His face is full of regret until a shy grin turns the corner of one side of his lips. When my feet are no longer made of concrete, I walk his way. Our mutual friends part like the Red Sea as I move through them.

'I got this,' I say to Olivia.

'Sweets, I can—'

'I don't need saving, Alex. I can take care of myself.' I hold a hand his way. Immediately he steps back, looking annoyed as he walks away towards the bar, Gunner following him.

Olivia takes to the stage behind me, attempting to turn the room's attention. However, I feel like all eyes are still staring our way, so I decide to give things a moment to settle with his 'Royal' presence. I walk past him, knocking my shoulder into his bicep to get by even though there isn't a crowd big enough to make that necessary. He sighs heavily as I continue to the bar.

'Two tequila shots,' I say to the bartender.

I feel Will walk up behind me. Even if I didn't know he was here, I'd know he's close. He sits on the barstool next to me as the bartender pours the shots. I grab both, finally turning to look him in the face, holding the glasses in the air between us.

He shakes his head. 'I can't, Berx, I—'

'I wasn't *offering* you one,' I say, cutting him off and downing them back-to-back, slamming the glasses onto the bar top as I do.

His eyes follow the shot glasses.

'I was saying a silent prayer to the tequila gods for help *not* to murder you in public. Word of warning, counting these two...' I add up the shots I've done since I walked in here less than an hour ago. 'I dunno, things are getting fuzzy, but I'm pretty sure I'm four or five shots in, *plus* a beer, so let's cross our fingers, shall we?' I cross fingers on both my hands, waving them in the air like a moron.

'You're *four* or *five* shots in?' he asks, looking me up and down with worried eyes. 'You never drink like that and you weigh nothing. You'll be full tilt in minutes.'

'A game you know well,' I say snidely.

He rolls his eyes, nodding his head, a guilty smile on his still pretty face.

'Why would you show up unannounced on my *birthday*?' I ask, the words leaving my lips angrily.

'I'm here for you, baby.' His voice is all soft and gooey, like a chocolate chip cookie straight from the oven.

I was beginning to think my heart was a goner. Charred in the flames that were once William Adler. But nope, it clearly exists, and it's definitely not beating correctly in his presence.

Pull yourself together, Berkley. If you're about to die of a heart condition you didn't know you had, at least tell him off first. He deserves that.

'No,' I say firmly. 'Do not "baby" me, Adler.'

'So, you hate me?' he asks curiously.

I nod. 'Hate. Loathe. Resent. With the venom of a thousand cobras.'

And hello, tequila. Oh, boy. It's really setting in fast now.

'That's a lot,' he says, nodding his head like he's impressed. 'I suppose I deserve that.'

'You *deserve* to let me punch you in the junk, film it, then tag you on all the social media so your adoring fans can see what a lying, crap-wagon, douche-lord you really are.'

He cracks a smile, leaning forward, resting his elbows on the bar. He fidgets with a bracelet I don't recognize around the wrist that doesn't sport his thirty-thousand-dollar Rolex.

'Did *Danika* give that to you? A token of her love to remember her while you come back to waffle stomp my heart?'

This time he laughs out loud.

'Seriously?' I ask, pissed he thinks this is a joke. 'I'll *let* Olivia murder you, and then I'll *help* her bury your body. And I probably won't mark your grave *or* visit.'

He wipes the smile off his face. 'It's not funny, Berx. I just...' The way he looks at me makes my heart weak. If I'm not careful, it'll start making decisions for me and not punish him the way I want. 'I missed your fiery mouth, that's all.'

I roll my eyes. 'You never answered my question. Did Danika give you that?'

He looks at the bracelet in question before glancing at me with his brow furrowed, shaking his head. 'Dani and I officially broke up a long time ago. We were never as serious as the show made it seem either.'

'You're *single*? No way.'

'Why is that unbelievable?'

'Uh, because you look like this.' I motion my hands over him obnoxiously.

His smile grows until he's again laughing to himself under his breath.

'Your obvious amusement is pissing me off, Adler. Do *not* take those words as me telling you how fucking handsome you are. 'Cause it's not. I mean, it *kinda* is, but it's *not*. It's complicated, OK? I'm just saying...' I let out a frustrated sigh, unsure of what I'm trying to say. I didn't expect to be this mad *and* completely heart-broken all at once.

'You know, I rarely think of you anymore,' I spout.

Lie. *Stop talking, Berkley.*

'Or miss your stupid handsome face.'

Lie. *Why are you still talking? Shut up!*

'The way you'd hold me...'

Fuck, uh, where ya going with this, Berx?

'You always had the power to make me feel like everything's somehow OK even when it wasn't.'

Jesus criminy, I am *bad* at this making him pay game. As his gaze softens with my words, my speech gets slower as my heart takes over, taking complete advantage of my head going suddenly fuzzy. His face softens as he listens to me.

Ten minutes of me spouting nonsense his way and him protesting only a little, the room suddenly shifts under my feet. I reach out to stabilize myself with the bar top, but I grab Will's forearm instead.

'You alright?' he asks, standing from his barstool, ready to either hold me up or help me to the bathroom. 'What are we doing here, Berx?' He's clearly worried, judging by his tone.

'Bathroom,' I say, taking a single step towards the door a dozen feet from us before the floor drops out from underneath me.

Without saying a word, he reads the signs and whisks me into the ladies' room, pushing into a stall, getting me there just in time. He's kneeling behind me, gathering my hair into his hand while I humiliate myself and yak way more tequila than I remember drinking into the throne.

When it's over, I sit back onto my heels, knocking him into the wall next to us, and fall into his lap. I rest my head on his shoulder, my forehead tucked into the hollow of his neck.

'If I could move, I would, but if I do, I'll puke again, and I feel like I've embarrassed myself about as much as I'm willing to tonight.'

'You don't need to move anywhere. This is the only place I want to be.'

'*Since. When?*'

'I needed to become the man you deserve, Berx. I'd lost him.'

'The man I deserve. Could you have taken *longer*? Now look at the mess you've caused.'

'I take full responsibility. That's why I'm here, to fix things.'

I notice ink on his left inner forearm as his hand rests on my knee. I've wondered about this for months. I grab his hand, lifting his arm to read it.

'This is... *my name*?' I run my fingers over the scrolling ink, tracing the black letters. This is my name.

'I know they say tattooing someone's name is a bad decision but you're sitting in my lap right now after not seeing you in what feels like forever. So, I call bullshit on that.'

'Why would you do this?'

He adjusts himself underneath me, careful he doesn't jostle me too much, his hand coming to a rest on my lower back, encouraging me to lean into him. This is the first time I've felt like I could relax into someone in a long time.

'I wanted you to know I'm yours.'

'You're *mine*?' I'm so confused. 'I hope you know I'm going to have a lot to say about this when I can think straight.'

'Honestly, I'm looking forward to it.' I can hear the smirk on his face.

'You're looking forward to fighting with me later?'

'Fighting is talking. I'd be more worried if you had nothing to say. I've messed up a lot, Berx. For years. When we'd fight, I'd get scared I'd never see you again, so I took whatever I could.'

We're silent for a few moments while I think about this.

'Took whatever you could and only gave back the minimum required of you. You're kind of a selfish bastard for that.'

'I am and I apologize, sincerely. I loved you selfishly for too long.'

'*What is happening?*' I ask. 'You're taking responsibility? Not blaming your parents, your asshole friends, or whatever stupid fucking contract you've signed?'

'I and I alone fucked this up. I'm taking responsibility for all of it.'

I don't know what to say to that. Suddenly, I heave. That seems right. I lean towards the toilet until it passes, then I relax back into him. Why must he feel like home even while we sit on the floor of a public bathroom stall?

He hesitantly takes my hand in his, the pad of his thumb grazing over my skin repeatedly, distracting me and giving my head somewhere to be beside the toilet bowl. Listening to his heart beating is somehow comforting and I want to sit here all night and just listen to him exist.

'I'm about to say something my sober self might regret.' The words tumble out of my mouth without any thought at all.

'Alright.'

'I missed you *so* much.' And the words barely leave my lips before tears follow.

He leans his head into mine, wrapping his arms around me. 'I missed you too. I'm sorry figuring out my shit took longer than I planned. I didn't want to half-ass this. You deserve so much more from me than that.'

For a moment, we're both silent. Our faces close, our hands on each other. I could kiss him I'm so close. My head is spinning, my loins are sparking and my heart is confused as fuck.

'When do you start filming again?' A trick question my wit has pushed through the tequila.

'I quit the show. I only came back for you.' His voice is so sincere and gentle as he says it that I have to close my eyes so the tears can't fall again.

'You did not. You came back for the show and quit me, William.'

'I'm serious, Berx. No more *Royals*. If we could just talk, I can expla—'

The bathroom door creaks open, both of us going silent.

'Berkley?' Bianca steps further into the bathroom, her footsteps suddenly stopping behind me. 'There you are— *oh*.' Her surprised voice. 'Are you guys good?'

'She's got a touch of the tequila flu,' Will says, a hint of laughter under his breath that I notice because my head is still resting on his shoulder.

I jab him in the ribs, earning a grunt as he grabs my hand.

'Alex is looking for you,' Bianca says. 'Pretty sure he won't hesitate to come in he—'

The door opens suddenly, cutting her off mid-word.

'Berx?' He says my name.

'Shit,' I groan.

'What the fuck are *you* doing?' His words clearly aren't directed at me.

My back is to the bathroom, but I'm getting the vibe that Alex isn't thrilled to see me sitting in Will's lap. Shocker.

'Nothing,' Will says calmly like it's not a big deal. 'She got sick, and I was there. I got her in here, she fell over and here we are. I don't want to make things worse by moving her.'

'Well, I got it from here, pal,' Alex bellows.

'*Pal?*' Will says with an irritated laugh.

Alex grabs my upper arm, pulling me from Will's lap.

'I can't—' I end up with my head in the toilet again, my arm in Alex's hand above my head.

'Will you stop?' Will asks, his voice calm but elevated as he stands from the floor, removing Alex's hand from my arm. 'She's sick; we're fine,' he says, once again gathering my hair as I puke things up from my childhood.

'I said, *I* got it.' Alex tries again, nearly knocking me into the toilet head first this time.

'Stop!' Will commands, just before someone grunts as they're slammed against a wall. My guess would be Alex considering I still feel Will's hand on my back.

'You stupid fucker,' Alex says, clearly pissed. Which kind of surprises me. We aren't serious enough for him to want to fight for me, so *what* is this?

'Bryce!' Bianca opens the bathroom door, hollering for help.

'Don't!' Will yells, his voice loud enough it makes me jump. He never yells. At least not with me around. I can tell he's standing right behind me still, probably preventing Alex from getting in.

'Get out!' Alex yells.

'If she needed you, she'd have come to you. She didn't,' Will says.

Alex grunts an unmistakably pissed-off laugh.

'Hey!' Bryce bolsters. 'What's going on?'

'He's making it worse. We were just talking, and all he wants to do is fight for her. She's sick. Can you get him outta here?' Will thunders.

'Alex, maybe you should go?' Bryce suggests.

'Fuck that!' Alex argues. 'Willy can go. If anyone is taking care of her, it's me. Berkley's *mine* now, jackass.'

I'm *his* now? Like he *owns* me? I think the fuck not.

'I am nobody's property!' I muster up the energy to yell. My voice echoes through the bathroom then all goes silent. 'Will was just helping but if you're going to fight, just get out. *Both* of you!'

'I wasn't fighting him,' Will defends himself. 'You're sick. I can't leave you in here alone with him after watching him yank you up like that...' His voice fades as someone, probably Bryce, directs him out of the bathroom.

'I got this, ya tool,' Alex says, spit dripping in his tone.

My heart slows at the thought of Will disappearing again before I can talk to him. This is not the hate I'd planned.

'Alex, why don't you go too?' Bianca says sternly. '*I'll* take care of her.'

The door slams against the back wall as Alex exits with a frustrated groan. The room finally settles as I sit back down, without the cushion of Will beneath me this time. I lean against the stall wall, pulling my knees to my chest and resting my forehead on them.

'Well,' Bianca says with a laugh. 'I didn't expect all hell to break loose tonight, did you?'

I glance up. She stands just outside my stall, her arms crossed over her chest and the exact face Mom would have if she were standing here. Disappointment, pity and a hint of amusement.

'You couldn't have warned me he was coming?'

'I honestly didn't know. If Bryce did he's kept it on the down-low.' She says the words gently, so I know she's not lying. We're twins and sisters; we don't always say things gently.

The bathroom door swings open, and Olivia bursts in. 'Oh my God, they *fought*? Like fists and everything?' she asks, glancing between Bianca and me, wide-eyed.

'Nobody swung,' Bianca informs her. 'But if I had to guess, that wouldn't be the case next time.'

'Alex just stormed out with Gunner, so I don't think there will be a next time tonight.'

'He *left*?' I ask. He drove me here and he just left? 'He's not worried at all about how him leaving might shove me right into the arms of— *wait*.' I glance at Olivia. 'Is *he* still here?'

'If by *he* you mean Will? Yes. He said he'll bring you home.'

'Oh,' Bianca swoons. 'He's claiming you by not asking if he can, just saying he will. Grew himself a spine while he was away, did he? How do you feel about that?'

I drop my head to my knees again. 'I don't know how I feel about any of this. He says he's here for me and wants to talk, yet I can hardly think beyond trying not to be sick. What do I do?'

'How about we go back out there? The puke parade seems to have passed,' Bianca says, flushing the toilet. 'We'll get you some water or coffee and just try and relax. This doesn't need to ruin our night. You two have been friends for a long time. You can handle *one* night with him.'

Handling one night with Will is the exact problem. One night turns into two. Two nights turn into us pretending we're back together. Then, suddenly, the igloo is on fire, and as Bianca so elegantly said earlier, all hell breaks loose. But tequila thinks I can do it, so I nod my head like it's a great idea, raise my hands and allow them to pull me off the floor to face the good prince himself.

'Let's just...' Bianca looks me over, running her fingers through my hair. She pulls a bobby pin from her bag, slipping it in and adjusting it until she's happy. Then she touches up my makeup, slathering lipstick onto my lips. She quickly checks my outfit. Then she slips me a breath mint.

'OK,' I say, pushing her away from me. 'How do you have that much crap in your purse? I'm good.' I take a few breaths as I step away from her and Liv, balancing myself with a hand on the wall, feeling real *not* good but steady enough to at least get to our table.

Will immediately stands as we approach, offering me his spot.

'Hey,' he says softly. 'I got you water, coffee, Gatorade, crackers, Tylenol.'

I glance between him and the table of offerings.

'What? No jewelry or gold bars?' Liv asks, attitude slung his way.

He chuckles. 'If she wants gold bars and jewelry, I'll get her gold bars and jewelry,' he says, his eyes on me.

'Thank you?' I slowly sit in the chair he's offering me, trying not to jostle anything internally. How in the hell did he put all this together so fast? We're in a bar. I get the coffee and water, but Gatorade, crackers and Tylenol? Did he ask for donations?

Wait.

There's a drugstore across the street. He bought all this stuff for me in the last five minutes. Shit. He's being sweet.

'We're up, woman,' Bryce says to Bianca, waggling his eyebrows as he directs her to the karaoke stage.

I lean forward, resting my head in my hands. Suddenly, I feel Will's hand on my back, gently gliding over my shirt in a circular motion. Now that the shock of him being here has faded, every nerve in my body lights up like an old power plant coming back to life after being dead for a very long time. Buzzing, sparking and electricity surge through every part of me.

After a few minutes, he leans forward, kissing the back of my shoulder; the smell of his cologne fills my head. Woodsy but sweet. He's either still wearing the Le Labo cologne he knows I like, or he put it on just for this. I breathe him in for a moment, and I swear he knows; that's why he's lingering so closely.

'You doin' alright?' he asks softly into my ear. 'I can take you home whenever you're ready.'

I turn my head on my hands, looking over at him. *Why?* Why must he be so fucking handsome? What is this look he's giving me? Some mix of regret, worry and adoration. Like I'm someone he's sincerely missed. He flashes me a panty-melting smile, and without me telling it to, my face matches his. It just responds to him however it fucking wants.

'How dare you walk in here, looking all super-hot Clark Kent while I look like booze-flu Barbie.'

He bursts out laughing.

'I kind of want to punch you in your pretty stupid face.'

'There she is!' Cole says with a laugh. 'Want us to bring him outside? Bryce and I can hold him down, and you can kick him in the balls?'

'Hey,' Will protests, obviously not thrilled with this idea, as he reaches down to cup his jewels with his free hand. My eyes follow. He notices and grins. 'Do I get a say in this?' His voice is soft and innocently intoxicating, like when we're alone.

'No,' Olivia snaps, interrupting our little moment. Little moments that continue to happen and make me want to know exactly why he's here.

'You get no say, and if ya fight it, maybe all three of us ladies kick you in the gonads. We will decide on your punishment based on your crime-s.' She adds in the plural as an afterthought.

'How about we let Berkley decide my punishment?' Will suggests, his gaze still on me.

'You sure you want to knock at that door?' I ask. 'I'm the one at this table that should hate you the most.'

'*Should?*' He picks up on it immediately.

I glare. 'How about this: you want me to hear your stupid explanation?'

'Yes.'

'Sing,' I say, grabbing the bottle of Gatorade, twisting the cap with all my might, but it doesn't budge. He takes it from me, opening it easily before handing it back.

'Thank you.' I lift the drink. 'You want to have a private conversation with me? The girl whose heart you destroyed. You have to sing.' I point to the stage.

'Seriously?' he asks. 'Me singing badly will make you feel better enough to talk?'

'You're a professional party boy, Adler. Don't pretend you've never drunkenly done karaoke. The whole world has watched you do it. Now get your pretty ass up there and sing me something.'

He stares at me, challenging me with his big brown eyes with gold flecks that sparkle anytime he looks at me. I remember them so well. I could stare into them all day and never feel lost.

'What's a conversation with me worth to you?' I ask.

With that, he flashes a confident smile and stands from his chair. 'Alright. I'll sing something. For *you*.' He makes his way to the guy that DJs this place. They talk for a few moments then Will takes the stage.

Tables of women cheer for him, realizing who he is immediately. I wouldn't be surprised if the stage was covered in panties when he's done. Then the music starts, and I'm suddenly invested.

'Oh. My. God,' Olivia says with a swoon. 'He's doing a song from one of her favorite movies.'

My heart slows as I realize the same thing – a movie I've made him watch a hundred times, easy. A rom-com involving Heath Ledger and Julia Stiles. *10 Things I Hate About You*. A classic.

Will grins my way, singing the song animatedly, reminding me he's a reality star with zero shame, pointing to me in all the right spots. The entire room's invested in this performance. People have their phones out to record every second. Everyone trying to glimpse who this Portland Royal is singing his heart out to.

Bianca sits next to me, watching him with the same stupid smile I probably have. 'How drunk is he? 'Cause he seems shockingly sober for a karaoke performance like this.'

'He's three months sober,' Cole says.

My head snaps from Will to Bianca to Cole. '*What?*'

Cole nods slowly. 'I probably shouldn't say anything more.'

My gaze moves back to Will. We're in a bar, and he's sober? Here I am, literally puking drunk, something I never ever do, and I find out he's sober. Why didn't he tell me?

He sings the words he used to say to me daily, throwing his arms out exaggeratedly in my direction. Yes, I'm ear-to-ear grinning, enjoying every single second of this as he embarrasses himself with an impromptu performance that he's selling in a way my poor heart is tossing money at.

When the song's over, the crowd applauds him as he walks back over to us, his hands shyly shoved into his pockets, a goofy grin on his face and a hint of pink in his cheeks that wasn't there before. He stops at the table, looking at me.

'Well?'

'That was, uh...' I laugh to myself, unable to look away from him. 'Pretty adorable, if I'm honest.'

I'm caving. I *want* to hear what he has to say. 'You wanted to talk?' I ask.

'Yeah.'

'My driver left without me, so I need a ride home.'

I can feel our friends' heads flipping between us, following the conversation, but our eyes are only on each other.

'I'll drive you,' he offers, pulling his keys from his pocket and extending a hand my way.

It takes her multiple tries to get the correct code into the security system, and considering I no longer know it, I can't help besides offering to call her sister, which she refuses. Third try's a charm and it turns out I did know it. The security code for the store is my birthday. Which has me wondering if her hating me with the venom of a thousand cobras might be a bit of an exaggeration?

'No Williams or Willys in my room, so don't even try it. I had to have an exorcism of you after you left, so don't undo what cost me a hundred bucks to do, Adler,' she says, struggling with the key in her apartment door.

'You had your room *exorcised* of me?' I laugh out loud. 'Like I was a guy haunting you?'

She turns to me suddenly, her back against her door. 'More like you were a demon poking my heart,' she says like I'm a total imbecile, jabbing her finger into my chest.

When she's satisfied that I understand, she goes back to the lock, turning the key, and opening her apartment door. I glance around her place with a relieved sigh. Everything is exactly as I saw it last and though I've never lived here like we'd planned so long ago, the place feels like home. A feeling I haven't had in a very long time.

I close the door behind me, and when I turn back her way, she suddenly throws her arms around my neck, a mess of tears sliding down her cheeks.

'Do you have any idea how worried I was?' she asks through sobs.

I wrap my arms around her, holding her close. 'I'm sorry,' I say. 'Honestly, I was a little scared you really did hate me.'

For a moment we just hold each other tightly. I breathe her in, wishing I never had to let her go again and that I never had to begin with.

'My emotions were all over the place at the bar. I wanted to hug the hell out of you, but I needed to hate you too. What happened? Where did you go? I can barely sleep I've been so worried.'

'You have? All this time you've made it seem like letting me go was so easy for you.'

'Ha! Behind the scenes it was torture, like someone ripping off my fingernails. I still can't find all the piece of my heart so I decided to miss you silently, and only on days that end in y.' She pulls away, giving me a slight – yet hesitant – smile.

Unfortunately, I have no words because I'm finally able to look her over and she's so much prettier than she was. Wearing a short black skirt with a slit up one side and a Blondie T-shirt tied at her waist, the strappy heels I bought her so long ago on her feet. Her hair's now faded into a caramelly brown color that I'm quickly falling in love with.

'First things first, happy birthday. You told me how pretty I was earlier, so it's only fair I do the same. You're even more gorgeous than the last time I saw you.'

She blushes, attempting – yet failing – to hide the grin sneaking up on her. 'Thanks.'

'The pleasure is all mine,' I say, wandering her apartment, taking it all in. This place is completely her, yet I see memories of us everywhere. I can't decide if that hurts or makes this all a little better.

'How drunk are you right now?' I ask. 'On a scale of one to ten.'

'Six?' she says, dropping onto her couch, her hand resting on her head. 'Although the headache says seven, I think it's fading. I'm not drunk enough not to remember this or do something stupid. Just fuzzy.'

'Alright, fuzzy works,' I say, inhaling deeply as I walk to her, sitting next to her. 'I've bee—'

'Why would you do that, William?'

'What part specifically are you referring to?'

'*Royals*, Danika, drinking yourself nearly to death, all the flirting, and partying, and then disappearing for months. *Why?*'

'Headed right into the battlefield, are we?'

'Did you *really* not want me anymore?'

'*What?*' I ask, surprised to hear her say those words. '*All* I wanted was you, Berx. But you insisted I do this on my own. Then we fought all the time. Every time I saw you I could see your disappointment in me.'

'That wasn't disappointment, William.'

'What was it?'

She sighs, looking at me sadly. 'Heartbreak? A crushed soul? I missing piece of me that no one could ever replace?'

'Berx... I was feeling all the same things. I tried to make this work but you were right, the show changed me and I hated what I'd turned into. I hated that one second it seemed like you wanted me and the next you didn't. What was I supposed to do?'

'You were supposed to stop hurting me.' She squeezes her eyes shut, tears escaping once again.

Damn it. I've been in her apartment five minutes, and she's cried twice. Hesitantly, I take her hand in mine, fully expecting her to jerk it away but instead, she holds it tightly.

'I was twenty-*three*, Berx. I didn't realize what I'd do to us by jumping all in with the show.'

'Well, isn't hindsight twenty-twenty? Now you think you can just come back and fall right back into where we were three years ago?'

'*No*, I don't think that. You told me the night of the Halloween party to find what makes me happy and it took me way longer than it should have but I found it. That's why it took me so long to get here.'

'What kind of change required you to flee my world without another word?'

I don't know why these words are so hard to say when I'm so proud of them. Maybe because most of my family and 'friends' act like this was the most selfish thing I could have done.

'I spent a while spiraling out of control while I lost my mind, knowing I'd fucked up so big I'd probably lost you for good, then when I hit rock bottom, someone laid my options out for me clearly, gave me some much-needed advice, and I did what you asked. I went to rehab.'

'Please, if that someone was Danika Frost, don't tell me.'

She still hates her and I don't blame her one bit. I feel exactly the same way about Alex.

'Danika only made it worse. It was your mom, Berkley.'

'My *mom*?'

I nod slowly. 'One night I ended up in jail with multiple charges that have only recently been settled. I called Bryce, but he was working, so he called Bianca and *she* called your mom. It's probably the thing that saved my life.'

'She never told me—'

'I know. She didn't want to hurt you more than I already had.'

Berkley frowns, wiping tears from her face.

'She was right. About everything. I needed to fix what was broken in me before I could fix what I'd broken in you. So, that's what I did.'

For a moment, she stares at me, confusion all over her face. 'You're really sober? And you faced temptation by coming to a bar to talk to me?'

'Berkley, I'd face a fucking dragon for you. And yes, I'm three months sober officially, and I now have hundreds of hours of therapy in the books.'

'And you actually quit the show? No more *Royals*, for *real*?'

I nod. 'I paid a price, trust me, but it's all over. The network high-ups call me daily but I've blocked all their numbers and I'm now officially out.'

She stares at me silently, shock on her face. She has her doubts.

'I had to save myself, baby. Nobody could do this for me. My world on the show was chaotic, shallow and complete bullshit. And the life I wanted was right in front of me, yet like a total fuckwit I didn't take it. You deserved better than who I was. So I became that better before I tried again.'

'I know I'm asking the same questions over and over but my heart and head are having a hard time understanding this. This is you here to try again or is this just one of your twelve steps – to make amends to the people you've hurt?'

'I'm here because I want another chance, Berkley. You're the only woman I've ever loved and I'll do *anything* to make all of this up to you.'

Her brows squish together. 'I dunno...' she says. 'I've had this dream before – you in my living room apologizing. What if I wake up tomorrow, and none of it's real? *Again*.'

God, she's dreamed of this, while I had nightmares she was marrying Alex. I really broke this woman's heart while I broke my own. Taking a chance, I reach up, wiping away her tears with my thumb.

'I'm really here, Berx, and it's literally the only place I want to be. But if you don't feel the same anymore – if you tell me you no longer love me – I'll walk away.'

She stares into my eyes, hers glazed over with tears. The silence hurts. Her answer here is all I've worried about since I came up with this plan.

'I can't say I don't love you,' she says, as she slides her thumb over my hand. 'It never went away no matter how much I tried to force it.'

Thank. Fucking. God.

'Then I'll still be here tomorrow and every day after that until we are either back to how we were, or you decide you don't want me.'

'I've never not wanted you,' she says, lying back against the couch, her hand on her head.

'Ditto,' I say, so glad to hear those words. 'We were made for each other, Berx. I believed it the day I met you and I still believe it now.'

'Really?'

'Absolutely.'

She rubs her temples gently, clearly still feeling the tequila from earlier. She's in no shape to talk any more than we already have.

'How about for now, we get you into bed to sleep this off?'

'I'd say no, but my head is pounding.'

She takes her time brushing her teeth, then stripping her clothes off in a striptease I didn't ask for but that I can't physically turn away from, so I don't doubt she'll regret making this such a show tomorrow. Once she's in one of my old T-shirts and a pair of skimpy panties – I try not to look directly at her for fear it'll prove my thoughts aren't entirely innocent when it comes to her – she climbs into bed.

I grab the trash can from her bathroom and a water from her fridge, sitting them near her, just in case. Her eyes are closed as I kneel bedside her to say goodbye, so instead, I brush her hair from her face and press my lips to her forehead. The smell of her vanilla shampoo reminds me of the old us.

'Goodnight, Berx. We'll talk tomorrow.' I stand to walk away, but she grabs my hand before I can.

'Will?'

Hearing her sweet voice again tears at my chest. I want to make every way I've wronged her right.

'Yeah?'

'Do you *have* to go?'

'You said no Williams of any variety were allowed in your room, so I'd guess yes?'

She laughs drunkenly. 'Like you ever followed the rules. I'm drunk, Will, and I'm never drunk. I don't want to be alone.'

My heart stumbles through my chest. I fully expected her to hate me with the fire of a thousand suns. Or, in her words, the venom of a thousand cobras. I've earned it. I absolutely will not be surprised when she wakes up tomorrow back to feeling precisely that. But I can't say no to her right now when I'm here to win her back. Leaving when she wants me to stay might worsen things, and I can't risk that.

'Are you sure? I don't know that Alex will be pleased with me staying the night. He wasn't overly happy with you in my lap earlier.'

'Alex and I aren't even *really* a thing anymore. We're just fuck-bud—UGH,' she groans. 'You weren't supposed to know that so pretend I didn't just say it.'

'What if he shows up here while I'm here?'

'He'd have to call first because he's got no access to the building like you always have.'

Wow. They've been off and on for how long, and he can't get into the building without permission. That makes me feel a little better.

'Fuck Alex, anyway,' she half slurs. 'He left when I was in crisis earlier. Plus I'm pretty sure he's just with me to get laid. But you always knew how to...' She stops, finally opening her eyes, looking up at me, adjusting her hand in mine but never letting go. 'You always knew how to make me feel better. Please, stay?' She pats the other side of her bed.

'In your bed?' I ask, making certain she understands what she's asking.

'This is totally stupid and if you tell anyone I let you in this easy I'll – I don't know – I just, maybe you could stay and hold me. Like you used to?'

She wants me to hold her like I used to? Maybe now's not the time to play the gentleman? Like being respectful of whatever she and Alex have going on will get me where I want to be. Cole's words play in my head. *You gonna wait until she's completely unavailable?* No.

'Sure, Berx. I'll stay. Let me just turn off the lights and lock up.'

I don't want to say I'm giddy as I lock her front door, flipping off the lamps, before heading back to her room but I absolutely am. She's asking me to stay here. Please, let this be a good sign.

I slip off my shoes, emptying my pockets onto her dresser, then crawl into her bed next to her fully clothed, lying flat on my back, almost afraid to touch her. She's got no such fear as she eases herself into my side, resting her head on my chest, her hand on my stomach. I hold her – like I used to, finally feeling complete again.

'I shouldn't tell you this, but I missed you *so* much.' Her voice wavers. She must not remember saying this multiple times already. She's too fucking adorable.

'I missed you too, baby. More than words can describe.'

24

WILL

I slept in her bed last night. Clothed and not one time did I try to kiss her or do anything to make her uncomfortable. We didn't even really talk much, but we also hardly slept; we just existed in the same space and I held her like she asked. It was literally – and this is no lie – the *best* night of my life.

Considering I've been a nervous wreck over all this for months, and sleeping at rehab was impossible with all the thoughts running through my head, I probably could have slept last night. But I didn't let myself because, at some point, I realized she may wake up feeling completely different than her tipsy self did last night. No way did I want to tempt the airplane nightmare back.

It's now eight in the morning, and I got up an hour ago. I've showered and I'm wearing yesterday's clothes still, standing at her stove, barefoot, making her breakfast while she sleeps. I had to do *something*. I don't know what her reaction to me will be so if last night is the last time I'll ever hold her, I want to remember every second and at least *try* to unsink this ship.

Her stumbling out of bed is what pulls me from my head. I turn on one heel and walk to her doorway, glancing at her now steadying herself, one hand on her dresser and the other on her head.

'Fuck-ing hell,' she groans. 'Why did I drink so mu—' She lifts her head, her eyes meeting mine. 'Holy tits.' She drops her hand from her head, a smile slowly filling her face. 'I didn't dream it.'

She looks genuinely happy to see me. My heart could probably light the whole damn world right now. Based on her shock that I'm standing in front of her, I'm willing to bet she doesn't remember everything that happened last night.

'You didn't dream it, but do you regret it?'

Her eyes grow wide with my question. 'Did we...' She points back at the bed, glances down at herself, then back up at me, my heart slowing as she takes her time looking me over, motioning between us.

'No,' I tell her with a laugh. God, she's cute. 'We weren't sexually active,' I say obnoxiously. 'But we *did* sleep together. My plan was to let you sleep off the tequila last night, alone, but you asked me to stay.'

'I *asked* you to stay?'

I nod. 'And hold you like I used to, because I always knew how to make you feel better. Your words.'

'So you—'

'Couldn't possibly say no to that,' I say, cutting her off. 'So, I did exactly that, just a lot less handsy than previous days, and that's it.' I turn, walking away from her and back to the kitchen like it's no big deal. She follows.

'No clothes came off?'

'I literally wore this,' I say, motioning over me. 'But *you*, on the other hand, happily stripped right in front of me, completely topless at one point, wearing the skimpiest pair of panties I've ever seen, and one of my old T-shirts that you took your sweet time putting on. Tempted as I was after that, I *just* held you.'

A shy smile creeps across her face. 'Hang on,' she says, veering into her bathroom, never closing the door behind her, just sitting down and peeing right in front of me.

I go back to the stove where every burner is in use, all to make sure she doesn't have a hangover from hell and starts her day off right.

'I slept with Alex,' she says when she emerges from the bathroom like she's throwing all her guilt onto the counter to deal with. Her frown says she's disappointed with herself.

Boner. Killer.

'And I slept with Danika,' I admit.

She frowns. 'Was it... good?'

I laugh. 'Not even a little bit. My heart was hiding and I was usually drunk as a skunk but it happened. Are you mad?'

'Are you mad about Alex?'

I shrug. 'I mean, *technically*, we were on a break,' I joke, quoting one of the scenes she hates the most from *Friends*. 'We hadn't seen one another in a long time by the time either of us attempted to move on so I can't be mad. Are *you* mad?'

'We were broken up; I couldn't be mad. But I'll admit, I was jealous as hell. I'll be happy if I never hear her name again.' She meanders to a stool, sitting down, then laying her head on the counter with a thud. 'Ouch.'

'That I can make happen,' I tell her. 'Here.' I hand her water and the bottle of Tylenol I found in her bathroom earlier. 'Drink this and take these. I'm working on the hangover cure that took me years to perfect. Crispy, greasy bacon, heavily buttered slightly burned toast, and scrambled eggs.'

'Seems like I'm in good hands, considering you are the hangover king,' she says into the counter before lifting her head and swallowing down a couple of Tylenol.

'*Was* the hangover king,' I correct her. 'Tell me you at least remember *some* of our conversation last night?'

'Things are slowly coming back to me. Just trying to process all of it.' After a few silent moments of her nursing her headache with her fingers on her temples, she speaks. 'Did you ever tell her you loved her?'

'*No*,' I say with a chuckle. 'Did you?' I'm afraid to turn around in case her answer is yes.

'Never,' she says.

'So, we can both breathe a sigh of relief that our hearts never let us truly move on,' I say, handing her steaming-hot coffee in a mug I found deep in the back of the cabinet that says 'Waiting on Prince Charming...' but someone crossed out the 'Charming' and in its place is her least favorite prince's name. Willy. I'd bet money Bryce is behind this and if so, thanks from the bottom of my heart, bro.

She smiles sweetly, forcing it away quickly as her eyes drop to her coffee mug. 'I still *have* this? Ugh,' she groans. 'Bianca swore it was in the donation box last year with the rest of your stuff you left here. I got rid of all of it because I couldn't stand looking at it anymore.'

I glance around the room, seeing many things of mine still in her possession. She follows my line of sight, her gaze stopping on the ridiculous *Mario Kart* trophy she won last time and still has displayed on her shelves full of books arranged by color.

'You sure about that?'

'Fine,' she admits reluctantly. 'Maybe I didn't get rid of you completely. God, Will. Do you know what a fucking mess I've been? Alex and I broke up around the time you disappeared and my family thought I was insane, mourning for a guy I hardly even liked. But it wasn't him I was missing. It was you and with every flower delivery I missed you a little more.'

I dish up her food and set the plate in front of her.

'I dunno if I can eat.' She rubs her stomach.

'Why not?'

'I blame the tequila – not to mention my heart that's on life support is slowly coming alive in your presence and giving me all sorts of awkward sensations I've never felt before.'

'If you eat, I brought you a present.' I reach over the bar, grabbing the gift and setting it between our plates.

She grins. 'You brought me a gift? *Why?*'

'Yesterday was your birthday, remember? Those usually have presents, so yeah. I was going to give it to you last night but the timing was off so I left it in my SUV and grabbed it this morning.'

'That's right!' she says suddenly. 'You weren't driving your Jeep last night. Where is it?'

'I sold it. I figured if I'm going for a new me, I had to change all of it. So, I bought the Range Rover while I was in rehab, and picked it up when I landed the other day.'

'Oh,' she says, her eyes on the gift bag next to her.

'Open it,' I say, then sip my coffee. 'I know you're dying to.'

Without wasting another second, besides popping a piece of bacon in her mouth, she tosses the lavender tissue paper from the bag and pulls out the box. She reads the back, glancing at me with her brows pinched together. 'One for each of us?'

'Yeah,' I say, sitting my fork on my plate and taking the box from her. 'They're touch bracelets. You touch your charm, my bracelet vibrates, and vice versa. I, uh – well, confession time,' I say nervously. 'I know pretty much everything about you and Alex thanks to Bryce having a big mouth and being engaged to your sister, who also can't keep a secret. Since I didn't think you were exactly single, and you don't owe me a second chance, I figured when I came back to do this, us texting or calling each other wouldn't be something you could easily do without explaining yourself but I wanted to be available to you at all times so you know how serious I am about this.' I glance at her once I've got her bracelet out of the box and on her wrist.

'Now, keep in mind I'm not suggesting we have some secret relationship like before and you give Alex up just because I'm back. I thought maybe we could use these to ease back into being friends again. Disclaimer: this is *not* a booty-call bracelet, so all those dirty things you want to do to me, push them out of your head – for now – because I'm not here for the sex. I'm here to win back the love of my life.'

'You still think I'm the love of your life?'

'Always have. So, these are cool.' I touch the bracelet charm already on my arm. 'No one will know what they are, and if I'm thinking of you, I'll be able to silently tell you, no words needed.'

'Oh my God,' she says, glancing at her now buzzing bracelet, then looking at mine. 'That's the bracelet I harassed you about last night. You were already wearing yours?'

I nod. 'Truthfully, I was a tad afraid you wouldn't want to see me at all, so I was prepared to leave the gift with a note and hope you pressed the button when you were ready to talk.'

She smiles sweetly, touching the charm, so my bracelet vibrates. 'I love it, Will. Thank you.'

'You're welcome. I'm seriously here to prove how much I still love you however you need me to.'

'I know,' she says shyly. 'I just need some time.'

I lean into her, resting my hand on her back and kissing her temple. It's not awkward or weird. In fact, it feels pretty damn good to have her sitting next to me again.

'Where are you staying?' she asks after we eat silently for a few minutes.

'A hotel not far from here.'

'A hotel? Why?'

Her phone buzzes on the counter in front of her, and she frowns when she glances at it.

'Shoot,' she says to herself. 'I forgot about this.' She taps the screen, texting someone back, before setting it back down. 'Alex has a game this afternoon, and that's him, letting me know everything's set for Liv, Gunner and me to go. I already told him I'd be there. I'm sorry.'

I blow out a breath, dragging my hand through my hair.

You knew this wouldn't be easy, Will. She's got a life that no longer includes you. This was your doing, ass-face. Reassure her that her moving on was alright.

'No need to be sorry. I'm alright on my own. I need to look for a place to live, so I can do that.'

She nods, her gaze lingering.

'Anyway, the bracelet thing – tap that charm and no matter what I'm doing, I'm yours. Anytime you need or want me, you get my full attention. Alright?'

She flashes me an unsure smile. 'OK.'

25

BERKLEY

This morning, right when I'd planned to really let him have it (after remembering he was even there), he was playing the part of the perfect gentleman. A man I once knew. Being sweet and listening to me, not blaming contracts or his family for his past stupidity. I don't know how to feel about him right now but hate isn't on the list.

Gunner, Olivia and I are once again at Providence Park Stadium, just behind the barriers that separate the fans from the field. I've never been here when the place isn't overflowing with soccer fans, exactly as it is now.

'You OK?' Liv asks as she and Gunner return from buying food and drinks for the three of us.

Gunner let it slip that Alex has something planned. Something for me. I'm worried. Please don't let him publicly humiliate me on what feels like the most confusing day of my life.

'Yeah, just keep the stadium wieners far away from me because if they plaster my face on the jumbotrons like I suspect they're going to, *with* a wiener in my mouth, I will die,' I say dramatically, earning a roll of Gunner's eyes.

'Do you know what he's doing?' I ask him again, even though he's refusing to speak to me or even make eye contact.

He's upset I let Will stay the night and most certainly doesn't believe I didn't sleep with him. I'd be lying if I said I didn't wake up at about four in the morning and momentarily consider seducing him. But he was so sweet, holding me with both his arms around me, one leg thrown over mine like he never wanted to let me go. I've never felt so in the right place.

'Come on, Gun,' I beg. 'Give me a heads-up. I have enough to deal with right now. How embarrassed am I about to be?'

'Very,' he says, his mouth full. 'For the record, before I get blamed for this, I tried to stop him because I know you'll hate it, but after Willy's sudden arrival last night, Alex feels like he needs to impress you and discourage him.'

Oh, God. He wants to discourage Will? Then last night is clearly at the forefront of his mind. This can only be one thing, an attempt to one-up Will. We're in high school all over again.

'He's not proposing, is he?' That would be insane, but Alex is competitive. I start to panic internally, my breathing speeding towards full-on get-me-a-brown-paper-bag-before-I-die levels. He can't be. 'Olivia.' I turn to her. '*Please* tell me if that's it?'

She lifts her shoulders while the crowd erupts in cheers as the team run onto the field.

'HELLO, TIMBERS FANS!' The announcer's voice rumbles through the overhead speakers. 'We've got a special announcement from one of the players tonight. Please, help me welcome Alex Donovan to the field!'

'Oh, fuck,' I say in a sing-song voice as I stand up from my seat to watch him walk to center field.

'What's up, Timbers fans?!' Alex hollers into the mic, getting the crowd riled up with his energy, bouncing to their cheers. 'I want to call down my lady, Berkley Kaine, who turned twenty-five yesterday. She's officially a quarter of a century old! Where you at, baby?'

My heart stops in my chest when he calls me 'baby'. No. I'm frozen in place. He wants me to go *down* there? In front of everyone? Has he lost his ever-loving mind?

'Berx.' Liv pokes me. 'He wants you to go out there. You heard that part, right?'

'You guys – I can't—'

'*GO*,' Gunner yells, now shoving me gently towards Olivia.

I stumble past her, making my way down the stairs towards the barrier, which security helps me over. Slowly and painfully, with security at my side, I walk towards Alex. People cheer me on even though they don't know me. I feel like Drew Barrymore in that movie *Never Been Kissed*. I *hate* that movie. I suddenly wish I'd just seduced Will this morning and never showed up.

'Isn't she gorgeous?' Alex asks the crowd, encouraging them to applaud. 'Well done me,' he says, high-fiving himself.

When I finally reach him, he grabs my hand.

'I don't say this lightly because I'm not usually a man of public declarations or romance. I prefer to keep it more in the bedroom and off the television.'

Trust me, Alex, it's not even there. But how nice of him to direct a slam at Will first thing. And not even subtly.

'But,' he continues, waving at his teammates, who all have flowers in their hands, 'I just wanted to say happy birthday, Berx. You have stolen my heart, you little thief!' He laughs into the mic, the crowd laughing along. 'That is why I love you.' He drags the last three words out, saying them slowly and intently.

He *loves* me? No thank you. We aren't even officially dating anymore. He's not even looking at me. The words were directed at the crowd, the cameras. *Why* do I choose men obsessed with cameras? I glance back at where I was sitting, desperately trying to see if Olivia is seeing this. Duh, she obviously is, considering it's playing on every big screen around the stadium. People are watching this from their homes.

Hell. In. A. Handbasket.

I told Will where I'd be today. He's undoubtedly watching too. Watching me, the moment a man says he loves me and my response as of now is...

'Thank you?'

Alex looks confused but motions for his teammates to hand me the flowers. 'You guys know what to do.' He points the mic towards the crowd, who break into a rendition of 'Happy Birthday'.

As if having your family do this once a year isn't bad enough. Imagine having thousands of soccer fans do it. My face is bright red; I just know it. Every part of me is buzzing with humiliation. Being singled out, the center of attention, in front of a crowd or the public is my idea of a nightmare and I'm currently living it.

I take the flowers from the guys; security helps, taking most of them from me since I am obviously just one small woman with only two hands and an entire soccer match to sit through after this.

'I did this for you, babe,' Alex says proudly, his hand on my back.

No, Alex. This was *not* for me. This was for your ego. How dumb does he think I am?

'I just, uh – I...' I swallow the lump in my throat, preventing words. 'I'm not good at crowds, but I love it.' I lie. I'd also love to murder him right now. But too many witnesses.

I like Alex. Over the last year he's become less douchey than I previously thought but I *don't* love him. I gotta give him something, though. I've got no more words so I flash him a smile, and before I know it, without warning, he's kissing me, with tongue, in front of thousands of people, now roaring as he dips me back, embarrassing the fuck out of me.

I didn't see this getting worse than it was, but here we are. How in the hell did I end up in this mess? I don't like cameras. I hate public displays of affection. Yet here I am, mid-field with a professional soccer player proclaiming his love for me, while I die a little more inside by the second. Without even thinking about it, I touch the charm on the bracelet Will gave me.

Minutes (that felt like hours) later, I'm back at the stadium seating, whisked off the field by security so the match can begin. I'm stunned silent. Two handfuls of loose flower stems, and the knowledge that a man just said he loves me on live television and I said 'thank you' float through my head like spider-webs. Sticky, icky and not easy to forget.

'That was hard to watch,' Olivia says as I walk the last few stairs to my seat. 'Like seriously, I was cringing for you.'

'You said "*thank you*"?' Gunner asks, clearly disappointed in me.

'Yep. "Thank you". I said "thank you" but I meant "*no* thank you".'

'Once more, the Timbers wish Berkley a happy birthday!' the announcer says, bringing a camera back to me, my face once again flashing on the screens around the stadium.

I plaster on an uncomfortable smile. *Do not cry, Berkley. This isn't the worst moment of your life. It just feels like it is.*

'*What* are you going to do?' Olivia asks through a clenched jaw, ventriloquist style, a conversation tactic we've used many times in the past.

'I don't know, Liv. There isn't a word big enough for how humiliating that wa—'

Right then, my bracelet buzzes on my wrist three times. Three times. When Will and I were teenagers, as he'd pull away from my house, he'd tap his brakes three times for 'I love you'.

My phone dings in my pocket with an incoming text. I pull it out. *Will Adler*. I unblocked him this morning after he left because it felt like the right thing to do after he was so lovely last night. Suddenly, I have never been so glad he exists.

If you need me, I'm outside the stadium gates.

He came down here? Which means he saw it. He saw it, and he knew.

'I gotta go,' I say, grabbing my things and running up the stairs towards the exit.

'Where are you...' Olivia calls after me, her voice fading as I run through the stadium away from her.

I step out onto the sidewalk, spotting him standing across the street almost immediately. I look both ways, so I'm not smeared by a bus because my luck's clearly not great today, then run across the road, stopping in front of him.

'My hotel is three blocks from here. I watched the whole thing on TV. After I got your buzz, I ran,' he says through heavy breaths, obviously having run.

'You *ran* to get here?'

He nods. 'Are you alright?'

My God. He sprinted to get to me when he knew I wasn't OK. That is probably the absolute nicest thing he's ever done for me. I slide my arms around his sides to his back and press my face into his shoulder. He seems almost surprised by this but doesn't hesitate to hold me close.

'Thank you,' I say, desperately trying not to cry. Only this time I mean it and I'm unsure what I'm crying over. The fact that Will finally stood up and fought for me? Or am I overly embarrassed by what just happened? Maybe both?

'Why would he do that? How doesn't he know me at all? Why am I so terrible at relationships?' I rattle off the questions I know he has no answers for. 'I *don't* love him,' I say, under my breath, unsure

I want Will to hear the words but needing to say them to someone. 'I could never fall in love with him because I can't ever *un*love you.'

'I know,' he says, matching my tone, holding me tightly. 'Why do you think I'm standing here right now?'

How can he somehow make me feel like everything will be alright when I'm in this position at all *because* of him? I should be getting the opposite feeling from him.

'Why are you doing all this? Rehab? Singing? Staying the night and never trying to seduce me? Making me breakfast? Buying me gifts? Running three blocks to save me?'

He steps away from me, a shy smile on his face. 'Because you're still my one, Berkley. I'll do anything to get back what we had.'

My heart slows as he says the words I'm sure he said last night, but tequila was making everything seem way less serious than it probably was. It *feels* serious now. Droplets of water hit my bare shoulders. It's nearly eighty degrees today and now it's going to pour down in a summer shower.

Will looks up, raindrops splattering on the lenses of his glasses. He raises a hand over his face. 'Can we hit pause on this?' he asks. 'I'm staying at Hotel Deluxe; it's fancy. Want to come over before we get soaked?' One flash of his smile and I can't say no.

'Yeah.'

He extends his hand. 'I don't *expect* anything, just trying to help you escape an embarrassing situation and get us out of the rain.'

I take his hand shyly, like it's the first time I've ever held it. 'Why are you staying in a hotel?' I meant to ask him this earlier but Alex texting me interrupted.

'For three months, I've been in what you would call a "rich boy" rehab center in California. I had no place to go when I got back, and I didn't want to just assume you'd want me back.'

'What about your parents' place?'

'That's no longer an option.'

'Why?'

'I don't need them anymore so I gave it all up.' He glances over at me. 'For us.'

'*All?*'

He nods.

'Prince Willy!' someone across the street yells and instinctively he lifts a single fist into the air, rolling his eyes.

'That's not going away anytime soon, and I'm sorry.'

26

WILL

We're back at my hotel. Berkley is on her phone, explaining why she ran out to Olivia, who's not taking it lightly from the way it sounds, when my phone rings.

Lloyd. Shit. I forgot about this.

'Hey, Lloyd. How'd it go?' I walk from the suite's sitting room into the bedroom.

'You *might* want to sit down,' he suggests.

'Bad?'

'Three point two million dollars.'

I choke out a heaving breath, dropping onto the bed next to me. 'Three point two *million*? They pushed it that high?'

That's the most I'll have paid for one singular thing, ever. I'd have paid anything to keep Berkley from my parents' wrath. I just don't want her to feel like I'm buying *her*. Especially since one of the reasons she went out with me to begin with was with the promise that I wouldn't treat her like she was incapable of taking care of herself and pay her way through life.

'Paperwork is being drawn up as we speak. How do you want to break the news to Berkley? Either you tell her first, or Frank announces it to her unexpectedly, and considering he just made bank, I don't doubt he'll make that announcement soon.'

I drop my head into my hand. 'She's going to be pissed both ways. When she finds out *I* bought her beloved bookstore *without* telling her after she's insisted all these years that she make her own way in life...'

'Well,' Lloyd says. 'It was nice knowing ya.'

I laugh nervously. 'You'll come visit my grave?'

'Probably after they find your body.' He laughs. 'Should we reconsider Berkley being the beneficiary on literally everything you have before you do this?'

'No,' I say without hesitation. 'What's mine is hers. I want to keep all that intact. Thanks, Lloyd.' I hang up, sitting on the bed for a few minutes.

How the hell do I tell her this? Tear it off like a Band-Aid? I could bookend it in 'I love you's and hope she'll only hear those. Or maybe I should take good old Calvin Klein's advice and strip naked to distract her. *Just say it, Will. Honestly. Blurt it out and deal with the consequences.* I walk back into the sitting room – fully clothed – and find her on the edge of the couch, casually watching the Timbers game still playing on my screen.

'I bought To Be Read, Berkley.'

'*What?*' Her head snaps my way, and she drops her phone into her lap. '*Why?* How – *how* do you even know about the store being up for sale? I just found out myself!'

I sit down next to her, resting my hand on her back. 'I didn't know, until yesterday. As soon as I was back, my parents requested my presence. They're pissed about how I ended things with the show and dumped Danika. I refused a new contract, I won't reconsider, so the network is close to canceling us altogether. They were once again up my ass, so I made some threats.'

She scrunches her face like she's disappointed in me.

'I know, baby, that's not usually like me, but I've learned how to play their game. Unfortunately, they hit back by threatening to buy the store and shut you down.'

She gasps, her entire face dropping.

'You're my kryptonite, Berkley. They *know* that. I'm sorry.' I lean into her. 'They didn't win. It's taken a couple days, but I just found out I won the bidding war.'

'It was a war?'

I nod repeatedly, the amount with every single zero included floating through my head like a NASDAQ ticker. 'A war that cost over three million dollars.'

She drops her head into her hands. '*William Alexander Adler.*' The way she says my full name says she's not thrilled, but the fact that it wasn't followed by swearing is a good sign.

'I know, I promised I wouldn't get involved in your finances a long time ago, but I couldn't let them steal your dream. That store is your life. *It's your home.*'

She looks over at me, her expression slack, her voice flat. 'I wanted to do this myself. Now I really am just the sugar baby everyone says I am.' She says the words with a heavy sigh.

'Who says you're a sugar baby?'

'Uh, the tabloids. I've dated two wealthy, influential men now and they make me seem like I'm some gold-digging, wallet-humping bimbo.'

'Berx, the tabloids make me seem like a douchey arrogant yet somehow charming fuckboy who isn't completely in love with his ex. You're *not* my sugar baby.'

She sighs heavily. 'The building and the business combined aren't worth three million dollars. I don't want you wasting money on me like this. Had I lost the store, I'd have figured out something else,' I lie. I was worried about exactly this.

'You are worth so much more than I could ever spend. You have to know that? I'd have spent everything to make your dreams come true. Call and ask Lloyd; I *said* that. Spend it all if you have to. But only the money was mine, Berx. This is *your* deal. I bought the building, not the business you've poured your soul into. Nothing's changed, and everything is going in your name.'

'Great!' she snaps. 'Now I feel like I owe you three million bucks, and that'll take me forever to pay off.'

'I'll never accept that and you know it. You owe me exactly nothing so stop that kind of talk now. If you want both our names on everything, so you don't feel like you owe me anything, I'm happy to do that. This isn't a loan. It's an investment. I'm investing in *you*, Berx. This was *our* dream. To do life together. Remember? We designed your apartment and you've turned it into the only place that's ever felt like home for me. I still want that life together. Whatever you want to do, I'll do with you. Wherever you are, I want to be. I may have gotten lost in myself for a while, but I'm back, and I'm ready to help you with the store.'

'Don't do that.' She crosses her arms over her chest.

'Don't do what?'

'Pretend like you're sticking around to "help me". Besides the time you insisted you put in a security system, you've never stuck around or helped with the store. You've always been too busy helping yourself. It's been twenty-four hours of you being back; how am I to know if that'll last?'

Ouch. I mean, she's not wrong but the words still sting a bit.

'I made every wrong decision before. But I swear it, I'm in this now. I'm here because my heart won't let me stay away, Berkley. Go on a date with me and let me prove it?'

'Go on a date with you?' she asks. 'Are you totally dicked in the head? I'm sitting here right now because I needed to escape and—' She stops talking, furrowing her brow. 'Damn it, Adler. How am I supposed to date you with this guy waiting in the wings to one-up you at every turn?' She motions to the TV screen, where Alex kicks the ball into the fucking goal like it was scripted to fit this exact moment.

'Ugh,' I groan, running a hand through my hair. 'You think that's what that was earlier? One-upping me?'

'Was that not your guys' "game" in high school? Without a doubt, this was him getting back at you for last night. He told Gunner he wanted to impress me and discourage you. Alex is very... *well*, he wants to be the most important person in every area of his life. I apparently am drawn to arrogance.'

I laugh to myself. 'Your *only* flaw.'

She rests her hand on my thigh hesitantly. 'I thought Alex and I would go on a date or two. I never expected it to turn into all this but I was lonely and he sometimes made me smile.'

I frown, mostly disappointed in myself. 'Don't be sorry; I totally deserve it. I just never wanted to lose you to that twat.'

'You think you've *lost*? Need I remind you that *you* are the one who came home with me on my birthday and took care of drunk me. Alex didn't even call or text to check on me after leaving the bar without saying goodbye and he was my ride.'

'If you don't love him, why not dump him?'

'Technically Alex and I aren't "dating" anymore, so I didn't think a dumping was necessary. But how would I do that now anyway? "Oh hey, Alex, you've been cool enough but since my ex – the new and improved version – who fucked me over for years is suddenly back after breaking my heart repeatedly, I think I want to run back to him like I'm being chased by a serial killer, hand him what's left of my heart and hope he doesn't obliterate it until I have zero capability of ever loving anyone again."' She cocks her head, lifting her eyebrows as she waits for my response.

I grimace. 'I wouldn't use those *exact* words,' I say with a guilty grin. 'But you're right; I get it. That probably won't go over well, knowing Alex. And if he hurts you, I'll have to kill him, and then I'll end up in jail, and we'll have to start this all over in thirty to fifty years.'

She rolls her eyes playfully, crossing her arms over her chest.

'For the record, I'm not here to obliterate your heart, Berx. I have all the pieces I took and I'd like to put it back together. Then once we're no longer just a couple of broken hearts, maybe we can trade again? I'll take care of yours, and you can take care of mine. Like we used to. Only, I *promise* to better this time.'

The look on her face as she stares at me. Her lips parted, her eyes fill with... hope? She sinks further into my side. 'That's possibly the sweetest thing you've ever said to me. But I'm gonna need you to prove it.'

'Is this you giving me permission to go all out and try to win you back?'

'Yep. *Go all out.* Do whatever it takes. Prove *I'm* the woman you want to spend your life with. Your *entire* life, William. Not just a few weeks or months until the next big break comes for you. Choose me first; just don't do it mid-soccer field, with cameras or a side dose of public humiliation.' She stands from the couch.

'Duh,' I say like I'm not a complete idiot. 'I know you better than that. I know you so well, I sprinted three blocks to get to you in a moment I knew you were mortified just to comfort you. You think that was the action of a guy who's going to disappear in a few weeks?'

'You should have done this years ago.'

I stand from the couch, taking the few steps to her, stopping right in front of her. Nervously, I reach up and rest my hand on the side of her neck like I used to, brushing my thumb across her cheek.

'You're right. I regret that I didn't every day since.'

She stares into my eyes, finally letting out a sigh. 'Against my better judgment, which is finally back after I attempted to drown it last night, you've got two weeks. I'm done if I don't see what I need to see. I can't waste any more of my time on you if you're not serious.'

'I promise, Berx, I don't even need that long.' I press my lips to her forehead. She leans into it, resting a free hand on my forearm.

'Gawd, this is gonna hurt if you screw up again,' she says nervously. 'I should go. I promised Olivia I'd come back, and I need to deal with Alex.'

I don't love the idea of her doing anything with Alex, but by 'deal', I hope to God she means 'dump'.

27

BERKLEY

PDX ROYALS – DOUBLE STORY ALERT!

First up, home from rehab? Is that where Willy's been all this time? According to his brother, that's exactly where he was. Mikey didn't seem all that thrilled with his choice but we say, good for you, Willy! We hated watching you destroy yourself in recent years. Hopefully now he can find whatever happiness he's been searching for.

Mikey also told us that all is not well in Adler-land. As soon as he arrived home, he was at his parents' place requesting to be expelled from the family and all that goes with that – trust fund included. Knowing what we know about his family, I'd bet that didn't go over very well. What's his plan now? We don't know, but we'll keep digging until we find out.

LOVE TRIANGLE?

Berkley Kaine (current girlfriend of Portland Timbers star Alex Donovan) and her twin sister, Bianca (fiancée of Willy's best friend, Bryce Turner), turned twenty-five recently! The two aren't 'official' Royals, but these gorgeous girls graced our screens a few times. They are the definition of sugar and spice, fraternal twin sisters who seem to have each other's back through anything.

They were all spotted at Sing! recently as they celebrated, and to our surprise, Willy made an appearance. We don't want to swoon too hard, but be still our beating heart! This video of him serenading Berkley at her birthday party is possibly one of the most adorable things we've ever seen.

According to the woman who sent this video, Alex was present but stormed out of the bar moments before she captured this. Did Willy and he have an altercation over the woman tying them together? Will's been back mere days, and the drama is already following him. The show may be over, but our obsession with this group is not. Time will tell, Royals fans.

For now, the remaining season of the show airs on E! every Sunday at 9:00 p.m. PST.

* * *

'We're having this conversation because Will's back?' Alex asks frustratedly, his eyes on my TV as he watches highlights of the game he just played in.

That was his only requirement of us 'talking and not fucking' (his words, and our usual after-game routine) – that he watches his highlights. Honestly, I'm a little surprised he doesn't want to do this *while* we fuck. Maybe then he'd be better at it since he seems more in love with himself than me?

'No. Until last night, I had no idea Will was coming back at all. It's just a weird coincidence.'

'What was that in the bathroom then? You two seemed pretty chummy, if you ask me.'

'That was literally him noticing his two choices were either I barf *on* him, or he could rush me to the bathroom, so I didn't totally humiliate both of us. After I yakked up everything from the many shots of tequila to the gum I swallowed seven years ago, I drunkenly fell into him and couldn't move.'

He grunts a disbelieving laugh. 'He was being a decent human for once?'

Isn't that the pot calling the kettle black?

'Will's *not* a bad guy. He's just a terrible decision-maker,' I say to Alex, pleading a little too hard and earning a side-eyed glare from him.

Bianca was right. End. This. For. Good. Berkley. You two don't click. He's sort of a douche. He's terrible in bed. And you don't owe him anything. Just say the words. I don't love you. You embarrassed the hell out of me. Go home. Watch some instructional videos on the art of the orgasm then call someone else.

How in the hell do I say this without making it seem precisely like he suspects?

He lounges on my couch, eyes on the TV when the security pad by my front door starts beeping. Saved by the pizza delivery guy.

'I'll just go grab that,' I say, half running down the stairs to the side door of the building. I yank it open and freeze.

Fiddle. Dicks.

'Melinda?' I act like I'm not sure it's her, eyes wide. Why is *she* here? I haven't seen this woman face to face since she tried to pay me to leave her son.

'I need to speak to William,' she snaps, hardly making eye contact with me.

'He uh, doesn't live here?'

She laughs, but not because she thinks I'm funny; that part is clear. 'Tell him his mother is here.'

'I'm serious; Will's not here.'

'You haven't seen him?'

'I've *seen* him, but he's not here currently.'

'We need to find him, and he's not answering our calls. So do whatever it is that you do to get him here.'

'*We?*' I ask, suddenly noticing Mike and Jacob exiting Mike's fancy, blacked-out-windows-so-dark-I can't-see-through-them SUV.

I stand against the open side door, completely confused. 'Why are you *all* here?' As I say the words, I'm frantically pressing the bracelet charm, pulling my phone from my pocket and calling him as quickly as I can.

'What's wrong?' he answers, worry in his voice.

'I've got a bit of a problem at the shop.'

'What?' I hear shuffling on his end. 'I can be there in five minutes. Are you alright? Is it Alex? Did he hurt you? Berx. Talk to me; *what's wrong?*' He's starting to panic.

'I'm not sure?' I ask as a question, my voice raising with each word. 'Your family is here. At the store. After hours. All of them. Either I'm about to go missing, or they're here to burn the place down.'

'*What?*' he barks into the phone, his voice raised so loud Mike hears him and snatches the phone from my hand.

'Get here and she'll leave unscathed, pretty boy,' he says with a douchey laugh, ending the call and handing my phone back to me. 'There ya go.' He flashes me a soulless grin as he walks past me into my store like he was invited. 'I know he'll never quit you, so if he's really not here, he will be soon.'

Truthfully, I'm a little worried about what's happening. I don't think I can handle these people alone without accidentally committing a crime. I pull up Alex's contact. It rings once. Twice.

Thrice. *Fuck*, Alex. He finally answers midway through the fourth ring.

'Babe, I'm sort of in the middle of something. Just tell me whatever it is up here.'

'I need you down here. I think I'm being kidnapped? Or murdered? Maybe burned at the stake? I dunno.'

'What?' He chokes out a laugh. 'By a Domino's delivery guy? Just take the pizza and close the door.'

'*Alex!*' I hiss. 'How much of an idiot do you think I am?' I yell it in a loud whisper, turning away from the Adlers now meandering through my bookstore like they belong here. 'I need your help so if you could hit pause on fangirling yourself on TV and get down here, that'd be great.'

He groans, clearly not thrilled. 'Might I remind you that you yelled at me last night in front of a room full of people that you don't need to be saved?'

'Oh, my God. *That* hurt your ego? Jesus, Alex. You're so fragile. *Just get down here, please.*' I hang up on him, shoving my phone into my pocket and turning back towards my uninvited guests.

'I thought you said he wasn't here?' Melinda asks, turning to look at me.

'*He's* not.'

After seconds that feel like hours, Alex rounds the corner into the hallway from my office, stopping in his tracks.

'Who is—?' He looks around before dropping his head. 'Fucking Adlers. Man, you just can *not* leave these people alone, can you?'

Like I invited them.

'So, William *has* been here,' Melinda says with a smirk, picking up on Alex's words.

'Alex Donovan,' Mike says with a grin. 'Dude, you were fucking stellar today. I mean, besides falling for this hot mess.' He throws a thumb my way before lifting a hand that Alex actually high-fives. 'She must be a real vagician to have both you and Willy after her, eh?'

Vagician?! '*Mike!*' I groan.

But Alex is laughing. 'Vagician. I like that.' He doesn't stand up for me. Doesn't ask Mike not to badmouth me. Just high-fives him.

How did I not see this before? *I'm casually dating a Mike.* How the fuck did I let *that* happen?

I'm still standing in the doorway when I hear tires screeching around the corner a block up, *Tokyo Drift* style. A little overly dramatic, but I'll give him a couple points for effort. Will flies to the bookstore, skidding to a stop at the curb, throwing his new fancy-schmancy SUV into park, and jumping from the driver's seat. I look like I'm hosting a secret service dinner party with these blacked-out SUVs parked along the curb.

'Are you alright?' he asks, his hands on my shoulders as he looks me over when he suddenly notices them in my store over my shoulder. 'Why are you here?' He practically growls the words at them, charging their way.

Jeesh. I know he mentioned them pulling some triggers against one another but damn, he's pissed to even see their ugly mugs.

'Damn it,' he groans, stopping in his tracks when he spots Alex, a hand now in his hair as he turns towards me, his face scrunched.

Sorry, I mouth, his face softening a little.

Alex throws out his arms. 'Little Willy finally shows,' he says. 'Tell ya the truth, I'm a little tired of seeing you. Why don't you go take a long walk off a short pier?'

'We're doing insults?' Will asks like he's excited about it. 'Perfect. You, my

"friend", are about as useful as a lighthouse in a desert, bright but not needed.'

'Pfft,' Alex says. 'Don't act like *I'm* the unwanted guest here. Why don't take your assholes back home and follow them there.'

'She *just* called me and asked me to cover over, *dickweed*, so do not—' Will says, taking a step in Alex's direction.

'*Or what?*' Alex bolsters.

'*Or* I'll kick you *all* out,' I answer for both of them, stopping them in their tracks, taking the pizza from the guy now standing at my open door.

'Fine,' Alex says, irritation in his voice. 'Looks like little Willy's here to save you again so I'm going back upstairs.'

I told him I thought I was being kidnapped, and this is his response? Sure, I was exaggerating and didn't expect Will to get here so quickly but damn, Alex. For a guy who just proclaimed his love for me to the entire city, what a mighty protector of me you are.

'Work this shit out, Berx. Get rid of 'em. *All* of them,' Alex demands, grabbing the pizza box from my hands, shaking his head as if he's sincerely disappointed in me as he turns to go back to my apartment like he owns the place.

When I'm at his place, I'm so uncomfortable it hurts, yet at mine, he's got no problem stripping to his underwear, lounging on my couch and telling me who's allowed and who's not. We aren't close enough for that.

'No!' I yell at Alex, following him into my office and up the stairs behind him. 'You don't get to be this casual in my apartment. We aren't even dating anymore.'

'What are you talking about? I just told you I loved you.'

Ugh. Right. I should deal with that right now. 'I know I've avoided this conversation so far tonight but what you did today embarrassed the hell out of me.'

'*Why?*' He looks back at me, legit confused. 'Do you have any idea how many women would love to be in your spot? It was totally romantic.'

'It was, for a girl who likes that kind of attention. I don't. Why do you think Will and I never worked out?'

'Because he's a drunk and a big fat liar?' He chortles.

'*Because* I didn't want to be some reality star. I didn't want the whole world to know me and judge my every move. You did that to me tonight. Tomorrow I'll be in every tabloid and I hate it.'

'How would I know you didn't like public attention? I assumed you did, considering you date some pretty well-known dudes,' he says, opening the pizza box and grabbing a slice.

'You say that like I sought you both out for that reason alone. How can you pretend like there was no other way to know how to say those words for the first time?' I ask, my voice now raised. 'We've dated off and on for a year now – admittedly it's not been a direct flight to relationship bliss – but that's a long time, Alex, and you don't even know the basics of me!'

'I do, too!' he says defensively.

'What's my favorite color?'

He lifts a shoulder, glancing around the room. 'Pink.'

'Wrong,' I snap. 'My middle name is?'

He lifts a hand, palm up, clearly taking a shot into the wind. '*Marie?*'

'Wrong again, Alexander *Walter* Donovan. What section of the store is my specialty?'

'The whole store is your specialty, sweets. You're the manager.'

I roll my eyes so hard it physically pains me. 'Wrong. How old was I when I had my first kiss?'

'Pass. Will's territory.'

'Pass? What, because you weren't first on ride Berkley? I wasn't your first kiss, and yet I'm not jealous of the twelve-year-old girl named Sandy who was. Or the girl who gave you your first taste of tongue, Jasmine, who did indeed resemble the Disney Princess, at summer camp when you were thirteen.'

He crosses his arms over his chest, a piece of pizza in one hand as he listens.

'I know you lost your virginity at seventeen to Alisha Pennington in the back of her Honda at a kegger in the woods, but you lied and told your friends it was when you were fifteen with McKenzie Tipton after homecoming. If I remember right, McKenzie said no to your advances, so you mouthed off to your friends later that she "gave you her flower". To, ya know, "teach her a lesson".'

I actually heard this story via Bryce and Bianca but didn't want to believe it was true because it's just too awful and Alex does have a sweet side. It rarely surfaces but I know him well enough to have seen it a time or two. I gave him the benefit of the doubt thinking maybe he'd grown up. I am officially an idiot.

'Do you have any idea what that kind of lie can do to a high-school girl? God, that alone should have been a giant red flag and yet I gave you another chance.' I say that last part to myself, a hand now on my forehead out of frustration.

'What are you talking about, red flags?'

'You get a red card on-field, you're suspended for the next game, right?'

He nods.

'A red *flag* is what should have led to your suspension with me a long-ass time ago, but I needed a distraction from my life and was hopeful that God wouldn't fuck me over by bringing me two beautiful idiots.'

I don't even *like* soccer and I've learned about it for this moron.

'Now I'm an idiot?'

'You're absolutely clueless, Alex.'

'That's ridiculous,' he says, propping his feet back on my coffee table. 'Clueless about what exactly?'

'Uh, *me!*' I let out a long sigh. 'I know technically we aren't together but I think we should break up. For good this time. I'm sorry. Trust me when I say you're not the complete problem here. It's mostly me. I just can't do this anymore.'

'Well, you and the asshole downstairs.' Alex stands from my couch, slowly getting dressed. 'I don't understand why you can't let that clown go. You realize you're just his backup ass, right? He shows up here whenever someone better isn't available. He's been using you for sex for a decade, and you've been using him for money.'

Using him for money? 'Excuse me!?'

If only I could shoot fire from my eyeballs, Alex would be a pile of ash on my hardwood floors.

'That's the rumor around town.'

'The *rumor*? What are we, fifteen?' Ugh! The balls on this guy. 'Firstly, that's not true. Secondly, I'm not about to discuss my financial life with you.'

'All I'm saying is that if it *is* true, that kind of makes you a high-profile prostitute. He's buying you!'

I clench my jaw so hard I'm afraid I might break a tooth. A high-profile prostitute? Is he serious right now?

'It's not about money with Will and me. *I. Love. Him!*' When the words leave my lips without being in the past tense, I stop breathing. Holy fuck. I did *not* just say that.

Alex catches it immediately, now moving quickly to get the hell out of my place, slipping on his shoes. He grabs the pizza box as he heads for my still-open front door.

'Sounds like you've made your choice here. Good luck with that. He'll be here for a few weeks, and then he'll skip into the sunset with someone far more influential than you. That's how it always goes with you two.'

In Will's defense, he's never done that. Looking back, Will's fought for us for a long time. Alex is repeating old tabloid headlines. Even though he's tried, Will's never 'fallen' for someone else. Just like I haven't. We even confirmed it with one another just this morning.

Alex jogs down my stairs, me right behind him.

'I guess thanks for the ass?' he says with a laugh, turning to look over his shoulder at me as we walk through my office. 'I can see why he keeps coming back.'

'Don't be a dick.'

'What? I didn't say you're bad at it. You're not, trust me.' He laughs under his breath. Finally, he stops walking and turns towards me, his face softening a bit. 'Truth is, I went out with you for two reasons. Number one, you're hot as fuck.' His eyes dart over me with a smile that says he'll be sad to let me go for this reason alone.

'I don't regret that. Number two, Will stole my girlfriend when we were fourteen, so when I found how his lady was hot for me, I jumped all in.' He says it casually, lifting a single shoulder.

'What?' I ask, confused. 'Did you forget we went to school together and I know the stories. He didn't steal your girlfriend and even if he did it was over a decade ago. Why would you still be holding a grudge?'

He shrugs. 'Paybacks are a bitch.'

'You actually went out with me to have sex with me and get back at Will?' I mean, I know I've pretty much done the same thing but how did I have no idea about his reasoning?

He nods proudly. 'You're totally worth it. Top three for me. And I've slept with a lot of women.'

I burst out a laugh, the two of us now stopping in front of the bookstore entrance.

'Why's that funny?'

'Well,' I say calmly. 'It's funny because you think I'm insecure about my skills in the bedroom. Like being in Alex Donovan's top

three lays is some kind of medal I should wear with pride. I've literally only slept with two people and you're not even in the top three.
A little advice: you could use some lessons.'

'*Me?*' He balks like it's not possible.

'How has no one told you this before?' I ask myself. 'There's no
easy way to say this, so I'm just going to tear off the Band-Aid so to
speak. The clitoris is the gatekeeper of the orgasm. It's that tiny
button at the front of the vagina. *I hope you find it one day!*'

He pulls his head back like I've deeply offended him. '*What* are
you even talking about? You loved it. I was there, *remember*?'

'Oh, I remember,' I say with a judgmental laugh. 'But not the
way you do. I faked *all* those orgasms. That one, and that one, oh
and that one over there too!' I point around the hallway like
orgasms are raining down around us. Not that he'd ever notice. 'You
might be a natural at kicking a ball, but the art of the orgasm has
evaded you!'

'Shut up.' He groans, turning towards the store side exit.

'Want me to prove it?'

An irritated laugh leaves his lips as he turns back towards me.
'How are you going to prove that?'

I clear my throat, ready to put on a show of a lifetime.

'Oh, Alex. Yeah, baby. Right there.' I moan his name, getting a
little bit louder with every word. 'Oh, God. Fuck, yeah. Keep going.
That's it. Don't stop. Harder, Alex, harder.'

His eyes widen, and his jaw drops a little further with each cry
of fake ecstasy.

'Yes. Yes. Fuck, yes, Alex! Holy hell, that's it, babe. Don't stop. Oh
my God. Yes! Yes! Yes! YES!' I yell and dramatically go on just like I
do when I'm lying underneath him, even the out-of-breath part.

'*Are. You. Fucking. Kidding. Me!?*' He says the words so slowly I
wonder if he'll ever finish his sentence.

The shock on his face feels good. I think I've just changed this guy's life. Or at least inspired him to do a little research, so the next woman he touches doesn't walk away wondering how God keeps screwing up these overly beautiful men.

'Say one word about me to any tabloid, and the whole world finds out,' I say, walking his way, shoving him out the door and grabbing the pizza box from his hands before he can object. 'Bye, Alex.'

The door slams shut behind him and I turn to go back to my apartment, but the sound of clapping stops me in my tracks. I glance into the semi-dark bookstore and see Mike giving me a standing ovation. My heart seizes in my chest.

'I forgot you people were here.' I drop my head. Mortification activated. Come on, sinkhole. Just swallow the whole damn store, would ya?

28

WILL

'What are you people doing here?' I ask my family, whose heads are all turned to hear Berkley and Alex fighting as they walk away.

'Marcus is in some trouble,' Dad says.

Marcus is their financial adviser.

'What does that have to do with me or Berkley?'

'He's been arrested, and raided, then the IRS showed up at the house this afternoon. They're seizing everything. Our cars, the house and everything inside, our vacation homes, our bank accounts...' Mom says, her voice quivering with emotion as she speaks.

The IRS is seizing their shit? I want to say I'm surprised but this feels a little more karma than 'oh no'. My parents are the royalty of fucking over everyone around them. I just fought to practically financial death to buy this bookstore that they wanted just to screw me over. Their son. Finally someone is taking revenge and it's the one organization that has the power to do so.

'If Marcus is to blame, why are they seizing your things?'

'Because it's not entirely Marcus's fault,' Dad says, pointing to Mom without her noticing because she and Mike are now fully invested in the yelling echoing through the building from upstairs.

'Did you two do this?' Dad snaps.

'Us two?' I ask, confused, as I glance at Mike.

'You and *Berkley*? Did you tip them off?'

I laugh. 'Pretty sure it takes more than a phone call to the IRS to get to this level of fuckery. How would I know anything about your finances, anyway? And *how* is it Mom's fault? You got some Ponzi scheme in the works?'

She looks guilty as fuck, refusing to make eye contact and glaring at my dad.

'Are you *kidding* me?' I ask at her lack of response.

'It's not about money with Will and me. *I. Love. Him!*' Berkley's voice is loud and clear.

My heart slows to a near stop. She loves me? God, I was terrified this would all go the opposite direction and now that it's not, I'm nervous. There are a lot of emotions swirling inside me right now and the part I feel I need to focus on is holding her own. I know for a fact she doesn't want me to save her from this. I glance back at my family and all eyes are on me. They're hearing the same things I am. But no way am I discussing any of it with them.

'Am I harboring fugitives with you three here?'

'I'm Melinda Adler,' Mom reminds me. 'Adlers do not go to jail. We pay off lawyers just like every other millionaire does.'

'Well.' Mike laughs. 'Unless you're Will. He's been to jail, haven't ya, baby bro?'

I nod, confirming it. 'Difference is, I didn't pay off my lawyers to get out. I paid up because I was an idiot and took my punishment like a fucking man. Something the three of you'd know nothing about.'

It was all over the tabloids for months. One of the rumors after I disappeared to rehab was that I'd been sent to prison for murder because the guy I assaulted (or who assaulted me) died. He didn't. I know because he sued the fuck out of me. Another was that I was running because I'd ruined my reputation. Only partially true. I care about what exactly one person thinks of me.

'I can *not* go to jail, William. You pee in public. It's like a zoo, only worse.' Mom's gripping my shirt like I have any control over this situation.

'Pretty sure worse things than peeing in public happen in prison.'

Suddenly both Alex and Berkley storm down the stairs, their voices getting louder by the second. Every word out of his mouth is obviously meant to hurt her and I want to step in, but she's giving it right back and making me proud.

All of us go silent as she and Alex stand in front of the open entrance to the bookstore. The four of us are in the reading area in the dark, probably just out of her sight. When she yells at him for not knowing what a clitoris is, we all gasp. Those are words a man never forgets.

When he challenges her to prove she's faked every orgasm, I laugh under my breath. Until I notice the look on her face. Oh, shit. No she's not... yep, she is. I drop my head into my hands, wishing I wasn't hearing it.

Mike is all smiles and even my mom has a smirk on her face as Berkley demonstrates that she's been faking things for their entire relationship. Ouch.

After it's over, Alex is stunned silent, then she kicks his ass out and, like an idiot, Mike stands, clapping his hands and whistling obnoxiously.

She glances in at us, shock on her face. 'I forgot you people were here.'

'That was beautiful. Absolute perfection. Until now I wasn't your biggest fan but damn, girl, that deserves an award.'

She's so frustrated she storms off towards her apartment. I punch Mike for her on my way past him to follow her. 'I'm here for *her* so you three are going to have to patiently wait while I make sure she's alright.'

'My God,' Dad says with a groan. 'What is it with him and this girl?'

Asshole. I want to storm back to him and punch him for being such an insensitive twat but Berkley is more important right now. I half jog up her stairs, knocking lightly on her door before opening it. Never in a million years did I think I'd walk into them having a relationship that was already near crumbling before I even made a move. I mean, thank God, maybe my timing isn't as off as I'd feared.

'Berx?' She's face down on her couch, sobbing into a pillow.

'Why are men such ass-faces?' she mumbles through tears.

I sit on her coffee table near her. 'Must be a part of our DNA?' I joke. 'Honestly, I don't know.'

'All I want is someone who puts me first as a human, not as a piece of ass they want to keep around. Is that too much to ask?' She turns her head, looking at me with tears still streaming down her face.

'No, it's not too much to ask. You deserve that and more.'

'Am I just your backup ass? The girl who will never quite be enough? Is that why you've always kept me around? I mean, he said—'

'I know what he said,' I interrupt her. 'I heard every word. Not one of them was true, either. Alex was mad. You were dumping him, kind of, in front of the competition and we both know he *has* to win. Not to mention your words were things that I don't doubt shattered the guy's ego. He'd have said anything that hurt you. You've *always* been enough. More than I deserve, truthfully.'

She forces a sad smile, wiping her eyes and sitting up, crossing her legs beneath her. 'This has been the most confusing twenty-four hours of my life.'

'Want to know what I think?'

She shrugs.

'I'm pretty sure you just won that fight,' I say with a proud smile. 'What you said to Alex...' I chuckle. 'Guys don't forget words like that. They're now burned into his brain in a way I don't doubt the first thing he does when he gets home is a little Google search on orgasms and the clitoris. He'll never forget you, and some other woman may one day thank you, that's for damn sure.'

A smile crosses her face as she wipes away more tears. 'You heard *everything*?'

I nod. 'Old building. Voices carry. Pretty sure your door was open.'

She lets out a heavy sigh. 'Even when I said I love—'

I take her hand in mine. 'Even then. In your defense, though, you probably felt like you were being attacked. I'm sure it slipped out.' I stroke the back of her hand with my thumb, her eyes on our hands in her lap.

'If someone or something better comes around, are you going to disappear?' She glances up at me.

I shake my head. 'Baby, you're the love of my life that I somehow let slip through my fingers, and I'm desperately trying to get back what I lost. You're still the one I want, no one else.'

She silently thinks about what I've said.

'What did you lose?' she asks timidly.

Of course she'd ask this. I don't blame her. After what I just witnessed and our past, she needs confirmation.

'That's a big question with an even bigger answer but I'll try to put it into words.' Please let me choose the right ones here. 'I hurt my best friend so badly that I lost her. I broke her trust and for a while I kept her on a string while I lived life without her, making decisions she should have been involved in. Turns out, I'm not whole without her. I needed her then; I'm desperate for her now. And in case you were wondering, my best friend is this beautiful, funny, smart, mouthy woman, who has the biggest heart of anyone I've ever known and can fake a hell of an orgasm.'

She laughs under her breath. 'Why are you so sweet?' she asks like she hates it, but her face says that's a lie.

Knock. Knock. Knock.

We both glance at the front door.

'Hello?' Mikey's voice fills the room as he cracks open the door. 'Willy, you forget we're in the middle of a conversation downstairs?'

Ugh, these cockroaches will never go away no matter how much I try.

'*Why* are they here?' Berkley asks.

I lift a single finger, walking to the door and pushing Mike's head out with a hand on his forehead. 'Give me five minutes, buttmunch.'

He glares. 'Seriously, *five* minutes or those two are going to self-destruct, and I'm gonna have to watch.' He throws a thumb towards the bookstore downstairs.

'If they do, they do. I'll be down in five.'

Mike rolls his eyes, walking back down the stairs. I close the door, locking it shut this time, then head back to Berkley.

'They have had some financial troubles. The IRS has been tipped off to some fraudulent activity, their financial guy is sitting in the slammer on federal charges, Mom's done something probably corrupt as fuck, and they think we are the ones who tipped them off.'

'*Us?*' she asks, pointing to herself. 'As in you and me, we?'

I nod.

She narrows her eyes, tilting her head. 'And they're here to make you save them?'

I shrug.

'Ugh,' she groans. 'Are you kidding me? Those assholes had the balls to come down here and ask *you* for help?'

'Money doesn't buy class, Berx.'

'No kidding,' she says. 'They're broke? Like *actually* broke, not have a million dollars in savings they don't want to disturb or a vacation home in Italy they can disappear to?'

'I'm guessing they're penniless if they're coming to me. IRS seized everything, the house, their cars, their bank accounts.'

She gasps, but with a huge grin. 'What are you going to do?' she asks, getting up off the couch.

'Tell them to fuck off?'

'No.' She shakes her head, now approaching me. 'They've spent how many years trying to tear us apart? Now's our chance to get even.'

'*Get. Even?* With my parents? I don't know if that's smart.' But, I admit, I'm curious. 'What did you have in mind?'

A sly grin grows on her face as she walks towards her closet. 'I have a pull-out couch in the stockroom and a fold-down chair in my office. Both are beyond uncomfortable. Whaddya say we set up Hotel Adler and make them miserable for a bit? We'll feed them food they'll hate and force them to work for once in their lives.'

'You want to get revenge on them?'

She lifts a shoulder as she pulls bedding from a closet, sitting it on her kitchen island.

'I mean, not to death. Probably. Do the words "twenty-five thousand dollars" mean nothing to you? They tried to ruin my life, Will. I'd be lying if I said I haven't dreamed of this. Just let me make them uncomfortable for a day. Please?'

'Um...'

'Will.' She walks over to me, stopping inches from me, staring up at me with her big brown eyes, her hand on my chest turning my decision-making skills to complete mush. She could ask me for absolutely anything right now and I'm sure my answer would be yes.

'They tried to pay me to leave you. Not one of them ever cared what you wanted or how that made you feel. They only cared about what benefited their lives. Don't offer them a dime. Let's make 'em sweat.'

'I'm not paying even a nickel to save them.'

'You won't have to.' She drops her hand from my chest, lacing her fingers through mine slowly. 'I'm volunteering.'

Against my better judgment, I nod. 'Alright. You're the boss. I'll back anything you say. Just don't make me bury any bodies.'

She smiles wide. 'I promise if it came to that, Olivia and Gunner would help there,' she teases. 'As of right now, you're broke too, so play along.' With that she grabs the stack of bedding from the island and piles it into my arms, leading the way to my family, who are probably not so patiently waiting on us.

29

BERKLEY

They're here to ask – or maybe force – Will for help. These people hate him, yet when they're down they turn to him? Un-fucking-believable. It's been twenty-four hours from hell so I've got some shit to say to these people. I just told off one rich asshole; might as well go for the gold and get all the others I know, right?

'How's your night going, Adlers? Heard the IRS is up your ass. That's unfortunate,' I say with a chuckle as Will and I walk back into the bookstore.

The three of them have made themselves somewhat comfortable in my reading area, Mike lying across one couch and his parents sitting at the edge of their seats on the sofa across from him like they might catch a disease from pre-owned furniture. Offensive, really.

Mike rolls his eyes. 'Did Willy get you all calmed down after humiliating yourself?'

'Please.' I laugh. 'I don't doubt you took notes because if I had to guess, I'd bet you need the same speech.'

He glares.

'Can we act like adults for once and talk this out?' Jacob snaps.

I laugh like he's just told a joke. 'Are you kidding me, right now?'

'We need Will to put us in a hotel for a bit until we can figure this out,' Melinda says as if she's innocent of all wrongdoing and it's all just a big misunderstanding.

'Never gonna happen,' Will says to her.

'Why's that?' Jacob barks.

'I don't support criminals,' he says. 'I *have* morals.'

The look on his mother's face right now is a picture. I may need to prevent whatever scene is about to unfold.

'What he means to say,' I say quickly, sidling up to him and taking over, 'is that because Will was cursed with the last name Adler—'

'Blessed,' Melinda corrects me.

I roll my eyes and not subtly. 'The IRS are investigating him too. He *can't* help. All his accounts are frozen as well.'

Every one of their faces drops. God, I love it. Will uses his newly acquired 'acting' skills and matches their moods perfectly, dropping onto the couch next to his brother.

'But no worries, *I've* volunteered to help,' I chirp.

Melinda's jaw hits the floor like I've just said the most offensive thing ever.

'How are *you* gonna help us?' Mike asks, sitting up as Will shoves his legs off the couch.

I flash him a douchey grin, one I know he can relate to. 'I know this is hard for you to understand but I do work for a living, which means I get a regular paycheck, so I'm not completely destitute.'

'Why would you do that?' Melinda asks, her face somber in a way I've never witnessed.

'Because I'm *not* an ass-face, you're down on your luck and I *have* a heart. But you'll be getting the necessities only with this little deal.'

'Deal?' Jacob asks. He undoes his tie, letting it drape down his chest.

'Yes. The deal is that I'll help you. All you need to do is give me your souls in return.'

'What?' Jacob and Melinda ask in unison.

I laugh. 'I'm kidding. What the hell would I want three demented souls for?'

Will laughs too, not even attempting to stifle it this time.

'That's a hard no on your souls; no doubt you already made deals with the devil ages ago and I wouldn't want to fight him for them. Basically, you have three options. Door number one: I will house you, feed you, allow you to use my kitchen and shower – temporarily, until you figure this all out – and in return, the three of you will help around the store.'

Mike chokes. 'You want us to *work* for you? *Here?* In a ri*dork*ulous bookstore?'

'You got another option, *King* Mikey?' I ask.

He cocks his head, his lips pinched the same way Melinda's are, then makes himself busy on his phone without answering my question.

'What's door number two?' Jacob asks.

'I'm so glad you asked! Door number two is that I let Will make the rules,' I say, glancing between the three of them, who all look to each other in a visible panic. 'I doubt that will be a pleasant path, as he doesn't seem happy with any of you, but that's your call.' I glance back at Will, who grins, nodding my way like he's proud. 'Door number three: we wave goodbye as the three of you leave us the hell alone. What'll it be? This is a limited-time offer and the clock is ticking.'

Jacob sighs heavily. I've convinced him, or maybe conned him. Oops. 'I guess we'll take door number one, Monty.'

I clap my hands together in front of me. 'Excellent choice, sir.

Welcome to Hotel Adler. Unfortunately, we don't qualify for your usual five-star requirements, but considering your situation and all, I wouldn't complain. We have two room options. For our happy couple...' I grab some of the bedding from the coffee table and walk towards the stockroom. 'Follow me,' I say, pushing through the double swinging doors and flipping on the light. 'We have a lovely 1997 queen-size pull-out couch, straight from my grandparents' basement. Hardly slept on, but mostly because sleeping on this lumpy old thing will make you wish you had a bed of gravel.'

Melinda is horrified. And I love every second of it.

'Don't fret, what we lack in comfort, we make up for in entertainment.' I motion towards the store. 'Borrow any reading material you want, just put it back when you're done. Here's your bedding.'

'Thread count?' Melinda asks.

'They've got threads,' I answer, knowing full well these sheets also came from my grandparents' place. I drop the bedding onto the couch.

At their house, they sleep in separate bedrooms, probably on sheets spun with gold thread. But tonight, they get used everything. Bwa-ha-ha-ha. That's my evil laugh. The villain they've always pretended I am has settled in, it seems.

'Bathroom is down the hall, and should you want to shower or cook, please text Will to schedule that.'

'We have to *schedule* our bathroom visits?' Melinda gawks.

'No,' I say. 'Public bathrooms are always open, and if scheduling a shower is too inconvenient, sponge baths are good enough for medical patients; I'm sure you'll do just fine.'

Melinda huffs a breath, crossing her arms over her chest and giving Will the stink-eye. 'You're OK with this?'

'More than, actually,' he says, a wide grin on his face.

I flash him a smile.

'And for our single guest, right this way...' I say to Mike, shoving him back through the double doors ahead of me.

He half stumbles the first couple of steps.

'You're gonna let her abuse us too?' he asks Will, who's now walking a few steps behind us, the bedding for Mike in his arms.

He nods.

'Oh, please. I'm probably the first person to touch you that you haven't paid.'

I stop just inside my office, pointing to the oversized lounge chair. 'That opens out into a single bed. Almost. It's a tad shorter and it's like sleeping on the worst cabin cot ever. And, bonus, I chased a spider that disappeared into the cushions recently, so sleep tight, princess.' I grab the bedding from Will, shoving it into Mike's chest as he takes a step away from the chair.

Spiders. Mike's number one fear.

He looks from the chair to me. 'How big of a spider?'

'Big enough I saw all eight eyeballs but it probably wasn't venomous and it wasn't aggressive; I mean, it didn't want to die but... I bet you'll be fine.'

'Seriously?' Mike asks Will. 'You're going to let her treat me like this?'

'Yep,' Will says with a nod.

'You two are assholes.' Mike tosses the bedding onto the chair.

'We're just getting started, sugar. Now, the alarm is already set, so if you leave the building and set it off, I'll just call the security center and let them know what's happening and ask them to leave it on to annoy you. So don't try sneaking out to party and think you'll somehow get back in. 'Cause until the store opens tomorrow at ten, you won't.'

'She's kinda mean,' Mike says.

'Yet I've never been more attracted to her than I am right now.'

I smile proudly.

'Since you're doing this little "goodness of your heart" scam prison-style, can we at least get our bags or did you have a jumpsuit you want us to wear?' Mike asks me.

'You've got five minutes,' I say, walking to the alarm keypad just outside my office and punching in the code. 'Your time starts now, and we lack a bellboy, so you'll have to get your criminal parents to help you.'

Mike groans as he pulls his keys from his pocket, yelling for his folks.

'I'm seeing a little bit of evil in you, Berx,' Will says with a crooked grin, clearly enjoying it.

'They just bring it out in me. I didn't even have to try,' I say, not feeling even an ounce of remorse. It's a little scary.

'If the bookstore thing ever didn't work out, I'm thinking prison guard might,' he jokes. 'You're even more amazing than I remembered.'

'Me tormenting your family gets you off, does it? I feel like I should be worried about that.'

He shakes his head. 'You do realize I can't let you stay here with them alone, right? I don't trust even one of them. If I have to, I'll sleep in the office chair and Mike can sleep on the floor.'

'If you *have* to? Is there another place you assumed you were sleeping?' I ask like I don't already know exactly what he's thinking.

He laughs to himself. 'Yeah,' he says, glancing at me with puppy-dog eyes. 'There is *one* place I'd rather sleep.' The way he holds my gaze while he says the words sends a flutter of butterflies through my body.

'Where?' I keep playing the game.

'You *know* where, Berx.'

'Perhaps I have some idea, but I could be way off so I'm afraid I'll need you to spell this out for me.'

'I want to be where I was last night. Holding you in my arms again. Though I'd literally sleep on a bed of nails outside the shop's front doors if that's what you preferred.'

'Hmm... tempting, but I don't think that'll be necessary. We could probably work something out,' I tease right as his family walks back in, every one of them mumbling about how mean I am. Mission accomplished. And we've only just begun.

30

BERKLEY

Once the demons downstairs are tucked in for the night, Will and I lock ourselves into my apartment. I'm walking out of my bedroom in my pajamas to find Will standing at my kitchen island, working on the cold pizza I forgot about.

'Is it weird I'm eating a pizza Alex ordered?' he asks.

'Nah,' I say, grabbing a bottle of water from the fridge and hopping onto the counter a few feet from where he's at. He sure is taking his time with all this. Maybe he's just being respectful but I'm tired of waiting.

'Why haven't you kissed me yet?'

He practically chokes on the pizza he just took a bite of. 'Uh.' He clears his throat, turning his attention to me. 'Two reasons. One, I thought you wanted to make me pay, and wasn't sure you were done with that yet. Two, you literally dumped a guy thirty minutes ago. Is there not a timeframe you give a woman recently single before you start begging her back?'

I laugh to myself. 'Yet here you are, in my apartment *after* said break-up, *after* telling me you came back for me, and *after* saying you want to sleep in my bed, and you're more interested in the pizza he ordered?'

Will tosses the slice of pizza in his hands back into the box, walking to where I am sitting, and stands between my legs.

'I didn't realize you wanted to just get down to business.' He shyly slides his hands up my thighs to my hips, pulling me closer.

'That's what we do, Will. We get down to business and deal with the fallout later.'

'Exactly,' he says. 'I don't want to do that again. I want more.'

'Well, welcome to club "I've always wanted more". Took ya *forever* to get here.'

Ha laughs. 'I'm trying to be romantic here. I've got a whole plan to earn you back.'

Do I want him to be romantic? Yes. Am I afraid of just taking what I want from him? For years, yes. But that's gotten me nowhere, so no more. From here on out I tell him what I want no matter how difficult that might be.

He's leaning into me, his hands on my hips, his face inches from mine as he stares at me. Hesitantly, I reach up, rest my hands on either side of his neck then press my lips to his. He gasps like he didn't expect it, then kisses me back like a soldier home from war. God, I missed him. He guides my legs around his waist, pulling me closer. The power plant from the karaoke bar just flipped back on. Full power. Sweet Lord, I wanna do the hell out of him right now. And I can. I'm suddenly single. He's single. Sure, I've got a building full of monsters downstairs, but the one kissing me desperately seems to have come to his senses. I've never seen him so present. No phone. No distractions. Just him and me, like he's suddenly grown up and knows what he wants. *Me*. Finally.

His fingers in my hair send shivers down my spine, practically knocking the breath right out of me. I haven't kissed him in a long time, and it feels nothing like I remember. It's... better? Like electricity is indeed surging through me to him. A moan leaves my lips, and he takes this as his cue to move down my neck, kissing softly to my collarbone then back to my ear.

'Oh my God, please just do me,' I say.

He laughs, lifting me from the counter, his hands on my ass and mine around his neck. He never removes his lips from mine, just carries me backward towards my room, ramming me into the door frame in our anxiousness to get there.

'Oh, shit,' he says with a laugh, touching the back of my head. 'You alright?'

'Very, very alright,' I say.

'Maybe we should do this with our feet on the floor,' he suggests, setting me down, then shoving me against the door, kissing me so hard I'm weak in the knees.

He pulls away, suddenly glancing into my room. 'Am I allowed in here again? I don't want to ruin the demon-purging séance you mentioned.'

I giggle, shoving him onto my bed. 'I'll allow it.'

'Whoa,' he says, scooting back and extending a hand for me. 'You're sure you want to do this now? 'Cause if we have sex, I'm going to be under the impression that we're getting back together. That's why I'm here, Berkley. To be your boyfriend again. You sure you don't want to torment me a touch longer? I'm sure I deserve it.'

'I'm sure,' I say, crawling over him and straddling his hips. I grind my pelvis into his, watching him close his eyes, letting out a groan he can't contain, his hands on my hips immediately. I like being able to do this to him. I lean down, kissing his neck to his jawline before looking him right in the eye. 'This is the most important makeup sex you'll ever have and you've got a lot to apologize for.'

'Yes, I do,' he says. 'I promise you will not be disappointed.'

And I'm not. No after-show solo bathroom trips needed – he just sends me to heaven and back again. Multiple times.

* * *

It's the slamming of my front door that wakes us up the next morning.

'What is it?' Will sits up suddenly, practically yelling the words as he throws an arm over me, probably to protect me from whatever the intrusion is but instead nearly throwing me from the bed in the process.

'Ow,' we both groan.

'Oh, babe.' He reaches for me.

'Why "ow" for you? What's wrong?'

He shakes his head. 'It's nothing. Just my back. Having sex all night kind of... fucked my back,' he says, waggling his eyebrows. 'I knew partway through and soldiered on. Totally worth it.'

'You two did *not!*' Olivia hollers from my bedroom doorway.

'Shit,' I moan. 'My *mom* caught us.'

'Olivia, get the hell outta here,' Will says, tossing a pillow in her direction with a laugh. 'You two have zero boundaries.'

'You *seduced* him? On night *two*!? You *temptress!*'

'Temptress?' I ask. 'You've been spending way too much time with Gunner.'

They aren't dating. They're flirting. Obnoxiously so, for far too long. Olivia even joined one of his reading groups, so now they speak a secret fantasy/sci-fi language I don't. I will get them together, if only so Liv will stop having larger-than-needed reactions to whatever this is that Will and I've got going on. The heart wants what it wants; who am I to tell it no?

'I didn't *seduce* him. It just happened.'

'Right...' she says, with disbelief. 'I have so many follow-up questions that we'll get to later. For now, I'd like to start with the most pressing one. *Why is our store full of Adlers?*'

'Ugh,' I groan, dropping back against my headboard. 'I forgot about them.' My gaze snaps to Will. '*Oh. My. God.* Do you think they heard us?'

He laughs. 'Without a doubt, but probably less than they heard you get off for Alex a few hours prior.'

'Pardon me?' Olivia asks with a ridiculous British accent.

'Liv...' I pull my sheets across my chest tightly, turning towards her as I cross my legs beneath me. Will's now sprawled out in front of me, his hand on my thigh under the blankets and even that send shivers through me. I explain the situation with Alex. Every humiliating detail. A smile grows on Olivia's face as I speak, her eyes darting to Will, who nods to confirm.

'So then yesterday was a *real* bad day for you,' she says before laughing.

'Real bad, so I turned to my ex,' I say, with a guilty grin.

But I don't want him to be my ex anymore. I never actually did, but last night decided it. And it's not the sex. It's him. The way he looks at me. The way he touches me. I see my Will in there that I've spent so long missing and he's all I want, still.

'I don't regret anything,' I say.

Will has that stupid adorably crooked grin on his face with my words. He sits up, kissing my shoulder, holding his lips there for a moment, glancing at me with only his eyes. That look is what I'm talking about. I haven't seen this in so long.

'The twat-waffles downstairs – they're Berkley's prisoners,' he says to Olivia.

'You *kidnapped* them? I assumed they fluttered in from the underworld as demons do.' She laughs at her own joke. 'What am I supposed to do with them? It's like a zoo down there. They're asking me to feed them and you know I'm not an animal person. I don't even like chasing Pokémon. *Why are they here and asking me for food?*

'Because they're suddenly broke,' Will says, now fishing his underwear from the floor with his foot and flawlessly pulling them on without ever flashing either of us. Liv and I exchange curious glances, then watch him nod like he's proud of this feat. 'That's a little trick I eventually learned after being on television for years.' He waggles his eyebrows, grabs the rest of his clothing from my floor, and heads out to the living room.

Olivia follows, drilling him about his family as I put on some clothing while she's distracted. Obviously him being half-naked on TV for years has her a little too comfortable fighting with him while he's in his underwear. They've known one another forever but it's still a sight to see.

'How do you go from multi-millionaire to broke overnight?' she asks, as I walk into the front room now clothed.

'By fucking over the IRS,' Will says. 'I'll take care of them. I need to go take a shower and change. I'll bring them with me.'

'No!' I blurt, crossing the room to him as he pulls on his jeans. 'They need to think you're broke. If you waltz them into Hotel Deluxe, they're not leaving until you've bought the place for them. Stay in character. You're broke.' I walk to my purse, pulling out some cash. 'You're paying for breakfast with the cash Berkley gave you, got it?' I coach him.

'Why would *you* pay?' Liv asks.

'We've convinced his parents that Will is broke too.'

She stands before us, a blank stare on her face. 'Just kick them all out. This is *our* store, no Adlers allowed, remember?'

I heave a sigh. 'Yeah, so, remember Frank calling to announce he's selling the store?'

'Yes...' Olivia says curiously.

'It sold,' I say nervously. 'To Will.'

'A freaking Adler got involved in our business?' she snaps, glaring at Will as he pulls his shirt over his head.

'His family bid against him hoping to put us out of business.'

She seethes. '*Estúpidos jodidos Adlers.*'

'I understood two words of that and I agree,' Will says. 'Don't worry, everything is going in Berkley's name. This is you girls' store, *not* mine.'

'And I'm just supposed to accept that my livelihood is now owned by an Adler?'

Will shrugs. 'If Berkley forgives me, isn't it best friend law or something that you have to as well?'

Liv rolls her eyes, a sly smile on her face. 'Isn't it boyfriend law that you don't continually act like a moron?'

He sits down on the couch, putting on his shoes. 'So, we're at war?'

'You ran away like a coward while I was the one to make sure she was alright through all this while you lived your life as a professional party boy whose longtime girlfriend waited in the wings for you to pull your head from your ass. So, until I see you wavin' a white flag, yes, we're at war.'

Will stands from the couch, nodding his head until he finally sighs, shoving his hands in his pockets as he approaches her.

'You're absolutely right. Thank you for picking up where I failed. I let down all my real friends for people who made me miserable because I thought it would get me somewhere in life. Turned out that place was heartbreak island and rehab. I promise, Liv, I'm not here just to make up with Berkley. There's you, Bryce, Bianca and even Gunner. I'm sorry I was a dick.'

She wants to be pissed; I can see it on her face. 'Damn it, he *is* charming isn't he?' she says to me. 'But I'm watching you, Adler.' She motions from her eyes to his. 'Consider yourself on probation.'

'Deal,' he says, glancing back at me. 'I'm gonna go. Change.

Shower. Grab something for breakfast I know they won't enjoy, maybe something partially frozen?' he suggests.

There's my Will. 'That's perfect!'

'We'll have a chat with them when I get back and get them settled into their new positions. Liv, you can handle the store for a few today while we deal with this, right?'

'That depends,' she says.

'On what?' he asks.

'I have some questions that need answering first.'

Of course she does.

Will sits on the edge of the couch next to me like we're back in the principal's office in trouble and headed to detention together. Which has previously happened more times than either of us would like to admit.

'Does the night of love-making mean you're back together?'

I grimace. 'You know I hate that word.'

'Answer the question.'

Will and I exchange a glance. 'You said no last time I asked but I'm not too proud to ask again. Go on a date with me?' he asks me, right in front of Olivia.

'What?'

'That plan I mentioned, it begins with a start-over date. So, please, go on a date with me tonight?'

Like I'm going to say no. 'Um – sure. Let's start over,' I say.

He grins, the tiny lines at the edges of his lips appearing as he rests a hand on the side of my neck, sliding his thumb down my jawline, planting a kiss on my lips.

'You two do realize I'm still here, right?' Liv asks.

He pulls away, heading towards my room. 'I'll be back. Stay away from the animals, take a shower, whatever; I'll be back in an hour at most.' He grabs the things he offloaded from his pockets in my room. 'Liv, you want anything?' he says on his way to the front door.

'A gift certificate to the BMW dealership? Preferably one with five digits ahead of the decimal,' she says with an actual straight face.

'Ha!' He laughs. As he exits he does his thing, pointing to his heart then to me, causing me to swoon like it always did.

'Look at you!' Olivia says as soon as the door clicks closed. 'You're already smitten with him. I can't believe you caved so soon.'

'I didn't cave. I just...' I sigh. 'I tried to hate him, and I couldn't. I don't know how to explain it. With him here, it's like I can breathe again.'

'You're just going to trust him?'

'No,' I say quickly. 'There is one thing, though.'

'What?'

'I feel a little insecure. Like at any moment, he'll just be gone. I'll wake up, and this will all be a stupid dream pining for what I can't have.'

'Insecure?!' She balks. 'You bagged Alex Donovan *and* Will Adler. You're like the queen of boning famous men of Portland.'

'It's felt a little more flaw than skill, but here we are.'

'Well, nothing is without flaws. We're human.'

I stand from the couch, hugging her around the neck tightly. 'You are the best friend ever, you know that?' I ask. 'I promise, Liv, I'm being careful.'

31

WILL

We're sitting in Berkley's apartment because the store is open and busy already. I have a feeling this might get loud. She thought this place needed an exorcism before? Ha!

I bought the breakfast I knew my family would hate, but Berkley would love. McDonald's pancake platters. Fake processed sausage patties, pressed deep-fried potatoes, warmed frozen pancakes, and so much butter and syrup you could save some for later.

My parents sit uncomfortably at the bar while Mike is on Berkley's couch, his eyes on the television.

'How'd you guys sleep?' I ask. 'I know I slept great. Better than I have in years.'

'You *slept*? 'Cause had it been quieter, maybe I could have,' Mike says, shooting both Berkley and I the stink-eye.

I laugh. 'Not even a little bit sorry.'

'Please, Mike,' Berkley says. 'You're the biggest sleaze here; no doubt you recorded it. Maybe tonight you put in headphones?'

She's thinking about tonight? Good to know I didn't disappoint her with my performance and she wants a repeat. The last thing I wanted was the speech Alex got.

'I take it you two are back together? You can't seem to keep your eyes off each other,' Mom says.

That seems like a sweet statement, unless you factor in the horrified face she said it with.

'Um...' Berkley says the word that started the implosion of my world, a flash of regret on her face.

'There's a lot I need to fix before we label it, but yeah, we're getting there.' I take the heat, seeing how uncomfortable she is to admit the thing my parents have fought against for years.

'We don't care,' Dad says flatly. 'You've let her torture us for a night; now cut the crap and loan us some money.'

My smile fades as my gaze moves to my father. I hate that this man can turn me into an insecure little boy so easily. I don't get it. Is he disappointed I exist or that I'm not a carbon copy of him?

'Don't be a dick to him,' Berkley snaps before I can speak. 'If you want to treat him like shit in your home – which is really dick-ish by the way – go ahead. But you're in *our* home now, and you will not disrespect him while you're here.'

Dad raises his eyebrows. '*Our* home?'

Of course he catches it. I caught it. I glance over at her. 'Can you guys give us a second?' I ask, motioning for her to follow me to her room. I can't just blow by this. I need to know what she meant.

She walks into her room behind me, her plate of food still in her hand, and she looks nervous. I close the door, turning to her slowly.

'*Our* home? You haven't said that since—'

'Since we called it that during the remodel, before I knew *Royals* was a thing? It sort of just slipped out. I wasn't sure you'd even notice it.'

I nod. 'I might not have if it hadn't stood out like a tiger in a grocery store. Berx, this is all I ever wanted. Since the day I made the decision to do the stupid show I've been searching for home, and this is the only place that makes me feel like I've found it.'

'Really?' she asks, like she didn't already know.

'Really.'

She blows out a relieved breath. 'Good. Because all I could think about last night was us being back together "officially" and what that could mean. Ya know? You *did* just buy the place, so technically, it's *all* yours.'

'It's all *ours*, Berx. I want to do this *with* you. I used to be good at the bookstore gig. I've got a way with words,' I remind her. 'I'm sure I could fall back into it. Let's do this, finally.'

She laughs nervously, shoving a forkful of pancakes into her mouth, probably hoping to give herself time to think.

'Are you seriously not thinking what I'm thinking?'

She swallows hard. 'I *am*,' she says. 'But then I look back and you've been back two days, Will. *Two* days and I've dumped my sort of "boyfriend", slept with you, and now your entire family is living here. This isn't exactly how I expected this to all go down. Isn't this too fast after all we've been through? Liv thinks I should torture you for a while.'

Of course she does. 'You *should* torment me. But us living together will only make that easier. You can flush while I shower. Dye all my whites pink. Control the remote. Make me do the dishes. Buy me an assless chaps butler uniform and I'll be at your beck and call with a smile on my face.' I can feel the goofy grin on my face as I suggest ways for her to torment me.

'You'd like that last one way too much; no waiting would be done and definitely no butlering...' She laughs.

'We've been together off and on for ten years. We were barely adults when we broke up. Now we're actual grown-ups in our mid-twenties and we can do anything we want. Fuck what anyone else things. My parents included. The only people we need to make happy are us. Let's do this, Berx. Let's live the life we planned so long ago.'

'You'd be moving in as my boyfriend?'

As her boyfriend. Final-fucking-ly. Part of me never thought this would happen. I could give her the ring right now, ask her to be my wife as opposed to my girlfriend and it'd probably go over exactly as I'd hoped. But she deserves more than a last-minute proposal in her bedroom with my family in the next room.

'Tonight, we're going on a date. Maybe we can make the boyfriend/girlfriend thing official then?'

She searches my eyes, like she's attempting to see into my soul to ensure I'm being serious. 'OK... so we're moving in together. For real? Romantically? Like, this is *finally* happening?'

'Exactly the way we'd always planned.'

She scrunches her face. 'Maybe not exactly. And you're *sure* sure that this is what *you* want?'

The way she's covering all her bases to make sure she's asked the question in every possible way is adorable.

I touch her chin. 'I've never been surer of anything.' I press my lips to hers gently.

'Wow!' she says timidly. 'I sort of never thought we'd get here.'

God, she's gorgeous. We're moving in together. Holy hell. There's nothing left to stand between us, and I'm not even scared. I feel like I did when my parents announced we were going to Disneyland when I was ten. I couldn't sleep the entire night before out of sheer excitement. I feel that right now.

Suddenly her bedroom door slams against my spine, making me groan.

'My eyes are closed so just get dressed and stop boning,' Mike says.

'We're not boning, you freak.'

'Word of advice,' Berkley says, stepping between Mike and me.

'I'm pushing my luck even having your brand of moron in my apartment. You're definitely not stepping foot in my room, so learn to knock.'

Before she can leave, I grab her hand, causing her to look back at me. 'We will celebrate this later, alright?'

She flashes me an *I can't wait* smile, the two of us exiting her room, hand in hand as we head back to her living room.

'Where were we?' I ask, standing opposite the kitchen island from my parents.

'*Our* home,' Dad says, his sausage patty on his fork as he inspects it closely. 'I don't think this is real sausage.'

Mom nods, agreeing with him.

'Right,' I say. '*Our* home – she didn't misspeak. We designed this apartment a long time ago, and recently we bought the building, so we've decided to move ahead with our prior plans.'

Dad drops the fork and sausage patty onto his Styrofoam plate, taking a moment to breathe over the fact that I'm moving in with the love of my life and the enemy of theirs. Insanity. Who could hate this woman? I'm beginning to wonder if the man needs to be institutionalized over his narcissism. It can't be healthy. I'm nearly twenty-six years old. I will choose who I love, and he will have absolutely zero say in that.

'*You* bought the store?' he asks curiously, crossing his arms over his chest.

'We,' I correct him. '*We* bought the store.'

He shakes his head. 'Berkley doesn't have three million dollars, son.'

'Neither do you,' I remind him with a chuckle.

He rolls his eyes. 'You've got money.' His mouth might not say it, but his eyes are screaming *give it to me*. Greed is scary. I know what people say about my father. He's an arrogant, narcissistic, egotistical, greedy asshole. I see it right now more than I ever have. 'Enough of this nonsense,' he snaps. 'Just loan us some money.'

Berkley suddenly drops her fork and goes from visibly excited about our new plans to pissed. Her eyes are on my father.

'Why would he help you with anything? My *God*, you are a selfish prick. For the entire time I've known Will, not once have you treated him as a father should – yet here you are, demanding he loan you money after you fucked yourselves over by being the corrupt queen and king of Portland.'

'Well, technically, I'm still the king,' Mike says under his breath from across the room.

'Ugh,' Berkley groans. 'You know what money can't buy? *Manners*.'

Everyone's heads snap in her direction. I can't help but smile. She would stand up for me to the scariest person on earth. If there's one thing no one does, it's backtalk my father.

'She's right, ya know. I'm not exactly the favorite son. For that reason alone, even if I had money, you wouldn't get a dime,' I say, my eyes on his.

Dad glares.

'All you've done my entire life is try to ruin me. Now the tables are turned. I'm not helping you, but Berkley offered because she has more of a heart than I do.'

'God damn it, William!' Dad barks, standing from his stool and pacing the room. 'You'd do this? Abandon your own family in a time of need?'

I snort then continue to laugh, looking at Berkley, sincerely shocked to hear these words come from this man. Slowly – and honestly terrified – I walk towards him, stopping so we can talk face to face.

'I almost died after a car accident in college and not once did you come to visit me in the hospital. Instead, once I'd recovered enough to not need life support, your lawyer called me to remind me that my drunken stunts were an embarrassment to the family and I'd be paying the hospital bill myself. You tried to *pay* my girl-friend to leave me. You talked me into contract after contract, with either bribes or threats, the entire time telling me that Berkley would forgive me, as "she always does for some reason" – *your words*. You pushed and pushed me onto a woman I had no interest in, who wanted exactly what you *don't* want Berkley to have. My entire life, you've threatened my trust fund, cars, parties, vacations, my future, if I didn't behave exactly as you wanted. You even threatened to fire Sylvia once when I mistakenly called her "Mom". I was *six*.'

'*That* was your mother's doing,' he snaps, calling out my mom like he's not the one who made the threat. What a fucking coward.

'This is where I get the blaming others from. By watching you blame someone else for everything and never taking responsibility for yourself.'

'Not true,' he argues.

'You know, I've never lived a life where I thought I could relax – without booze – because God-fucking-forbid I do or say the wrong thing and disappoint you. What would you do to make me pay? Nothing I've done is ever enough for you, while Mikey over here is the fucking golden boy.'

'William,' Melinda scolds. 'That is not true.'

'Isn't it?' I ask. 'I graduated from both high school and college with honors. I've built up my own bank accounts. I know what I'm doing enough to make the last chaotic few years work for me and, luckily, I found a woman with a heart bigger than I'd ever known who never gave up on me. She made sure I knew right from wrong, and the only times I've ever struggled with that was when you people were involved. Maybe I screwed up with her for a while, but she's always been the angel on my shoulder. While you idiots have forever been the demons. Now you want to guilt me into helping because we're *family*?'

Dad listens to my words silently, the two of us now in a stare-down that, I'm not gonna lie, kind of scares me. The true 'king' Adler – the one Mike's always worshiped – has been stripped of his power, and the spare son is finally standing his ground. This took way too long.

'Um...' Berkley says behind me.

I laugh. Of course, her word brings me peace as she takes the chance and interrupts, stepping up to my side, gripping my hand tightly. She's afraid of nothing. With this woman by my side, I will never have to fight a battle alone.

'Obviously, we're not working out all your relationship kinks in a day. If you don't want to stay here, surely you guys have friends who can help?' Berkley asks.

Silence.

'Extended family?'

Nothing.

'People, who owe you?'

Crickets.

'*Someone* in the city you haven't blackmailed or fucked over?'

A needle could crash to the floor and sound like a rockslide in this silence.

'Jesus, Adlers. This may be a wake-up call that you're not the stand-up folks you think you are. 'Cause if I'm your only hope, a woman you've tormented for a decade, you're on thin ice of ever pulling out of this.'

'Did you check *all* the credit cards?' Mom yells at Dad, ignoring Berkley completely.

'He'll help us,' Dad says, his eyes still locked with mine.

'He won't. Berkley might still be up for it, although I'd rather she didn't,' I say, shaking my head, my face casual, like none of this bothers me. Truthfully, if I still drank, I'd need one after this.

'*Fix this*,' Mom snaps, grabbing Dad's arm, clearly pissed as she motions between him and me. 'He's your son. Nearly twenty-six years old and already more of a respectable man than you've ever been.'

Whoa, so things aren't bliss like they pretend they are. I can't say I'm surprised by that.

'*Is* he my son, Mel? We don't really know the answer to that, do we?' Dad snaps back, my, Berkley and Mike's heads all whipping their direction.

Wait.

A.

Second.

Did he just say—

'*What?*' The three of us say the word in unison, glancing between one another.

Berkley's gaze is complete worry, Mike's is shock and I feel like I just had the wind knocked out of me. How has this never come up?

'*Is* he my son?' I repeat his words, fidgeting with the clasp on the watch I've worn daily since he gifted it to me the day I graduated high school. It's my tell. When I'm worried, I click the clasp on it nervously.

Mom looks at Dad like she's a deer caught in the headlights with nowhere to run. She stands from her chair slowly, causing both me and Berkley to back away from them.

'*Jacob Francis Adler*,' Mom scolds. 'How *dare* you say that out loud. We had a deal.'

'Deal's off,' Dad says. 'It's time he knew the truth about what you did.'

The more they speak, the more I feel like a thick fog of lies has settled over me, and I'm rethinking my entire life like I'm near death. Suddenly the watch I'm fidgeting with catches my attention. Dad made a speech at dinner after I graduated college when he gave me this watch. 'I'm proud of you, son.' That was all he said. Mike got a fucking slideshow of memories, literal fireworks over the lake at dusk, and the same watch. I got five words and a thirty-thousand-dollar Rolex I've let become so important to me that I never take it off. It represented the *one* thing I wanted from this man and now I know it's a lie. I yank it off and toss it onto the coffee table in front of Mike.

'Dude,' Mike says, grabbing it. 'This is a *Rolex*, man. Don't throw it down on the table, dumbass. You'll scratch it.'

'Why would it matter? It's nothing but a lie anyway.'

'Son, that watch wasn't cheap.'

'Don't you dare "son" me, you liar. You three are more concerned over a damn watch then me when my entire existence is suddenly in question.'

I need to get out of here for a minute. I storm out the front door, through Berkley's office and out the side door to the sidewalk. I could really use a cigarette right now and I've never smoked. Maybe a triple shot of Jack Daniel's. Ugh. I lean against the brick wall, sliding down to the sidewalk, closing my eyes and feeling the memory of Jack settling this without even taking a sip.

'Will?' Her voice is small and scared. I am an idiot. I scared her. 'Are you OK?'

I nod. It's partially a lie but I don't want her to worry. I extend a hand to her, helping her down to me, where she sits against the wall at my side.

'Have you ever had the absolute worst and the outright best day of your life all in the same twenty-four-hour period? 'Cause that's how I feel right now.'

'Yes,' she says with a chuckle. 'Twenty-four hours ago.'

'Also my fault,' I say, leaning into her. 'Never in a million years did I expect a bomb of bullshit to implode in every area of my life by coming back. I just wanted to come home and win over the woman of my dreams and now everything is a mess and if you weren't in the picture I'd be headed to the bar right now.'

She tucks her hand into the crook of my arm. 'They don't have to stay here. I didn't realize how miserable they're still making you.'

'I'm *not* his kid, Berx – it's all making sense now. He's fought me his whole life because I'm not his. Part of me is like, *yes!* Then another part is like, *fuck!* Who am I, then?'

'I'm sorry,' she says, sliding her hand down my arm to my hand. 'What do you want to do?'

'I don't kn—'

The back door slams open, nearly crushing Berkley as I pull her to me. Mike walks out, his fingers pinched together in front of him.

'What do *you* want?' I ask angrily.

'You got a zip-lock bag or something?'

'Why?' Berkley asks.

'DNA sample, anyone?' He stares at us, his arrogance fading as he notices how upset I am.

I lean forward, inspecting what he's displaying before my face. 'You ripped out the man's hair?'

He nods proudly. 'I prefer low-key violence to asking him to power-wank into a cup,' he says with a shiver. 'Listen, I'm a dick.'

Berkley and I both laugh.

He lowers his chin. 'I'm possibly the worst older brother in the history of brothers. I mean, if you don't count biblical brothers. That said, I saw the look on your face just now when he made his pissed-off announcement, and even you didn't deserve that. Take this and get a DNA test. Maybe you'll get lucky, and you're really *not* the Adler you never wanted to be. Perhaps you're one of those babies kidnapped at birth and this will eventually make a great Lifetime movie.'

I cock my head, rolling my eyes, but at this point I wouldn't put anything past my mother.

'Why would you volunteer to help me? I thought you hated me?'

'When you're unnecessarily sleeping in a bookstore listening to your little brother have loud sex, you've got some time to think.'

'*Unnecessarily?*' Berkley asks.

Mike smirks. 'I'm not *exactly* in their situation.' He lifts both shoulders to his ears guiltily. 'I suspect you aren't either? They might be terrible parents but they didn't raise idiots.'

'You *have* money?' Berkley asks. 'And you're just—'

'Lying?' Mike laughs. 'Yeah, I'm an Adler, remember? Lying is my game. I can't tell them; Jesus, they'd milk me dry if they knew. Plus, I was living at their place when all this went down and didn't have a place to go and figured why waste money on a hotel if it's not necessary? I tend to overspend on ridiculous shit, and don't exactly have a job right now thanks to someone insisting he get sober to get laid – so here I am, becoming a tight-ass.'

I stare at my smarmy brother, trying to process all this. He's lying about being broke and sleeping on an uncomfortable pull-out bed just to save some money? Isn't it just like him to play this out until he can figure out how best to use it to his advantage.

'Well?' he asks. 'You gonna come clean?'

He's right, he's a dick, yes, but like he said, he's not a total idiot.

'Fine,' I admit. 'I'm not broke. But I'm also not giving them a penny and I refuse to let Berkley waste money on them either. So, now what?'

After I've gathered my father's hair sample from Mike, he shoves his hands into his pockets, now leaning against the side of the building, looking down at us. 'I honestly don't know. If Berx wants to torment them for a while, God knows they deserve it. They've spent a lot of time making her miserable.'

'*They?*' she asks, standing from the sidewalk and shooting daggers his way.

'Me too,' he says flatly. 'I'm sure I owe you an apology, but none of this is really me, so give me a bit, would ya? I just learned my parents have been lying to me since Will was born. One life lesson at a time, please.'

'Wait,' I say, trying to get up off the ground but my back isn't cooperating and Berkley notices. She extends both hands to me, in an assist to pull me up.

'You have to go have your back checked out,' she says with worry.

'I'll be alright,' I insist, before turning my attention to Mike. 'You really knew none of this?'

Mikey shakes his head slowly. 'No idea. Though it's now making sense of why he's always told me how much better than you I am.'

'He *told* you that?'

'Oh yeah,' he confirms. 'He'd badmouth the hell out of you and convince me all of it was true. I'm starting to see that maybe he was lying. Did he really threaten to fire Sylv because you called her "Mom"? Because let's face it, Sylvia *is* our mom.'

I nod. 'She was helping me with homework, and the word just slipped out. Mom overheard it and practically jerked my arm from the socket when she dragged me to my room to wait for Dad. After he lectured the hell out of me and threatened to fire her, he then made sure I understood to never make the mistake again, *or else.* Who throws an *or else* at a six-year-old?'

I never told Berkley this story. It always felt too humiliating. I was a rich kid who was constantly told how 'blessed' I was but I felt lost. I had no idea why I had to act a certain way, kissing people's asses from a young age. Neither of my parents acted like they loved me so I sincerely thought of my nanny as my mom. Sylvia, who doted over me and made a big deal about coming in second at a grade-school science fair. She said it meant I had room to grow and growing smarter was never a bad thing. My actual mother told me only first place is the winner, everyone else is a loser, and wanted to know what I'd do next time to make sure I wasn't a loser. She'd be proud when I brought home the winner's trophy and only then. Her actual words. Until recently, I didn't realize how much damage some of this stuff did. I've worked through a lot of it in rehab during counseling sessions but this is brand new information and I'm not sure how to accept it or move past it.

Mike's face is scrunched, and honestly, this is the first time I've ever seen him be this human. I'm truly shocked. I didn't think demons had souls.

'Assholes do that,' Mike says. 'I'm not a father – here's hoping I never am – but even I know that's not right. I always knew things were different between us in his eyes but never saw through it until today. I guess that makes me a bigger dick than I thought, eh?' He laughs.

He thinks this is funny? I feel like my whole world just crashed to the ground from a high shelf, and it was made of glass.

'Dad told you I was a piece-of-shit child, and you just believed the man? The same guy who told you to walk off a broken arm when you were thirteen because docking the boat to get you to a hospital would cut into his vacation?'

Mike frowns. 'I'd forgotten about that. Fair point. But he's convincing as hell and scary. I've seen full-grown dudes cower at his presence. There was no fucking way I was challenging anything he said. Somehow, he convinced me you would ruin us with your rebellious ways. He said you were going against the family. God, now that I think on this, it's reminding me of those Mafia movies he likes. Jesus.'

I rub my forehead, my brain suddenly throbbing against my skull.

'Anyway, according to him, he needed to break you, so you'd calm down and do as you were told. That sounded bad, and I didn't want him doing it to me, so I listened.' He shrugs like still believing any of this at twenty-eight is normal.

I can't believe these people.

'I could help get them out of here if you want,' he suggests.

'How?'

'Last night, as I lay awake wishing the building was more sound-proof than it is, I found a place. My assistant is making an offer today. I'm not taking them with me, but I'll help get them out of here.'

'You have an assistant?' Berkley balks.

Mike smirks. 'I'm a twenty-eight-year-old rich guy who's never worked a day in my life. Of course I have an assistant.'

Berkley laughs, shaking her head.

'You seriously want to help after letting me spend a night thinking you were a bigger fucking moron than I thought? You are too good a liar,' I say. 'Why didn't you just tell me you weren't hit by the IRS?'

'Uh, newsflash, baby bro: you're lying pretty convincingly too. If that makes me a dick, so are you. Plus, I wasn't sure if I could trust you. We're not exactly BFFs.'

'Why are you being human?' Berkley asks a valid question.

He shrugs. 'A lot of stuff was said up there, and things started clicking in my head. For a long time, I truly thought Will was the problem in our family. But it turns out money can turn people into monsters. I know because I've been one. I've watched the show, I see it and I'm not exactly proud of it. Get the DNA test.'

Berkley and I exchange glances. He's admitting he's a tool and ashamed of it? Well, this is a new Mikey I don't know.

'I'll get the test,' I say. 'Now what do we do about the mutants inside?'

A few ideas are discussed and we agree on the one that will piss off my parents the most. As we walk back to Berkley's apartment, she stops me.

'Hey,' she says. 'You're *limping*. I thought you said you were alright?'

'Another lie. My back still hurts after last night,' I admit. 'Worth it, though, Berx. I promise I'll go have it checked later. First I need to check out of my hotel and move into my new place. Which won't take that much work considering I've only got a couple bags with me.'

Her smile. I want to kiss the hell out of it but I've got a couple idiots to torment first.

'Happy first day to our newest To Be Read employees,' I say after the drama has settled and everyone is back in the store, making a big deal about it as I flip on the overhead lights in the stockroom, Jacob, Melinda and Mike following behind.

Our plan is to make them miserable for a couple days then Mike and Will will each give them money, boundaries and move them the hell out of here. The idea seems flawless, but I think we all know it won't be. It took a game of rock, paper, scissors to decide who was stuck with which Adler 'employee'. Olivia got Mike. Gunner got Jacob. And I got Melinda.

Now everyone is in their assigned departments, except Will, who ran to drop off the DNA test and refill one of his regular prescriptions he uses for his back.

Melinda glances at me silently, both of us standing at the front desk uncomfortably. Besides asking her why she's such a yuppity bitch, I can't think of a single thing to talk about.

A woman walks up, setting a stack of books in front of Melinda. She checks the woman's purchases out, as I supervise over her shoulder, without a single question and she only watched me do it twice.

'Wow,' I say, legitimately surprised. 'You picked up on this quick.'

Melinda's shoulder-length dark hair is lying limp without her cabinet of potions and on-call hairdresser, and for the first time ever, she seems almost human. No color-coordinated jewelry sets that complement her eyes or her sweater, and not a stitch of makeup on her face.

'Was it supposed to be hard?' she asks snidely.

'No,' I say. 'I just—'

'I was a lawyer, Berkley. I'm not brain-dead.'

My jaw drops open involuntarily. Melinda rolls her eyes.

'You were a lawyer?' I'm just realizing I know pretty much nothing about this woman. I've never asked, and Will doesn't like to talk about them.

'How do you think I met Jacob?'

'I kind of assumed it was in the realms of the underworld as you battled for the most power.'

A pinched smirk crosses her face. 'It was an evil lawsuit and I got him out of it. We were married six months later.' The way she CliffsNotes the story makes it seem so unromantic. Obviously, Will didn't get that from his parents.

There's a slap on the counter that makes me jump, and when I look over, Mike is standing in front of me.

'This isn't your department,' I remind him.

'I know. I have a question, though.' He motions for me to follow him. Reluctantly I do. All the way into the horror department, where he stops in front of the display I built of the Royals' tell-all book that released last summer. 'I stumbled upon this masterpiece this morning. What the hell is it and why are we in the horror section?'

I laugh. I'd forgotten about this since I can't see it from the front desk. I received the book at an unfortunate time, just after Alex and I had broken up, so Olivia suggested we build it a fitting display. A four-foot penis built of books with all the Royals' faces on them. It seems to have developed a bit of a tilt, which makes it funnier if you ask me.

'It is what you think it is: a giant meat twinkie with your face on it.'

He bursts out laughing, turning away from me for a second before finally facing me with a straight face. 'Why?'

'Because y'all were giant tools, and I built a display I thought would represent the show.'

He rolls his eyes dramatically. 'Has Will seen this?'

'I dunno? It's sort of hard to hide a four-foot penis made of books.'

'Are you not afraid you'll break his heart by making fun of him?'

'No.' I laugh. 'I stand by this thing. If he was still on the show, he'd still be a big dick. Trust me, this is probably the most accurate book display for the Royals' book in the city.'

He shakes his head. 'You should ask Mom about Will,' he says, under his breath like we're staging some kind of evil plan together.

'Absolutely not.'

'Why?' he asks. 'You want answers. She'll most likely talk when my dad isn't standing by her side.'

'This is a family problem, and three out of the four of you have made it very clear I'm not a part of your family. Why don't you grow a set and finally stand up to your parents yourself?'

He shakes his head as if that's impossible. 'I'll never understand why Will likes you.'

'And despite your heartwarming apology earlier, I'll never question why he doesn't like you.'

He huffs. 'Fine, you coward, I'll do it,' he says, suddenly marching towards the front desk.

'Mike!' I hiss his name as I follow behind him. My gut is telling me this isn't a good idea.

'Mom,' he thunders, not keeping his voice down one bit. 'What's the deal with Will? Is what Dad said true?'

Melinda sets the book she's reading on the counter gently, taking her time to meet Mike's gaze with a sigh, her eyes moving to me as I walk back around the counter.

'Where is he?' she asks, her gaze burning through my skin.

'He had some errands to run.'

In my defense, I didn't mean to ruin his back last night. And it's not entirely my fault. When we were in college, Will was on a drinking binge with a guy he was supposed to be studying with. Instead, they went to a party, got utterly hammered and, like an idiot, he let his wasted friend drive them home. They didn't make it. Instead, they crashed on the freeway, plowing into a concrete barrier on Will's side. The driver walked away from the accident nearly unscathed, but Will had a burst fracture in his spine, four broken ribs, a punctured lung, a broken shoulder, collarbone and arm.

I was legit terrified when I got the call. For the first twenty-four hours he was on a ventilator. Things were touch and go. It was the scariest day of my life. Bryce and I were the only two who showed up at the hospital. His family couldn't have given a shit. In fact, when Mike finally showed up a week later, it was to make sure he understood what this embarrassing event did to the Adler reputation.

Somehow everything makes more sense now that I know about Jacob. He really does treat Will differently. I was never imagining it. All because he knew Will probably wasn't his. But whose is he? Suddenly, I'm on board with Mike's verbal assault on his mother.

Melinda and Mike exchange glances.

'Come on, Mom. He *has* to know. Who Darth Vader-ed Will?'

She frowns. 'Jacob should have kept his mouth shut. It's probably nothing.'

'*Probably* nothing? *Mom*,' Mike says seriously. 'Will's dropped samples off with a DNA lab. Your "probably nothing" has a truth that he will soon find out. Don't you think it should come from you? He deserves at least that.'

'You're standing up for your brother?' She pulls her head back like she's shocked by this.

'There's a first time for everything and this is kind of a big deal. You just crushed the guy's entire world.'

'He's crushed?' she asks, looking at me with worry.

I nod. 'Imagine discovering the guy who's spent his life harping at him with disappointment might not even be his own dad? Yeah,' I say, agreeing with Mike. 'He's crushed.'

Melinda crosses her arms over her chest, shaking her head like this disturbs her. It should.

'It wasn't meant to happen,' she says suddenly, her back to us as she speaks while she paces behind the front counter next to me. 'I was mad, and I did something with someone your father was intimidated by. I thought if I threatened it he'd back down but he didn't.'

'Back down from what?' Mike asks.

'Jacob went against a deal we had, and I needed leverage. His stubbornness forced me to follow through. After I played my hand, I discovered I was pregnant.'

'You used *sex* with someone who intimidated your husband as leverage because he broke a deal you had?' I ask, with shock. I thought these types of things only happened in soap operas.

'Money complicates things, sweetheart. I wouldn't expect you to understand.'

Bitch.

'Unfortunately, thanks to this family, I *do* understand.'

She rolls her eyes, turning back to Mike. 'I told your father, and we agreed a baby could be good for you growing up and kept it quiet for that reason alone.'

Mike looks at me, his eyebrows raised. 'Please tell me that leverage lay did not come from who I think it did?'

'I'm not confirming or denying anything.'

'Mom. Only *one* man intimidated Dad. Will's going to find out.'

One man? Mike knows!

'Well, it won't be from me,' she says flatly.

'You'd rather save yourself from retaliation than tell your son the truth?' I ask, not completely surprised to hear which way she's leaning here, but shocked anyone could be this cold towards their own flesh and blood.

'I have to take care of myself,' she says, picking back up the book she's reading. 'This conversation is over. I'm taking a break.'

'A break from what?' I call after her as she disappears into the stockroom, leaving Mike and me staring at one another. 'Who is it?' I snap at him.

'Has Will ever mentioned Uncle Teddy?'

'Uncle Teddy?' I shake my head.

'He was Dad's little brother.'

Holy... 'Wait. Are you saying your mom slept with her husband's little brother to get back at him?'

'It's looking that way,' Mike says as if it disgusts him too. 'It *has* to be him. I've seen photos of Teddy in his younger years, and Will's always looked just like him.'

'Blech.' I practically gag. 'She slept with her brother-in-law to piss her husband off, and he knocked her up?'

The horror on his face no doubt matches my own.

'This is insane, even for my family,' he says. 'I'm starting to loathe being an Adler too.' He drags a hand down his face.

'Tell me about Teddy. Is this good or bad?'

'He and Dad hated each other. They tried to outdo one another both financially and personally pretty much their entire lives. Dad always said Teddy needed to be taught a lesson.'

Suddenly, a visible light bulb goes off in his head, and he lets out a weird gasp. 'Jesus Christ, Dad was trying to make me hate Will in the same way he hated Teddy. And I fucking fell for it.' His hand is in his hair the same way Will's is when he's stressed.

'You were a kid, Mike. You couldn't have possibly kno—'

'Hey.' Will interrupts our conversation, suddenly walking our way from the back hallway.

Mike's eyes go wide, his back to his brother. Will side-eyes him as he rounds the front counter to me. 'Is this sleazoid bothering you?'

'Yes.' I smirk Mike's way. 'But he's not being a total cockroach, so I can deal.'

'You drop the sample off at the lab?' Mike asks, pretending we didn't just find out what we did.

'It is in process.' Will nods. 'Now we wait.' He glances at me. 'I also checked out of my hotel and picked up the muscle relaxers the doctor called in for me.'

'William.' Melinda acknowledges his presence as she walks back to us, her glare quickly moving to Mike and me as she passes.

'Mom.' Will returns her manners, not noticing the looks she's spearing my way.

'Well, this hasn't been fun at all,' Mike says, backing away from us towards Liv's department. 'I have books to put on the shelf backward, so if you'll excuse me...'

That explains why I walked into my office this morning to find every other book facing the wrong way on my office shelves.

'I can help you bring your bags in,' I suggest, glancing back at Melinda. 'Think you can handle the front desk alone for a few?'

'I was a lawyer,' she reminds me, saying the words slowly, proving that she may currently look human but the demon within hasn't yet left.

'And that means... yes?' I ask, matching her douchiness.

'Go.' Her dead stare gives me the reason to back away from the counter.

I can't possibly tell Will what I just found out. Not yet. I'll have Mike do some research and find out for sure before I go freaking him out. Here I thought Mike and Will's relationship was fucked up. Those two suddenly seem very vanilla.

33

WILL

I know Berkley is enjoying tormenting my parents a bit, but I don't get why Mike seems suddenly on board with everything she says. Those two have never bonded and the fact they have now worries me. Because my mother has had enough of the 'public', she's disappeared to the storeroom with a 'headache'. I think really it's just a deep heartache at her situation. I know she was some high-powered lawyer at one time but she just took a sick day on the first day of a new job. Her résumé won't thank her for this and I have a feeling she'll be needing one soon.

'Hello, ladies.' I glance through the books they've set on the counter in front of me. I took over for my mom so Berkley could take care of other things. 'Romances, eh? Did you know we have the largest romance collection in the city?' I ask, flashing the two women a smile. 'The owner of the store is a huge fan so if you ever need a recommendation, she knows every romance book in this place. She's like a walking card catalog.'

'Aren't you... Prince Willy of the Royals?' one of them asks.

I nod. 'I am. Interested in finding out some of my secrets?' I grab one of the Royals books that Berkley mentioned haven't really sold well, and scribble my name inside, sitting it on the top of the stack. 'Five bucks and you can know it all.'

'Five dollars?' she asks. 'Sure!'

'Flash sale. I just made it up; tell your friends.' I bag their books and hand them the bag, noticing Berkley walking my way as the two women exit.

'You're selling yourself short,' she says. 'Those are worth at least a tenner.'

'Yet, they're marked at $24.99.' I laugh. 'No secret of mine is worth that much.'

'Are you good running the front desk? I need to run to the bank.'

'I was good at this at sixteen; I'm even better now.'

She flashes me a grin. 'I'll be back in an hour or less.'

'Take your time. I got it all covered,' I say confidently. This is my new life now; I'm embracing it and actually enjoying it.

When Berkley leaves the store, and there are few customers meandering, I catch Liv watching me from her desk across the room. I straighten up the front counter, but feel her stare boring a hole through me the entire time.

'What's up?' I ask.

'Excuse me?' she says like she's no idea why I'm now standing at her desk.

I laugh. 'I feel like you've got something to say. Let's hear it.'

She sighs heavily, as if she's been caught and now the truth must be told. For a second she continues working, a book in one hand, her eyes on the computer in front of her until she finally sets the book on the stack and turns to me with a straight face.

'Is this all for real? Or is it an act to make yourself feel better before you disappear and become the next Bachelor? 'Cause that'll kill her, you know that, right? The girl has been desperately in love with you since high school and no matter what kind of idiot you act like, it never goes away and she's tried.'

'I'm serious as a heart attack, Liv.'

She clearly doesn't believe me.

'Can I trust you?' I ask.

'Duh,' she says with a roll of her eyes.

'I bought a ring.'

Slowly, her jaw drops. 'As in a diamond?' Her gaze never leaves mine.

I nod. 'A big one. From a store famous for their little blue boxes.'

'*Santa mierda, pequeño diablo furtivo.*' The way she rattles off her initial thoughts in Spanish cracks me up because she knows only one of us in this store speaks it fluently and it's not any of us Adlers or Kaines. 'Then you plan to keep your previously agreed-upon life plans?'

'I've always wanted to keep those plans. I just got caught up in myself for a while.'

'If you're hoping I'll tell you you're not an idiot, you've come to the wrong girl.'

I chuckle. 'Not what I'm fishing for. We agreed to move in together, as boyfriend and girlfriend. That's huge. There's just one problem.'

'What?' she asks with worry.

'We go on our start-over date tonight and I'm hoping to make her my fiancée as opposed to my girlfriend. Too soon?'

'*Too soon?*' She bursts out a laugh. 'You're nearly three years too late, dumbass.'

'We on a break?' Gunner asks, entering Liv's section, a sandwich in his hand. 'Or is this the gossip section now?'

'Gossip,' Liv says, zero hesitation. 'They're moving in together and Will's going to ask Berkley to marry him, tonight.'

I cock my head, a little annoyed. 'I *just* asked if I could trust you and two minutes later you blurt my secret out to someone.'

'If you didn't want anyone to know, you should have led with that. Gunner is a part of the secrets club. He knows everything.'

He's now staring at me while eating his sandwich. 'Really? You're going to propose?'

I nod. I know Gunner. Not super well, but enough to know he genuinely has Berkley's best interests at heart. He's also a tad protective over both these women he spends his days with.

'Please tell me you're not thinking of doing it on camera in the middle of a soccer field? I didn't get great feedback with that one,' he says.

'No,' I say with a laugh. 'I *actually* know her.'

Gun wipes a hand on his jeans then extends it my way. 'Considering you're the only man she's ever truly wanted, congratulations.'

I take his hand, feeling almost giddy inside. Congratulations on my hopeful upcoming engagement. My chest bubbles with excitement. I've never had this feeling. Not on the show. Not over money. Not even over my ex-BFF Jack Daniel's. Only Berkley does this to me.

'This is a secrets circle, right?' I ask.

The two of them nod. 'Well, pillow talk has informed me that you two are into one another as more than just friends and co-workers. Maybe you two should finally have that conversation?' As the words leave my lips, I'm backing away from Liv's desk, leaving them alone.

Her jaw drops and her glare is meant to drop me dead, but Gunner's eyes are on her and the goofy grin on his face as he attempts to act casual and eat his lunch says Berkley's not wrong. Maybe they just needed a push?

'William.' Almost as soon as I'm back at the front counter, my father – or rather the man who probably is *not* my father – approaches me slowly. I say nothing, just straighten up the front counter, looking busy.

'I overheard you talking to Olivia and Gunner.'

Fuck.

'Did you *really* buy her an engagement ring?'

'You're the person whose opinion I want the least on this,' I admit.

'Fine. But I've been married thirty-plus years so I know a bit about the process.'

'If we were looking for a marriage to influence us, it wouldn't be yours.'

Dad nods, his head full of dark hair disheveled in a way it usually isn't. He's still wearing a suit, like he's headed to work. I don't think he has casual clothes as I've never seen him in anything besides slacks and dress shirts.

'I realize you think you know everything but—'

'I think no such thing,' I say, cutting him off. 'But I do know you don't actually give a shit about anything I do. You're toxic. I told you I want out of this family and I meant that. Especially knowing what I now know. The only reason you're here is because Berkley doesn't have the heart to let someone be homeless. Enjoy it, 'cause once I can convince her to kick you out, I don't ever want to see you again.'

'That's a little harsh, don't you think?'

'Not really. I think it's only fair you know I'm disappointed in you and literally only trying to save myself here.'

'Because you had it so bad? You got everything you wanted in life. Had experiences most people never get.'

'I did. The kind that leave you with lasting memories I'll cherish forever, and then there are the experiences that have me questioning my existence and leaving me with scars so deep I don't know how to heal them but am desperately trying.'

'You're hurt because I gave you a good life? That's rich—' His voice bellows through the store.

'Stop. It. Jacob.' Mom's voice drowns his, as she suddenly is standing behind him, speaking loud enough that Mike pops out of Liv's department to watch.

'I thought you had a headache?' Jacob asks her.

'I lied,' she says, like lying is just a normal thing in this family. No wonder I'm so fucked up. 'Working in a bookstore isn't my cup of tea. I'm above this.'

'You're *above* this?' I laugh. 'You might want to rethink that considering the Feds are possibly going to be throwing you both into the slammer, you're that corrupt. You think working in a bookstore will be worse than working in the kitchen at a federal prison?'

'Nobody is going to prison,' Mom says with a roll of her eyes.

'It's Teddy,' Mike says loudly, from where he stands across the room.

'*Michael!*' Mom scolds.

'Oh, please,' he says with an attitude he's never had with our parents. 'He's not five. It wasn't that hard a case to crack and this affects his life. He deserves to know.'

'Teddy?' I ask, my heart stalled in my chest. 'As in *dead* Uncle Teddy?'

Based on the seething look now filling Jacob's face (I'm no longer calling him Dad), I'd say Mike guessed correctly. I look at my mom, attempting to hide the horror but unsuccessfully, based on the guilt now spreading across her face.

Teddy is my dad? I mean, I guess it makes sense considering I look just like him but I thought that was just genetics. Jacob *hated* Teddy. With a passion I never understood because even though I barely knew him, he seemed like a stand-up guy. He was the Sean Penn of the Adler family, using his money for humanitarian causes, a real philanthropist running into war zones and unsafe countries to help people suffering. He died in a helicopter crash when I was ten during one of these trips. It was my first experience with death and considering I only knew what Jacob had told me about Teddy –

none of it good – I was unfazed, really. Until right this second, I never understood why Sylvia dressed me up and snuck me out of the house that day to bring me to his funeral. On the way there she'd said, 'One day you'll understand this.' She had to have known the truth the whole time.

'You had an affair with your husband's little brother?' I ask, a hand now firmly in my hair.

'It was more complicated than that,' Mom says.

Jesus. I just wanted to win back my girlfriend and now I'm fatherless, housing my asshole family in a bookstore, and shit's constantly blowing up in my face. They are ruining this for Berkley and me, again. If they scare her away with their bullshit…

The two of them stare at me as I process this information, like I'm being unreasonable to want to know who my real father is.

'Is Teddy my *real* dad?' I ask my mom, completely ignoring Jacob. 'Keep in mind I've got a DNA test at the lab so I *will* soon know whether you decide to be honest or not.'

Mom drops her head. 'Yes.'

'Holy shit…' I walk away from the counter, my hands on the back of my head, the exact stance the cameras loved to find me in as it meant I was losing it and about to jump into a bottle of booze. This time, I'm wandering into the romance department, instead wishing this building was a fucking bar.

'Hey!' Berkley chirps as she enters the store, stopping in her tracks when she notices my family all standing at the front desk where she was probably expecting to see me. She looks around, noticing me as I disappear down an aisle of colorful books about love.

'He knows,' Mike tells her.

She doesn't say anything, just approaches me and wraps her arms around me.

'It's Teddy,' I say, holding her back, resting my chin on her head. 'He's my dad.'

'Mike was *right*?'

'You *knew*?' I lean back, my hands on her shoulders, confused how she found out before me.

She grimaces. 'Barely. Mike suggested it based off something your mom said earlier but we didn't know for sure so I didn't want to say anything yet. I should have, though. I'm sorry.'

'Why are you sorry?'

'I should have told you immediately; instead, I did exactly to you what I was always so mad you were doing to me – I kept it from you because I thought I was protecting you and now you've found out from someone else.'

She seems worried as she says this, like I'm going to be mad at her. Like it'll start our years of fighting all over again. But I've done so much therapy. Is all this a shock to me? Like discovering Bigfoot is real, yes. I can't be mad at her, though. I know I kept secrets from her because I knew that was best for me, not her. She's never been like that and I've learned a huge lesson through all this. Open communication is the only way relationships survive.

I pull her to me again, kissing the top of her head. 'Berkley, our relationship will never be perfect. We're going to fuck up, piss each other off, annoy one another. It's inevitable. I screwed up because I was thinking about me first before. But you are always thinking of me first, you last. I want to do the same for you now, so if we have things we think might hurt one another, whether it was done intentionally to spare the other's feelings or accidentally, we need to talk about it. It won't end us. I promise.'

'You grew up on me, Adler. I was so scared you'd turned into Prince Willy for good, but you didn't. I see my Will again, only now you're a grown man and I like it.'

I've got to shove all this family crap aside and do what I came here to do. They can't ruin this for her.

'Wait until this grown man sweeps you off your feet on our date tonight,' I say, hinting it's going to be epic and having no doubt it will.

34

BERKLEY

I am on a date with Will. It's been a long time since we did this. He's holding my hand to his chest as he drives, occasionally lifting it to his lips. This is the Will I knew. He's being sweet, romantic and so incredibly attentive.

'Where are we headed?' I ask as he pulls into a Goodwill parking lot.

'One time when I was filming, you told me a story about one of your college interns going on a date where they had to choose one another's outfits at the Goodwill and wear them for the entire night. You laughed the whole time you told me about it.'

'That was *so* long ago. I can't believe you remember. You seriously want to walk in here and walk out wearing *used* clothing? *Who* are you, and *what* have you done with my Will?'

He smiles wide. 'I missed that,' he says softly. 'The "*my* Will" thing.'

'Well, get used to it because we live together now and I don't doubt I'm going to call you a lot of things. Most of them probably even nice...' she kids.

He laughs, nodding his head like he's completely alright with that. 'I'm more than happy to wear used clothing if the outfit fits the rules of the night.'

'Rules of the night?' I ask, taking his hand as he helps me out of his SUV. 'What might those be?'

He laces his fingers through mine, and it feel so normal. Yet also so new? I don't know. All I do know is that I missed this. Him. All of it.

'We're going fancy schmancy. Top shelf. If it's on a mannequin, check it out. You choose my outfit; I choose yours.'

I laugh out loud, following him through the front doors and into the store. 'You might regret this.'

'I hope I do,' he says. 'Meet back here in fifteen?'

'Sure.'

With a single wink, he backs away from me into the women's department. A few heads turn, one woman says his name, and he stops, casually chatting with her, now signing something she's handing him, but he's clearly on a mission.

I turn to the men's section, my gaze landing on the perfect outfit almost immediately. He was right. Mannequins are where the good stuff is.

'Hey,' I say to a guy who works here. 'I need that.' I point to the two-piece suit I somehow just know will fit him. Navy plaid. Slim fit. I search the dress shirt racks for one of those ruffled-front seventies button-up shirts and find one that entices a laugh out of me. It's grass-green, with white piping along the ruffles at the chest. It's ridiculously perfect.

'What's your name?' I ask the guy now lugging the mannequin from the display to the ground where I can strip this plastic man of his dignity.

'My friends call me Big Jim.'

I look him over. He's only a couple inches taller than me. Huh. It must be one of those ironic nicknames.

'Well, Big Jim.' I toss the ruffled shirt over my shoulder. 'We're about to strip this guy nude together. How about you do his top? I'll do his bottom.'

He nods.

'Have you ever seen *PDX Royals*?' I ask as we work, feeling like I need to fill the air with words.

'My wife watches it. Likes that Willy character.' He lifts a shoulder like he could take him or leave him.

'Then your wife will be thrilled to know that this suit will be gracing the world on Willy's back in about ten minutes.'

Big Jim looks down at me as he peels the jacket over the headless mannequin's arms. 'You serious?'

'Done,' Will says from behind me as I literally yank the mannequin's pants down to his knees.

'Holy crap,' Big Jim says, his gaze now lingering behind me.

I look over my shoulder, catching Will laughing at the sight of me, a coy grin on his face.

'You've been gone five minutes,' I say, standing to inspect the dress in his hands. Black, shiny, ruffly and short short. 'Nineties prom night does it for ya?'

His eyebrows are raised as he stares at the nearly nude mannequin standing between Jim and me. 'Steampunk does it for you?' he asks as I drop back down to my knees to yank the pants off my new mannequin friend.

'Fair point. Will, this is Big Jim; his wife's a fan of yours.'

'Oh yeah?' Will asks, extending his hand to Jim.

Jim wipes his hands on his pants before taking Will's hand, nodding his head silently.

'You helped this weirdo choose this?' Will asks.

'*Nooo*,' Jim says uncomfortably. 'Just helped her undress him. She's kind of bossy.' He whispers that last part, but not quietly enough.

'*Jim.*' I say his name like I'm offended, earning a grin from the stout, serious man.

Will nods his head, glancing around the place like he's about to tell Jim a secret. 'I can't take her anywhere. Look at her,' he jokes, his eyes on me while my head is at this mannequin's waistline, trying to yank the pants off him.

I burst out a laugh as Jim nods like he agrees.

'We ready?' Will asks as Jim hands me my newly acquired clothes.

'Thank you, Jim,' I say to him before walking away with Will. 'Are we wearing these out?'

'If you think I'm touching anything in those dressing rooms, you're nuts. I brought Febreze and Lysol for the clothes, even. My car has dark windows. We'll change in the back seat and no one will be the wiser.'

'Yeah.' I laugh. 'That doesn't sound like a dangerous idea.'

Will flashes me a smile as he hands the lady at the register his debit card. He looks totally handsome even in his T-shirt with the word 'DORK' across his chest.

'Thirty-two bucks?' he asks, laughing as she shoves the nicest clothes we could find into two used Walmart bags.

'I think you may be a little too "rich boy" to make this your regular clothing store. I bet your underwear cost more than that,' I say to him as I crawl into the back seat of his SUV.

He stands outside the car, Lysoling the hell out of everything we bought, tossing them in to me one by one, before getting in and closing the door behind him.

'Are you sure nobody can see through the windows?' I ask.

'The only person looking at you right now is me.' He winks, not wasting a moment stripping off his shirt and undoing his jeans, shoving them to his knees as I sit next to him.

I remove my shirt and throw it at him to make the playing field even, pulling off my jeans and tossing those his way too.

His gaze is on me until he finally lets out a breath and runs a hand through his hair, looking away with a laugh. He pulls off his glasses, setting them on the center console in front of us.

'What are you doing?'

'The only thing I know to do so I don't accidentally seduce you.' I laugh.

'You were definitely right,' he says, his eyes on me. 'Changing in my car might have been a bad idea.'

'What do we do?' I ask, afraid to look at him, holding a hand his way so I can't see him even though I'm not trying very hard as I separate my fingers to look through them.

'We shouldn't touch.'

'OK...' I say, reaching for the dress he's chosen.

He goes to grab his stuff, but the jacket falls to my feet, almost as if it was pushed by him. He leans forward, brushing his arm against my calf intentionally as he grabs for it.

'Oops,' he says, kissing my knee.

'I thought we shouldn't touch?' I ask, a heavy breath leaving my lips as he kisses my thigh.

'I can't help it.'

'I like this Will.'

'Good,' he says. 'Maybe by the end of the night you'll love him?'

What that, he slides back on his glasses and grabs the plaid dress pants, pulling them on. He then steps out of the SUV in only his pants, standing in the door so no one can see past him to me. Luckily, I've already got the dress over my head when he opens his door.

'Holy hell,' he says, shaking a leg, adjusting things inside the pants. 'I'm not gonna lie; I bet my ass looks fantastic,' he says with a turn, displaying his ass, glancing over his shoulder as he attempts to see it for himself.

'Yes, Will. Your ass looks, uh, *good* good.'

'Then, I love 'em. Consider these my new favorite pants,' he says, grabbing the dress shirt.

I try not to watch as he buttons up his shirt, tucking it into the pants, but he's boiling hot. I do eventually force my eyes away from him and strap on the shoes he requested I bring with me tonight, making absolutely no effort to make it graceful or tactful when I notice his eyes meandering to me and my panties. This feels incredibly flirty, and I like how it reminds me of us so long ago.

'Can you zip me?' I ask, stepping out of his car once my shoes are laced up.

'If I do, can I *un*zip you later?'

'I probably won't say no.'

He grins, slipping on his shoes before walking around his SUV to me, zipping the back of my dress, kissing the tattoo of his initial on the back of my shoulder as he does. He then steps back to look me over as he pulls the jacket over his green ruffled shirt.

'Wow,' he says, running a hand through his hair. 'I thought you'd look good but damn, girl, you're gorgeous.'

He squeezes past me, reaching into his car and pulling out the Febreze, giving us each a once-over. When I can no longer breathe through the cloud of chemicals in the air, he tosses the bottle back into his car.

'Weirdo!'

He laughs, nodding his head to confirm. 'Ready for the next part?'

'The *next* part?'

'You thought the outfits were it?' He holds up three fingers. 'There are three parts of tonight's date. Ready for part two?'

He's put some work into this. 'More than ready,' I say, my insides filled with a cloud of butterflies that are spreading through my entire body with every glance, word, touch.

'Next up, Ground Kontrol,' he says, getting into the driver's seat.

'The arcade?'

Without a word, he lifts the center console lid and pulls out the trophy from our high-school days. A *Mario Kart* toy glued to the top of a bowling trophy. When he was sixteen, he sawed off the bowler on top and created this ridiculous masterpiece that still graces my apartment to this day. I didn't think he'd noticed it.

'You stole this from me?!'

'I happened upon it and thought what better way to re-introduce our relationship than with a *Mario Kart* war like we used to have. Maybe I'll win this back tonight? If I do, it's moving to my bedside table until you earn it back.'

'No way will you win,' I tease. As we drive, I realize I'm not really wearing shoes for 'driving'. 'You chose these shoes because it'll be impossible for me to win, didn't you?'

'I chose those shoes because I love them. When I go to sleep tonight, I'm dreaming of you in an arcade seat, in *only* those shoes.'

'Can't say I hate that dream...'

He laughs as he drives towards an arcade one might assume will be full of children, but it's primarily adult dudes reliving their childhoods. We strut through the place, people turning to look and realizing who he is. He's cordial, shaking people's hands if they approach him, but ultimately his eyes are on me, and he's reading my every expression. He grips my hand tightly in his, our gaze now on the *Mario Kart* games. A rope sits across the chairs with a handwritten 'RESERVED – ADLER' sign hanging from it.

'You reserved these? I didn't even know you could do that.'

'The right amount of money can buy you anything, Berx.'

'You *paid* to reserve these?' I ask with a laugh. 'That's ridiculous.'

'Well, I'm ridiculously in love with you, so it's fitting. You ready for this, Kaine?'

He removes the rope, motioning for me to have a seat, then sits in the chair next to me.

'Did you just call me by my last name?' He used to do this all the time. This is totally all-in, fun, flirtatious Will. No more feeling like we have to walk on eggshells around each other.

'I did,' he confirms with a nod. 'I don't want to get too personal for when I kick your ass.'

'Ha!' I burst out. 'Good luck, Adler. Er...' Shit. I grimace. He's really pushed away whatever feelings he's having over discovering who his father is and I haven't asked, knowing he's not ready. Maybe I shouldn't call him Adler for now?

'It's alright,' he says, noticing my face. 'No matter what happens, technically, it's looking like I'm still an Adler.'

'From here on out, you're just Will to me,' I tell him, extending a hand his way, a good-luck handshake that he eyes, but ultimately, he shakes his head. 'You seem a little competitive tonight. Shall we put money on this?'

'One million dollars,' he says with a straight face.

'You realize if I win, I'll be paying you with your own money?'

He shrugs.

'I was thinking, like, twenty bucks.'

'Twenty bucks it is,' he says with a nod, placing his hands on the video game steering wheel. 'Ready?'

'Yes.'

'No cheating.'

I motion crossing my heart. A lie I intend to keep. As the game starts, I tug my already short skirt up my leg closest to him. He eyes my thigh but says nothing. Gonna have to go bigger here.

'Remind me to stop by the store for some massage oil later,' I say casually. 'I'm nearly out and I like the kind that tastes like strawberries. You know...' I glance over at him. 'In case it ends up in your mouth. Or my mouth. Who knows?'

'*What?*' he says, his voice high as he looks over at me. His eyes move straight to my lap, where I'm pulling up my skirt a little further, and he lets go of the wheel to pull it down, immediately falling behind.

I blow by him; this will be so much easier than when we were teenagers. I yank my skirt up again; this time he notices much quicker and pulls it down, holding one hand on my lap, his fingers gripping the hem of my dress.

'I'm not afraid to have an accidental nip slip in here. It'll probably be the only nipple most of these guys will ever see in the flesh.'

He's laughing so hard, he can barely drive his car. 'They'll put your picture on the wall.'

'They'll put a picture of my nipple on the wall, more likely.'

'If you say that word one more time...'

'What? You'll lose? *Tragic.*' I laugh. '*Nipple. Nipple. Nipple. Nipple.*' I chant it as I drive, earning the attention of some guys near us.

'Berkley,' he half growls, playfully, his voice low, the goofy grin on his face adorable and full of lust as he glances between the screen in front of him and me.

Once I realize people are recognizing him and starting to gather, my confidence and concentration go out the window. He notices and exaggeratedly lets me win.

'Woo! Girl, you kicked my ass, again. I guess that trophy is still yours.'

Why is the attention he brings about such a big deal for me? Am I afraid some woman will catch his attention and sincerely steal him away from me? Ugh, *yes.* Sigh. This part isn't his problem; it's mine. We walk back to his car quietly, my hand in his. He opens my door but turns me to face him before I can get in, his hands on my waist.

'I adore you, Berkley. I always have. When I'm with you, you're all I see. When I'm away from you, you're all I think about. I know you hate the attention, but people recognizing me will probably fade with time. You can trust me. I worked out my issues. No one will ever steal me away from you. I promise.'

He read my mind. I didn't have to tell him how I felt for once; he saw it. I pull him to me by his jacket lapels and kiss his lips. The way he touches my face and neck when he kisses me makes me weak at the knees.

'If we're not careful, we won't make it to part three and that's the best part,' he says.

I'm already having so much fun with him I can't picture it getting better.

35

WILL

'The Rose Festival fair?' she asks with a laugh as we walk from the parking garage.

'I feel like winning ya something,' I say with a wink. 'I haven't been to this in years. Last time was with you.'

I pay the entrance fee, buy some ride tickets and hold her hand as we walk, heading right to the Ferris wheel. The sweet smell of funnel cakes and deep-fried everything is intoxicating. Colorful lights flash, and children's laughter fills the air. A few people glance our way, but nothing overwhelming. She doesn't seem to notice.

'You *remember* this?' she asks as we approach the wheel.

'Of course I remember this. I got to second base with you on a Ferris wheel once. Maybe even this exact one.'

We get in line behind a few other people. Berkley looks beautiful. The dress reminds me of when we went to our high-school prom.

'I asked you to be my girlfriend and told you I loved you for the first time on this Ferris wheel,' I remind her, lifting her hand to my lips. 'Do you remember that?'

'That's what I was talking about,' she says, rolling her eyes playfully.

It was the summer after we met. I was nearly sixteen and she'd just turned fifteen. I was desperately trying to be romantic. Until then we'd just casually dated as young teenagers do. But that night, I worked up the courage to say the words I'd never said to anyone. Like, *anyone*. Not even my family.

'You're beautiful even in someone else's dress, Berx,' I say, stepping up in line as it moves forward. Just saying the words makes my insides all fuzzy in the best way. That's how I know she's the one. She's always been the one.

'Thank you,' she says shyly. 'I like how you look at me lately.'

'I can't take my eyes off you.'

She smiles sweetly, squeezing my hand in hers. 'You're easily the most handsome man I've ever seen. *GQ* with an IQ. Absolutely dashing. A real Hottie McNaughty.' She's enjoying messing with me way too much, but not nearly as much as I am. Every word out of her mouth, I fall for her a little bit more, and she has no clue. Honestly, I wasn't sure I could love her any more but tonight has proved me wrong.

'Seriously.' She glances at me as we take another step forward. 'I find myself looking at you with heart-eyes, and I see no wrong. That scares me a little bit, considering our past.'

I get it, I do. Hopefully the move I'm about to make wipes all that worry away. We step up to the ride, sitting in the chair we've been directed to. The ride attendant makes sure we're seated before pulling down the overhead bar to keep us from falling to the ground.

'I'm not perfect, Berx. I've got plenty wrong, and I know I've wronged you more times than I can count. It's alright to see that.'

'Are you saying you're OK with me still being a little mad at you while also falling for you?'

The ride moves, causing her to tighten her grip on my arm.

'You're falling for me?'

She nods, pressing her face into my shoulder. 'I wanted to make this harder for you,' she says, her voice muffled. She sits back again. 'I feel like I should be madder than I am, considering I told you it was your last chance like thirty chances ago, and yet here I am giving you one last shot. I *want* to fall – I mean, not from here...' She motions to the ground now far beneath us, doing the most adorable Hail Mary. 'I can't seem to be mad at you; my heart won't let me. But none of this feels like it did before...'

'In a bad way?' I ask, suddenly nervous.

'No,' she says softly. 'In a grown-up way so good that if it doesn't work out this time—'

'Berkley,' I interrupt her. I don't want her considering what it might be like if we didn't work out. We will work; she's my soulmate and I've never felt more sure of something than right now. 'I didn't wake up one morning and decide to try and get you back. You're who I've always wanted. I got rid of all the distractions from before. I've dealt with my demons and each time I had a breakthrough moment, I wanted the same thing. You. *Us*.'

She's holding my arm tight, not because she's scared – the girl is fearless – but because we're as high as we're going to get and looking into the city.

'Would it make you feel better if I admit I'm scared too?'

'Why are you scared?' She seems truly surprised by this.

'Because if I don't do things right this time, I risk losing you forever. The last three years have nearly killed me. I love you with everything I am, Berx, and if I lose you for good, I don't kno—'

She pulls me to her by my jacket, kissing me. It only lasts a moment before she pulls away, looking into my eyes. 'I love you too.'

I pull away, cocking my head, staring at her, completely bewildered by what she's just said. She hasn't said those words since that day she found out I'd signed on to do the show. Maybe I didn't hear her right?

'You love me? Like in the *present* tense?'

She nods. 'I couldn't say it until I knew you were mine, and tonight you made me feel like you were.'

I let out a long nervous breath. 'Baby, I need to ask you something.' I've known this woman my entire adult life and I definitely didn't expect to be this nervous to say four words that'll forever change my life for the better. Hopefully our lives for the better.

'OK...' she says nervously, her eyes growing wide as I reach into the inside pocket of this ridiculous jacket. I had the ring in my car and I grabbed it in the darkness of the parking garage while she wasn't looking.

'When you told me off at that Halloween party – or pretty much any time you've let me have it – I already knew what I wanted. What made me happy in life. I went to every counseling session available while in rehab. I even did yoga therapy, and you know how good I am at yoga.'

She laughs. Once I went to a yoga class with her. Once. That was all it took to know I hated it.

'I needed something to keep me going. A reminder of what it was that made me happy so I could work towards getting there.' I pull my hand from my jacket, the diamond now on my little finger. 'So I wore this the entire time, to remind me of where I wanted to end up.' I open my right hand and her eyes move right to it.

She gasps, but not like she's in shock, more *final-fucking-ly*. 'Is that a—'

'Yeah,' I say with a nod. 'Bought just for you on my way to rehab in preparation for this moment. I wore it just like this and anytime I felt like I couldn't keep going I looked at it and immediately I knew

I had it in me. You inspired me to become a better version of myself, Berx.'

She grins, but her chin quivers and her brows push together as her eyes glaze over.

'I don't want you to be my girlfriend, baby. I want you to be my forever. Maybe this is too soon, considering everything that's happened, but I don't want to wait another second to ask you this...'

'Yes!' she says excitedly, not allowing me to actually ask.

'I haven't even said the words yet,' I say through a chuckle, an absolute giddy grin on my face.

'Well, could you say them already?' she says.

'Berkley,' I say, a little less nervously knowing her answer already. I pull the ring off my finger, hoping to God I don't drop it to the ground from where we are. 'You're my best friend, and the love of my life. I never want to spend another day without you. Will you marry me?'

I thought about doing this a million ways. Skywriting. Using her favorite romance novel. At the store. In front of her friends and family. But ultimately I know Berkley, and just the two of us, without the eyes and ears of anyone else, is how she'd want this.

'*Yeah* I will! *Hell* yes! *Finally, yes!*' Her hand shakes as she holds it out for me, allowing me to slip the ring on her finger and when I do she sighs with relief. 'I love you *so* much,' she says gleefully, planting a kiss on my lips.

'I've never loved you more. So, we're doing this?'

'We're doing this!' she says, now staring at her hand, held out in front of her. 'Holy Moses, this thing is gorgeous. *Please* tell me it's insured?'

'It's insured,' I reassure her. 'Berkley...' I slide my hand down her thigh. She looks up from the ring, tears falling down her face, but this time happy ones. 'You're going to be my *wife*.'

'Your *wife*,' she repeats. 'Wow. Which means you'll be my *husband*... oh, I like the way that sounds.'

'Me too.'

The ride slows to a stop, and once we unload we walk slowly hand in hand down the waterfront walkway, towards my car. Every few seconds Berkley lifts her hand to look at the ring.

'It's so beautiful, Will. You did good.'

'I know you pretty well.'

'Want to know something that might surprise you?' she asks. 'I don't want a big wedding. Your life has been public for so long. I think I want to do this just us.'

'You want to elope?' I didn't expect this. I thought for sure she'd want the huge white wedding she deserves. 'No big white dress, none of your family or friends?'

She shakes her head. 'I'm thinking... Vegas.'

Vegas? I love it. 'You know I could make that happen tonight. *If* you want to?'

36

BERKLEY

'I can't believe we're doing this right now!' I chirp as we ride through Sin City in the back of a cab on our way to One Love Wedding Chapel, where 'Elvis' has agreed to marry us, tonight. That's right, we got engaged four hours ago and are already in Las Vegas after a last-minute chartered flight, and we haven't even changed out of our secondhand date clothes.

'Do we look ridiculous?'

'Ridiculously *perfect*,' Will says. 'Elvis won't have a single complaint.'

He called ahead and 'Elvis' is awaiting us. He's a fan of the show and can't wait for us to arrive, but we requested something lower-key. The last thing we need is this all over the tabloids before we even get home. Will's exact words were, 'Treat us like the most normal couple you've ever met.'

While he made that call, I called his brother and told him we'd gone on an adventure but would be back by the end of the weekend and have decided we want their parents out before we get back. He's agreed. If I never see their faces again, I could give two shits. Harsh? Maybe. Also, though, necessary for both our mental health. Will can one day make that call if he ever wants to repair that relationship.

Our car pulls to a stop outside the chapel and Elvis – in a blue suede suit – greets us with an arm windmill directing the driver to a parking spot.

'We're here!' I say with a giggle. My insides feel like champagne spilling over, in the best of ways. The two of us exit the car, and Elvis greets us with open arms.

'If y'all's temperature is rising, it's because of this flaming love of yours!' he says, extending a hand to Will. 'Introduce me to this lovely lady by your side,' he says.

'This is Berkley Kaine, the love of my life.'

'*Enchanté.* Aren't you just the prettiest gal alive?' Elvis lifts my hand to his lips, planting a wet kiss on the back. He suddenly covers his eyes. 'Sparks are flying off you two. Let's hurry,' he says, ushering us into the building.

It's a whirlwind of choosing the room we want to get married in (the all-white one – like heaven), flowers, veil, and we each decide to wing the vows. Elvis promises he'll make this easy as pie. Actually, his exact words are, 'If drunk folks can do it, it should be no problem for the sober.'

'Here we go, kids. The road to love is full of danger signs, a road you both know well.' He winks at Will. 'When y'all kiss, are your hearts on fire?'

'On fire and burning with desire,' Will says, playing along.

'I second that,' I pipe. I feel like a little kid and my insides are dancing.

'Talk to each other,' Elvis directs. 'William, you first.'

He smiles, holding both my hands in his as Elvis holds my bouquet. 'I've made a lot of mistakes in my life, Berkley. But falling in love with you was never one of them. I'll be forever thankful that you've given me this one last shot. I promise I won't let you down, baby.'

'Like poetry, my reality-star friend. Berkley, you're up, little lady.'

I don't know if I can even speak; his words have taken my breath away and my heart has never beat louder.

'Despite me trying to play it cool, you stole my heart the moment you sat in front of me in homeroom so long ago. Every time we reunite it's like we never spent time apart. We made some mistakes, but no one else has ever stood a chance. It's always been you, Will. Until the end of time.'

'Are we writing a love song here because I'm fallin'!' Elvis bolsters. 'Love her tender, love her true, William Adler. Will you love this woman until the end of time? If so, say "I do".'

Will nods and I swear I see a golden sparkle in his eyes. A sparkle that's been missing since that day so long ago when everything fell apart.

'I do.'

'Well, this ain't no one-sided love affair now, is it? If you want to be loved by the one your heart longs for, you've got to "I do" him too...'

'I absolutely do.' My insides are smiling right now.

'By the power invested in me, may the fire you spark in one another's souls, while husband and wife, never fizzle out. Kiss this beautiful woman, your new wife, and seal the deal, William.'

He kisses me gently yet with everything in him, dipping me back, and my heart never worries he'll let go. Elvis claps, before breaking out his guitar and singing a little 'Love Me Tender' to set the mood.

If I had any doubts Will's finally choosing me, I don't anymore. Standing here, sharing our first dance with him (and Elvis), despite all the turmoil we've been through, he was the only one my heart could ever see no matter what was going on in our lives. Love can hurt at times. That's for damn sure. But the fact that I'm deliriously happy right now, after so much heartbreak, makes it all worth it. I just married my best friend after truly believing I'd lost him. Maybe meeting your soulmate as a teenager doesn't make things as complicated as I thought it did. It just helped me love him through things I never thought possible until the timing was finally perfect.

EPILOGUE
WILL

* * *

Three Weeks Later, June 2023

PDX ROYALS – PRINCE WILLY IS OFFICIALLY UNAVAILABLE, LADIES!

That's right, he married her, *Royals* fans. No, we're not talking about the princess of the show, or her best friend, but Berkley Kaine, the girl who's held his heart since he was just a teenager. In a late-night impromptu ceremony with only Elvis present, these two said the words 'I do' and seem blissfully happy based on the photos we captured of them walking the streets of Portland, hand in hand, having the time of their lives.

It's also become mainstream news that the Adlers have fallen from the kingdom and mommy and daddy dearest are currently sitting in jail cells awaiting trial on multiple financial fraud charges. Oh how the rich have fallen. That's unfortunate, but they likely only have themselves to blame.

Join us in wishing Will (he's dropped the y) and Berkley Adler the best in their new adventure. Give us a shout out sometime, would you!

ALSO – SURPRISE *ROYALS* NEWS

You're reading it here first, *Royals* fans: *PDX Royals* will live on with a brand new set of trust-funded young adults moving into the condo and bringing us the drama (and sometimes love stories) that we're absolutely addicted to with this first crew! We can't wait to meet the new housemates, so stay tuned!

The show will once again air on E! every Sunday at 9:00 p.m. PST.

* * *

'Berkley *Adler*?!' Olivia yells from the magazine department.

We knew the article was coming out; that's why we planned a 'birthday' party for my twenty-sixth birthday today. Only it's not a party; it's a reception.

'Uh-oh,' Berkley says, glancing my way with her eyes wide. 'It's happening.'

Liv storms the front counter, Gunner by her side. 'You *married* him and didn't tell us?! I thought you two went away for a long weekend.'

'Time for my break,' I say. Berkley glares. 'I'm kidding.' I laugh. 'Liv, you knew I had a ring. I told you I was proposing. How did you not put the pieces together?'

'That – *that's* not important. Did you two really get married?'

'We did,' Berkley says with a giggle. 'But you can't be mad because it was totally last-minute and even we didn't know we were going to do it. Plus, tonight we were going to announce it so, really, you're the first to know!'

Gunner laughs to himself. 'You think maybe *you* have something to tell them first now?' he asks Olivia.

'Shush,' she says to him.

Berkley and I exchange curious glances. I think I know what Gunner is referring to but I want to hear it from their lips before I guess.

'My God!' Mike pops out of the horror section, a stack of books in his hands. He enjoys coming to the shop now as he's gotten into reading about the horrors that are not his family. That and he's met a woman who he waits for, just to talk to her, and she's made it very clear she's not got the time. I think maybe she's just playing hard to get, but considering Mike's most recent 'fame', maybe she's just not a fan. Time will tell.

'Just tell them already,' he groans. 'Because if I have to walk in on it one more time, I'm going to gouge my eyes out right in front of you.'

'Walk in on *what*?' I ask.

Olivia glares. 'You're the one who lit the fuse, so you should know.'

'Oh. My. God,' Berkley says suddenly, knowing immediately probably based on the way Gunner is looking at Olivia alone. 'You two did it!'

'My man, Gun! You did it!' I lift a hand, which he meets.

'*It* has a name,' Olivia snaps, a smirk on her face. 'And we didn't *just* do it, we're *officially* dating. We're coming up on our one-month anniversary. It's no big deal, just the longest relationship I've ever had. And let me be the first to say that there were things about Gunner we did *not* know...' She waggles her eyebrows at Berkley.

'Jesus.' Gunner drags a hand down his face.

'Ugh,' Mike groans. '*Why* did I think reading would help me with the boredom after discovering none of my friends were *really* my friends? I've seen their tongues in one another's mouths for far too long.'

I cock my head. 'You're jealous now? Why don't you go to work so you can watch other people tongue, then?'

Yep, Mike got an *actual* job that isn't at the bookstore. He's been signed on for the new *Royals* as the 'elder housemate'. He doesn't love the title, but I'm into it. The former 'king' gets to supervise the house, so the network doesn't have any more 'Willy'-type behavior. Apparently they were worried I might die during filming and they're hoping to prevent that this time around. He'll give his opinion and try to smother the flames before the whole show is on fire again.

For the most part, we've forgiven each other. I mean, our parents are sitting in jail so all we have is each other now. And, oddly enough, without them around, things are peaceful – for the most part. He can still be a real douche, but things are getting better. He's also seeing a therapist, and I've truthfully never been happier. Life is amazing.

'Enough about us – I can't believe you two got married in secret! Where's the photos?' Liv asks, enticing Berkley to pull out her phone to excitedly show them to someone other than me. Gunner, Olivia and Mike look through the photos but eventually Mike comes to my side of the counter.

'Ya did it. You won her back. Honestly, I wasn't sure it was going to happen, little brother. Are you finally happy?'

I glance to the woman who literally saved my life many times over, as beautiful as the day I met her. 'I don't think there's any way I could be happier.'

ACKNOWLEDGMENTS

To my loyal readers: so many of you found me through my *He Loves Me, He Loves Me Not* trio of books. Because I love you all so, there will soon be a 'final chapter' of that series available to subscribers of my newsletter. It will be a short story, told from all six leads of the three books. So, let me be the first to request your presence to the wedding of Dax Hartley and Hollyn Matthews.

This is the first book I've ever written with a critique partner. I was a nervous wreck because my books change SO much from first draft to final and I was afraid she would hate everything I wrote. But she didn't! Actually, her words gave me so much confidence to keep going and that maybe I do have what it takes to do this as a career. To you, Carrie Lomax, I thank you. This book is better because of you.

I'd like to thank my usual cheerleaders in life: my family, kids, parents, dedicated readers across social media, and my tiny circle of writer friends. You know who you are; I don't know what I'd do without you. We're all going to make it in this gig. I feel it in mah bone. I mean, bones. ;)

Boldwood Books – the reason you get to read these books. Everyone in this company makes my life easier. They're friendly, welcoming, don't tell me I suck or ask if I've had my meds, but they talk to me and keep me updated on how things are going and what's going on. They're a dream publisher and I'd like to thank each one of you that I work with regularly, not to mention those I don't. I appreciate you all believing in me enough to help make my dreams come true. On to book five!

(What's it gonna be about? I don't even know yet...)

A NOTE FROM THE AUTHOR

Hello! I just wanted to touch base and let you know that I'm aware I do sometimes write about heavier topics in my books – then call them a rom-com. If only rom-dramedy was a 'thing'. I think it's important to acknowledge real-life situations, hard as they can be, because nobody's life is perfect. If you are triggered, I apologize, that's not my intention. I truly try to write both the heartwarming and the turmoil in all my stories. Along with my usual sweary, immature sense of humor. I may be forty-five (and a grandmother by the time this book comes out. Welcome to the world, Ava Elizabeth. Promise Mimi you won't read this book until you're a teenager!) but my mind doesn't agree.

I'd also like to point out that I do use real and fictional places in Portland, Oregon as my setting. I lived there for many years and was born and raised in Oregon. I write about the Portland I knew, so maybe it doesn't match what it is now, but when I lived there, Portland was my dream city and forever holds a piece of my heart. I like to embrace my weird and this city allows me to do so through my best friends (that I made up).

I'm around on social media, you can find me on: Facebook, Twitter, Threads, Instagram, LUV and Litsy.

Sign up for my newsletter and stay up to date with all my new releases, giveaways, sales and more.

If I can ask one quick favor, it would be for you to leave a short review on Amazon (or wherever you bought this book, but Amazon is the big one). Reviews help Amazon bring my book to new readers and each one helps my books' ranking. Seems like I shouldn't be worried about those things but it's how I get paid and though I adore this job just for the stories I get to make up alone, it's nice to pay the bills too.

Thank you for reading. I can't wait to bring you my next. Happy reading!

Aimee

PLAYLIST

'Butterflies' – MAX & Alie Gatie

'Karma' – AJR

'Maybe You're The Problem' – Ava Max

'I Don't Like Myself' – Imagine Dragons

'Time Machine' – Cuco

'Worth It (feat. Kid Ink)' – Fifth Harmony

'Cursed' – King Princess

'Stunnin' (feat. Harm Franklin)' – Curtis Waters

'Glimpse of Us' – Joji

'Girlfriend' – Avril Lavigne

'ilu' – elijah woods

'MyBoi (TroyBoi Remix)' – Billie Eilish

'Tainted Love' – Milky Chance

'Nonsense' – Sabrina Carpenter

'I Don't Know (with ELIO)' – Peter Fenn

'Better Days' – NEIKED, Mae Muller & Polo G

'Big Energy' – Latto

'Stranger' – Lauv

'What's Next' – Austin Millz & Pell

'I Still See You At Parties' – Port Cities & Emma-Lee

'26' – Lauv

'Love/Hate Letter To Alcohol (feat. Fleet Foxes)' – Post Malone

'Sick of U (feat. Oliver Tree)' – BoyWithUke

'When It Ends (feat. JORDY)' – Avery Lynch

'goodbye' – Billie Eilish

'this is what losing someone feels like' – JVKE

'Never Been Better (feat. Orla Gartland)' – half·alive

'hate me' – aldn

'I Will Survive' – Cake

'I miss you, I'm sorry' – Gracie Abrams

'Can't Take My Eyes Off You' – Muse

'Easy' – Tayla Parx

'Hold Me Like You Used To' – Zoe Wees

'Love of My Life' – Harry Styles

'No Thank You' – Ella Bleu

'Still the One' – Emilee

'idk' – Haley Joelle

'Read the Room' – ELIO

'Hate Our Love' – Queen Naija & Big Sean

'Evil' – Daughtry

'Heaven' – Maude Latour

'Fairytale' – Milky Chance

'Sharks' – Imagine Dragons

'UH OH!' – Sub Urban & BENEE

'sheluvme' – Tai Verdes

'What Lovers Do (feat. SZA)' – Maroon 5

'I Love You Baby' – Emilee

'Love Me Tender' – Elvis Presley

ABOUT THE AUTHOR

Aimee Brown is the bestselling romantic comedy author of several books including *The Lucky Dress*. She's an Oregon native, now living in a tiny town in cold Montana and sets her books in Portland.

Sign up to Aimee Brown's mailing list here for news, competitions and updates on future books.

Visit Aimee Brown's website: https://aimeebwrites.com

Follow Aimee Brown on social media:

X x.com/aimeebwrites
f facebook.com/authoraimeebrown
instagram.com/authoraimeeb
BB bookbub.com/authors/aimee-brown

ABOUT THE AUTHOR

Aimee Brown is the best-selling romantic comedy author of several books including *The Lucky Dress*. She's an Oregon native, now living in a tiny town in cold Montana and sets her books in Portland.

Sign up to Aimee Brown's mailing list here for news, competitions and updates on future book.

Visit Aimee Brown's website: https://aimeebrownwrites.com

Follow Aimee Brown on social media:

ALSO BY AIMEE BROWN

He Loves Me, He Loves Me Not

Love Notes

Stuck With You

Can't Take My Eyes Off You

LOVE NOTES

LOVE IN EVERY CHAPTER

WHERE ALL YOUR ROMANCE
DREAMS COME TRUE!

THE HOME OF BESTSELLING
ROMANCE AND WOMEN'S
FICTION

 WARNING:
MAY CONTAIN SPICE

SIGN UP TO OUR
NEWSLETTER

https://bit.ly/Lovenotesnews

Boldwood

Boldwood Books is an award-winning fiction publishing company seeking out the best stories from around the world.

Find out more at www.boldwoodbooks.com

Join our reader community for brilliant books, competitions and offers!

Follow us
@BoldwoodBooks
@TheBoldBookClub

Sign up to our weekly deals newsletter

https://bit.ly/BoldwoodBNewsletter

Milton Keynes UK
Ingram Content Group UK Ltd.
UKHW041638050124
435535UK00012B/166

9 781804 268360

Berkley Kaine was lucky enough to meet her perfect
man at a young age.

Blissfully in love, she's about to graduate college, take on her dream job
and has never been more optimistic for the future.

Will Adler has been in love with Berkley Kaine since
the moment he laid eyes on her.

But ever since they became a couple, Will and Berkley have had to conten
with his socialite family who have never thought Berkley is good enough
Determined to drive the young lovers apart, Will's family reveal the secre
he's yet to tell her – he's signed on to be a part of a reality TV show called
PDX Royals, as apparently money is all it takes to be 'royalty' in America.

Can the couple survive the pressure of Will's crazy family and
a TV show they never expected to blow up the way it did?

Perfect for all fans of Sariah Wilson, Lindsey Kelk
and Abby Jiminez.

ISBN 978-1-80426-836-0

90000

9 781804 268360

www.boldwoodbooks.com